D1551664

The Wide, Carnivorous Sky

HIPPOCAMPUS PRESS LIBRARY OF FICTION

Edith Miniter, *Dead Houses and Other Works* (2008)
Jonathan Thomas, *Midnight Call and Other Stories* (2008)
————, *Tempting Providence and Other Stories* (2010)
Ramsey Campbell, *Inconsequential Tales* (2008)
Joseph Pulver, *Blood Will Have Its Season* (2009)
————, *Sin and Ashes* (2011)
————, *Portraits of Ruin* (2012)
Michael Aronovitz, *Seven Deadly Pleasures* (2009)
Donald R. Burleson, *Wait for the Thunder* (2010)
W. H. Pugmire, *Uncommon Places: A Collection of Exquisites* (2012)
Peter Cannon, *Forever Azathoth: Parodies and Pastiches* (2012)
Alan Gullette, *Intimations of Unreality* (2012)
Richard A. Lupoff, *Dreams* (2012)
————, *Visions* (2012)
Richard Gavin, *At Fear's Altar* (2012)
Jason V Brock, *Simulacrum and Other Possible Realities* (2013)

The Wide, Carnivorous Sky
and Other Monstrous Geographies

John Langan

Hippocampus Press

New York

Copyright © 2013 by Hippocampus Press

Works by John Langan © 2013 by John Langan
"Reading Langan" © 2013 by Jeffrey Ford
"Note Found in a Glenfiddich Bottle" © 2013 by Laird Barron

Published by Hippocampus Press
P.O. Box 641, New York, NY 10156.
http://www.hippocampuspress.com
All rights reserved.
No part of this work may be reproduced in any form or by any means
without the written permission of the publisher.

Cover art © 2013 by Santiago Caruso (www.santiagocaruso.com.ar)   .
Hippocampus Press logo designed by Anastasia Damianakos.

First Edition
1 3 5 7 9 8 6 4 2

ISBN13: 978-1-61498-054-4

For Fiona

Understand Death? Sure. That was when the monsters got you.
—Stephen King, *'Salem's Lot*

Contents

Introduction: Reading Langan

In recent years, the horror genre has given rise to a number of exceptionally talented short story writers—Caitlín R. Kiernan, Laird Barron, Joe Hill, Brian Evenson, M. Rickert, Gary A. Braunbeck, Kaaron Warren, Glen Hirshberg, Ekaterina Sedia, to name only a few. These are incredibly adept stylists, and yet they never forget to deliver the chills both physical and metaphysical. The work of each of them is idiosyncratic. It would be a disservice to try to corral them together under the banner of some movement. John Langan is most certainly an important voice in this bumper crop of creators. His excellent fiction simultaneously honors and violates traditions in the genre, giving rise to mutations that stalk off in new directions.

Langan's short fiction might, at first, seem daunting, because it's rarely short. The guy is in no hurry. He writes long and he gives good weight on the detail. It doesn't take many pages after entering one of these stories, though, to understand why. In adopting a concern for Gravity and Time (two key ingredients of the Gothic) in his work, Langan is able to create fictional effects you can't get with the brief or minimal. The pacing of his stories and the manipulation of the passage of time, its effects on the characters, its warping of the plot, are ingenious and seem organic. Years often pass as these stories unfold, or there are sudden leaps in time, or the sequence of events is subtly rearranged. As in the world of physics, the rate of Time is influenced by Gravity, and through the varying weight of the description in these stories Langan directs this magic, sometimes to hallucinatory effect. When I speak of the weight of description, I don't mean a cluttering of sentences. The read is always smooth and the flow of language carries you. Instead, I'm talking about the quality of description, its ability to convince the reader of the physical nature of the world of the story. This is important because Langan's horror is vitally physical as well as psychological and philosophical. For a good example in this collection, I'd point to the opening paragraphs of "City of the Dog."

Although the influence of the Gothic and of Poe in particular are evident everywhere in these stories, I wouldn't say that Langan is so much working in a tradition as through it. He is garnering fictional effects from it and employing them in new ways, but he is also busy dissecting that tradition. If you notice, many of these stories have an analytical aspect and some take the obvious form of anatomies. Langan is a scholar of fantastic fiction and a professor, a fact he openly embraces in his stories. What better voice or persona for a fascinating, creepy, cockeyed lecture on "The Masque of the Red Death" or a disquisition on the werewolf story? He is pinning up traditional tropes of the genre and taking a scalpel to them. The point isn't simply to analyze—this is not a research project—but to dig down to the core of these old monsters and change them. "How the Day Runs Down," a zombie story that first appeared in the John Joseph Adams anthology *The Living Dead,* is a good example: it is a zombie story structured around Thornton Wilder's iconic play *Our Town.* Langan uses the classic horror trope to dissect the classic American dream/nightmare and vice versa. The fiction that results from the process, a mutation, is brimming with original energy.

The most interesting aspect of the stories in this collection, though, comes through the characters and the drama. Langan gives us a chance to get to know the characters—you get a feeling of lives being lived—and become immersed in their realities. He is great at conveying character through dialogue or monologue. The gravity of the description pulls you toward its center. And the way things transpire seems always immediate, even in the past tense, as if these stories are being discovered as they are written. Langan is an explorer, and he has got the courage to follow the story where it takes him. There is an organic feel to the fiction, the unpredictability of journeys and visions, which makes the real realer and the weirdness weirder. This and all the various aspects of Langan's fiction I've mentioned to this point come across as totally unpremeditated on his part. There is a unity to these stories that strikes me as having less to do with calculation and more some kind of fictional intuition, but that too could be art.

Ultimately, what awaits you in this collection are gravity and time, weird stories, supernatural and unsettling, physical horror, madness, monsters, hallucination, philosophical haunting, mutation at the core. And all of this, all of it, in glorious Technicolor.

—JEFFREY FORD

The Wide, Carnivorous Sky

Kids

These were not his students. For one thing, he'd never taught kids this young: the oldest couldn't be more than six or seven, and the majority of the group crowding through his classroom door looked nearer four or five. For another thing, these children were beyond dirty, they were filthy: hair matted, skin thick with dirt, clothes a motley of stains. Not to mention the smell they brought with them: the pungence of garbage bags heaped high on the sidewalks outside cheap restaurants. For a moment, he was possessed by the conviction, by the absolute certainty, that he had stepped into a novel—*Oliver Twist*, perhaps, the Artful Dodger and his crew come calling, or possibly *Maggie: A Girl of the Streets*, the denizens of Crane's Manhattan paying a visit—which his mind quickly corrected: *I haven't stepped into the novel; the novel's stepped into me.* The sensation gave him an odd vertigo; he reached out a hand to his desk to steady himself. Behind the six- or seven-year-old, the children shuffled into the room en masse. Finding his voice, he said, "Can I help you?" and was surprised to hear the quaver in his words.

The children stopped where they were, the expressions on their faces those of small animals suddenly discovered by a predator. The possibility that this was some kind of strange joke, one of the seniors playing freak-out the hardass English teacher, flashed through his mind, only to be rejected as paranoia. Anyway, there was too much about the scene in front of him that didn't make joke-sense. It wasn't as if he were teaching Dickens right now—as if he ever taught Dickens, or Crane, for that matter. That he could recall, he'd never made mention of any phobias involving groups of small, dirty children, either. He stepped around the desk, closer to the kids. "Are you guys okay?" The children's eyes tracked him as he drew closer to them, bent over slightly as he said, "Are you lost? Were you on your way someplace?" Maybe a student organization was doing something with kids from one of the more run-down sections of Worcester, having them to lunch or something. Although, Jesus, if that were the case, you'd think the kids' parents could have done a little more to clean them up. Not that they had to be wearing dresses and suits, but still . . . He looked at the children's eyes looking at him. How dark they all were, that dark brown that can seem indistinguishable from black. Strange to find a group of kids this size all with the exact same eye color. "Tell you what: why don't you come with me, and we'll see if we can't find out where you're supposed to be." He started to walk past them, toward the door.

He didn't see which one tripped him, was on the floor so quickly that it took a moment for his brain to register what had happened. "What . . ." He was all right, but he'd come this far away from braining himself on one of the students' desks. Probably an accident. "Hey," he said as he went to turn over.

The pain in his calf was sharp and burning. He shouted and swung his hand back without thinking. It connected with a child's head with a loud smack, rolled the kid off and away from him. *Shouldn't have done that,* he thought as he tried to stand. *But OW, the little punk bit me, look at that, he bit right through the leg of my pants.* It was true: the brown fabric was torn, along with the skin beneath. Blood was literally running out of the wound, tickling down his leg, damping his sock. *What the hell?* "All right," he said.

He wasn't all the way to his feet when the children broke over him. This time his head did connect with the corner of a desk. There was a flare of white light and then a gap, a moment when the world went far away. It returned on a wave of pain. His legs, his arms, his side—all on fire with, with . . . *Oh Christ, they're biting me! Good Lord, the little—they're biting me!*

They were. Looking at their mouths smeared with red, you might have thought they were playing at clowns, applying their mothers' lipstick with children's enthusiastic spasms. But one of them was licking her lips; another was *chewing,* for the love of God; a third was jerking his head back the way you do when you're trying to alley-oop a piece of food from your lip into your mouth. They were eating him. He could feel their teeth ripping pieces of him away. He tried to flail his arms, kick his legs, roll one way or the other, but they had him pinned to the classroom floor. His shirt, pants—what hadn't been torn away—were sticking to him with his own blood. He tried to raise his head, to see what was being done to him, but all he could make out were small heads whose thick hair was slick with blood, with his blood. They pushed and shoved one another, jostling for the best places at the dinner table he had become.

No sound, he thought as consciousness spiraled down the drainpipe. They weren't talking, laughing, crying, making any of the sounds a group of children might make. There was only the noise of eating, flesh tearing, teeth clicking, lips smacking together.

How the Day Runs Down

(The stage dark with the almost-blue light of the late, late night, when you've been up well past the third ranks of late-night talk shows, into the land of the infomercial, the late show movies whose soundtrack is out of sync with its characters' mouths and which may break for commercial without regard for the action on the screen, the re-broadcast of the news you couldn't bear to watch the first time. It is possible—just—to discern rows of smallish, rectangular shapes running across the stage, as well as the bulk of a more substantial, though irregular, shape to the rear. The sky is dark: no moon, no stars.

(When the STAGE MANAGER snaps on his flashlight—a large one whose bright beam he sweeps back and forth over the audience once, twice, three times—the effect of the sudden light, the twirl of shadows around the theater, is emphasized by brushes rushing over drums, which give the sound of leaves, and a rainstick, which conjures the image of bones clicking against one another more than it does rain.

(Having surveyed the audience to his apparent satisfaction, the Stage Manager trains his light closer to home. This allows the audience to see the rows of tombstones that stretch the width of the stage, two deep in most places, three in a couple. Even from his quick inspection of them, it is clear that these are old tombstones, most of them chipped and worn almost smooth. The Stage Manager spares a moment for the gnarled shape behind the tombstones, a squat willow, before positioning the flashlight on the ground to his left, bottom down, so that its white light draws a cone in the air. He settles himself down beside it, his back leaning for and finding a tombstone, his legs gradually crossing in front of him.

(It has to be said, even with the light shining right beside him, the Stage Manager is not easy to see. A reasonable guess would locate him somewhere in his late forties, but estimates a decade to either side

17

would not be unreasonable. His eyes are deep set, sheltered under heavy brows and the bill of the worn baseball cap on his head. His nose is thick and may have been broken in some distant confrontation; the shadows from the light spilling across his face make it difficult to decide if his broad upper lip sports a mustache, although his solid chin is clear of any hair. His ethnicity is uncertain; he could put in an appearance at most audience members' family reunions as a cousin twice-removed and not look out of place. He is dressed warmly, for late fall, in a bomber jacket, flannel shirt, jeans, and heavy boots.)

Stage Manager: Zombies. As with most things in life, the reality, when compared to the high-tech, Hollywood gloss of the movies, comes as something of a surprise. For one thing, there's the smell, a stench that combines all the worst elements of raw sewage and rotted meat, together with the faint tang of formaldehyde. Folks used to think that last was from the funeral homes—whatever they'd used to pickle dear Aunt Myrtle—but as it turned out, this wasn't the case. It's just part of the smell they bring with them. Some people—scientists, doctors—have speculated that it's the particular odor of whatever is causing the dead to rise up and stagger around; to which speculations I gather there are objections from other scientists and doctors. But you don't have to understand the chemistry of it to know that it's theirs.

For another thing, when it comes to zombies, no one anticipated how persistent the damned things would be. You shoot them in the chest, they keep on coming. You shoot them in the leg—hell, you blow their leg clean off with your shotgun at point-blank range—they fall on their side, flop around for a minute or two, then figure out how to get themselves on their front so they can pull themselves forward with their hands, while they push with their remaining leg. And all the time, the leg you shot off is twitching like mad, as if, if it had a few more nerve cells at its disposal, it would find a way to continue after you itself. There is shooting in the head—it's true, that works, destroy enough brain matter and they drop—but do you have any idea what it's like to try to hit a moving target, even a slow-moving one, in the head at any kind of distance? Especially if you aren't using a state-of-the-art sniper rifle, but the snub-nosed .38 you bought ten years ago when the house next door was burglarized and haven't given a thought to since—and the face you're aiming at belongs to your pastor, who just last Saturday was exhorting the members of your diminished congregation not to lose hope, the Lord was testing you.

(From high over the Stage Manager's head, a spotlight snaps on, illuminating OWEN TREZZA standing in the center aisle about three-quarters of the way to the stage. He's facing the back of the theater. At a guess, he's in his mid-thirties, his brown hair standing out in odd directions the way it does when you've slept on it and not washed it for several days running, his glasses duct-taped on the right side, his cheeks and chin full of stubble going to beard. The denim jacket he's wearing is stained with dirt, grass, and what it would be nice to think of as oil, as are his jeans. The green sweatshirt under his jacket is, if not clean, at least not marred by any obvious discolorations, although whatever logo it boasted has flaked away to a few scattered flecks of white. In his outstretched right hand, he holds a revolver with an abbreviated barrel that wavers noticeably as he points it at something outside the spotlight's reach.)

Owen: Oh, Jesus. Oh, sweet Jesus. Stop. Stop right there! Pastor Parks? Please—don't come any closer. Pastor? It's Owen, Owen Trezza. Please—can you please stay where you are? I don't want to— You really need to stay there. We just have to make sure—Jesus. Please. Owen Trezza—I attend the ten o'clock service. With my wife, Kathy. We sit on the left side of the church—our left, a couple pews from the front. Pastor Parks? Can you please stop? I know you're probably in shock, but—please, if you don't stop, I'm going to have to shoot. It's Owen. My wife's expecting our first child. She has red hair. Will you stop? Will you just stop? Goddamnit, Pastor, I will shoot! I don't want to, but you're giving me no choice. Please! I don't want to have to pull this trigger, but if you don't stay where you are, I'll have to. Don't make me do this. For Christ's sake, won't you stop? I have a child on the way. I don't want to have to shoot you.

(From outside the range of the spotlight, the sound of inexpensive loafers dragging across the carpet.)

Owen: Pastor Parks—Michael—Michael Parks, this is your final warning. Stop right there. Stop. Right. There.

(The shoes continue their scrape over the carpet. From the rear of the theater, a terrible odor rolls forward, like the cloud that hangs around the carcass of a deer two days dead and burst open on a hot summer afternoon. Owen's hand is shaking badly. He grabs his right wrist with his left hand, which steadies it enough for him to pull the trigger. The gun cracks like an especially loud firecracker and jerks up and away. Owen brings it back to aim.)

Owen: Okay—that was a warning shot. Now please stay where you are.

(The rough noise of the steps is joined by the outline of a figure at the edge of the spotlight's glow. Owen shoots a second time; again, the gun cracks and leaps back. He swings it around and pulls the trigger four times, straining to keep the pistol pointed ahead. Now the air is heavy with the sharp smell of gunsmoke. Hands at its sides, back stiff, swaying like a metronome as it walks, the figure advances into the light. It is a man perhaps ten years Owen's senior, dressed in a pair of khaki slacks and a black short-sleeved shirt whose round white collar is crusted with dried blood. Except for a spot over his collar, which is open in a dull, ragged wound the color of old liver, his skin is gray. Although it is difficult to see his face well, it is slack, his mouth hanging open, his eyes vacant. The hammer clacks as Owen attempts to fire his empty gun.)

Owen: Come on, Pastor Parks. I'm sorry I called you Michael. Come on—I know you can hear me. Stop. Please. Stop. Will you stop? Will you just stop? For the love of Christ, will you just fucking STOP!

(PASTOR MICHAEL PARKS—or the zombie formerly known by that name—does not respond to Owen's latest command any more than he has those preceding it. Owen's hands drop. A look passes over his face—the momentary stun of someone recognizing his imminent mortality—only to be chased off by a surge of denial. He starts to speak.

(Whatever he was about to say, whether plea or threat or defiance, is drowned out by a BOOM that staggers the ears. Simultaneously, the back of Pastor Parks's head blows out in a spray of stale blood and congealed brains and splinters of bone that spatters those sitting to either side of the aisle. The minister drops to the floor.

(The Stage Manager has risen to his feet. In his right hand, he holds out a long-barreled pistol trailing a wisp of smoke. For what is probably not more than five seconds, he keeps the gun trained on the pastor's unmoving body, then raises the revolver and returns it to a shoulder holster under his left arm. Owen Trezza continues staring at the corpse as the spotlight snaps off. The Stage Manager resumes his seat.)

Stage Manager: No, there are some marksmen and—women about, that's for sure, but it's equally sure they're in the minority. Most folks have to rely on other methods. A few would-be he-men have tried to play Conan the Barbarian, rushed the zombies with a hatchet in one hand, a butcher knife in the other. One particularly inspired specimen, a heavyset guy named Gary Floss, rip-started the chainsaw he'd bought to take down the line of pines in front of his house. (This was a mistake: then everyone saw what lousy shape Gary kept his house in.) The problem is, that hatchet you have in your right hand isn't a weapon; it's a tool you've used splitting wood for the fireplace, and while it's probably sharp enough for another winter's worth of logs, it's not going to separate someone's head from their shoulders with a single blow from your mighty arm. The same thing's true for the knife sweating up your left hand: it's cutlery, and if you recall the effort it takes to slice a roast with it—a roast that is not trying to find its way inside your skull with its persistent fingers—you might want to reconsider your chances of removing limbs with ease. Even if you have a razor-sharp ax and an honest-to-God machete, these things are actually fairly difficult to use well. The movies—again—aside, no one picks up this kind of weapon and is instantly skilled with it; you need training. In the meantime, you're likely to leave your hatchet lodged in a collarbone, the pride of your assorted knives protruding above a hip.

As for Gary Floss and his chainsaw—you want to be careful swinging one of those around. A man could take off an arm.

(To the right and left of the theater, the snarl of a chainsaw starting. It revs once, twice, a third time, changes pitch as it catches on something. It blends with a man's voice shrieking—then silence.)

Stage Manager: What works is fire. Zombies move away from fire faster than they move toward a fresh kill. The problem is, they're not especially flammable—no more than you or I are—so you have to find a way to make the fire stick. For a time, this meant Billy Joe Royale's homemade napalm. A lingering sense of civic responsibility precludes me from disclosing the formula for Billy Joe's incendiary weapon, which he modified from suggestions in—was it *The Anarchist's Cookbook*? or an old issue of *Soldier of Fortune*? or something he'd watched on the Discovery Channel, back before it stopped broadcasting? (It's the damnedest thing: do you know, the History Channel's still on the air?

Just about every other channel's gone blue. Once in a while, one of the stations out of the City will manage a broadcast; the last was a week and a half ago, when the ABC affiliate showed a truncated news report that didn't tell anyone much they hadn't already heard or guessed, and a re-run of an episode of *General Hospital* from sometime in the late nineties. But wherever the History Channel is located, someone programmed in twenty-four hours' worth of old World War II documentaries that have been playing on continuous loop ever since. You go from D-Day to Pearl Harbor to Anzo, all of it in black and white, interrupted by color-ful ads for restaurant chains that haven't served a meal in a month, cars that no one's seen on the road for as long, movies that never made it to the theater. Truth to tell, I think the folks who bother to waste their generator's power on the TV do so more for the commercials than any nostalgia for a supposed Greatest Generation. These days, a Big Mac seems an almost fabulous extravagance, a Cadillac opulent decadence, a new movie an impossible indulgence.)

That's all a bit off-topic, though. We were talking about Billy Joe and his bathtub napalm. By the time he perfected the mixture, the situation here had slid down the firepole from not-too-bad to disastrous, all within the matter of a couple of days. Where we are—

Son of a gun. I never told you the name of this place, did I? I apolo-gize. It's—the zombies have become so much the center of existence that they're the default topic of conversation, what we have now instead of the weather. This is the town of Goodhope Crossing, specifically, the municipal cemetery out behind the Dutch Reformed Church. Where I'm sitting is the oldest part of the place; the newer graves are . . .

(The Stage Manager points out at the audience.)

Stage Manager: Relax, relax. While there's nowhere that's completely safe anymore, the cemetery's no worse a danger than anyplace else. For the better part of—I reckon it must be going on four decades, local regulations have decreed that every body must be buried in a properly sealed coffin, and that coffin must be buried within a vault. To prevent contamination of groundwater and the like. The zombies have demon-strated their ability to claw their way out of all sorts of coffins time and again, but I have yet to hear of any of them escaping a vault. Rumors to the contrary, they're not any stronger than you or me; in fact, as a rule, they tend to be weaker. And the longer they go without feeding, the weaker they become. Muscle decay, you know. Hunger doesn't exactly kill them—it more slows them down to the point they're basically motionless. Dormant, you might say. So the chances are good that anyone who might have been squirming around down there in the dirt has long since run out of gas. Granted, not that I'm in any rush to make absolutely sure.

It is true, those who passed on before the requirement for a vault were able to make their way to the surface. A lot of them weren't exactly in the best of shape to begin with, though, and the ordeal of breaking out of their coffins and fighting up through six feet of earth—the soil in these parts is dense, thick with clay and studded with rocks—it didn't do anything to help their condition, that's for sure. Some of the very old ones didn't arrive in one piece, and there were some who either couldn't complete the trip or weren't coherent enough even to start it.

(Stage right, a stage light pops on, throwing a dim yellow glow over one of the tombstones and JENNIFER and JACKSON HOWLAND, she standing behind the headstone, he seated on the ground in front of and to its right. They are sister and brother, what their parents' friends secretly call Catholic or Irish twins: Jennifer is ten months her brother's senior, which currently translates to seventeen to his sixteen. They are siblings as much in their build—tall yet heavy—as they are in their angular faces, their brown eyes, their curly brown hair. Both are dressed in orange hunting caps and orange hunting vests over white cable-knit sweaters, jeans, and construction boots. Jennifer props a shotgun against her right hip and snaps a piece of bubble gum. Jackson has placed his shotgun on the ground behind him; chin on his fists, he stares at the ground.)

Jennifer: I still say you're sitting too close.

Jackson: It's fine, Jenn.

Jennifer: Yeah, well, see how fine it is when I have to shoot you in the head to keep you from making me your Happy Meal.

(Jackson sighs extravagantly, pushes himself backwards, over and behind his gun.)

Jackson: There. Is that better?

Jennifer: As long as the person whose grave you're sitting on now doesn't decide your ass would make a tasty treat.

(Jackson glares at her and climbs to his feet.)

Jennifer: Aren't you forgetting something?

(She nods at the shotgun lying on the ground. Jackson thrusts his hands in the pockets of his vest.)

Jackson: I'm sure there'll be plenty of time for me to arm myself if anything shows up.

Jennifer: Don't be so sure. Christine Compton said her family was attacked by a pair of eaters who ran like track stars.

Jackson: Uh-huh.

Jennifer: Why would she make that up?

Jackson: She—did Mr. Compton kill them?

Jennifer: It was Mrs. Compton, actually. Christine's dad can't shoot worth shit.

Jackson: Regardless—they're both dead, these sprinting zombies. Again. So we don't have to worry about them.

Jennifer: There could be others. You never know.

Jackson: I'll take my chances. (Pauses.) Besides, it's not as if we need to be here in the first place.

Jennifer: Oh?

Jackson: Don't you think, if Great-Grandma Rose were going to return, she would have already? I mean, it's been like, what? ten days? two weeks? since the last ones dug themselves out. And it took them a while to do that.

Jennifer: Right, which means there could be others who'll need even longer.

Jackson: Do you really believe that?

Jennifer: Look—it's what Dad wants, okay?

Jackson: And we all know he's the poster-child for mental health these days.

Jennifer: What do you expect? After what happened to Mom and Lisa—

Jackson: What he says happened.

Jennifer: Not this shit again.

Jackson: All I'm saying is, the three of them were in the car—in a Hummer, for Christ's sake. They had guns. How does that situation turn against you? That's an honest question. I'd love to know how you go from that to—

Jennifer: Just shut up.

Jackson: Whatever.

(The siblings look away from each other. Jackson wanders the graves to the right, almost off-stage, then slowly turns and walks back to their great-grandmother's grave. While he does, Jennifer checks her gun, aims it at the ground in front of the tombstone, and returns it to its perch on her hip. Jackson steps over his shotgun and squats beside the grave.)

Jackson: Did Dad even know her?

Jennifer: His grandmother? I don't think so. Didn't she die before he was born? Like, years before, when Grandpa Jack was a kid?

Jackson: I guess. I don't remember. Dad and I never talked about that kind of stuff—family history.

Jennifer: I'm pretty sure he never met her.

Jackson: Great.

(Another pause.)

Jennifer: You want to know what I keep thinking about?

Jackson: Do I have a choice?

Jennifer: Hey, fuck you. If that's the way you're going to be, fuck you.

Jackson: I'm sorry. Sorry, geez.

Jennifer: Forget it.

Jackson: Seriously. Come on. I'm sorry.

Jennifer: I was going to say that, for like the last week, I haven't been able to get that Thanksgiving we went to Grandpa Jack's out of my head. That cranberry sauce Dad made—

Jackson: Oh yeah, yeah! Man, that was awful. What was it he put in it . . .

Jennifer: Jalapeño peppers.

Jackson: Yes! Yes! Remember, Grandpa started coughing so hard—

Jennifer: His teeth shot out onto Mom's plate!

Jackson: Yeah . . . (He wipes his eyes.) Hey. (He stands, stares down at the grave.) Is that—what is that?

Jennifer: What?

Jackson (pointing): There. In the middle. See how the ground's . . .

(Jennifer positions her gun, setting the stock against her shoulder, lowering the barrel, and steps around the headstone.)

Jennifer: Show me.

(Jackson kneels, brings his right hand to within an inch of the ground.)

Jennifer: Not so close.

Jackson: You see it, right?

(Jennifer nods. Jackson rises and steps back onto his gun, almost tripping over it.)

Jennifer: You might want to cover your ears.

(Jennifer fires five times into the earth. Jackson slaps his hands to either side of his head as dirt jumps up from the grave. The noise of the shotgun is considerable, a roar that chases its echoes around the inside of the theater. There's a fair amount of gunsmoke, too, so that when Jennifer steps back and raises her gun, Jackson coughs and waves his arms to clear the air.)

Jackson: Holy shit.

Jennifer: No sense in doing a half-assed job.

Jackson: Was it her?

Jennifer: I think so. Something was right at the surface.

Jackson: Let's hope it wasn't a woodchuck.

Jennifer: Do you see any woodchuck guts?

Jackson: I don't see much of anything. (He stoops, retrieves his shot-gun.) Does this mean we can go home?

Jennifer: We should probably wait a couple more minutes, just to be sure.

Jackson: Wonderful.

(The two of them stare down at the grave. The stage light pops off.)

Stage Manager: Siblings.

Right—what else can I tell you about the town? I don't imagine latitude and longitude are much use; I'm guessing it'll be more helpful for me to say that New York City's about an hour and a half south of here, Hartford an hour and a half east, and the Hudson River twenty minutes west. In an average year, it's hot in the summer, cold in the winter. There's enough snow to give the kids their fair share of snow days; you can have thunderstorms so fierce they spin off tornadoes like tops. At one time, this was IBM country; that, and people who com-muted to blue-collar jobs in the City at places like Con Ed. That changed twice, the first time in the early nineties, when IBM collapsed and sent a host of middle-aged men and women scrambling for work. The second time was after 9/11, when all the affluent folks who'd

suddenly decided Manhattan was no longer their preferred address realized that, for the same amount of money you were spending on your
glorified walk-in closet, you could be the owner of a substantial home
on a reasonable piece of property in place that was still close enough to
the City for you to have a manageable commute.

Coming after the long slowdown in new home construction that
had followed IBM's constriction, this sent real estate prices up like a
Fourth of July rocket. Gentrification, I guess you'd call it. What it
meant was that your house significantly appreciated in value in what
seemed like no more than a month—it wasn't overnight, no, not that
fast, but fast enough, I reckon. We're talking thirty, forty, fifty percent
climbs, sometimes higher, depending on how close you were to a Me-
tro-North station, or the Taconic Parkway. It also meant a boom in
the construction of new homes—luxury models, mostly. They didn't
quite achieve the status of McMansions, but they were too big on the
outside with too few rooms on the inside and crowded too close to
their neighbors, with a front yard that was just about big enough to be
worth the effort it was going to cost you to yank the lawnmower to life
every other Saturday. If you owned any significant amount of property,
the temptation to cash in on all the contractors making up for lost time
was nigh-irresistible. That farm that hadn't ever been what you'd call a
profit-machine, and that had been siphoning off more money that it
gave back for more years than you were comfortable admitting, became a dozen, fifteen parcels of land, a new little community with a
name, something like Orchard Hills, that you could tell yourself was an
acknowledgment of its former occupant.

What this expansion of houses meant was that, when the zombies
started showing up in significant numbers, they found family after
family waiting for them in what must have seemed like enormous lun-
chboxes.

(From the balcony, another spotlight snaps on, its tightly focused
beam picking out MARY PHILLIPS standing in front of the orchestra
pit. Although she faces the audience, her gaze is unfocused. She cannot
be thirty. Her red hair has been cut recently—poorly, practically
hacked off in places, where it traces the contours of her skull, and only
partially touched in others, where it sprouts in tufts and a couple of
long strands that suggest its previous style. The light freckles on her

face are disturbed by the remnants of what must have been an enormous black eye, which has faded to a motley of green and yellow, and
a couple of darker spots, radiating out from her right eye. She is wearing a white dress shirt whose brownish polka dots appear to have been
applied irregularly, even haphazardly, a pair of almost-new dark jeans,
and white sneakers clumped with mud. She keeps her hands at her
sides in tight fists.)

Mary: I was in the kitchen, boiling water for pasta. We'd had a gas delivery a couple of weeks before—it's funny: everything's falling to
pieces—this was after the first outbreak had been contained, and all
the politicians and pundits were saying yes, we'd had a close call, but
the worst was past—what had happened in India, Asia, what was happening in South America—none of that was going to happen here. No
matter that there were reports the things—what we were calling the
eaters, because zombies sounded too ridiculous—the eaters had been
sighted in a dozen different places from Maine to California, none of
them previously affected. You heard stories: my next-door neighbor,
Barbara Odenkirk—she was the HR director for an ad agency in Manhattan, and she commuted to the City every day, took the train from
Beacon. The last time we talked, she told me that there were more of
them, the eaters, along the sides of the tracks every trip. She said none
of the guys on the train acted particularly concerned—if an eater came
too close to a moving train, it didn't end well for them. I asked her
about the places alongside the tracks, what about them, the towns and
cities and houses—I'd taken that same ride I don't know how many
times, when Ted and I first started seeing one another, and I remembered all the houses you saw sitting off in the woods. Oh, Barbara said,
she was sure the local police were on top of the situation. They weren't, of course, not like Barbara thought. I don't know why. When
that soccer game in Cold Spring was attacked—we were so surprised,
so shocked, so outraged. We should have been packing our cars,
cramming everything we could fit into our Volvos and BMW's and
heading out of town tires screaming. Where, I'm not sure. Maybe
north, up to the Adirondacks—I heard the situation isn't as bad there.
Even the Catskills might have been better.

But the gas truck pulled into the driveway the way it did every six
months, and the power was on more than it was out, and we could

drive to Shop Rite—where, if the shelves were stocked thinner than we'd ever seen them, and the butcher case was empty, not to mention the deli and fish counters, we could fill our baskets with enough of the foods we were used to for us to tell ourselves that the President was right, we were through the roughest part of this, and almost believe it. Ted had bought a portable generator when the first outbreak was at its height and it looked as if Orlando would be overrun; everyone else was buying whatever guns they could lay their hands on, and here's my husband asking me to help him unload this heavy box from the back of the car. He was uptight—I think he was expecting me to rake him over the coals for not having returned from Wal-Mart with an armful of rifles. I wasn't angry; if anything, I was impressed with his foresight. I wasn't especially concerned about being armed—at that point, I still believed the police and National Guard were capable of dealing with the eaters, and if they weren't, I was surrounded by neighbors who were two steps away from forming their own militia. The blackouts, though—we were lucky: the big one only lasted here until later that same night. According to NPR, there were places where the lights were out for a week, ten days. But there were shorter outages every few days, most no more than five or ten seconds, a few a solid couple of hours. Having the generator—not to mention the big red containers of gas I had no idea how Ted had obtained: rationing was already in effect, and most gas stations were pretty serious about it—that generator gave me a feeling of security no machine gun could have matched. To tell the truth, I was more worried by Ted's insistence that he could hook it up himself. Being in IT does not give you the magical ability to master any and all electrical devices—how many times had I said that to him? Especially when Sean Reynolds two houses over is an electrician who loves helping out with this kind of stuff. But no, he's fully capable of doing this, which is what he'd said about the home entertainment system he tripped half the circuit breakers in the house setting up. What was I supposed to do? I made sure to unplug the computers, though, as well as the entertainment center.

Somehow—with a lot more cursing than I was happy with the kids hearing from their father—he succeeded, which is why, on that particular afternoon, I was standing at the kitchen stove waiting for a pot of water to reach the boil. Robbie had asked for mac and cheese again, and I wasn't inclined to argue with her, since Brian would eat it, too, and we had more than enough boxes of it stacked in the pantry. It was the organic kind that only needed a little bit of milk added to make the sauce, which I thought was more economical; although the stuff had cost more to begin with, so where's the sense in that? The power had gone out an hour earlier, and while we tried to use the generator prudently, starting it up now didn't seem especially extravagant. I waited until I was ready to start dinner, then ran out onto the back porch, down the stairs, and under the porch to where Ted had installed the generator. When Ted was home, the moment he heard that lock click, he dropped whatever he was doing to dash into the kitchen and asked if I'd made sure it was safe to go outside. No matter what I replied, he'd insist on checking, himself—as if he could see better through his glasses than I could with 20/20 vision. I got that it was a guy thing, and in its own way I suppose it was kind of sweet. Really, though— unless there was an eater standing outside the door, I didn't think I had anything to worry about. They weren't much for running—most of them had trouble walking. Okay, high school track was ten years and two kids in my past, but I was still in good enough shape from chasing after those kids to leave Ted eating my dust. Granted, my husband's idea of exercise was putting away the dishes; the point is, I wasn't concerned about being caught by an eater. From what I'd heard on the radio, they were most dangerous in large numbers, when they could trap you. Sure, there were woods at the edge of the backyard that could have hidden a decent-sized group of them, but I was fairly confident my well-armed neighbors would mow the lot of them down the second they staggered into the open. We were pretty anal about checking the tree line; I tried to do it at least once an hour, usually on the hour when the hall clock played its electronic version of the Westminster Chimes, but some of the neighbors were at their windows every fifteen or twenty minutes. Matt Odenkirk had a pair of high-powered binoculars—they looked like they cost a bundle—and he would stand on his back porch staring into the woods for minutes at a time. It was as if he was certain the eaters were out there, doing their best to blend in with the foliage, and all he needed was to catch one of them moving to reach for the equally expensive-looking rifle balanced against the railing and be the hero of the neighborhood. Which never happened. I don't think he fired that gun once—I don't think it was in his hands when—when they—when he—

The generator started no problem; I was out and in the house almost before the kids realized. I turned on the stove light and filled a pot with water from the cooler—which always drove Ted crazy. "That's for drinking only," he'd say. "Use the water from the filter jugs for cooking." But our water tasted funny; I'm sorry, it did, and no matter how many times you passed it through those jugs, it was like drinking from a sulfur spring. "What do you mean?" Ted would—he'd insist. "It tastes fine." Okay, I'd say, then you can drink it, which he would, of course, to prove his point. When he wasn't home, though—on a day like today, when he'd driven in to IBM because they were open—I can't imagine what they could have been doing, what business they could have been conducting, with everything the way it was—on a day like today, we used the bottled water for cooking.

I lit the burner, set the pot on it, and switched on the transistor radio. Usually, I kept the radio quiet, because who knew what the news was going to be today? Granted, NPR wasn't as bad as any of the TV channels, which, as things had deteriorated in Florida and Alabama, had taken to broadcasting their raw footage, so that when Mobile was overrun, you saw all the carnage in color and up close and personal. But NPR had sent a reporter to Mobile, and when the National Guard lines collapsed, she was caught on the wrong side—trapped inside a car. The eaters got her, and you heard pretty much everything. First, she's saying "Oh no, oh please," as they pound on the car windows. Then the windows shatter, she screams, and you can hear the eaters, the slap of their hands on the upholstery as they grab her at her and miss, the rip of the reporter's clothes where they catch her, and their voices—I know there's a lot of debate about the sounds they make, whether they're expressions of coherent thought or just some kind of muscle spasm, but I swear, I listened to that broadcast all the way through, and those were voices, they were saying something. I couldn't make out what, because now the reporter was shrieking, emptying her lungs in panic and pain. I thought that was as bad as it would get—as it could get—but I was wrong. There was a sound—it was the sound a drumstick makes when you twist it off the Thanksgiving turkey, a long tearing followed by a pop—only it was . . . wet. The reporter's voice went from high to low, from scream to moan, and that moan—it was awful, it was what comes out of you the moment you set one foot into death and feel it tugging the rest of you after. The rest—one of the eaters figured out how to open one of the car doors. Whatever the reporter was wearing rasped on the seat as she was dragged out, her moan rising a little as she realized this was it, and then there was a noise like the rest of that Thanksgiving bird being torn apart in all directions, this succession of ripping and snapping, and then you hear the eaters feeding, stuffing pieces of the reporter into their mouths, grunting with pleasure at the taste. It—

Robbie was old enough to understand what was on the radio, and even Brian picked up on more than you expected. I didn't want to expose them to something like that. As it was, they heard too much from the other kids in the neighborhood, especially the McDonald girls. Alice, their mother, was one of those parents who likes to pretend they're treating their kids with what they call respect, when really, all they're doing is exposing them to all kinds of things they're too young to handle. A parent—a mother isn't supposed to—that's not your job. Your job—your duty, your sacred duty—it is your sacred duty to protect those children, to keep them safe no matter what—you have to protect them, no matter—

Well, I was. With the generator running, I could let them watch a DVD, which had gone from a daily occurrence—sometimes twice daily—to a treat, just as going to the movies had been when I was their age. They were so thrilled Robbie was willing to sit down to *The Incredibles,* which Brian adored, although it didn't do anything for her. So with the two of them safely seated in front of the TV, I was safe to turn on the radio, low, and try to catch up with what news I could as the water came to a boil.

And you know, the news wasn't bad. I wouldn't call it good, exactly, but the National Guard seemed to be making progress. They'd held on to Orlando, although apparently Disneyworld was the worse for it; and they'd caught a significant number of the eaters on one of the major highways—I can't remember the number; it may have been Highway 1—where they'd brought in the air power, let the planes drop bombs on the eaters until they were in so many microscopic pieces. Given what we learned about them in the weeks after, this was about the worst thing that could have happened, since it spread bits of them and their infection to the four winds, but at the time it sounded like a step forward. There was talk of retaking Mobile; a team of Navy SEALs had rescued a group of survivors holed up in City Hall, and a squad of Special Forces had made an exploratory journey into the city that had brought them to within sight of the harbor. Of course, the powers-that-be are going to tell you that things are better than they are, but I was willing to believe them.

I heard the truck pull up outside, heard the slow rumble of its engine, the squeal and hiss of its air brakes. I noticed it, but I wasn't especially concerned. The Rosses had sold their house across the street to a couple from the City who supposedly had paid them almost a million dollars for it. The news made our eyes goggle; Ted and I spent a giddy couple of hours imagining how we might spend our million. Once we went online to check housing prices in the Adirondacks, though, all our fantasies came crashing down. Up north, a million was the least you'd pay for a place not even half the size of ours. We knew Canada had closed the border, but we looked anyway. With the state of the U.S. dollar, it was more like 1.5 million for the same undersized house. It appeared we would be staying where we were. And we'd have new neighbors, whose moving truck had arrived.

Sometimes, I think about that driver. I don't know anything about him—or her, it could have been a woman; although, for some reason, I always picture a man. Not a kid: someone in his fifties, maybe, kind of heavyset, with a crewcut that doesn't hide the gray in his hair. He's been around long enough to have seen all kinds of crises, which is why he doesn't panic, keeps working through this one. No one else at the delivery company wants to make the drive upstate with him, risk the wilds to the north, but he's happy to leave the City for a day. Everybody's on edge. There are soldiers and heavily armed police clustered at all the docks, the airports, the train stations, the bus terminals. Everyone who arrives in the City is supposed to be examined by a doctor flanked by a pair of men who keep the laser-sights of their pistols centered on the traveler's forehead for the duration of the exam. The slightest cause for concern—fever, swollen and tender glands, discolored tongue—is grounds for immediate quarantine. Protest, and those men to either side of the doctor are expressly authorized to put a pair of bullets in your head. What's worse is, with the police largely off the streets, groups of ordinary citizens have taken it on themselves to patrol the City for eaters. They've given themselves license to stop and question anyone they consider suspicious, and if you ask what gives them the right, they'll be only too happy to show you the business ends of their assorted pistols and rifles. There's been at least one major shootout between two of these patrols, each of whom claimed they thought the other were eaters. Cops had to be pulled off port duty to bring it under control, which they did by shooting most of the participants.

I can't imagine anything happened to the driver while he was in the City. My guess is, he passed through the checkpoints and was on his way without a hitch. It was a nice, early fall morning, the air cool but not cold, the leaves on the verge of losing their green, the sun bright but not oppressive. Maybe he had the radio on, was listening to one of the AM stations out of the City. He heard the news out of Florida and thought, *I knew it.* He decided to take the next exit, stop at a Dunkin' Donuts for a celebratory coffee and a Boston Cream.

As he steered into the parking lot, maybe he noticed the absence of any other cars. Or maybe he saw the lights on in the donut shop and assumed he'd arrived during a lull in business. He parked the truck, climbed down from the cab, and walked toward the glass door. There are times I see him striding up to the counter, his eyes on the racks of donuts on the wall opposite him, not aware of anything unusual until he sees that all the racks are empty. In what feels to him like slow-motion, he turns to the tables to his right and takes in the floor slick with blood, the remains of the last patrons scattered across the tables. Then I think, *That's ridiculous—there's no way he would not have seen all of that right away.* The second he swung open the door, he would have smelled it. Chances are, he wouldn't have had to go that far—he would have seen the blood splashed across the windows and immediately turned around. Either way—whether he bolts out of the place or walks away without going in—he would be distracted, shocked by what he's (almost) seen. Maybe the closest he's been to something like this has been an image on the TV. It's the reason he doesn't pick up on the feet dragging across the tarmac until the eater is out from around the front of the truck and practically on him. The driver's eyes bulge; if he's never been this close to such carnage, you can be sure he's never had an eater lurching toward him, either. His feet catch on one another and he trips, which causes the eater to trip and fall on top of him. For one horrifying moment, he's under the thing, under that stink, the teeth clacking in his ear as it tries to take a bite out of him, those hands pawing at him. He drives his right elbow back and up into its face. Fireworks of pain burst in his arm, but the eater rolls off him. He scrambles to his feet, kicking at the eater's hands as they try to drag him down again, and climbs up and into the truck's cab. Maybe he jumps when the eater slaps the door, almost drops the keys his fingers can't fit into the ignition. The eater pounds the door, throws itself against it, actually makes the truck rock ever so slightly. The key slides into place, the engine turns over, and the driver grinds the gears, putting the truck into first. He speeds out of that parking lot so fast the rear end of the truck bashes a telephone pole, throwing open one of the rear doors and tumbling a couple of plastic crates out onto the road. His foot doesn't leave the gas pedal. Let them take it out of his pay. His heart is hammering, his hands trembling on the wheel. If he smokes, he's desperate for a cigarette; if he quit, he wishes he hadn't; if he never has, he wishes he'd started.

It wouldn't have been until that Dunkin' Donuts was a good thirty, forty minutes in his rearview mirror that the driver would have felt his right elbow throbbing. When he glances down, he sees blood on the seat and floor. He turns his arm over. His stomach squeezes at the torn skin bright with blood, the pair of broken teeth protruding just above the joint. His foot relaxes on the gas; the truck slows to the point it is barely moving. His vision constricts to a tunnel; he wonders if he is about to faint. He takes the wheel with his right hand, reaches around with his left, and feels for the jagged edges of the eater's teeth. The blood makes them slippery, hard to keep hold of. He digs his fingers into his skin, seeking purchase, but that only squeezes out more blood. There is no choice; he has to stop. He clicks on the hazards, steers to the shoulder, and sets the brake. He does not turn off the engine. He leans over and slides the first aid box out from under his seat. His fingers slip on the catch. Once he has it open, he finds the bottle of sterile saline and the stack of gauze bandages. He sprays half the bottle over his elbow, unwraps a couple of bandages, and wipes his skin. There is a pair of tweezers in the box; despite his shaking hand, he succeeds in tugging one, and then the other, tooth from his arm. Their extraction causes more bleeding. He drops the tweezers on the floor, next to the teeth, and empties the remainder of the saline on his elbow. There are enough gauze pads left for him to wipe his elbow off and improvise a bandage using the roll of surgical tape.

No one really understood what brought the eaters out of the ground, up off their tables in the morgues and funeral homes, in the first place. There was all kinds of speculation, some of it ridiculous. Hell was full: Ted and I had a good laugh over that one. Some of it was more plausible but still theoretical: NPR had on a scientist from the CDC who talked about a kind of super-bacteria, like a nasty staph infection that could colonize a human host in order to gain more flesh to consume; although that seemed like a lot for a single microorganism to accomplish. Besides, none of the eaters the government had captured showed the slightest response to any of the antibiotics they were injected with. I wondered if it was a combination of causes, several bacteria working together, but Ted swore that was impossible. Because the IT thing made him an expert in bacteriology, too.

What we did know was that, if an eater got its teeth in you, even if you escaped becoming its next meal, you were finished all the same. It just took longer—between thirty minutes and forty-eight hours. The initial symptoms were a raging fever, swollen and tender glands, and a tongue the color of old meat; in short order, these were followed by hallucinations, convulsions, and death. Anywhere from five minutes to two hours after your heart had ceased beating, your body—reanimated was the technical term. It was incurable, and if you presented to your doctor or a hospital ER with the telltale signs, you were taken as fast as possible to a hospital room, hooked up to monitors for your heart rate and blood pressure, and strapped onto a bed. If there was an experimental cure making the rounds that day, it would be tested on you. When it didn't work, you would be offered the services of the clergy and left for the inevitable. An armed guard was stationed outside your door; after the monitors had confirmed your death, he would enter the room, unholster his pistol, and make sure you didn't return. At first, the guards were given silencers, but people complained, said they felt better hearing the gunshot, knowing they were safe.

I don't know how much of this the driver knew, but I'm guessing he'd heard most of it, which is why he didn't take himself to the nearest hospital as soon as he realized what had happened to him. Instead, he switched off the hazards, released the brake, and headed back out onto the road. It could be he was thinking he had to make this last delivery while he could, but I doubt it. He was already dead; his body simply needed to catch up to that fact. His mind, though—his mind was not having any of this. As far as his mind was concerned, he'd scraped his arm, that was all, hardly enough to have turned him into one of those things, and if he went on with this day the way he'd intended, everything would be fine. If he had to roll down his window, because the cab had grown so hot he checked to be sure he hadn't turned the heater on high, he must be fighting off the cold that was making the rounds at work. That same cold must be what was causing the skin under his jaw to feel so sore. The temptation to tilt the rearview mirror so he could inspect his tongue must have been almost too much to resist.

If the driver heard anything moving in the back of the truck, he probably assumed it was more of the plastic crates come loose, maybe a piece of furniture that had broken the straps securing it. Of course, by then his fever would have ignited, so the eaters could have banged around the inside of that container for the hours it took him to complete what should have been a sixty-minute trip, and I doubt he would have noticed. Or the sounds might have registered, but—you know how it is when you're that sick: you're aware of what's going on around you, but there's a disconnect—it fails to mean what it should. How else do you explain what led this guy to drive a large moving truck full of eaters into the middle of a neighborhood—into the middle of our neighborhood—my neighborhood, the place where I lived with my husband and my kids, my girl and my boy—how else do you explain someone fucking up so completely, so enormously?

That's right—the truck that came to a stop outside the house as I watched bubbles forming at the bottom of the pot of water I was heating was full—it was packed with eaters. Don't ask me how many. And no, I don't know how they got in there. I'd never heard of anything like that before. Maybe the things were chasing someone who climbed into the back of the truck thinking the eaters wouldn't be able to follow them and was wrong. Maybe the eaters started as a group of infected who were in the same state of denial as the driver and wanted to hide themselves until they recovered—which, of course, they didn't. Maybe they didn't jump into the truck all at the same time: maybe a few were in pursuit of a meal, a few more were looking to hide, and a few others thought they'd found a cool place to escape the sun. As the fever soared within him, his neck ached so bad swallowing became agony, his tongue swelled in his mouth, the driver must have let the truck slow to a stop over and over again, leaning his head on the steering wheel for whatever comfort its lukewarm plastic could provide. There would have been plenty of opportunities for eaters to hitch a ride with him.

I don't know what that man's fate was, whether he died the moment he set the parking brake, or opened the door and stepped down from the cab to let his customers know their furniture had arrived, or if the eaters figured out the door handle and dragged him from his seat. But I hope they got to him first; I hope he found himself in the middle of a group of eaters and had consciousness left to understand what was about to happen to him. I hope—I pray; I get down on my knees and plead with God Almighty that those things ripped him apart while his heart was still beating. I hope they stripped the flesh from his arms and legs. I hope they jammed their fingers into him and rooted around for his organs. I hope they bit through his ears the way you do a tough piece of steak. I hope he suffered. I hope he felt pain such as no one ever felt before. That's why I spend so much time imagining him, so that his death can be as real—as vivid—to me as possible. I—

The first bubbles had lifted themselves off the bottom of the pot and drifted up through the water to burst at the surface. On the radio, the report about the Special Forces in Mobile had ended, and the anchor was talking about sightings of eaters in places like Bangor, Carbondale, and Santa Cruz, which the local authorities were writing off as hysteria but at least some of which, the anchor said, there was disturbing evidence were true; in which case, they represented a new phase in what he called the Reanimation Crisis. From the living room, Brian yelped and said, "Scary!" which he did when something on the screen was too much for him; Robbie said, "It's okay—Vi's gonna get them out. Watch," one of those grace notes your kids sound that makes you catch your breath, it's so unexpected, so pure. There was a knock at the front door.

It sounded like a knock. When I rewind it and play it again in my mind, it still sounds like a knock, no matter how I try to hear it otherwise. None of the descriptions of the eaters mentioned anything about knocking. Besides, I hadn't heard anyone's gun going off, which I fully expected would announce the arrival of eaters in our neck of the woods. Of course, this was because everyone was watching the treeline behind the houses; I realize how ridiculous it sounds, how unforgivably stupid, but it never occurred to any of us that the eaters might walk right up to our front doors and knock on them. Or—I don't know—maybe we were aware of the possibility, but assumed there was no way a single eater, let alone a truckload of them, could appear in the middle of the street without someone noticing.

I left the pot with the wisps of steam starting to curl off the water and walked down the front stairs to the door. At the top of the stairs, I thought it might be Ted home from work, but on the way down I decided it couldn't be him, because he wouldn't have bothered knocking, would he? It had to be a neighbor, probably the McDonald girls come to ask if Robbie wanted to go out and play with them. They were forever doing things like that, showing up five minutes before dinner and asking Robbie to play with them—which, the second she heard their voices, Robbie naturally was desperate to do. I tried to compromise, told Robbie she could go out for a little while after she was done with her food, or invited the McDonald girls to join us for dinner, but Robbie would insist she wasn't hungry, or the McDonald girls would say they had already eaten, or were going to have pizza later, when their father brought it home. At which, Robbie would ask why we couldn't have pizza, which Brian would hear and start chanting, "Piz-za! Piz-za! Piz-za!" Sometimes I let Robbie run out and kept a plate warm for her, let her eat with Ted and me when he got home, which she loved, being at the table with Mommy and Daddy and no little brother. Sometimes, though, I told the McDonald girls to return in half an hour, Roberta was sitting down to her dinner—and prepared myself for the inevitable storm of protests. I hadn't made up my mind what my decision this time would be, but my stomach was clenching. I turned the lock, twisted the doorknob, and pulled the door open.

They say that time slows down in moments of crisis; for some people, maybe it does. For me, swinging that door in was like hitting the fast-forward button on the DVD player, when the images on the screen advance so fast they appear as separate pictures. One moment, I'm standing with the door in my hand and a trio of eaters on the front step. They're women, about my age, I think—the one nearest me is missing most of her face. Except for her right eye, which is cloudy and blue and looks as if it's a glass eye that's been scuffed; I'm staring at bare bone adorned with tatters and shreds of muscle and skin. Her mouth—her teeth part, and I have the absurd impression she's about to speak to me.

The next moment, I'm scrambling up the stairs backwards. I could leap them three at a time—I have in the past—but there's no way I'm turning my back on the figures who have entered the house. The pair behind the faceless one don't appear nearly as desiccated: their skin is blue-gray, and their faces show no expression, but compared to what's raising her right foot to climb the stairs after me, they're practically normal.

The moment after that, I'm in the kitchen, one hand reaching for the handle of the pot of water, which hasn't come to full boil yet. Behind me, I can hear the stairs shifting under the eaters' weight. I can smell them—God, everything I've heard about the way the things smell is true. I want to call to the kids, tell them to get in here with me, but it's all I can do not to vomit.

That second, the second my fingers are closing around the handle—that's the one I return to. When I replay the three minutes it took for my life to disintegrate, I focus on me in the kitchen. I can't remember how I got there. I mean, I know how I went from the stairs to the kitchen, I don't know why. Once I reached the top of the stairs, it would have been easy enough to haul myself to my feet and run into the living room, to Robbie and Brian. We could have—I could have shoved the couch out from the wall, used it to delay the eaters while we ran for the back door—or even around them, back down the stairs and out the front door, or into the downstairs rec room. We could have barricaded ourselves in the garage. We—instead, I ran for the kitchen. I realize I must have been thinking about a weapon; I must have been searching for something to defend myself—us with, and the pot on the stove must have been the first thing that occurred to me. This has to be what made me choose the kitchen, but I can't remember it. All I have is me on the stairs, and then my fingers curling around that piece of metal.

Which isn't in my hand anymore; it's lying on the kitchen floor, and Miss Skull-Face's right eye has sagged downwards because the pot has collapsed her cheek where it struck it. The hot water doesn't appear to have had any effect on her, although a couple of the pieces of flesh dangling from her face have fallen onto her blouse. She's moving toward me fast, her hands outstretched, and I see that she's missing two of the fingers on her left hand, the ring and pinkie, and I wonder if she lost them trying to prevent whoever it was from tearing off her face.

The next thing, I'm on the floor, on my back, which is numb. My head is swimming. Across the kitchen tiles from me, Miss Skull-Face struggles to raise herself from her back. At the time, I don't know what's happened, but I realize now the eater's rush has carried us into the wall, stunning us both. The other eaters are nowhere to be seen.

And then I'm on the other side of the kitchen island, which I've scooted around on my butt. I'm driving the heel of my left foot straight into the eater's face, the shock of the impact traveling through the sole of my sneaker up my leg. I feel as much as hear the crunch of bone splintering. I'm as scared as I've ever been, but the sensation of the eater's face breaking under my foot sends a rush of animal satisfaction through me. Although I'm intent on the web of cracks spreading out from the sudden depression where Miss Skull-Face's nose and cheeks used to be, I'm aware that her companions are not in the kitchen.

I must—if I haven't before, I must understand that the other eaters have left Miss Skull-Face to deal with me and turned in search of easier—of the— I know I pull myself off the floor, and I'm pretty sure I kick the same spot on the eater's face with the toe of my sneaker, because afterwards it's smeared with what I think are her brains. What I remember next is—

(To the front, rear, left, and right of the theater, the air is full of screaming. At first, the sound is so loud, so piercing, that it's difficult for anyone in the audience to do anything more than cover her or his ears. Mary raises her hands to either side of her head; it does not appear that the Stage Manager does, even as the screams climb the register from terror to pain. Muffled by skin and bone, the screams resolve themselves into a pair of voices. It is hard to believe that such noises could issue from the throats of anything human; they seem more like the shrieks of an animal being vivisected. As they continue for four, five, six seconds—an amount of time that, under other circumstances, would pass almost without notice but that, with the air vibrating like a plucked guitar string, stretches into hours—it becomes possible to distinguish the screams as a single word tortured to the edge of intelligibility, made the vessel for unbearable pain: "Mommy."

(The screaming stops—cut off. Mary removes her hands from her ears hesitantly, as if afraid her children's screams might start again.)

Mary: That's—there are—they—there are some—I don't—there are some things a mother shouldn't have to see, all right? My parents—I—when I was growing up, our next-door neighbor's oldest son died of leukemia, and my mother said, "No parent should outlive their children." Which is true. I used to think it was the worst thing that could happen to you as a parent, especially of small children. But I was wrong—I was—they—oh, they had them in their teeth—

(Now Mary screams; head thrown back, eyes closed, hands clutching her shirt, she opens her mouth and pours forth a wail of utter loss. When her scream subsides to a low moan, her head drops forward. She brings her hands to her head, runs one over it while the other winds one of the long strands of her hair around itself.)

(From the front of the theater, Mary's voice speaks, but from the echoey quality of the words, it's clear this is a recording.)

Mary's Voice: That second, the second my fingers are closing around the handle—that's the one I return to. When I replay the three minutes it took for my life to disintegrate, I focus on me in the kitchen. I can't remember how I got there. I mean, I know how I went from the stairs to the kitchen, I don't know why. Once I reached the top of the stairs, it would have been easy enough to haul myself to my feet and run into the living room, to Robbie and Brian. We could have—Robbie and Brian. I didn't want to expose them to something like that. A parent—a mother isn't supposed to—that's not your job. Your job—your duty, your sacred duty, is to protect those children, to keep them safe no matter what—we—instead, I ran for the kitchen. I realize I must have been thinking about a weapon; I must have been searching for something to defend myself—us with, and the pot on the stove must have been the first thing that occurred to me. This has to be what made me choose the kitchen, but I can't remember it. You have to protect them, no matter—

(The recording stops. The spotlight snaps off, and Mary is gone, lost to the darkness.

(Slowly, the Stage Manager comes to his feet. Once he is up, he looks away from the audience, toward the willow behind him. He takes a deep breath before turning towards the audience again.)

Stage Manager: Here's the problem. When you sign up for this job— when you're cast in the part, if you like—you're told your duties will be simple and few. Keep an eye on things. Not that there's much you can do—not that there's anything you can do, really—but there isn't much that needs doing, truth to tell. Most of the business of day-to-day existence takes care of itself, runs ahead on the same tracks its used for as long as there've been people. Good things occur—too few, I suppose most would say—and bad things as well—which those same folks would count too numerous, I know—but even the very worst things happen now as I'm afraid they always have. Oh, sure, could be you can give a little nudge here or there, try to make sure this person won't be at work on a June morning that'll be full of gunfire, or steer the cop in the direction of that house she's had a nagging suspicion about, but mostly you're there to watch it all take place.

Then something like this—then this, these zombies, folk getting up who should be lying down—it overtakes you, sweeps across the world and your part of it like—like I don't know what, something I don't have words for. You do the best you can—what you can, which mostly consists of putting on a brave face and not turning your eyes away from whatever horror's in front of you; although there may be opportunities for more direct action.

(Through his jacket, the Stage Manager pats his gun.)

Stage Manager: You try to maintain some semblance of a sense of humor, which is not always as hard as maybe it should be. There's something to the old saw about horror and humor being flip sides of the same coin. An idiot takes his arm off with his chainsaw trying to play hero—I grant you it's pretty grim fodder for laughs, but you make do with what's to hand—so to speak.

A situation like this, though, like this poor woman and her children—those children—I know what she saw when she ran into that living room. I know what that is on her shirt, and how it got there. I can't—I don't have the faintest idea what I'm supposed to do with that knowledge. I could tell you, I suppose, but to what end? You know what those things—those eaters, that's not a bad word, is it?—you know what they did to that little girl and that little boy. There's no need for the specifics. Maybe you'd rather hear about the scene that greeted Mary when she fled her house in horror, or maybe you've guessed that, too: her neighbors' houses overrun, pretty much without a single shot being fired.

This is the beginning of the second phase of the zombie trouble—what did that newscaster call it? The Reanimation Crisis? From something people were watching on their TVs, or seeing outside the windows of their trains, zombies become something that's waiting for you when you go to get in your car, that clatters around your garage, that thumps on your door. Situation like this, where folks have known the world's going to hell and been preparing themselves for it—which mostly means emptying their bank accounts accumulating as many guns as Wal-Mart'll sell them—you'd expect that all that planning would count for something, that those zombies never would have made it up Mary's front walk, that one or the other of her neighbors would have noticed what was tumbling out the back of that delivery truck and started shooting. There'd be lot of noise, a lot of mess, possibly a close call or two, but everything would turn out well in the end. Mary would be home with her kids, her neighbors would be patting themselves on the backs with a certain amount of justifiable pride, and at least one zombie outbreak would have been contained. Instead, Mary's the only one to escape alive, which she accomplishes by running screaming out of her house, up the street and out onto Route 376, where she's struck by a red pickup truck driven by an eighteen-year-old girl who received it as a birthday present from her parents last month.

Mary avoids being hit head-on, which would have killed her, but she's tossed to the side of the road. To her credit, the girl stops, reverses, and leaves the truck to see to the woman who collided with it. Actually it's a risky move—for all the girl knows, she could have knocked down a zombie. Mary's pretty seriously concussed, but it's clear to the girl she hails from one of the big houses on the side street—the houses from which a few zombies are emerging, doused with blood. The girl doesn't waste any time: she hustles Mary into her truck and literally burns rubber racing away. The girl—who deserves a name: she's Beth Driscoll—Beth takes Mary into the center of Good-hope Crossing, to the new walk-in emergency-care place, and stays with her as the doctor examines her with an openly worried expression on his face. Mary's in what he's going to call a fugue state—like being part of the way into a coma—and she's never going to surface from it. The doctor—Dr. Bartram, for the record—tries to arrange for an ambulance to transfer her to one of the local hospitals, but all at once the ambulances are very busy. By the time he considers driving her himself, the police will have told everyone to stay off the roads. When those same police start stumbling through the front doors with wounds of their own for the doc to treat, Mary will be placed on a cot in one of the hallways and left there. Beth will check on her as she's able, which won't be much, because she'll be busy helping the doc and his staff with the injured. After the medical facilities are transferred to St. Pat's church hall, Mary's installed there, given a futon-bed and a molded plastic chair and a garbage bag full of assorted sweatpants, T-shirts, underwear, and socks. Beth tends to her as she can.

Ted doesn't show up looking for his wife. In fairness to him, that's due to his having parked in front of his house about two minutes after Beth sped off with Mary. Once he realized what was taking place, he bolted his car for the house, whose front door he'd noticed open and which had him dreading the worst. The worst met him at the door, in the form of the pair who'd devoured his children, one of whom was holding Brian's stuffed frog, which was dark with blood. You may consider it a kindness that Ted died without seeing what was left of his beloved daughter and son upstairs.

Mary can eat and drink, use the toilet if you take her to it. Speak to her, and she'll bob her head in your direction. There are times, after Beth has sat with her for an hour, maybe read to her from the Bible (which Beth secretly hopes might produce a miraculous cure), the girl looks at Mary half-slumped in her chair, or reclining on her bed, and wonders if Mary isn't lucky to be like this, safe from the chaos that's descended on the world. She has no idea—she can have no idea that deep within Mary's psyche, she's standing at that stove for the ten thousandth time, watching a pot full of water begin to boil, waiting for her children to start screaming.

(The Stage Manager sighs, looks up, looks down, rubs his hands together half-heartedly, sighs again.)

Stage Manager: I never finished telling you about the town, did I? Not that it makes much difference at this point, but maybe one or two of you are curious.

(Once more, the Stage Manager settles himself on the ground, against the headstone; although he appears to have more trouble finding a comfortable position than previously.)

Stage Manager: All right. What more is there to say about Goodhope Crossing? The longer-term history of the town isn't that much different from that of any other in this neck of the woods. There were farms around these parts as far back as the Dutch, but Goodhope Crossing, as the name suggests, owes itself to the railroads. In the years after the Civil War, when track was stitching up the country everywhere you looked, three north-south lines and one east-west line met one another right here.

(From the orchestra pit, a quartet of wooden train whistles sound softly.)

Stage Manager: There was a long, low hill to the east of the junction, a stream and some flatter land to the west. The town was plotted on that axis, the poorer folk crowding their small houses together on the hill, the better off setting up Main Street and its larger dwellings on the other side of the stream. From those two locations, the town spread outward, most of the commercial establishments opening on the other side of the hill, while the majority of new homes went up on and just off Main Street. Lot of Irish settled here; Poles and Italians, too. Big Catholic population: the local church, St. Patrick's, started on Main Street and by the turn of the century had moved across the stream to the top of another hill just south of the one most of its parish lived on. St. Pat's was part of the Archdiocese of New York; right before everything fell apart, they were the third or fourth largest congregation in the fold.

Interestingly—you might even say ironically—enough, pretty much the entire surviving population has relocated to the hill, which remained a location of more . . . affordable housing. Control the high ground: it's what a military strategist will tell you, and it's a good plan, for zombies as much as anything. Once the half-dozen or so who'd staggered up Concord Street were dealt with, and all the dwellings had been checked and double-checked to be sure they were clear, folks started putting up the best barrier they could as fast as they could around the foot of the hill, tipping over cars; running barbed wire; propping up old boxsprings, mattresses; piling whatever looked as if it might hold a walking corpse at bay long enough for you to have a clear shot at it: sofas, bureaus, bookcases, china cabinets.

(From either side of the theater, the sounds of men and women grunting, furniture creaking atop other furniture.)

Stage Manager: Hillary Schwabel, who used to manage the local True Value hardware, strung some wires all the way around what people already had christened the Wall and hooked them to several of her louder alarms; she also hung a dozen motion-detector lights from trees and houses next to the Wall. Things are so sensitive a cat'll trip them, but it beats the alternative. As a rule, zombies travel in numbers; when you see one of them, you see ten, twenty, sometimes as many as fifty, a hundred. A significant percentage of that group is going to be limber enough to make a try at getting past the Wall—and all it takes is for one of them to succeed, grab someone and start biting, for you to want to know they're moving in your direction while they're still a safe distance away. It's another myth that they only, or mostly, move at night. Their eyesight's poor-to-nonexistent—apparently, the ravages death inflicts on the eyes are exacerbated by the process of reanimation. Although they never stop moving completely, if you should have the misfortune to come across them after dark, they're likely to be shuffling their feet, practically standing in place. No, they prefer the light; the dawn pouring through the trees sets them going. A bright day is practically a guarantee you're going to see some of them.

All that said, a few of them have been known to travel by night, especially if the moon is full. And even inching forward a little bit at a time will bring you somewhere, eventually. Better safe than sorry, right?

Have you noticed how disasters bring out the clichés in droves? Why is that? Is the trite and overused that consoling? Or is it that, even though the brain is short-circuiting, it still wants to grasp what's going on, so it reaches for whatever tools are at hand, no matter how worn and rusted? Or is the language breaking down along with everything else? I've never been what you'd call a poet, but I have always prided myself on my phrasing, on a knack for finding a fit and even memorable form for whatever sentiment I'm attempting to convey. Lately, though—lately, I swear I sound more and more like a parody of a Good Ole Boy, your folksy uncle with his bucket of country wisdom.

Nor is that the worst. Before everything went down the crapper, one of my—you might say duties, although I considered it more a responsibility, if that distinction means anything to you—anyway, one of the things I did was to help those who'd shuffled off their mortal coils come to grips with their new condition. Mostly, this meant talking with them, taking them for a last look at their loved ones, about what you'd expect. In a few cases, I let them have one of their days over again, which, knowing what they knew now, tended to be a more unhappy experience than they'd anticipated. Even after I'd spoken to them, showed them what I could, there were a few who refused to walk down the long dark hall to join the ranks of those who'd gone before, who insisted on remaining in their house, or at the spot they'd ceased breathing, which was a shame, but was allowed for.

Once the dead started to rise, though—for the one thing, death no longer separated what lasted from what didn't; instead, the two remained bound together as the one began its new existence. For another thing, the destruction of that second life—or un-life—didn't allow matters to proceed on their natural course. Instead . . . well, maybe you want to see for yourselves.

(The theater's lights come on. Their harsh brightness reveals the center aisle, side aisles, front, and rear of the theater crowded with figures—with zombies, it appears, since the men, women, and children surrounding the audience bear the familiar signs of decay. Whatever shock and fear the appearance of so many of them in such proximity engenders, however, is gradually tempered by their complete lack of movement. Indeed, with the exception of one figure shuffling its way from the very back of the theater up the center aisle, the apparent zombies might as well be mannequins.)

Stage Manager: Being chained to that body as it stumbles along in the single-minded pursuit of flesh, as it finds and kills and consumes that flesh—it isn't good for the other part, for what I call the spark—it twists it, warps it, so that when it's cut loose, this is how it appears. Mostly. A few—I haven't worked out the exact numbers, but it's something on the order of one in a thousand, fifteen hundred—they show up hostile, violent, as if what they last were in life has followed them across its borders. There's no talking to them, let alone reasoning with them. I'm not certain what they could do to me—there've been rumors through the grapevine, but you know how that it is—but I'm not inclined to find out.

(The Stage Manager rises to his feet, withdrawing his revolver from its shoulder holster on the way. In a continuous motion, he extends his arm, sights along the long barrel of the gun, and squeezes the trigger. The gun's BOOM stuns the air; the young man in the brown three-piece suit who is approximately halfway to the stage jerks as the back of his head detonates in a surprisingly solid clump. The young man falls against one of the motionless forms in the aisle, an old woman wearing a blue dress and a knitted white pullover, who barely moves as he slides down her to the floor. The Stage Manager maintains his aim at the young man for five seconds, then levels the gun and sweeps it across the theater. It is difficult to ascertain whether his eye is on the figures in the aisle, the audience in their seats, or both. Unable to locate any further threats, he re-holsters the pistol. He remains standing.)

Stage Manager: That's—there's nothing else I can do. It means—I don't like thinking about what it means. It's a step up from what a fellow like that was, but—it's not a part of the job I relish. Could be, it would be a service to the rest of these folks, but I haven't got the stomach for it.

(The Stage Manager lowers himself to the ground. The lights dim but not all the way. The forms in the aisles remain where they are.)

Stage Manager: Once in a while—it's less and less, but it still happens—a regular person finds his way here. That was how I had the chance to talk with Billy Joe Royale, he-of-the-famous-homemade-napalm. I'd witnessed his handiwork in action—must have been the day after the day after that truckload of zombies parked in the middle of Mary Phillips's neighborhood. The number of zombies had increased exponentially; the cops had been overrun in most places; the National Guard who were supposed to be on their way remained an unfulfilled promise. Those who could had retreated to the parking lot of St. Pat's, which, since the hill hadn't yet been fortified, looked to be the most defensible position. I reckon it was, at that. There wasn't time for much in the way of barriers or booby-traps, but those men and women—there were forty-six of them—did what they could.

(From the right and left of the theater comes a cacophony of gunfire; of voices shouting defiance, instructions, obscenity, encouragement; of screams. It is underscored by a frenzied, atonal sawing of the violins. It subsides as the Stage Manager continues to speak, but remains faintly audible.)

Stage Manager: In the end, though, no matter how much ammunition you have, if the zombies have sufficient numbers, there's little you can hope for aside from escaping to fight another day. These folks couldn't expect that much: they'd backed themselves against the church's north wall, and the zombies were crowding the remaining three sides.

Exactly how Billy Joe succeeded in evading the zombies, finding his way inside St. Pat's, climbing up the bell-tower, and shimmying out onto the roof—all the while carrying a large cloth laundry bag of three-liter soda bottles full of an extremely volatile mixture—I'd like to take credit for it, but I was down below, all my attention focused on the by-now forty-two defenders staging what I was sure was their updated Alamo. They were aiming to die bravely, and I was not about to look away from that. When the first of Billy Joe's soda-bottle-bombs landed, no one, myself included, knew what had just taken place. About twenty feet back into the zombies' ranks, there was a flash and a clap and an eruption of heavy black smoke. Something had exploded, but none of the men and women could say what or why. When the second, third, fourth, and fifth bombs struck in an arc to either side of the first, and smoke was churning up into the air, and the smell of dead skin and muscle barbecuing was suddenly in everyone's nostrils, it was clear the cavalry had arrived. A couple of guys looked around, expecting a Humvee with a grenade-launcher on top, or an attack helicopter whose approach had been masked by the noise of the fighting. The rest were busy taking advantage of the wall of fire the bombs had created, which separated the zombies on this side of it from those on the other, reducing their numbers from who-could-count-how-many to a more manageable thirty or forty. While they worked on clearing the zombies closest to them, Billy Joe continued to lob bottle after bottle of his fiery concoction, dropping some of them into the thick of the zombies, holding onto others almost too long, so that they detonated over the zombies, literally raining fire down on their heads. He'd stuffed twenty-three bottles into that laundry bag, and he threw all but one of them.

(The din of the battle rises again, accompanied by the pops of a drumstick tapping on a drum, and the lower thrum of viols being plucked. The pops increase, the thrums increase, then the violins scream an interruption and all noise stops.)

Stage Manager: That last bomb was what killed him, a single-serve Coke bottle that remained in his hand past the point of safety. It blew off his right arm to the elbow and hurled him flaming from the roof. He didn't survive the fall, which was just as well, since his burning corpse was shot by roughly half the people he'd saved. Stupid, but understandable, I guess.

He took longer to show up than I'd anticipated, the better part of a day, during which his identity and his actions had been discovered, along with the two hundred additional bottles of napalm standing row after row in his parents' basement. Unfortunately, he hadn't seen fit to leave the formula, but those bombs were a big down payment on buying those among the living sufficient time to move to the hill and begin the process of securing it. There've been a couple of tries at duplicating his secret mix, neither of which ended well.

(From the rear of the theater, the faint *crump* of explosions.)

Stage Manager: As for Billy Joe . . .

(Stage left, a stage light pops on, throwing a dim yellow glow over one of the tombstones and BILLY JOE ROYALE, who is a very young sixteen, his face struggling with its acne, a few longish hairs trying to play a goatee on his chin. He is dressed in an oversized blue New York Giants shirt, baggy jeans, and white sneakers. A backwards baseball cap lifts the blond hair from his forehead, which emphasizes the surprise smoothing his features. He hooks his thumbs in the pockets of his jeans in what must be an effort at appearing calm, cool. He sees the Stage Manager and nods at him. The bill of the Stage Manager's hat tilts in reply.)

Billy Joe: So are you, like, him?

Stage Manager: Who is that?

Billy Joe: You know—God.

Stage Manager: I'm afraid not.

Billy Joe: Oh. *Oh.* You aren't—

Stage Manager: I'm more of a minor functionary.

Billy Joe: What, is that some kinda angel or something?

Stage Manager: No. I'm—I meet people when they show up here, help them find their bearings. Then I send them on their way.

Billy Joe: Like a tour guide, one of those hospitality guys.

Stage Manager: Close enough.

Billy Joe: Where am I headed?

(The Stage Manager points stage right.)

Stage Manager: You see that hall over there?

Billy Joe: That looks pretty dark. I thought it was supposed to be all bright and shit.

Stage Manager: No, that's just an effect produced by the cells in your eyes dying.

Billy Joe: Oh. Where does it go?

Stage Manager: Where everyone else has gone.

(Billy Joe notices the figures in the aisles. He nods at them.)

Billy Joe: What about them? Are they—

Stage Manager: Yes.

Billy Joe: Shouldn't they be moving down that hall, too?

Stage Manager: They should.

Billy Joe: So why aren't they?

Stage Manager: I'm not sure. It's got something to do with what's going on—where you came from.

Billy Joe: These guys were like, the living dead?

Stage Manager: That's right.

Billy Joe: Wild. Any of them try to eat you?

Stage Manager: A couple.

Billy Joe: What'd you do?

Stage Manager: I shot them in the head.

Billy Joe: Huh. That work, here?

Stage Manager: It seemed to do the trick.

Billy Joe: It's just, I thought, you know, being where we are and all—

Stage Manager: Some things aren't all that much different. You'd be surprised.

Billy Joe: I guess so. Do you know, like, what caused all this shit—I mean, what brought all those guys back from the dead? Because Rob—he's this friend of mine—he was—anyway, Rob was like, It's all a big government conspiracy, and I was like, That's ridiculous: if it's a government conspiracy, why did it start in, like, fucking India? And Rob—

Stage Manager: I don't know. I don't know what started it; I don't know what it is.

Billy Joe: Really?

Stage Manager: Really.

Billy Joe: Shit.

Stage Manager: Sorry.

Billy Joe: Does anyone?

Stage Manager: What do you mean?

Billy Joe: Does anyone know what's going on?

Stage Manager: Not that I've heard.

Billy Joe: Oh.

Stage Manager: Look—maybe there's someplace you'd like to see, someplace you'd like to go . . .

Billy Joe: Nah, I'm good.

Stage Manager: Are you sure there's nowhere? Your house, school—

Billy Joe: No, no—I mean, thanks and all, but—it's cool.

Stage Manager: All right; if you're sure.

Billy Joe: So . . . that's it?

Stage Manager: What else would you like?

Billy Joe: I don't know. Isn't there supposed to be some kinda book, you know, like a record of all the shit I've done?

Stage Manager: That's Santa Claus. Sorry—no, there's nothing like that. All the record you have of what you've done is what you can say about it.

Billy Joe: Huh. So what's it like?

Stage Manager: What's what like?

Billy Joe: Wherever that hall leads.

Stage Manager: Quiet.

Billy Joe: Oh.

(Billy Joe crosses the stage slowly, passing behind the Stage Manager, until he stands as far stage right as he can without leaving the stage.)

Billy Joe: That's it.

Stage Manager: It is.

Billy Joe: Well, no point in delaying the inevitable, right?

Stage Manager: I suppose not.

Billy Joe: Can you tell me one thing—before I go, can you answer one question?

Stage Manager: I can try.

Billy Joe: We're fucked, aren't we?

(The Stage Manager pauses, as if weighing his words.)

Stage Manager: There's always a chance—I realize how that sounds, but there's just enough truth left in it to make it worth saying. Things could turn around. Someone could discover a cure. Whatever's driving the zombies could die out—hell, it isn't even winter yet. A couple weeks of freezing temperatures could thin their numbers significantly. Or someone could be resistant to their bite, to the infection. With seven-plus billion people on the planet, you figure there has to be one person it doesn't affect . . .

Billy Joe: Do you believe any of that shit?

Stage Manager: No.

Billy Joe: Yeah.

(He exits, stage right.)

Stage Manager: Understand, it's not that I don't want to believe any of it. I want to believe all of it. All that shit, as my young friend would say. But doing so has traveled past the point of hard to the point of no return. No, this—this, I fear, is how the day runs down for the human race. It's how *Homo sapiens sapiens* departs the scene, carried off a bite at a time in the teeth of the undead. If there weren't so much pain, so much suffering in the process, you could almost see the humor in it. This is the way the world ends, not with a bang, and not with a whimper, but with the bleak gusto of a low-budget horror movie.

(The Stage Manager reaches for his flashlight, which he shuts off and takes with him as he rises from his seat and walks to the back of the stage. He is visible against the bulk of the willow, and then the shadows have him. The theater lights come up, revealing the aisles still full of the dead. Men, women, old, young, most wearing the causes of their several demises, they encompass the audience, and do not move.)

Technicolor

Come on, say it out loud with me: "And Darkness and Decay and the Red Death held illimitable dominion over all." Look at that sentence. Who says Edgar Allan Poe was a lousy stylist? Thirteen words—good number for a horror story, right? Although it's not so much a story as a masque. Yes, it's about a masque, but it is a masque, too. Of course, you all know what a masque is. If you didn't, you looked it up in your dictionaries, because that's what you do in a senior seminar. Anyone?

No, not a play, not exactly. Yes? Good, okay, "masquerade" is one sense of the word, a ball whose guests attend in costume. Anyone else?

Yes, very nice, nicely put. The masque does begin in the sixteenth century. It's the entertainment of the elite, and originally, it's a combination of pantomime and dance. Pantomime? Right—think "mime." The idea is to perform without words, gesturally, to let the movements of your body tell the story. You do that, and you dance, and there's your show. Later on, there's dialogue and other additions, but I think it's this older sense of the word the story intends. Remember that tall, silent figure at the end.

I'm sorry? Yes, good point. The two kinds of masque converge.

Back to that sentence, though. Twenty-two syllables that break almost perfectly in half, ten and twelve, "And Darkness and Decay and the Red Death" and "held illimitable dominion over all." A group of short words, one and two syllables each, takes you through the first part of the sentence, then they give way to these long, almost luxurious words, "illimitable dominion." The rhythm—you see how complex it is? You ride along on these short words, bouncing up and down, alliterating from one *d* to the next, and suddenly you're mired in those Latinate polysyllables. All the momentum goes out of your reading; there's just enough time for the final pair of words, which are short, which is good, and you're done.

Wait, just let me—no, all right, what was it you wanted to say?

Exactly, yes, you took the words out of my mouth. The sentence does what the story does, carries you along through the revelry until you run smack-dab into that tall figure in the funeral clothes. Great job.

One more observation about the sentence, then I promise it's on to the story itself. I know you want to talk about Prospero's castle, all those colored rooms. Before we do, however, the four *d*'s. We've mentioned already, there are a lot of *d* sounds in these thirteen words. They thread through the line, help tie it together. They also draw our attention to four words in particular. The first three are easy to recognize: they're capitalized, as well. Darkness, Decay, Death. The fourth? Right, dominion. Anyone want to take a stab at why they're capitalized?

Yes? Well . . . okay, sure, it makes them into proper nouns. Can you take that a step farther? What kind of proper nouns does it make them? What's happened to the Red Death in the story? It's gone from an infection you can't see to a tall figure wandering around the party. Personification, good. Darkness, Decay, (the Red) Death: the sentence personifies them; they're its trinity, its unholy trinity, so to speak. And this godhead holds dominion, what the dictionary defines as "sovereign authority" over all. Not only the prince's castle, not only the world of the story, but all, you and me.

In fact, in a weird sort of way, this is the story of the incarnation of one of the persons of this awful trinity.

All right, moving on, now. How about those rooms? Actually, how about the building those rooms are in, first? I've been calling it a castle, but it isn't, is it? It's "castellated," which is to say, castle-like, but it's an abbey, a monastery. I suppose it makes sense to want to wait out the Red Death in a place like an abbey. After all, it's both removed from the rest of society and well fortified. And we shouldn't be too hard on the prince and his followers for retreating there. It's not the first time this has happened, in literature or in life. Anyone read *The Decameron*? Boccaccio? It's a collection of one hundred stories told by ten people, five women and five men, who have sequestered themselves in, I'm pretty sure it's a convent, to wait out the plague ravaging Florence. The Black Death, that one.

If you consider that the place in which we find the seven rooms is a monastery, a place where men are supposed to withdraw from this world to meditate on the next, its rooms appear even stranger. What's the set-up? Seven rooms, yes, thank you, I believe I just said that. Running east to west, good. In a straight line? No. There's a sharp turn every twenty or thirty yards, so that you can see only one room at a time. So long as they follow that east-to-west course, you can lay the rooms out in any form you like. I favor steps, like the ones that lead the condemned man to the chopping block, but that's just me.

Hang on, hang on, we'll get to the colors in a second. We need to stay with the design of the rooms for a little longer. Not everybody gets this the first time through. There are a pair of windows, Gothic windows, which means what? That they're long and pointed at the top. The windows are opposite one another, and they look out on, anybody? Not exactly: a chandelier hangs down from the ceiling. It is a kind of light, though. No, a candelabrum holds candles. Anyone else? A brazier, yes, there's a brazier sitting on a tripod outside either window. They're . . . how would you describe a brazier? Like a big metal cup, a bowl, that you fill with some kind of fuel and ignite. Wood, charcoal, oil. To be honest, I'm not as interested in the braziers as I am in where they're located. Outside the windows, right, but where outside the windows? Maybe I should say, What is outside the windows? Corridors, yes, there are corridors to either side of the rooms, and it's along these that the braziers are stationed. Just like our classroom. Not the tripods, of course, and I guess what's outside our windows is more a gallery than a corridor, since it's open to the parking lot on the other side. All right, all right, so I'm stretching a bit here, but have you noticed, the room has seven windows? One for each color in Prospero's Abbey. Go ahead, count them.

So here we are in this strange abbey, one that has a crazy zigzag suite of rooms with corridors running beside them. You could chalk the location's details up to anti-Catholic sentiment; there are critics who have argued that anti-Catholic prejudice is the secret engine driving Gothic literature. No, I don't buy it, not in this case. Sure, there are stained-glass windows, but they're basically tinted glass. There's none of the iconography you'd expect if this were anti-Catholic propaganda, no statues or paintings. All we have is that enormous clock in the last room, the mother of all grandfather clocks. Wait a minute . . .

What about those colors, then? Each of the seven rooms is decorated in a single color that matches the stained glass of its windows. From east to west, we go from blue to purple to green to orange to white to violet to—to the last room, where there's a slight change. The windows are red, but the room itself is done in black. There seems to be some significance to the color sequence, but what that is—well, this is why we have literature professors, right? (No snickering.) Not to mention, literature students. I've read through your responses to the homework assignment, and there were a few interesting ideas as to what those colors might mean. Of course, most of you connected them to times of the day, blue as dawn, black as night, the colors in between morning, noon, early afternoon, that kind of thing. Given the east-west layout, it makes a certain amount of sense. A few more of you picked up on that connection to time in a slightly different way, and related the colors to times of the year, or the stages in a person's life. In the process, some clever arguments were made. Clever, but not, I'm afraid, too convincing.

What! What's wrong! What is it! Are you all—oh, them. Oh for God's sake. When you screamed like that, I thought—I don't know what I thought. I thought I'd need a new pair of trousers. Those are a couple of graduate students I've enlisted to help me with a little presentation I'll be putting up shortly. Yes, I can understand how the masks could startle you. They're just generic white masks; I think they found them downtown somewhere. It was their idea: once I told them what story we would be discussing, they immediately hit on wearing the masks. To tell the truth, I half expected they'd show up sporting the heads of enormous fanged monsters. Those are relatively benign.

Yes, I suppose they do resemble the face the Red Death assumes for its costume. No blood splattered on them, though.

If I could have your attention up here, again. Pay no attention to that man behind the curtain. Where was I? Your homework, yes, thank you. Right, right. Let's see . . . oh—I know. A couple of you read the colors in more original ways. I made a note of them somewhere—here they are. One person interpreted the colors as different states of mind, beginning with blue as tranquil and ending with black as despair, with stops for jealousy (green, naturally) and passion (white, as in white-hot) along the way. Someone else made the case for the colors as—let me make sure I have the phrasing right—"phases of being."

Actually, that last one's not bad. Although the writer could be less obtuse; clarity, people, academic writing needs to be clear. Anyway, the gist of the writer's argument is that each color is supposed to take you through a different state of existence, blue at one end of the spectrum representing innocence, black at the other representing death. Death as a state of being—that's . . . provocative. Which is not to say it's correct, but it's headed in the right direction.

I know, I know: Which is? The answer requires some explanation. Scratch that. It requires a boatload of explanation. That's why I have Tweedledee and Tweedledum setting up outside. (Don't look! They're almost done.) It's also why I lowered the screen behind me for the first time this semester. There are some images I want to show you, and they're best seen in as much detail as possible. If I can remember what the Media Center people told me . . . click this . . . then this . . .

Voilà!

Matthew Brady's *Portrait* of Edgar, taken 1848, his last full year alive. It's the best-known picture of him; were I to ask you to visualize him, this is what your minds' eyes would see. That forehead, that marble expanse—yes, his hair does make the top of his head look misshapen, truncated. As far as I know, it wasn't. The eyes—I suppose everyone comments on the eyes, slightly shadowed under those brows, the lids lowered just enough to suggest a certain detachment, even dreaminess. It's the mouth I notice, how it tilts up ever so slightly at the right corner. It's hard to see; you have to look closely. A strange mixture of arrogance, even contempt, and something else, something that might be humor, albeit of the bitter variety. It wouldn't be that much of a challenge to suggest colors for the picture, but somehow black and white is more fitting, isn't it? Odd, considering how much color there is in the fiction. I've often thought all those old Roger Corman adaptations, the ones Vincent Price starred in—whatever their other faults, one thing they got exactly right was Technicolor, which was the perfect way to film these stories, just saturate the screen with the most vibrant colors you could find.

I begin with the *Portrait* as a reminder. This is the man. His hand scraped the pen across the paper, brought the story we've been discussing into existence word by word. Not creation *ex nihilo,* out of nothing, creation . . . if my Latin were better, or existent, I'd have a

fancier way to say out of the self, or out of the depths of the self, or—
hey—out of the depth that is the self.

Moving on to my next portrait . . . Anyone?

I'm impressed. Not many people know this picture. Look closely,
though. See it?

That's right: it isn't a painting. It's a photograph that's been
tweaked to resemble a painting. The portrait it imitates is a posthu-
mous representation of Virginia Clemm, Edgar's sweetheart and child
bride. The girl in the photo? She'll be happy you called her a girl.
That's my wife, Anna. Yes, I'm married. Why is that so hard to believe? We met many years ago, in a kingdom by the sea. From? "Annabel Lee," good. No, just Anna; although we did meet in the King of
the Sea Arcade, on the Jersey shore. Seriously. She is slightly younger
than I am. Four years, thank you very much. You people. For Halloween one year, we dressed up as Edgar and Virginia—pretty much from
the start, it's been a running joke between us. In her case, the resem-
blance is striking.

As it so happened, yes we did attend a masquerade as the happy
couple. That was where this photo was taken. One of the other guests
was a professional photographer. I arranged the shot; he took it, then
used a program on his computer to transform it into a painting. The
guy was quite pleased with it; apparently it's on his website. I'm showing it to you because . . . well, because I want to. There's probably a
connection I could draw between masquerade, the suppression of one
identity in order to invoke and inhabit another, that displacement, and
the events of our story, but that's putting the cart about a mile before
the horse. She'll like it that you thought she was a girl, though; that'll
make her night. Those were her cookies, by the way. Are there any
left? Not even the sugar cookies? Figures.

Okay, image number three. If you can name this one, you get an A
for the class and an autographed picture of the Pope. Put your hand
down, you don't know. How about the rest of you?

Just us crickets . . .

It's just as well; I don't have that picture of the Pope anymore.
This gentleman is Prosper Vauglais. Or so he claimed. There's a lot
about this guy no one's exactly sure of, like when he was born, or
where, or when and where he died. He showed up in Paris in the late

eighteen-teens and caused something of a stir. For one winter, he appeared at several of the less reputable *salons* and a couple of the . . . I wouldn't go so far as to say more reputable—maybe less disreputable ones.

His "deal"? His deal, as you put it, was that he claimed to have been among the quarter of a million soldiers under Napoleon Bonaparte's personal command when, in June of 1812, the Emperor decided to invade Russia. As some of you may remember from your European history classes, this was a very bad idea. The worst. Roughly a tenth of Napoleon's forces survived the campaign; I want to say the number who limped back into France was something like twenty-two thousand. In and of itself, being a member of that group is nothing to sneeze at. For Vauglais, though, it was only the beginning. During the more or less running battles the French army fought as it retreated from what had been Moscow, Vauglais was separated from his fellows, struck on the head by a Cossack's sword, and left for dead in a snow bank. When he came to, he was alone, and a storm had blown up. Prosper had no idea where he was; he assumed still Russia, which wasn't too encouraging. Any Russian peasants or what have you who came across French soldiers, even those trying to surrender, tended to hack them to death with farm implements first and ask questions later. So when Prosper strikes out in what he hopes is the approximate direction of France, he isn't what you'd call terribly optimistic.

Nor is his pessimism misplaced. Within a day, he's lost, frozen, and starving, wandering around the inside of a blizzard like the sort you read about, white-out conditions, shrieking wind, unbearable cold. The blow to his head isn't helping matters, either. His vision keeps going in and out of focus. Sometimes he feels so nauseated he can barely stand, let alone continue walking. Once in a while, he'll see a light shining in the window of a farmhouse, but he gives these a wide berth. Another day, and he'll be closer to death than he was even at the worst battles he saw—than he was when that saber connected with his skull. His skin, which has been numb since not long after he started his trek, has gone from pale to white to this kind of blue-gray, and it's hardened, as if there's a crust of ice on it. He can't feel his pulse through it. His breath, which had been venting from his nose and mouth in long white clouds, seems to have slowed to a trickle, if that. He can't see anything; although, with the storm continuing around him, maybe that isn't so strange. He's not cold anymore—or it's not that he isn't cold so much as it is that the cold isn't torturing him the way it was. At some point, the cold moved inside him, took up residence just beneath his heart, and once that happened, that transition was accomplished, the temperature outside became of much less concern.

There's a moment—while Vauglais is staggering around the way you do when you're trying to walk in knee-high snow without snowshoes, pulling each foot free, swiveling it forward, crashing it through the snow in front of you, then repeating the process with your other foot—there's a moment when he realizes he's dead. He isn't sure when it happened. Some time in the last day or so. It isn't that he thinks he's in some kind of afterlife, that he's wandering around a frozen hell. No, he know he's still stuck somewhere in western Russia. It's just that, now he's dead. He isn't sure why he's stopped moving. He considers doing so, giving his body a chance to catch up to his apprehension of it, but decides against it. For one thing, he isn't sure it would work, and suppose while he's standing in place, waiting to fall over, someone finds him, one of those peasants, or a group of Russian soldiers? Granted, if he's already dead, they can't hurt him, but the prospect of being cut to pieces while still conscious is rather horrifying. And for another thing, Prosper isn't ready to quit walking. So he keeps moving forward. Dimly, the way you might hear a noise when you're fast asleep, he's aware that he isn't particularly upset at finding himself dead and yet moving, but after recent events, maybe that isn't so surprising.

Time passes; how much, he can't say. The blizzard doesn't lift, but it thins, enough for Vauglais to make out trees, evergreens. He's in a forest, a pretty dense one, from what he can see, which may explain why the storm has lessened. The trees are . . . there's something odd about the trees. For as close together as they are, they seem to be in almost perfect rows, running away into the snow on either side of him. In and of itself, maybe that isn't strange. Could be, he's wandered into some kind of huge formal garden. But there's more to it. When he looks at any particular tree, he sees, not so much bark and needles as black, black lines like the strokes of a paintbrush, or the scratches of a pen, forming the approximation of an evergreen. It's as if he's seeing a sketch of a tree, an artist's estimate. The black lines appear to be moving, almost too quickly for him to notice; it's as if he's witnessing them being drawn and re-drawn. Prosper has a sudden vision of himself from high above, a small, dark spot in the midst of long rows of black on white, a stray bit of punctuation loose among the lines of an unimaginable text.

Eventually, Vauglais reaches the edge of the forest. Ahead, there's a building, the title to this page he's been traversing. The blizzard has kicked up again, so he can't see much, but he has the impression of a long, low structure, possibly stone. It could be a stable, could be something else. Although there are no religious symbols evident, Prosper has an intuition the place is a monastery. He should turn right or left, avoid the building: the Russian clergy haven't taken any more kindly to the French invaders than the Russian people. Instead, he raises one stiff leg and strikes off toward it. It isn't that he's compelled to do so, that he's in the grip of a power that he can't resist, or that he's decided to embrace the inevitable, surrender to death. He isn't even especially curious about the stone structure. Forward is just a way to go, and he does.

As he draws closer, Vauglais notices that the building isn't becoming any easier to distinguish. If anything, it's more indistinct, harder to make out. If the trees behind him were rough drawing, this place is little more than a scribble, a jumble of lines whose form is as much in the eye of the beholder as anything. When a figure in a heavy coat and hat separates from the structure and begins to trudge in his direction, it's as if a piece of the place has broken off. Prosper can't see the man's face, all of which except the eyes is hidden by the folds of a heavy scarf, but the man lifts one mittened hand and gestures for Vauglais to follow him inside, which the Frenchman does.

And . . . no one knows what happens next.

What do I mean? I'm sorry: wasn't I speaking English? No one knows what happened inside the stone monastery. Prosper writes a fairly detailed account of the events leading up to that point, which is where the story I'm telling you comes from, but when the narrative reaches this moment, it breaks off with Vauglais's declaration that he's told us as much as he can. End of story.

All right, yes, there are hints of what took place during the five years he was at the Abbey. That was what he called the building, the

Abbey. Every so often, Prosper would allude to his experiences in it, and sometimes someone would note his remarks in a letter or diary. From combing through these kinds of documents, it's possible to assemble and collate Vauglais's comments into a glimpse of his life with the Fraternity. Again, his name. There were maybe seven of them, or seven after he arrived, or there were supposed to be seven. He referred to "Brother Red," once; to "The White Brother" at another time. Were the others named Blue, Purple, Green, Orange, and Violet? We can't say; although, as an assumption, it isn't completely unreasonable. They spent their days in pursuit of something Vauglais called The Great Work; he also referred to it as The Transumption. This seems to have involved generous amounts of quiet meditation combined with the study of certain religious texts—Prosper doesn't name them, but they may have included some Gnostic writings.

The Gnostics? I don't suppose you would have heard of them. How many of you actually got to church? As I feared. What would Sr. Mary Mary say? The Gnostics were a religious sect who sprang up around the same time as the early Christians. I guess they would have described themselves as the true Christians, the ones who understood what Jesus' teachings were really about. They shared sacred writings with the more orthodox Christians, but they had their own books, too. They were all about *gnosis,* knowledge, especially of the self. For them, the secret to what lay outside the self was what lay inside the self. The physical world was evil, a wellspring of illusions and delusions. Gnostics tended to retreat to the desert, lead lives of contemplation. Unlike the mainstream Christians, they weren't much on formal organization; that, and the fact that those Christians did everything in their power to shunt the Gnostics and their teachings to the margins and beyond, branding some of their ideas as heretical, helps explain why they pretty much vanished from the religious scene.

"Pretty much," though, isn't the same thing as "completely." (I know: such precise, scientific terminology.) Once in a while, Gnostic ideas would resurface, usually in the writings of some fringe figure or another. Rumors persist of Gnostic secret societies, occasionally as part of established groups like the Jesuits or the Masons. Which begs the question, Was Vauglais's Fraternity one of these societies, a kind of order of Gnostic monks? The answer to which is—

Right: no one knows. There's no record of any official—which is to say, Russian Orthodox—religious establishment: no monastery, no church, in the general vicinity of where we think Prosper was. Of course, a bunch of Gnostic monastics would hardly constitute anything resembling an official body, and so might very well fly under the radar. That said, the lack of proof against something does not count as evidence for it.

That's true. He could have been making the whole thing up.

Transumption? It's a term from classical rhetoric. It refers to the elision of a chain of associations. Sorry—sometimes I like to watch your heads explode. Let's say you're writing your epic poem about the fall of Troy, and you describe one of the Trojans being felled by an arrow. Let's say that arrow was made from the wood of a tree in a sacred grove; let's say, too, that that grove was planted by Hercules, who scattered some acorns there by accident. Now let's say that, when your Trojan hero sinks to the ground, drowning in his own blood, one of his friends shouts, "Curse the careless hand of Hercules!" That statement is an example of transumption. You've jumped from one link in a chain of associations back several. Make sense?

Yes, well, what does a figure of speech have to do with what was going on inside that Abbey?

Oh, wait—hold on for a moment. My two assistants are done with their set-up. Let me give them a signal . . . Five more minutes? All right, good, yes. I have no idea if they understood me. Graduate students.

Don't worry about what's on the windows. Yes, yes, those are lamps. Can I have your attention up here, please? Thank you. Let me worry about Campus Security. Or my masked friends out there will.

Okay—let's skip ahead a little. We were talking about The Transumption, a.k.a. The Great Work. There's nothing in his other references to the Abbey that offers any clue as to what he may have meant by it. However, there is an event that may shed some light on things.

It occurs in Paris, toward the end of February. An especially fierce winter scours the streets, sends people scurrying from the shelter of one building to another. Snow piles on top of snow, all of it turning dirty gray. Where there isn't snow, there's ice, inches thick in places. The sky is gray, the sun a pale blur that puts in a token appearance for a few hours a day. Out into this glacial landscape, Prosper leads half a dozen men and women from one of the city's less disreputable *salons*. Their destination: the catacombs, the long tunnels that run under Paris. They're quite old, the catacombs. In some places, the walls are stacked with bones, from when they were used as a huge ossuary. (That's a place to hold the bones of the dead.) They're also fairly crowded, full of beggars, the poor, searching for shelter from the ravages of the season. Vauglais has to take his party deep underground before they can find a location that's suitably empty. It's a kind of side-chamber, roughly circular, lined with shelves full of skull piled on skull. The skulls make a clicking sound, from the rats shuffling through them. Oh yes, there are plenty of rats down here.

Prosper fetches seven skulls off the shelves and piles them in the center of the room. He opens a large flask he's carried with him, and pours its contents over the bones. It's lamp oil, which he immediately ignites with his torch. He sets the torch down and gathers the members of the *salon* around the skulls. They join hands.

It does sound as if he's leading a séance, doesn't it? The only difference is, he isn't asking the men and women with him to think of a beloved one who's passed beyond. Nor does he request they focus on a famous ghost. Instead, Vauglais tells them to look at the flames licking the bones in front of them. Study those flames, he says, watch them as they trace the contours of the skulls. Follow the flames over the cheeks, around the eyes, up the brows. Gaze into those eyes, into the emptiness inside the fire. Fall through the flames; fall into that blackness.

He's hypnotizing them, of course—Mesmerizing would be the more historically accurate term. Under the sway of his voice, the members of the *salon* enter a kind of vacancy. They're still conscious—well, they're still perceiving, still aware of that heap of bones burning in front of them, the heavy odor of the oil, the quiet roar of the flames—but their sense of their selves, the accumulation of memory and inclination that defines each from the other, is gone.

Now Prosper is telling them to think of something new. Picture the flesh that used to clothe these skulls, he says. Warm and smooth, flushed with life. Look closely—it glows, doesn't it? It shines with its living. Watch! watch—it's dying. It's growing cold, pale. The glow, that dim light floating at the very limit of the skin—it's changing, drifting up, losing its radiance. See—there!—ah, it's dead. Cool as a cut of meat. Gray. The light is gone. Or is it? Is that another light? Yes, yes it is; but it is not the one we have watched dissipate. This is a darker glow. Indigo, that most elusive of the rainbow's hues. It curls over the dull skin like fog, and the flesh opens for it, first in little cracks, then in long windows, and then in wide doorways. As the skin peels away, the light thickens, until it is as if the bone is submerged in a bath of indigo. The light is not done moving; it pours into the air above the skull, over all the skulls. Dark light is rising from them, twisting up in thick streams that seek one another, that wrap around one another, that braid a shape. It is the form of a man, a tall man dressed in black robes, his face void as a corpse's, his head crowned with black flame—

Afterwards, when the half-dozen members of the *salon* compare notes, none of them can agree on what, if anything, they saw while under Vauglais's sway. One of them insists that nothing appeared. Three admit to what might have been a cloud of smoke, or a trick of the light. Of the remaining pair, one states flat-out that she saw the Devil. The other balks at any statement more elaborate than, "Monsieur Vauglais has shown me terrible joy." Whatever they do or don't see, it doesn't last very long. The oil Prosper doused the skulls with has been consumed. The fire dies away; darkness rushes in to fill the gap. The trance in which Vauglais has held the *salon* breaks. There's a sound like wind rushing, then quiet.

A month after that expedition, Prosper disappeared from Paris. He had attempted to lead that same *salon* back into the catacombs for a second—well, whatever you'd call what he'd done. A summoning? (But what was he summoning?) Not surprisingly, the men and women of the *salon* declined his request. In a huff, Vauglais left them and tried to insert himself into a couple of even less disreputable *salons,* attempting to use gossip about his former associates as his price of admission. But either the secrets he knew weren't juicy enough—possible, but I suspect unlikely—or those other *salons* had heard about his underground investigations and decided they preferred the comfort of their drawing rooms. Then one of the men from that original *salon* raised questions about Prosper's military service—he claimed to have found a sailor who swore that he and Vauglais had been on an extended debauch in Morocco at the very time he was supposed to have been marching toward Moscow. That's the problem with being the flavor of the month: before you know it, the calendar's turned, and no one can remember what they found so appealing about you in the first place. In short order, there's talk about an official inquiry into Prosper's service record—probably more rumor than fact, but it's enough for Vauglais, and he departs Paris for parts unknown. No one sees him leave, just as no one saw him arrive. In the weeks that follow, there are reports of Prosper in Libya, Madagascar, but they don't disturb a single eyebrow. Years—decades later, when Gauguin's in Tahiti, he'll hear a story about a strange white man who came to the island a long time ago and vanished into its interior, and Vauglais's name will occur to him, but you can't even call that a legend. It's . . . a momentary association. Prosper Vauglais vanishes.

Well, not all of him. That's right: there's the account he wrote of his discovery of the Abbey.

I beg your pardon? Dead? Oh, right, yes. It's interesting—apparently, Prosper permitted a physician connected to the first *salon* he frequented to conduct a pretty thorough examination of him. According to Dr. Zumachin, Vauglais's skin was stubbornly pallid. No matter how much the doctor pinched or slapped it, Prosper's flesh remained the same gray-white. Not only that, it was cold, cold and hard, as if it were packed with ice. Although Vauglais had to inhale in order to speak, his regular respiration was so slight as to be undetectable. It wouldn't fog the doctor's pocket mirror. And try as Zumachin might, he could not locate a pulse.

Sure, Prosper could have paid him off; aside from his part in this story, there isn't that much information on the good doctor. For what it's worth, most of the people who met Vauglais commented on his skin, its pallor, and, if they touched it, its coldness. No one else noted his breathing, or lack thereof, but a couple of the members of that last *salon* described him as extraordinarily still.

Okay, back to that book. Actually, wait. Before we do, let me bring this up on the screen . . .

I know—talk about something completely different. No, it's not a Rorschach test. It does look like it, though, doesn't it? Now if my friends outside will oblige me . . . and there we go. Amazing what a sheet of blue plastic and a high-power lamp can do. We might as well be in the east room of Prospero's Abbey.

Yes, the blue light makes it appear deeper—it transforms it from ink-spill to opening. Prosper calls it *"La Bouche,"* the Mouth. Some mouth, eh?

That's where the design comes from, Vauglais's book. The year after his disappearance, a small Parisian press whose biggest claim to fame was its unauthorized edition of the Marquis de Sade's *Justine* publishes Prosper's *L'Histoire de Mes Aventures dans L'Etendu Russe,* which translates something like, "The History of My Adventures in the Russian," either "Wilderness" or "Vastness." Not that anyone calls it by its title. The publisher, one Denis Prebend, binds Vauglais's essay between covers the color of a bruise after three or four days. Yes, that sickly, yellowy-green. Of course that's what catches everyone's attention, not the less-than-inspired title, and it isn't long before customers are asking for *"le livre verte,"* the green book. It's funny—it's one of those books that no one will admit to reading, but that goes through ten printings the first year after its appears.

Some of those copies do find their way across the Atlantic, very good. In fact, within a couple of months of its publication, there are at least three pirated translations of the green book circulating the booksellers of London, and a month after that, they're available in Boston, New York, and Baltimore.

To return to the book itself for a moment—after that frustrating ending, there's a blank page, which is followed by seven more pages, each showing a separate design. What's above me on the screen is the first of them. The rest—well, let's not get ahead of ourselves. Suffice it to say, the initial verdict was that something had gone awry in the printing process, with the result that the *bouche* had become *bouché,* cloudy. A few scholars have even gone so far as to attempt to reconstruct what Prosper's original images must have been. Prebend, though—the publisher—swore that he'd presented the book exactly as he had been instructed.

For those of us familiar with abstract art, I doubt there's any great difficulty in seeing the black blot on the screen as a mouth. The effect—there used to be these books; they were full of what looked like random designs. If you held them the right distance from your face and let your eyes relax, almost to the point of going cross-eyed, all of a sudden, a picture would leap out of the page at you. You know what I'm talking about? Good. I don't know what the name for that effect is, but it's the nearest analogue I can come up with for what happens when you look at the Mouth under blue light—except that the image doesn't jump forward so much as sink back. The way it recedes—it's as if it extends, not just through the screen, or the wall behind it, but beyond all that, to the very substratum of things.

To tell the truth, I have no idea what's responsible for the effect. If you find this impressive, however . . .

Look at that: a new image and a fresh color. How's that for coordination? Good work, nameless minions. Vauglais named this *"Le Gardien,"* the Guardian. What's that? I suppose you could make an octopus out of it; although aren't there a few too many tentacles? True, it's close enough; it's certainly more octopus than squid. Do you notice . . . right. The tentacles, loops, whatever we call them, appear to be moving. Focus on any one in particular, and it stands still—but you can see movement out of the corner of your eye, can't you? Try to take in the whole, and you swear its arms are performing an intricate dance.

So the Mouth leads to the Guardian, which is waving its appendages in front of . . .

That green is bright after the purple, isn't it? Voila *"Le Récif,"* the Reef. Makes sense, a cuttlefish protecting a reef. I don't know: it's angular enough. Personally, I suspect this one is based on some kind of pun or word-play. *"Récif"* is one letter away from *"récit,"* story, and this reef comes to us as the result of a story; in some weird way, the reef may be the story. I realize that doesn't make any sense; I'm still working through it.

This image is a bit different from the previous two. Anyone notice how?

Exactly: instead of the picture appearing to move, the light itself seems to—I like your word, "shimmer." You could believe we're gazing through water. It's—not hypnotic, that's too strong, but it is soothing. Don't you think?

I'll take your yawn as a "yes." Very nice. What a way to preface a question. All right, all right. What is it that's keeping you awake?

Isn't it obvious? Apparently not.

Yes! Edgar read Prosper's book!

When? The best evidence is sometime in the early eighteen-thirties, after he'd relocated to Baltimore. He mentions hearing about the green book from one of his fellow cadets at West Point, but he doesn't secure his own copy until he literally stumbles upon one in a bookshop near Baltimore's inner harbor. He wrote a fairly amusing account of it in a letter to Virginia. The store was this long, narrow space located halfway down an alley; its shelves were stuffed past capacity with all sizes of books jammed together with no regard for their subject. Occasionally, one of the shelves would disgorge its contents without warning. If you were underneath or to the side of it, you ran the risk of substantial injury. Not to mention, the single aisle snaking into the shop's recesses was occupied at irregular intervals by stacks of books that looked as if a strong sneeze would send them tumbling down.

It's as he's attempting to maneuver around an especially tall tower of books, simultaneously trying to avoid jostling a nearby shelf, that Edgar's foot catches on a single volume he hadn't seen, sending him—and all books in the immediate vicinity—to the floor. There's a huge puff of dust; half a dozen books essentially disintegrate. Edgar's sense of humor is such that he appreciates the comic aspect of a poet—as he styled himself—buried beneath a deluge of books. However, he insists on excavating the book that undid him.

The copy of Vauglais's essay he found was a fourth translation that had been done by a Boston publisher hoping to cash in on the popularity of the other editions. Unfortunately for him, the edition took longer to prepare than he'd anticipated—his translator was a Harvard professor who insisted on translating Prosper as accurately as he could. This meant an English version of Vauglais's essay that was a model of fidelity to the original French, but that wasn't ready until Prosper's story was last week's news. The publisher went ahead with what he titled *The Green Book of M. Prosper Vauglais* anyway, but he pretty much lost his shirt over the whole thing.

Edgar was so struck at having fallen over this book that he bought it on the spot. He spent the next couple of days reading and re-reading it, puzzling over its contents. As we've seen in "The Gold Bug" and "The Purloined Letter," this was a guy who liked a puzzle. He spent a good deal of time on the seven designs at the back of the book, convinced that their significance was right in front of him.

Speaking of those pictures, let's have another one. Assistants, if you please—

Hey, it's Halloween! Isn't that what you associate orange with? And especially an orange like this—this is the sun spilling the last of its late light, right before all the gaudier colors, the violets and pinks, splash out. You don't think of orange as dark, do you? I know I don't. Yet it is, isn't it? Is it the darkest of the bright colors? To be sure, it's difficult to distinguish the design at its center; the orange is filmy, translucent. There are a few too many curves for it to be the symbol for infinity; at least, I think there are. I want to say I see a pair of snakes wrapped around one another, but the coils don't connect in quite the right way. Vauglais's name for this was *"Le Coeur,"* the Heart, and also the Core, as well as the Height or the Depth, depending on usage. Obviously, we're cycling through the seven rooms from "The Masque of the Red Death"; obviously, too, I'm arguing that Edgar takes their colors from Prosper's book. In that schema, orange is at the center, three colors to either side of it; in that sense, we have reached the heart, the core, the height or the depth. Of course, that core obscure the other one—or maybe not.

While you try to decide, let's return to Edgar. It's an overstatement to say that Vauglais obsesses him. When his initial attempt at deciphering the designs fails, he puts the book aside. Remember, he's a working writer at a time when the American economy really won't support one—especially one with Edgar's predilections—so there are always more things to be written in the effort to keep the wolf a safe distance from the door. Not to mention, he's falling in love with the girl who will become his wife. At odd moments over the next decade, though, he retrieves Prosper's essay and spends a few hours poring over it. He stares at its images until they're grooved into the folds of his brain. During one long afternoon in 1840, he's sitting with the book open to the Mouth, a glass of water on the table to his right. The sunlight streaming in the windows splinters on the waterglass, throwing a rainbow across the page in front of him. The arc of the images that's under the blue strip of the bow looks different; it's as if that portion of the paper has sunk into the book—behind the book. A missing and apparently lost piece of the puzzle snaps into place, and Edgar starts up from the table, knocking over his chair in the process. He races through the house, searching for a piece of blue glass. The best he can do is a heavy blue jug, which he almost drops in his excitement. He returns to the book, angles the jug to catch the light, and watches as the Mouth opens. He doesn't waste any time staring at it; shifting the jug to his right hand, he flips to the next image with his left, positions the glass jug over the Guardian, and . . . nothing. For a moment, he's afraid he's imagined the whole thing, had an especially vivid waking dream. But when he pages back to the Mouth and directs the blue light onto it, it clearly recedes. Edgar wonders if the effect he's observed is unique to the first image, then his eye lights on the glass of water, still casting its rainbow. He sets the jug on the floor, turns the page, and slides the book closer to the glass.

That's how Edgar spends the rest of the afternoon, matching the designs in the back of Vauglais's book to the colors that activate them. The first four come relatively quickly; the last three take longer. Once he has all seven, Edgar re-reads Prosper's essay and reproaches himself as a dunce for not having hit on the colors sooner. It's all there in Vauglais's prose, he declares, plain as day. (He's being much too hard on himself. I've read the green book a dozen times and I have yet to find the passage where Prosper hints at the colors.)

How about a look at the most difficult designs? Gentlemen, if you please . . .

There's nothing there. I know—that's what I said, the first time I saw the fifth image. *"Le Silence,"* the Silence. Compared to the designs that precede it, this one is so faint as to be barely detectable. And when you shine a bright white light onto it, it practically disappears. There is something in there, though; you have to stare at it for a while. More so than with the previous images, what you see here varies dramatically from viewer to viewer.

Edgar never records his response to the Silence, which is a pity. Having cracked the secret of Vauglais's designs, he studies the essay more carefully, attempting to discern the use to which the images were to be put, the nature of Prosper's Great Work, his Transumption. (There's that word again. I never clarified its meaning vis-à-vis Vauglais's ideas, did I?) The following year, when Edgar sits down to write

"The Masque of the Red Death," it is no small part as an answer to the question of what Prosper was up to. That answer shares features with some of the stories he had written prior to his 1840 revelation; although, interestingly, they came after he had obtained his copy of the green book.

From the looks on your faces, I'd say you've seen what the Silence contains. I don't suppose anyone wants to share?

I'll take that as a "No." It's all right: what you find there can be rather . . . disconcerting.

We're almost at the end of our little display. What do you say we proceed to number six? Here we go . . .

Violet's such a nice color, isn't it? You have to admit, some of those other colors are pretty intense. Not this one, though; even the image—"*L'Arbre*," the Tree—looks more or less like a collection of lines trying to be a tree. Granted, if you study the design, you'll notice that each individual line seems to fade and then re-inscribe itself, but compared to the effect of the previous image, this is fairly benign. Does it remind you of anything? Anything we were discussing, say, in the last hour or so?

Oh never mind, I'll just tell you. Remember those trees Vauglais saw outside the Abbey? Remember the way that, when he tried to focus on any of them, he saw a mass of black lines? Hmmm. Maybe there's more to this pleasant design than we'd thought. Maybe it's, not the key to all this, but the key trope, or figure.

I know: which means what, exactly? Let's return to Edgar's story. You have a group of people who are sequestered together, made to disguise their outer identities, encouraged to debauch themselves, to abandon their inner identities, all the while passing from one end of this color schema to the other. They put their selves aside, become a massive blank, a kind of psychic space. That opening allows what is otherwise an abstraction, a personification, to change states, to manifest itself physically. Of course, the Red Death doesn't appear of its own volition; it's called into being by Prince Prospero, who can't stop thinking about the reason he's retreated into his abbey.

This is what happened—what started to happen to the members of the *salon* Prosper took into the Parisian catacombs. He attempted to implement what he'd learned during his years at the Abbey, what he first had perceived through the snow twirling in front of his eyes in that Russian forest. To manipulate—to mold—to . . .

Suppose that the real—what we take to be the real—imagine that world outside the self, all this out here, is like a kind of writing. We write it together; we're continuously writing it together, onto the surface of things, the paper, as it were. It isn't something we do consciously, or that we exercise any conscious control over. We might glimpse it in moments of extremity, as Vauglais did, but that's about as close to it as most of us will come. What if, though, what if it were possible to do something more than simply look? What if you could clear a space on that paper and write something *else*? What might you bring into being?

Edgar tries to find out. Long after "The Masque," which is as much caution as it is field guide, he decides to apply Prosper's ideas for real. He does so during that famous lost week at the end of his life, that gap in the biographical record that has prompted so much speculation. Since Virginia succumbed to tuberculosis some two years prior, Edgar's been on a long downward slide, a protracted effort at joining his beloved wife. You know, extensive forests have been harvested for the production of critical studies of Edgar's "bizarre" relationship with Virginia; rarely, if ever, does it occur to anyone that Edgar and Virginia might honestly have been in love, and that the difference in their ages might have been incidental. Yet what is that final couple of years but a man grieving himself to death? Yes, Edgar approaches other women about possible marriage, but why do you think none of those proposals work out?

Not only is Edgar actively chasing his death, paddling furiously toward it on a river of alcohol; little known to him, death has noticed his pursuit, and responded by planting a black seed deep within his brain, a gift that is blossoming into a tumor. Most biographers have remained ignorant of this disease, but years after his death, Edgar's body is exhumed—it doesn't matter why; given who Edgar was, of course this was going to happen to him. During the examination of his remains, it's noted that his brain is shrunken and hard. Anyone who knows about these things will tell you that the brain is one of the first organs to decay, which means that what those investigators found rattling around old Edgar's cranium would not have been petrified gray matter. Cancer, however, is a much more durable beast; long after it's killed you, a tumor hangs around to testify to its crime. Your guess is as good as mine when it comes to how long he'd had it, but by the time I'm talking about, Edgar is in a pretty bad way. He's having trouble controlling the movements of his body, his speech; half the time he seems drunk, he's stone cold sober.

There's something else. Increasingly, wherever he turns his gaze, whatever he looks at flickers, and instead of, say, an orange resting on a plate, he sees a jumble of black lines approximating a sphere on a circle. It takes him longer to recall Vauglais's experience in that Russian forest than you'd expect; the cancer, no doubt, devouring his memory. Sometimes the confusion of lines that's replaced the streetlamp in front of him is itself replaced by blankness, by an absence that registers as a dull white space in the middle of things. It's as if a painter took a palette knife and scraped the oils from a portion of his picture until all that remained was the canvas, slightly stained. At first, Edgar thinks there's something wrong with his vision; when he understands what he's experiencing, he speculates that the blank might be the result of his eyes' inability to endure their own perception, that he might be undergoing some degree of what we would call hysterical blindness. As he continues to see that whiteness, though, he realizes that he isn't seeing less, but more. He's seeing through to the surface those black lines are written on.

In the days immediately prior to his disappearance, Edgar's perception undergoes one final change. For the slightest instant after that space has uncovered itself to him, something appears on it, a figure—a woman. Virginia, yes, as he saw her last, ravaged by tuberculosis, skeletally thin, dark hair in disarray, mouth and chin scarlet with the blood she'd hacked out of her lungs. She appears barefoot, wrapped in a shroud stained with dirt. Almost before he sees her, she's gone, her place taken by whatever he'd been looking at to begin with.

Is it any surprise that, presented with this dull white surface, Edgar should fill it with Virginia? Her death has polarized him; she's the lodestone that draws his thoughts irresistibly in her direction. With each glimpse of her he has, Edgar apprehends that he's standing at the threshold of what could be an extraordinary chance. Although he has discovered the secret of Prosper's designs, discerned the nature of the

Great Work, never once has it occurred to him that he might put that knowledge to use. Maybe he hasn't really believed in it; maybe he suspects that, underneath it all, the effect of the various colors on Vauglais's designs is some type of clever optical illusion. Now, though, now that there's the possibility of gaining his beloved back—

Edgar spends that last week sequestered in a room in a boarding house a few streets up from that alley where he tripped over Prosper's book. He's arranged for his meals to be left outside his door; half the time, however, he leaves them untouched, and even when he takes the dishes into his room, he eats the bare minimum to sustain him. About midway through his stay, the landlady, a Mrs. Foster, catches sight of him as he withdraws into his room. His face is flushed, his skin slick with sweat, his clothes disheveled; he might be in the grip of a fever whose fingers are tightening around him with each degree it climbs. As his door closes, Mrs. Foster considers running up to it and demanding to speak to this man. The last thing she wants is for her boarding house to be known as a den of sickness. She has taken two steps forward when she stops, turns, and bolts downstairs as if the Devil himself were tugging her apron strings. For the remainder of the time this lodger is in his room, she will send one of the serving girls to deliver his meals, no matter their protests. Once the room stands unoccupied, she will direct a pair of those same girls to remove its contents— including the cheap bed—carry them out back, and burn them until nothing remains but a heap of ashes. The empty room is closed, locked, and removed from use for the rest of her time running that house, some twenty-two years.

I know: what did she see? What could she have seen, with the door shut? Perhaps it wasn't what she saw; perhaps it was what she felt: the surface of things yielding, peeling away to what was beneath, beyond— the strain of a will struggling to score its vision onto that surface—the waver of the brick and mortar, of the very air around her, as it strained against this newness coming into being. How would the body respond to what could only register as a profound wrongness? Panic, you have to imagine, maybe accompanied by sudden nausea, a fear so intense as to guarantee a lifetime's aversion to anything associated with its cause.

Had she opened that door, though, what sight would have confronted her? What would we see?

Nothing much—at least, that's likely to have been our initial response. Edgar seated on the narrow bed, staring at the wall opposite him. Depending on which day it was, we would have noticed his shirt and pants looking more or less clean. Like Mrs. Foster, we would have remarked his flushed face, the sweat soaking his shirt; we would have heard his breathing, deep and hoarse. We might have caught his lips moving, might have guessed he was repeating Virginia's name over and over again, but been unable to say for sure. Were we to guess he was in a trance, caught in an opium dream, aside from the complete and total lack of opium-related paraphernalia, we could be forgiven.

If we were to remain in that room with him—if we could stand the same sensation that sent Mrs. Foster running—it wouldn't take us long to turn our eyes in the direction of Edgar's stare. His first day there, we wouldn't have noticed much if anything out of the ordinary. Maybe we would have wondered if the patch of bricks he was so focused on didn't look just the slightest shade paler than its surroundings, before dismissing it as a trick of the light. Return two, three days later, and we would find that what we had attributed to mid-afternoon light blanching already-faded masonry is a phenomenon of an entirely different order. Those bricks are blinking in and out of sight. One moment, there's a worn red rectangle; the next, there isn't. What takes its place is difficult to say, because it's back almost as fast as it was gone; although, after its return, the brick looks a bit less solid . . . less certain, you might say. Ragged around the edges, though not in any way you could put words to. All over that stretch of wall, bricks are going and coming and going. It almost looks as if some kind of code is spelling itself out using the stuff of Edgar's wall as its pen and paper.

Were we to find ourselves in that same room, studying that same spot, a day later, we would be startled to discover a small area of the wall, four bricks up, four down, vanished. Where it was—let's call what's there—or what isn't there—white. To tell the truth, it's difficult to look at that spot—the eye glances away automatically, the way it does from a bright light. Should you try to force the issue, tears dilute your vision.

Return to Edgar's room over the next twenty-four hours, and you would find that gap exponentially larger—from four bricks by four bricks to sixteen by sixteen, then from sixteen by sixteen to—basically, the entire wall. Standing in the doorway, you would have to raise your hand, shield your eyes from the dull whiteness in front of you. Blink furiously, squint, and you might distinguish Edgar in his familiar position, staring straight into that blank. Strain your gaze through the narrowest opening your fingers can make, and for the half a second until your head jerks to the side, you see a figure, deep within the white. Later, at a safe remove from Edgar's room, you may attempt to reconstruct that form, make sense of your less-than-momentary vision. All you'll be able to retrieve, however, is a pair of impressions, the one of something coalescing, like smoke filling up a jar, the other of thinness, like a child's stick-drawing grown life-sized. For the next several months, not only your dreams, but your waking hours will be plagued by what you saw between your fingers. Working late at night, you will be overwhelmed by the sense that whatever you saw in that room is standing just outside the cone of light your lamp throws. Unable to help yourself, you'll reach for the shade, tilt it back, and find . . . nothing, your bookcases. Yet the sensation won't pass; although you can read the spines of the hardcovers ranked on your bookshelves, your skin won't stop bristling at what you can't see there.

What about Edgar, though? What image do his eyes find at the heart of that space? I suppose we should ask, What image of Virginia?

It—she changes. She's thirteen, wearing the modest dress she married him in. She's nine, wide-eyed as she listens to him reciting his poetry to her mother and her. She's dead, wrapped in a white shroud. So much concentration is required to pierce through to the undersurface in the first place—and then there's the matter of maintaining the aperture—that it's difficult to find, let alone summon, the energy necessary to focus on a single image of Virginia. So the figure in front of him brushes a lock of dark hair out of her eyes, then giggles in a child's high-pitched tones, then coughs and sprays scarlet blood over her lips and chin. Her mouth is pursed in thought; she turns to a knock on the front door; she thrashes in the heat of the disease that is consuming her. The more time that passes, the more Edgar struggles to keep his memories of his late wife separate from one another. She's nine, standing beside her mother, wound in her burial cloth. She's in her coffin, laughing merrily. She's saying she takes him as her lawful husband, her mouth smeared with blood.

Edgar can't help himself—he's written, and read, too many stories about exactly this kind of situation for him not to be aware of all the ways it could go hideously wrong. Of course, the moment such a possibility occurs to him, it's manifest in front of him. You know how it is: the harder you try to keep a pink elephant out of your thoughts, the more that animal cavorts center-stage. Virginia is obscured by white linen smeared with mud; where her mouth is, the shroud is red. Virginia is naked, her skin drawn to her skeleton, her hair loose and floating around her head as if she's under water. Virginia is wearing the dress she was buried in, the garment and the pale flesh beneath it opened by rats. Her eyes—or the sockets that used to cradle them—are full of her death, of all she has seen as she was dragged out of the light down into the dark.

With each new monstrous image of his wife, Edgar strives not to panic. He bends what is left of his will toward summoning Virginia as she was at sixteen, when they held a second, public wedding. For an instant, she's there, holding out her hand to him with that simple grace she's displayed as long as he's known her—and then she's gone, replaced by a figure whose black eyes have seen the silent halls of the dead, whose ruined mouth has tasted delicacies unknown this side of the grave. This image does not flicker; it does not yield to other, happier pictures. Instead, it grows more solid, more definite. It takes a step toward Edgar, who is frantic, his heart thudding in his chest, his mouth dry. He's trying to stop the process, trying to close the door he's spent so much time and effort prying open, to erase what he's written on that blankness. The figure takes another step forward, and already is at the edge of the opening. His attempts at stopping it are useless—what he's started has accrued sufficient momentum for it to continue regardless of him. His lips are still repeating, "Virginia."

When the—we might as well say, when Virginia places one gray foot onto the floor of Edgar's room, a kind of ripple runs through the entire room, as if every last bit of it is registering the intrusion. How Edgar wishes he could look away as she crosses the floor to him. In a far corner of his brain that is capable of such judgments, he knows that this is the price for his *hubris*—really, it's almost depressingly formulaic. He could almost accept the irony if he did not have to watch those hands dragging their nails back and forth over one another, leaving the skin hanging in pale strips; if he could avoid the sight of whatever is seething in the folds of the bosom of her dress; if he could shut his eyes to that mouth and its dark contents as they descend to his. But he can't; he cannot turn away from his Proserpine as she rejoins him at last.

Four days prior to his death, Edgar is found on the street, delirious, barely conscious. He never recovers. Right at the end, he rallies long enough to dictate a highly abbreviated version of the story I've told you to a Methodist minister, who finds what he records so disturbing he sews it into the binding of the family Bible, where it will remain concealed for a century and a half.

As for what Edgar called forth—she walks out of our narrative and is not seen again.

It's a crazy story. It makes the events of Vauglais's life seem almost reasonable in comparison. If you were so inclined, I suppose you could ascribe Edgar's experience in that rented room to an extreme form of auto-hypnosis which, combined with the stress on his body from his drinking and the brain tumor, precipitates a fatal collapse. In which case, the story I've told you is little more than an elaborate symptom. It's the kind of reading a literary critic prefers; it keep the more . . . outré elements safely quarantined within the writer's psyche.

Suppose, though, suppose. Suppose that all this insanity I've been feeding you isn't a quaint example of early-nineteenth-century pseudo-science. Suppose that its interest extends well beyond any insights it might offer in interpreting "The Masque of the Red Death." Suppose—let's say the catastrophe that overtakes Edgar is the result of—we could call it poor planning. Had he paid closer attention to the details of Prosper's history, especially to that sojourn in the catacombs, he would have recognized the difficulty—to the point of impossibility—of making his attempt alone. Granted, he was desperate. But there was a reason Vauglais took the members of his *salon* underground with him—to use as a source of power, a battery, as it were. They provided the energy; he directed it. Edgar's story is a testament to what must have been a tremendous—an almost unearthly will. In the end, though, it wasn't enough.

Of course, how could he have brought together a sufficient number of individuals, and where? By the close of his life, he wasn't the most popular of fellows. Not to mention, he would have needed to expose the members of this hypothetical group to Prosper's designs and their corresponding colors.

Speaking of which: pleasant as this violet has been, what do you say we proceed to the *pièce de résistance*? Faceless lackeys, on my mark—

Ahh. I don't usually talk about these things, but you have no idea how much trouble this final color combination gave me. I mean, red and black gives you dark red, right? Right, except that for the design to achieve its full effect, putting up a dark red light won't do. You need red layered over black—and a true black light, not ultraviolet. The result, though—I'm sure you'll agree, it was worth sweating over. It's like a picture painted in red on a black canvas, wouldn't you say? And look what it does for the final image. It seems to be reaching right out of the screen for you, doesn't it? Strictly speaking, Vauglais's name for it, *"Le Dessous,"* the Underneath, isn't quite grammatical French, but we needn't worry ourselves over such details. There are times I think another name would be more appropriate: the Maw, perhaps, and then there are moments I find the Underneath perfect. You can see why I might lean toward calling it a mouth—the Cave would do, as well—except that the perspective's all wrong. If this is a mouth, or a cave, we aren't looking into it; we're already inside, looking out.

Back to Edgar. As we've said, even had he succeeded in gathering a group to assist him in his pursuit, he would have had to find a way to introduce them Prosper's images and their colors. If he could have, he would have . . . reoriented them, their minds, the channels of their thoughts. Vauglais's designs would have brought them closer to where they needed to be; they would have made available certain dormant faculties within his associates.

Even that would have left him with challenges, to be sure. Mesmerism, hypnosis, as Prosper himself discovered, is a delicate affair, one subject to such external variables as running out of lamp oil too soon. It would have been better if he could have employed some type of pharmacological agent, something that would have deposited them into a more useful state, something sufficiently concentrated to be delivered via a few bites of an innocuous food—a cookie, say, whose sweetness would mask any unpleasant taste, and which he could cajole his assistants to sample by claiming that his wife had baked them.

Then, if Edgar had been able to keep this group distracted while the cookies did their work—perhaps by talking to them about his writing—about the genesis of one of his stories, say, "The Masque of the Red Death"—if he had managed this far, he might have been in a position to make something happen, to perform the Great Work.

There's just one more thing, and that's the object for which Edgar would have put himself to all this supposed trouble: Virginia. I like to think I'm as romantic as the next guy, but honestly—you have the opportunity to rescript reality, and the best you can come up with is returning your dead wife to you? Talk about a failure to grasp the possibilities . . .

What's strange—and frustrating—is that it's all right there in "The Masque," in Edgar's own words. The whole idea of the Great Work, of Transumption, is to draw one of the powers that our constant, collective writing of the real consigns to abstraction across the barrier into physicality. Ideally, one of the members of that trinity Edgar named so well, Darkness and Decay and the Red Death, those who hold illimitable dominion over all. The goal is to accomplish something momentous, to shake the world to its foundations, not play out some hackneyed romantic fantasy. That was what Vauglais was up to, trying to draw into form the force that strips the flesh from our bones, that crumbles those bones to dust.

No matter. Edgar's mistake still has its uses as a distraction, and a lesson. Not that it'll do any of you much good. By now, I suspect few of you can hear what I'm saying, let alone understand it. I'd like to tell you the name of what I stirred into that cookie dough, but it's rather lengthy and wouldn't do you much good, anyway. I'd also like to tell you it won't leave you permanently impaired, but that wouldn't exactly be true. One of the consequences of its efficacy, I fear. If it's any consolation, I doubt most of you will survive what's about to follow. By my reckoning, the power I'm about to bring into our midst will require a good deal of . . . sustenance in order to establish a more permanent foothold here. I suspect this is of even less consolation, but I do regret this aspect of the plan I'm enacting. It's just—once you come into possession of such knowledge, how can you not make use—full use of it?

You see, I'm starting at the top. Or at the beginning—before the beginning, really, before light burst across the perfect formlessness that was everything. I'm starting with Darkness, with something that was already so old at that moment of creation that it had long forgotten its identity. I plan to restore it. I will give myself to it for a guide, let it envelop me and consume you and run out from here in a flood that will wash this world away. I will give to Darkness a dominion more complete than it has known since it was split asunder.

Look—in the air—can you see it?

The Wide, Carnivorous Sky

I

9:13 P.M.

From the other side of the campfire, Lee said, "So it's a vampire."

"I did not say vampire," Davis said. "Did you hear me say vampire?"

It was exactly the kind of thing Lee would say, the gross generalization that obscured more than it clarified. Not for the first time since they'd set out up the mountain, Davis wondered at their decision to include Lee in their plans.

Lee held up his right hand, index finger extended. "It has the fangs."

"A mouthful of them."

Lee raised his middle finger. "It turns into a bat."

"No—its wings are like a bat's."

"Does it walk around with them?"

"They—it extrudes them from its arms and sides."

"'Extrudes'?" Lee said.

Han chimed in: "College."

Not this shit again, Davis thought. He rolled his eyes to the sky, dark blue studded by early stars. Although the sun's last light had drained from the air, his stomach clenched. He dropped his gaze to the fire.

The Lieutenant spoke. "He means the thing extends them out of its body."

"Oh," Lee said. "Sounds like it turns into a bat to me."

"Uh-huh," Han said.

"Whatever," Davis said. "It doesn't—"

Lee extended his ring finger and spoke over him. "It sleeps in a coffin."

"Not a coffin—"

"I know, a flying coffin."

"It isn't—it's in low-Earth orbit, like a satellite."

"What was it you said it looked like?" the Lieutenant asked. "A co-coon?"

"A chrysalis," Davis said.

"Same thing," the Lieutenant said.

"More or less," Davis said, unwilling to insist on the distinction because, even a year and three-quarters removed from Iraq, the Lieutenant was still the Lieutenant and you did not argue the small shit with him.

"Coffin, cocoon, chrysalis," Lee said, "it has to be in it before sunset or it's in trouble."

"Wait," Han said. "Sunset."

"Yes," Davis began.

"The principle's the same," the Lieutenant said. "There's a place it has to be and a time it has to be there by."

"Thank you, sir," Lee said. He raised his pinky. "And, it drinks blood."

"Yeah," Davis said, "it does."

"Lots," Han said.

"Yeah," the Lieutenant said.

For a moment, the only sounds were the fire popping and, somewhere out in the woods, an owl prolonging its question. Davis thought of Fallujah.

"Okay," Lee said, "how do we kill it?"

II

2004

There had been rumors, stories, legends of the things you might see in combat. Talk to any of the older guys, the ones who'd done tours in Vietnam, and you heard about a jungle in which you might meet the ghosts of Chinese invaders from five centuries before; or serve beside a grunt whose heart had been shot out a week earlier but who wouldn't die; or find yourself stalked by what you thought was a tiger but had a tail like a snake and a woman's voice. The guys who'd been part of the first war in Iraq—"The good one," a sailor Davis knew called it—told their own tales about the desert, about coming across a raised tomb, its black stone worn free of markings, and listening to someone laughing inside it all the time it took you to walk around it; about the dark shapes you might see stalking through a sandstorm, their arms and legs a child's stick-figures; about the sergeant who swore his reflection had been killed so that, when he looked in a mirror now, a corpse stared back at him. Even the soldiers who'd returned from Afghanistan talked about vast forms they'd seen hunched at the crests of mountains; the street in Kabul that usually ended in a blank wall, except when it didn't; the pale shapes you might glimpse darting into the mouth of the cave you were about to search. A lot of what you heard was bullshit, of course, the plot of a familiar movie or TV show adapted to new location and cast of characters, and a lot of it started off sounding as if it were headed somewhere interesting then ran out of gas halfway through. But there were some stories about which, even if he couldn't quite credit their having happened, some quality in the teller's voice, or phrasing, caused him to suspend judgment.

During the course of his associate's degree, Davis had taken a number of courses in psychology—preparation for a possible career as a psychologist—and in one of these, he had learned that, after several hours of uninterrupted combat (he couldn't remember how many, had never been any good with numbers), you would hallucinate. You couldn't help it; it was your brain's response to continuous unbearable stress. He supposed that at least some of the stories he'd listened to in barracks and bars might owe themselves to such cause, although he was unwilling to categorize them all as symptoms. This was not due to any overriding belief in either organized religion or disorganized superstition; it derived more from principle—specifically, a conclusion that an open mind was the best way to meet what continually impressed him as an enormous world packed full of many things.

By Fallujah, Davis had had no experiences of the strange, the bizarre, no stories to compare with those he'd accumulated over the course of basic and his deployment. He hadn't been thinking about that much as they took up their positions south of the city; all his available attention had been directed at the coming engagement. Davis had walked patrol, had felt the crawl of the skin at the back of your

neck as you made your way down streets crowded with men and wom-
en who'd been happy enough to see Saddam pulled down from his pe-
destal but had long since lost their patience with those who'd operated
the crane. He'd ridden in convoys, his head light, his heart throbbing at
the base of his throat as they passed potential danger after potential
danger—a metal can on the right shoulder, what might be a shell on
the left—and while they'd done their best to reinforce their Hummers
with whatever junk they could scavenge, Davis was acutely aware that it
wasn't enough, a consequence of galloping across the Kuwaiti desert
with The Army You Had. Davis had stood checkpoint, his mouth dry as
he sighted his M-16 on an approaching car that appeared full of women
in black burkas who weren't responding to the signs to slow down, and
he'd wondered if they were suicide bombers, or just afraid, and how
much closer he could allow them before squeezing the trigger. However
much danger he'd imagined himself in, inevitably, he'd arrived after the
sniper had opened fire and fled, or passed the exact spot an IED would
erupt two hours later, or been on the verge of aiming for the car's engine when it screeched to a halt. It wasn't that Davis hadn't discharged
his weapon; he'd served support for several nighttime raids on suspected
insurgent strongholds, and he'd sent his own bullets in pursuit of the
tracers that scored the darkness. But support wasn't the same thing as
kicking in doors, trying to kill the guy down the hall who was trying to
kill you. It was not the same as being part of the Anvil.

That was how the Lieutenant had described their role. "Our
friends in the United States Marine Corps are going to play the Hammer," he had said the day before. "They will sweep into Fallujah from
east and west and they will drive what hostiles they do not kill outright
south, where we will be waiting to act as the Anvil. The poet Goethe
said that you must be either hammer or anvil. We will be both, and we
are going to crush the hostiles between us."

After the Lieutenant's presentation, Han had said, "Great—so the
jarheads have all the fun," with what Davis judged a passable imitation
of regret, a false sentiment fairly widely held. Davis had been sure,
however, the certainty a ball of lead weighting his gut, that this time
was going to be different. Part of it was that the Lieutenant had known
one of the contractors who'd been killed, incinerated, and strung up at
the Saddam Bridge last April. Davis wasn't clear exactly how the men

had been acquainted, or how well, but the Lieutenant had made no secret of his displeasure at not being part of the first effort to (re)take the city in the weeks following the men's deaths. He had been—you couldn't say happy, exactly, at the failure of that campaign—but he was eager for what was shaping up to be a larger-scale operation. Though seven months gone, the deaths and dishonorings of his acquaintances had left the Lieutenant an appetite for this mission. Enough to cause him to disobey his orders and charge into Fallujah's southern section? Davis didn't think so, but there was a reason the man still held the rank of Lieutenant when his classmates and colleagues were well into their captaincies.

The other reason for Davis's conviction that, this time, something was on its way to him was a simple matter of odds. It wasn't possible—it was not possible that you could rack up this much good luck and not have a shitload of the bad bearing down on you like a SCUD on an anthill. A former altar boy, he was surprised at the variety of prayers he remembered—not just the Our Father and the Hail Mary, but the Apostles' Creed, the Memorare, and the Hail, Holy Queen. As he disembarked the Bradley and ran for the shelter of a desert-colored house, the sky an enormous, pale blue dome above him, Davis mumbled his way through his prayers with a fervency that would have pleased his mother and father no end. But even as his lips shaped the words, he had the strong sense that this was out of God's hands, under the control of one of those medieval demigoddesses, Dame Fortune or something.

Later, recovering first in Germany, then at Walter Reed, Davis had thought that walking patrol, riding convoy, standing checkpoint, he must have been saved from something truly awful each and every time, for the balance to be this steep.

III

10:01 P.M.

"I take it stakes are out," the Lieutenant said.

"Sir," Lee said, "I unloaded half a clip easy into that sonovabitch, and I was as close to him as I am to you."

"Closer," Han said.

"The point is, he took a half-step backwards—maybe—before he tore my weapon out of my hands and fractured my skull with it."

"That's what I'm saying," the Lieutenant said. "I figure it has to be . . . what? Did you get your hands on some kind of major ordnance, Davis? An rpg? A Stinger? I'll love you like a son—hell, I'll adopt you as my own if you tell me you have a case of Stingers concealed under a bush somewhere. Those'll give the fucker a welcome he won't soon forget."

"Fucking-A," Han said.

"Nah," Lee said. "A crate of Willy Pete oughta just about do it. Serve his ass crispy-fried!"

Davis shook his head. "No Stingers and no white phosphorous. Fire isn't going to do us any good."

"How come?" Lee said.

"Yeah," Han said.

"If I'm right about this thing spending its nights in low-Earth orbit—in its 'coffin'—and then leaving that refuge to descend into the atmosphere so it can hunt, its skin has to be able to withstand considerable extremes of temperature."

"Like the Space Shuttle," the Lieutenant said. "Huh. For all intents and purposes, it's fireproof."

"Oh," Lee said.

"Given that it spends some of its time in the upper atmosphere, as well as actual outer space, I'm guessing substantial cold wouldn't have much effect, either."

"We can't shoot it, can't burn it, can't freeze it," Lee said. "Tell me why we're here, again?" He waved at the trees fringing the clearing. "Aside from the scenery, of course."

"Pipe down," the Lieutenant said.

"When we shot at it," Davis said, "I'm betting half our fire missed it." He held up his hand to the beginning of Lee's protest. "That's no reflection on anyone. The thing was fast, cheetah-taking-down-a-gazelle fast. Not to mention, it's so goddamned *thin* . . . Anyway, of the shots that connected with it, most of them were flesh wounds." He raised his hand to Lee, again. "Those who connected with it," a nod to Lee, "were so close their fire passed clean through it."

"Which is what I was saying," Lee said.

"There's a lot of crazy shit floating around space," Davis said—
"little particles of sand, rock, ice, metal. Some of them get to moving
pretty fast. If you're doing repairs to the Space Station and one of
those things hits you, it could ruin your whole day. Anything that's going to survive up there is going to have to be able to deal with something that can punch a hole right through you."

"It's got a self-sealing mechanism," the Lieutenant said. "When
Lee fired into it, its body treated the bullets as so many dust-particles."

"And closed right up," Davis said. "Like some kind of super-
clotting-factor. Maybe that's what it uses the blood for."

"You're saying it's bulletproof, too?" Lee said.

"Shit," Han said.

"Not—more like, bullet-resistant."

"Think of it as a mutant healing ability," the Lieutenant said, "like
Wolverine."

"Oh," Han said.

"Those claws it has," Lee said, "I guess Wolverine isn't too far off
the mark."

"No," Han said. "Sabertooth."

"What?" Lee said. "The fuck're you going on about?"

"Sabertooth's claws." Han held up his right hand, fingers splayed.
He curled his fingers into a fist. "Wolverine's claws."

"Man has a point," the Lieutenant said.

"Whatever," Lee said.

"Here's the thing," Davis said: "it's bullet-resistant, but it can still
feel pain. Think about how it reacted when Lee shot it. It didn't tear
his throat open: it took the instrument that had hurt it and used that to
hurt Lee. You see what I'm saying?"

"Kind of," Lee said.

"Think about what drove it off," Davis said. "Remember?"

"Of course," the Lieutenant said. He nodded at Han. "It was Han
sticking his bayonet in the thing's side."

For which it crushed his skull, Davis could not stop himself from
thinking. He added his nod to the Lieutenant's. "Yes he did."

"How is that different from shooting it?" Lee said.

"Your bullets went in one side and out the other," Davis said.
"Han's bayonet stuck there. The thing's healing ability could deal with

an in-and-out wound no problem; something like this, though: I think it panicked."

"Panicked?" Lee said. "It didn't look like it was panicking to me."

"Then why did it take off right away?" Davis said.

"It was full; it heard more backup on the way; it had an appointment in fucking Samara. How the fuck should I know?"

"What's your theory?" the Lieutenant said.

"The type of injury Han gave it would be very bad if you're in a vacuum. Something opening you up like that and leaving you exposed . . ."

"You could vent some or even all of the blood you worked so hard to collect," the Lieutenant said. "You'd want to get out of a situation like that with all due haste."

"Even if your healing factor could seal the wound's perimeter," Davis said, "there's still this piece of steel in you that has to come out and, when it does, will reopen the injury."

"Costing you still more blood," the Lieutenant said.

"Most of the time," Davis said, "I mean, like, nine hundred and ninety-nine thousand, nine hundred and ninety-nine times out of a million, the thing would identify any such threats long before they came that close. You saw its ears, its eyes."

"Black on black," Lee said. "Or, no—black over black, like the corneas had some kind of heavy tint and what was underneath was all pupil."

"Han got lucky," Davis said. "The space we were in really wasn't that big. There was a lot of movement, a lot of noise—"

"Not to mention," Lee said, "all the shooting and screaming."

"The right set of circumstances," the Lieutenant said.

"Saved our asses," Lee said, reaching over to pound Han's shoulder. Han ducked to the side, grinning his hideous smile.

"If I can cut to the chase," the Lieutenant said. "You're saying we need to find a way to open up this fucker and keep him open so that we can wreak merry havoc on his insides."

Davis nodded. "To cut to the chase, yes, exactly."

"How do you propose we do this?"

"With these." Davis reached into the duffel bag to his left and withdrew what appeared to be a three-foot piece of white wood, tapered to a point sharp enough to prick your eye looking at it. He passed the first one to the Lieutenant, brought out one for Lee and one for Han.

"A baseball bat?" Lee said, gripping near the point and swinging his like a Louisville Slugger. "We gonna club it to death?"

Neither Davis nor the Lieutenant replied; they were busy watching Han, who'd located the grips at the other end of his and was jabbing it, first underhand, then overhand.

"The people you meet working at Home Depot," Davis said. "They're made out of an industrial resin, inch-for-inch, stronger than steel. Each one has a high-explosive core."

"Whoa," Lee said, setting his on the ground with exaggerated care.

"The detonators are linked to this," Davis said, fishing a cell phone from his shirt pocket. "Turn it on." Pointing to the Lieutenant, Han, Lee, and himself, he counted, "One-two-three-four. Send. That's it."

"I was mistaken," the Lieutenant said. "It appears we will be using stakes, after all."

IV

2004

At Landstuhl, briefly, and then at Walter Reed, at length, an impressive array of doctors, nurses, chaplains, and other soldiers whose job it was encouraged Davis to discuss Fallujah. He was reasonably sure that, while under the influence of one of the meds that kept his body at a safe distance, he had let slip some detail, maybe more. How else to account for the change in his nurse's demeanor? Likely, she judged he was a psych case, a diagnosis he was half inclined to accept. Even when the Lieutenant forced his way into Davis's room, banging around in the wheelchair he claimed he could use well enough, goddamnit, Davis was reluctant to speak of anything except the conditions of the other survivors. Of whom he had been shocked—truly shocked, profoundly shocked, almost more so than by what had torn through them—to learn there were only two, Lee and Han, Manfred bled out on the way to be evac'd, everyone else long gone by the time the reinforcements had stormed into the courtyard. According to the Lieutenant, Han was clinging to life by a thread so fine you couldn't see it.

He'd lost his helmet in the fracas, and the bones in his skull had been crushed like an eggshell. Davis, who had witnessed that crushing, nodded. Lee had suffered his own head trauma, although, compared to Han's, it wasn't anything a steel plate couldn't fix. The real problem with Lee was that, if he wasn't flooded with some heavy-duty happy pills, he went fetal, thumb in his mouth, the works.

"What about you?" the Lieutenant said, indicating the armature of casts, wires, weights, and counterweights that kept Davis suspended like some overly ambitious kid's science project.

"Believe it or not, sir," Davis said, "it really is worse than it looks. My pack and my helmet absorbed most of the impact. Still left me with a broken back, scapula, and ribs—but my spinal cord's basically intact. Not that it doesn't hurt like a motherfucker, sir. Yourself?"

"The taxpayers of the United States of America have seen fit to gift me with a new right leg, since I so carelessly misplaced the original." He knocked on his pajama leg, which gave a hollow, plastic sound.

"Sir, I am so sorry—"

"Shut it," the Lieutenant said. "It's a paper cut." Using his left foot, he rolled himself back to the door, which he eased almost shut. Through the gap, he surveyed the hallway outside long enough for Davis to start counting, *One Mississippi, Two Mississippi,* then wheeled himself to Davis's head. He leaned close and said, "Davis."

"Sir?"

"Let's leave out the rank thing for five minutes, okay? Can we do that?"

"Sir—yes, yes we can."

"Because ever since the docs have reduced my drugs to the point I could string one sentence after another, I've been having these memories—dreams—I don't know what the fuck to call them. Nightmares. And I can't decide if I'm losing it, or if this is why Lee needs a palmful of M&Ms to leave his bed. So I need you to talk to me straight, no bullshit, no telling the officer what you think he wants to hear. I would genuinely fucking appreciate it if we could do that."

Davis looked away when he saw the Lieutenant's eyes shimmering. Keeping his own focused on the ceiling, he said, "It came out of the sky. That's where it went, after Han stuck it, so I figure it must have dropped out of there, too. It explains why, one minute we're across the courtyard from a bunch of hostiles, the next, that thing's standing between us."

"Did you see it take off?"

"I did. After it had stepped on Han's head, it spread its arms—it kind of staggered back from Han, caught itself, then opened its arms and these huge wings snapped open. They were like a bat's, skin stretched over bone—they appeared so fast I'm not sure, but they shot out of its body. It tilted its head, jumped up, high, ten feet easy, flapped the wings, which raised it another ten feet, and turned—the way a swimmer turns in the water, you know? Another flap, two, and it was gone."

"Huh."

Davis glanced at the Lieutenant, whose face was smooth, his eyes gazing across some interior distance. He said, "Do you—"

"Back up," the Lieutenant said. "The ten of us are in the courtyard. How big's the place?"

"I'm not very good with—"

"At a guess."

"Twenty-five feet wide, maybe fifty long. With all those jars in the way—what were they?"

"Planters."

"Three-foot-tall stone planters?"

"For trees. They were full of dirt. Haven't you ever seen those little decorative trees inside office buildings?"

"Oh. All right. What I was going to say was: With the row of planters at either end, the place might have been larger."

"Noted. How tall were the walls?"

"Taller than any of us—eight feet, easy. They were thick, too, a foot and a half, two feet. It really was a good spot to attack from. Open fire from the walls, then drop behind them when they can't maintain that position. The tall buildings are behind it, and we don't hold any of them, so they don't have to worry about anyone firing down on them. I'm guessing they figured we didn't know where we were well enough to call in any artillery on them. No, if we want them, we have to run a hundred feet of open space to a doorway that's an easy trap. They've got the planters for cover near and far, not to mention the doorway in the opposite wall as an exit."

"Agreed."

"To be honest, now that we're talking about it, I can't imagine how we made it into the place without losing anyone. By all rights, they should have tagged a couple of us crossing from our position to theirs. And that doorway: they should have massacred us."

"We were lucky. When we returned fire, they must have panicked. Could be they didn't see all of us behind the wall, thought they were ambushing three or four targets, instead of ten. Charging them may have given the impression there were even more of us. It took them until they were across the courtyard to get a grip and regroup."

"By which time we were at the doorway."

"So it was Lee all the way on the left—"

"With Han beside him."

"Right, and Bay and Remsnyder. Then you and Petit—"

"No—it was me and Lugo, then Petit, then you."

"Yes, yes. Manfred was to my right, and Weymouth was all the way on the other end."

"I'm not sure how many—"

"Six. There may have been a seventh in the opposite doorway, but he wasn't around very long. Either he went down, or he decided to season his valor with a little discretion."

"It was loud—everybody firing in a confined space. I had powder all over me from their shots hitting the wall behind us. I want to say we traded bullets for about five minutes, but it was what? Half that?"

"Less. A minute."

"And . . ."

"Our guest arrived."

"At first—at first it was like, I couldn't figure out what I was seeing. I'm trying to line up the guy who's directly across from me—all I need is for him to stick up his head again—and all of a sudden, there's a shadow in the way. That was my first thought: *It's a shadow.* Only, who's casting it? And why is it hanging in the air like that? And why is it fucking eight feet tall?"

"None of us understood what was in front of us. I thought it was a woman in a burka, someone I'd missed when we'd entered the courtyard. As you say, though, you don't meet a lot of eight-foot-tall women, in or out of Iraq."

"Next thing . . . no, that isn't what happened."

"What?"

"I was going to say the thing—the Shadow—was in among the hostiles, which is true, it went for them first, but before it did, there was a moment . . ."

"You saw something—something else."

"Yeah," Davis said. "This pain shot straight through my head. We're talking instant migraine, so intense I practically puked. That wasn't all: this chill . . . I was freezing, colder than I've ever been, like you read about in Polar expeditions. I couldn't—the courtyard—"

"What?"

"The courtyard wasn't—I was somewhere high, like, a hundred miles high, so far up I could see the curve of the Earth below me. Clouds, continents, the ocean: what you see in the pictures they take from orbit. Stars, space, all around me. Directly overhead, a little farther away than you are from me, there was this thing. I don't know what the fuck it was. Big—long, maybe long as a house. It bulged in the middle, tapered at the ends. The surface was dark, shiny—does that make any sense? The thing was covered in—it looked like some kind of lacquer. Maybe it was made out of the lacquer.

"Anyway, one moment my head's about to crack open, my teeth are chattering, my skin's blue, and I'm in outer space. The next, all of that's gone, I'm back in the courtyard, and the Shadow—the thing is ripping the hostiles to shreds."

"And then," the Lieutenant said, "it was our turn."

V

November 11, 2004, 11:13 A.M.

In the six hundred twenty-five days since that afternoon in the hospital, how many times had Davis recited the order of events in the courtyard, whether with the Lieutenant, or with Lee once his meds had been stabilized, or with Han once he'd regained the ability to speak (though not especially well)? At some point a couple of months on, he'd realized he'd been keeping count—*That's the thirty-eighth time; that's the forty-third*—and then, a couple of months after that, he'd realized that he'd lost track. The narrative of their encounter with what Davis continued to think of as the Shadow had become daily catechism, to be reviewed morning, noon, and night, and whenever else he happened to think of it.

None of them had even tried to run, which there were times Davis judged a sign of courage, and times he deemed an index of their collective shock at the speed and ferocity of the thing's assault on the insurgents. Heads, arms, legs were separated from bodies as if by a pair of razored blades, and wherever a wound opened red, there was the thing's splintered maw, drinking the blood like a kid stooping to a water fountain. The smells of blood, piss, and shit mixed with those of gunpowder and hot metal. While Davis knew they had been the next course on the Shadow's menu, he found it difficult not to wonder how the situation might have played out had Lee—followed immediately by Lugo and Weymouth—not opened up on the thing. Of course, the instant that narrow head with its spotlight eyes, its scarlet mouth, turned in their direction, everyone else's guns erupted, and the scene concluded the way it had to. But if Lee had been able to restrain himself . . .

Lugo was first to die. In a single leap, the Shadow closed the distance between them and drove one of its sharpened hands into his throat, venting his carotid over Davis, whom it caught with its other hand and flung into one of the side walls with such force his spine and ribs lit up like the Fourth of July. As he was dropping onto his back, turtling on his pack, the thing was raising its head from Lugo's neck, spearing Petit through his armor and hauling him toward it. Remsnyder ran at it from behind; the thing's hand lashed out and struck his head from his shoulders. It was done with Petit in time to catch Remsnyder's body on the fall and jam its mouth onto the bubbling neck. It had shoved Petit's body against the Lieutenant, whose feet tangled with Petit's and sent the pair of them down. This put him out of the way of Manfred and Weymouth, who screamed for everyone to get clear and fired full automatic. Impossible as it seemed, they missed, and for their troubles the Shadow lopped Manfred's right arm off at the elbow and opened Weymouth like a Christmas present. From the ground, the Lieutenant shot at it; the thing sliced through his weapon and the leg underneath it. Now Bay, Han, and Lee tried full auto, which brought the thing to Bay, whose face it bit off. It swatted Han to the ground, but Lee somehow ducked the swipe it aimed at him and tagged it at close range. The Shadow threw Bay's body across the courtyard, yanked Lee's rifle from his hands, and swung it against his head like a ballplayer aiming for the stands. He crumpled, the thing reaching out for him, and Han leapt up, his bayonet ridiculously small in his hand. He drove it into the thing's side—what would be the floating ribs on a man—to the hilt. The Shadow, whose only sound thus far had been its feeding, opened its jaws and shrieked, a high scream more like the cry of a bat, or a hawk, than anything human. It caught Han with an elbow to the temple that tumbled him to the dirt, set its foot on his head, and pressed down. Han's scream competed with the sound of his skull cracking in multiple spots. Davis was certain the thing meant to grind Han's head to paste, but it staggered off him, one claw reaching for the weapon buried in its skin. Blood so dark it was purple was oozing around the hilt. The Shadow spread its arms, its wings cracked open, and it was gone, fled into the blue sky that Davis would spend the next quarter-hour staring at, as the Lieutenant called for help and tried to tourniquet first his leg then Manfred's arm.

Davis had stared at the sky before—who has not?—but, helpless on his back, his spine a length of molten steel, his ears full of Manfred whimpering that he was gonna die, oh sweet Jesus, he was gonna fucking die, the Lieutenant talking over him, insisting no he wasn't, he was gonna be fine, it was just a little paper cut, the washed blue bowl overhead seemed less sheltering canopy and more endless depth, a gullet over which he had the sickening sensation of dangling. As Manfred's cries diminished and the Lieutenant told—ordered him to stay with him, Davis flailed his arms at the ground to either side of him in an effort to grip onto an anchor, something that would keep him from hurtling into that blue abyss.

The weeks and months to come would bring the inevitable nightmares, the majority of them the Shadow's attack replayed at half-, full-, or double-speed, with a gruesome fate for himself edited in. Sometimes repeating the events on his own or with a combination of the others led to a less disturbed sleep; sometimes it did not. There was one dream, though, that no amount of discussion could help, and that was the one in which Davis was plummeting through the sky, lost in an appetite that would never be sated.

VI

12:26 A.M.

Once he was done setting the next log on the fire, Davis leaned back and said, "I figure it's some kind of stun effect."

"How so?" Lee said.

"The thing lands in between two groups of heavily armed men: it has to do something to even the odds. It hits us with a psychic blast, shorts out our brains so that we're easier prey."

"Didn't seem to do much to Lee," the Lieutenant said.

"No brain!" Han shouted.

"Ha-fucking-ha," Lee said.

"Maybe there were too many of us," Davis said. "Maybe it miscalculated. Maybe Lee's a mutant and this is his special gift. Had the thing zigged instead of zagged, gone for us instead of the insurgents, I don't think any of us would be sitting here, regardless of our super powers."

"Speak for yourself," Lee said.

"For a theory," the Lieutenant said, "it's not bad. But there's a sizable hole in it. You"—he pointed at Davis—"saw the thing's coffin or whatever. Lee"—a nod to him—"was privy to a bat's-eye view of the thing's approach to one of its hunts in—did we ever decide if it was Laos or Cambodia?"

"No, sir," Lee said. "It looked an awful lot like some of the scenery from the first *Tomb Raider* movie, which I'm pretty sure was filmed in Cambodia, but I'm not positive."

"You didn't see Angelina Jolie running around?" Davis said.

"If only," Lee said.

"So with Lee, we're in Southeast Asia," the Lieutenant said, "with or without the lovely Ms. Jolie. From what Han's been able to tell me, he was standing on the moon or someplace very similar to it. I don't believe he could see the Earth from where he was, but I'm not enough of an astronomer to know what that means.

"As for myself, I had a confused glimpse of the thing tearing its way through the interior of an airplane—what I'm reasonably certain was a B-17, probably during the Second World War.

"You see what I mean? None of us witnessed the same scene— none of us witnessed the same time, which you would imagine we would have if we'd been subject to a deliberate attack. You would expect the thing to hit us all with the same image. It's more efficient."

"Maybe that isn't how this works," Davis said. "Suppose what it does is more like a cluster bomb, a host of memories it packs around a psychic charge? If each of us thinks he's someplace different from everybody else, doesn't that maximize confusion, create optimal conditions for an attack?"

The Lieutenant frowned. Lee said, "What's your theory, sir?"

"I don't have one," the Lieutenant said. "Regardless of its intent, the thing got in our heads."

"And stayed there," Lee said.

"Stuck," Han said, tapping his right temple.

"Yes," the Lieutenant said. "Whatever their precise function, our exposure to the thing's memories appears to have established a link between us and it."

Davis said, "Which is what's going to bring it right here."

VII

2004–2005

When Davis was on board the plane to Germany, he could permit himself to hope that he was, however temporarily, out of immediate danger of death—not from the injury to his back, which, though painful in the extreme, he had known from the start would not claim his life, but from the reappearance of the Shadow. Until their backup arrived in a hurry of bootsteps and rattle of armor, he had been waiting for the sky to vomit the figure it had swallowed minutes (moments?) prior, for his blood to leap into the thing's jagged mouth. The mature course of action had seemed to prepare for his imminent end, which he had attempted, only to find the effort beyond him. Whenever word of some acquaintance's failure to return from the latest patrol had prompted Davis to picture his final seconds, he had envisioned his face growing calm, even peaceful, his lips shaping the syllables of a heartfelt Act of Contrition. However, between the channel of fire that had replaced his spine and the vertiginous sensation that he might plunge into the sky—not to mention, the Lieutenant's continuing monologue to Manfred, the pungence of gunpowder mixed with the bloody reek of meat, the low moans coming from Han—Davis was unable to concentrate. Rather than any gesture of reconciliation toward the God with Whom he had not been concerned since his discovery of what lay beneath his prom date's panties junior year, Davis's attention had been snarled in the sound of the Shadow's claws puncturing Lugo's neck, the fountain of Weymouth's blood over its arm and chest, the wet slap of his entrails hitting the ground, the stretch of the thing's mouth as it released its scream. Despite his back, which had drawn his vocal chords taut, once the reinforcements had arrived and a red-faced medic peppered him with questions while performing a quick assessment of him, Davis had strained to warn them of their danger. But all his insistence that they had to watch the sky had brought him was a sedative that pulled him into a vague, gray place.

Nor had his time at the Battalion Aid Station, then some larger facility (Camp Victory? with whatever they gave him, most of the details a variety of medical staff poured into his ears sluiced right back out again) caused him to feel any more secure. As the gray place loosened its hold on him and he stared up at the canvas roof of the BAS, Davis had wanted to demand what the fuck everyone was thinking. Didn't they know the Shadow could slice through this material as if it were cling film? Didn't they understand it was waiting to descend on them right now, this very fucking minute? It would rip them to shreds; it would drink their fucking *blood.* At the presence of a corpsman beside him, he'd realized he was shouting—or as close to shouting as his voice could manage—but he'd been unable to restrain himself, which had led to calming banalities and more vague grayness. He had returned to something like consciousness inside a larger space in the CSH, where the sight of the nearest wall trembling from the wind had drawn his stomach tight and sped a fresh round of protests from his mouth. When he struggled up out of the shot that outburst occasioned, Davis had found himself in a dim cavern whose curving sides rang with the din of enormous engines. His momentary impression that he was dead and this some unexpected, bare-bones afterlife was replaced by the recognition that he was on a transport out of Iraq—who knew to where? It didn't matter. A flood of tears had rolled from his eyes as the dread coiling his guts had, if not fled, at least calmed.

At Landstuhl, in a solidly built hospital with drab but sturdy walls and a firm ceiling, Davis was calmer. (As long as he did not dwell on the way the Shadow's claws had split Petit's armor, sliced the Lieutenant's rifle in two.) That, and the surgeries required to relieve the pressure on his spine, left him, to quote a song he'd never liked that much, comfortably numb.

Not until he was back in America, though, reclining in the late medieval luxury of Walter Reed, the width of an ocean and a continent separating him from Fallujah, did Davis feel anything like a sense of security. Even after his first round of conversations with the Lieutenant had offered him the dubious reassurance that, if he were delusional, he was in good company, a cold comfort made chillier still by Lee, his meds approaching the proper levels, corroborating their narrative, Davis found it less difficult than he would have anticipated to persuade himself that Remsnyder's head leaping from his body on a jet of blood was seven thousand miles away. And while his pulse still quickened whenever his vision strayed to the rectangle of sky framed by the room's lone window, he could almost pretend that this was a different sky. After all, hadn't that been the subtext of all the stories he'd heard from other vets about earlier wars? Weird shit happened, yes—sometimes, very bad weird shit happened—but it took place over there, In Country, in another place where things didn't work the same way they did in the good old U.S. of A. If you could keep that in mind, Davis judged, front-and-center in your consciousness, you might be able to live with the impossible.

Everything went—you couldn't call it swimmingly—it went, anyway, until Davis began his rehabilitation, which consisted of: a) learning how to walk again and b) strength training for his newly (re)educated legs. Of course, he had been in pain after the initial injury—though shock and fear had kept the hurt from overwhelming him—and his nerves had flared throughout his hospital stay—especially following his surgery—though a pharmacopeia had damped those sensations down to smoldering. Rehab was different. Rehab was a long, low-ceilinged room that smelled of sweat and industrial antiseptic, at one end of which grazed a small herd of the kind of exercise machines you saw faded celebrities hawking on late-night TV, the center of which held a trio of parallel bars set too low, and the near end of which was home to a series of overlapping blue mats whose extensive

cracks suggested an aerial view of a river basin. Rehab was slow
stretches on the mats, then gripping onto the parallel bars while you
tried to coax your right leg into moving forward; once you could lurch
along the bars and back, rehab was time on one of the exercise machines, flat on your back, your legs bent, your feet pressed against a
pair of pedals connected to a series of weights you raised by extending
your legs. Rehab was about confronting pain, inviting it in, asking it to
sit down and have a beer so the two of you could talk for a while. Rehab was not leaning on the heavy-duty opiates and their synthetic
friends; it was remaining content with the over-the-counter options
and ice-packs. It was the promise of a walk outside—an enticement
that made Davis's palms sweat and his mouth go dry.

When the surgeon had told Davis the operation had been a success and that there appeared to be no permanent damage to his spinal
cord, Davis had imagined himself, freed of his cast and its coterie of
pulleys and counterweights, sitting up on his own and strolling out the
front door. Actually, he'd been running in his fantasy. The reality, he
quickly discovered, was that merely raising himself to a sitting position
was an enterprise far more involved than he ever had appreciated, as
was a range of action so automatic it existed below his being able to
admit he'd never given it much thought. He supposed the therapists
here were as good as you were going to find, but that didn't make the
routines they subjected him to—he subjected himself to—any easier or
less painful.

It was during one of these sessions, his back feeling as if it had
been scraped raw and the exposed tissue generously salted, that Davis
had his first inkling that Fallujah was not a self-contained narrative, a
short, grisly tale; rather, it was the opening chapter of a novel, one of
those eight-hundred-page Stephen King specials. Lucy, Davis's pri-
mary therapist, had him on what he had christened the Rack. His target was twenty leg presses; in a fit of bravado, he had promised her
thirty. No doubt, Davis had known instances of greater pain, but those
had been spikes on the graph. Though set at a lower level, this hurt
was constant, and while Lucy had assured him that he would become
used to it, so far he hadn't. The pain glared like the sun flaring off a
window; it flooded his mind white, made focusing on anything else
impossible. That Lucy was encouraging him, he knew from the tone of

her voice, but he could not distinguish individual words. Already, his vision was blurred from the sweat streaming out of him, so when the blur fractured, became a kaleidoscope-jumble of color and geometry, he thought little of it and raised his fingers to clear his eyes.

According to Lucy, Davis removed his hand from his face, paused, then fell off the machine on his right side, trembling and jerking. For what she called his seizure's duration, which she clocked at three minutes fifteen seconds, Davis uttered no sound except for a gulping noise that made his therapist fear he was about to swallow his tongue.

To the Lieutenant, then to Lee and eventually Han, Davis would compare what he saw when the rehab room went far away to a widescreen movie, one of those panoramic deals that was supposed to impart the sensation of flying over the Rockies, or holding on for dear life as a roller coaster whipped up and down its course. A surplus of detail crowded his vision. He was in the middle of a sandy street bordered by short buildings whose walls appeared to consist of sheets of long, dried grass framed with slender sticks. A dozen, two dozen women and children dressed in pastel robes and turbans ran frantically from one side of the street to the other as men wearing dark brown shirts and pants aimed Kalashnikovs at them. Some of the men were riding brown and white horses; some were stalking the street; some were emerging from alleys between the buildings, several of whose walls were releasing thick smoke. Davis estimated ten men. The sounds—it was as if the soundtrack to this film had been set to record the slightest vibration of air, which it played back at twice the normal level. Screams raked his eardrums. Sandals scraped the ground. Guns cracked; bullets thudded into skin. Horses whickered. Fire snapped. An immense thirst, worse than any he had known, possessed him. His throat was not dry; it was arid, as if it—as if he were composed of dust from which the last eyedropper of moisture had long been squeezed.

One of the men—not the nearest, who was walking the opposite direction from Davis's position, but the next closest, whose horse had shied from the flames sprouting from a grass wall and so turned its rider in Davis's direction—caught sight of Davis, his face contracting in confusion at what he saw. The man, who might have been in his early twenties, started to raise his rifle, and everything sped up, the movie fast-forwarded. There was—his vision wavered, and the man's gun dipped, his eyes widening. Davis was next to him—he had half scaled the horse and speared the hollow of the man's throat with his right hand, whose fingers, he saw, were twice as long as they had been, tapered to a set of blades. He felt the man's tissue part, the ends of his fingers (talons?) scrape bone. Blood washed over his palm, his wrist, and the sensation jolted him. His talons flicked to the left, and the man's head tipped back like a tree falling away from its base. Blood misted the air, and before he realized what was happening, his mouth was clamped to the wound, full of hot, copper liquid. The taste was rain falling in the desert; in three mighty gulps, he had emptied the corpse and was springing over its fellows, into the midst of the brightly-robed women and children.

The immediate result of Davis's three-minute hallucination was the suspension of his physical therapy and an MRI of his brain. Asked by Lucy what he recalled of the experience, Davis had shaken his head and answered, "Nothing." It was the same response he gave to the new doctor who stopped into his room a week later and, without identifying himself as a psychiatrist, told Davis he was interested in the nightmares that had brought him screaming out of sleep six of the last seven nights. This was a rather substantial change in his nightly routine; taken together with his recent seizure, it seemed like cause for concern. Perhaps Davis could relate what he remembered of his nightmares?

How to tell this doctor that closing his eyes—an act he resisted for as long as could each night—brought him to that yellow-brown street; the lime, saffron, and orange cloth stretching as mothers hauled their children behind them; the dull muzzles of the Kalashnikovs coughing fire? How to describe the sensations that still lived in his skin, his muscles: the tearing of skin for his too-long fingers; the bounce of a heart in his hand the instant before he tore it from its setting; the eggshell crunch of bone between his jaws? Most of all, how to convey to this doctor, this shrink who was either an unskilled actor or not trying very hard, the concentrate of pleasure that was the rush of blood into his mouth, down his throat, the satisfaction of his terrific thirst so momentary it made the thirst that much worse? Although Davis had repeated his earlier disavowal and maintained it in the face of the doctor's extended—and, to be fair, sympathetic—questions until the man left, a week's worth of poor sleep made the wisdom of his decision appear less a foregone conclusion. What he had seen—what he had been part of the other week was too similar to the vision he'd had in the courtyard not to be related; the question was, how? Were Davis to summarize his personal horror ride to the psychiatrist—he would have to tell him about Fallujah first, of course—might the doctor have more success at understanding the connections between his driver's-seat views of the Shadow's activities?

Sure, Davis thought, *right after he's had you fitted for your straitjacket.* The ironic thing was, how often had he argued the benefits of the Army's psychiatric care with Lugo? It had been their running gag. Lugo would return from reading his e-mail with news of some guy stateside who'd lost it, shot his wife, himself, which would prompt Davis to say that it was a shame the guy hadn't gotten help before it came to that. Help, Lugo would say, from whom? The Army? Man, you must be joking. The Army don't want nothing to do with no grunt can't keep his shit together. No, no, Davis would say, sure, they still had a ways to go, but the Army was changing. The kinds of combat-induced pathologies it used to pretend didn't exist were much more likely to be treated early and effectively. (If Lee and Han were present, and/or Remsnyder, they'd ooh and aah over Davis's vocabulary.) Oh yeah, Lugo would reply, if they don't discharge your ass right outta here, they'll stick you at some bullshit post where you won't hurt anyone. No, no, Davis would say, that was a rumor. Oh yeah, Lugo would say, like the rumor about the guys who went to the doctor for help with their PTSD and were told they were suffering from a fucking preexisting condition, so it wasn't the Army's problem? No, no, Davis would say, that was a few bad guys. Oh yeah, Lugo would say.

Before he and the Lieutenant—who had been abducted by a platoon of siblings, their spouses, and their kids for ten days in Florida— discussed the matter, Davis passed his nightly struggles to stay awake wondering if the psychiatric ward was the worst place he might wind up. His only images of such places came from films like *One Flew Over the Cuckoo's Nest, Awakenings,* and *K-PAX,* but based on those examples, he could expect to spend his days robed and slippered, possibly medicated, free to read what he wanted except during individual and group therapy sessions. If it wasn't quite the career as a psychologist he'd envisioned, he'd at least be in some kind of proximity to the mental health field. Sure, it would be a scam, but didn't the taxpayers of the U.S. of A. owe him recompense for shipping him to a place where the Shadow could just drop in and shred his life? The windows would be barred or meshed, the doors reinforced—you could almost fool yourself such a location would be safe.

However, with his second episode, it became clear that safe was one of those words that had been bayoneted, its meaning spilled on the floor. Davis had been approved to resume therapy with Lucy, who had been honestly happy to see him again. It was late in the day; what with the complete breakdown in his sleeping patterns, he wasn't in optimal condition for another go-around on the Rack, but after so much time stuck in his head, terrified at what was in there with him, the prospect of a vigorous workout was something he was actually looking forward to. As before, gentle stretching preceded the main event, which Lucy told Davis he didn't have to do but for which he had cavalierly assured her he was, if not completely able, at least ready and willing. With the second push of his feet against the pedals, pain ignited up his back, and his lack of sleep did not aid in his tolerating it. Each subsequent retraction and extension of his legs ratcheted the hurt up one more degree, until he was lying on a bed of fire.

This time

VIII

2:15 A.M.

"my vision didn't blur—it cracked, as if my knees levering up and down were an image on a TV screen and something smacked the glass. Everything spiderwebbed and fell away. What replaced it was movement—I was moving up, my arms beating down; there was this feeling that they were bigger, much bigger, that when I swept them down, they were gathering the air and piling it beneath them. I looked below me, and there were bodies—parts of bodies, organs—all over the place. There was less blood than there should have been. Seeing them scattered across the ground—it was like having a bird's- eye view of some kind of bizarre design. Most of them were men, twenties and thirties; although there were two women and a couple-three kids. Almost everybody was wearing jeans and workboots, sweatshirts, base-ball caps, except for a pair of guys dressed in khaki and I'm pretty sure cowboy hats."

"What the fuck?" Lee said.

"Cowboys," Han said.

"Texas Border Patrol," the Lieutenant said.

"So those other people were like, illegal immigrants?" Lee said.

The Lieutenant nodded.

Davis said, "I've never been to Texas, but the spot looked like what you see on TV. Sandy, full of rocks, some scrub brush, and short trees. There was a muddy stream—you might call it a river, I guess, if that was what you were used to—in the near distance, and a group of hills further off. The sun was perched on top of the hills, setting, and that red ball made me beat my arms again and again, shrinking the scene below, raising me higher into the sky. There was—I felt full—more than full, gorged, but thirsty, still thirsty, that same, overpowering dryness I'd experienced the previous . . . time. The thirst was so strong, so compel-ling, I was a little surprised when I kept climbing. My flight was con-nected to the sun balanced on that hill, a kind of—not panic, exactly: it was more like urgency. I was moving, now. The air was thinning; my arms stretched even larger to scoop enough of it to keep me moving. The temperature had dropped—was dropping, plunging down. Some-thing happened—my mouth was already closed, but it was as if it sealed somehow. Same thing with my nostrils; I mean, they closed themselves off. My eyes misted, then cleared. I pumped my arms harder than I had before. This time, I didn't lose speed; I kept moving forward.

"Ahead, I saw the thing I'd seen in the courtyard—a huge shape, big as a house. Pointed at the ends, fat in the middle. Dark—maybe dark purple, maybe not—and shiny. The moment it came into view, this surge of . . . I don't know what to call it. Honestly, I want to say it was a cross between the way you feel when you put your bag down on your old bed and, 'Mommy,' that little kid feeling, except that neither of those is completely right. My arms were condensing, growing sub-stantial. I was heading toward the middle. As I drew closer, its surface rippled, like water moving out from where a stone strikes it. At the center of the ripple, a kind of pucker opened into the thing. That was my destination."

"And?" Lee said.

"Lucy emptied her Gatorade on me and brought me out of it."

"You have got to be fucking kidding me," Lee said.

"Afraid not," Davis said.

"How long was this one?" the Lieutenant asked.

"Almost five minutes."

"It took her that long to toss her Gatorade on you?" Lee said.

"There was some kind of commotion at the same time, a couple of guys got into a fight. She tried to find help; when she couldn't, she doused me."

Lee shook his head.

"And you have since confirmed the existence of this object," the Lieutenant said.

"Yes, sir," Davis said. "It took some doing. The thing's damned near impossible to see, and while no one would come out and say so to me, I'm pretty sure it doesn't show up on radar, either. The couple of pictures we got were more dumb luck than anything."

"'We'?" Lee said.

"I . . ."

The Lieutenant said, "I put Mr. Davis in touch with a friend of mine in Intelligence."

"Oh," Lee said. "Wait—shit: you mean the CIA's involved?"

"Relax," Davis said.

"Because I swear to God," Lee said, "those stupid motherfuckers would fuck up getting toast out of the toaster and blame us for their burned fingers."

"It's under control," the Lieutenant said. "This is our party. No one else has been invited."

"Doesn't mean they won't show up," Lee said. "Stupid assholes with their fucking sunglasses and their 'We're so scary.' Oooh." He turned his head and spat.

Davis stole a look at the sky. Stars were winking out and in as something passed in front of them. His heart jumped, his hand was on his stake before he identified the shape as some kind of bird. The Lieutenant had noticed his movement; his hand over his stake; he said, "Everything all right, Davis?"

"Fine," Davis said. "Bird."

"What?" Lee said.

"Bird," Han said.

"Oh," Lee said. "So. I have a question."

"Go ahead," the Lieutenant said.

"The whole daylight thing," Lee said, "the having to be back in its coffin before sunset—what's up with that?"

"It does seem . . . atypical, doesn't it?" the Lieutenant said. "Vampires are traditionally creatures of the night."

"Actually, sir," Lee said, "that's not exactly true. The original Dracula—you know, in the book—he could go out in daylight; he just lost his powers."

"Lee," the Lieutenant said, "you are a font of information. Is this what our monster is trying to avoid?"

"I don't know," Lee said. "Could be."

"I don't think so," Davis said. "It's not as if daylight makes its teeth any sharper."

"Then what is it?" Lee said.

"Beats me," Davis said. "Don't we need daylight to make Vitamin D? Maybe it's the same, uses the sun to manufacture some kind of vital substance."

"Not bad," the Lieutenant said.

"For something you pulled out of your ass," Lee said.

"Hey—you asked," Davis said.

"Perhaps it's time for some review," the Lieutenant said. "Can we agree on that? Good.

"We have this thing—this vampire," holding up a hand to Davis, "that spends its nights in an orbiting coffin. At dawn or thereabouts, it departs said refuge in search of blood, which it apparently obtains from a single source."

"Us," Han said.

"Us," the Lieutenant said. "It glides down into the atmosphere on the lookout for likely victims—of likely groups of victims, since it prefers to feed on large numbers of people at the same time. Possibly, it burns through its food quickly."

"It's always thirsty," Davis said. "No matter how much it drinks, it's never enough."

"Yeah," Lee said, "I felt it, too."

"So did we all," the Lieutenant said. "It looks to satisfy its thirst at locations where its actions will draw little to no attention. These include remote areas such as the U.S.–Mexico border, the Sahara and Gobi, and the Andes. It also likes conflict zones, whether Iraq, Darfur, or the Congo. How it locates these sites is unknown. We estimate that it visits between four and seven of them per day. That we have been able to determine, there does not appear to be an underlying pattern to its selection of either target areas or individuals within those areas. The vampire's exact level of intelligence is another unknown. It possesses considerable abilities as a predator, not least of them its speed, reaction time, and strength. Nor should we forget its teeth and"—a rap of the artificial leg—"claws."

"Not to mention that mind thing," Lee said.

"Yes," the Lieutenant said. "Whether by accident or design, the vampire's appearance is accompanied by a telepathic jolt that momentarily disorients its intended victims, rendering them easier prey. For those who survive the meeting"—a nod at them—"a link remains that may be activated by persistent, pronounced stress, whether physical or mental. The result of this activation is a period of clairvoyance, during which the lucky individual rides along for the vampire's current activities. Whether the vampire usually has equal access to our perceptions during this time is unclear; our combined accounts suggest it does not.

"However, there are exceptions."

IX

2005

"I know how we can kill it," Davis said. "At least, I think I do—how we can get it to come to a place where we can kill it."

Lee put his Big Mac on his tray and looked out the restaurant window. The Lieutenant paused in the act of dipping his fries into a tub of barbecue sauce. Han continued chewing his McNugget but nodded twice.

"The other day—two days ago, Wednesday—I got to it."

"What do you mean?" the Lieutenant said.

"It was coming in for a landing, and I made it mess up."

"Bullshit," Lee said. He did not shift his gaze from the window. His face was flushed.

"How?" the Lieutenant said.

"I was having a bad day, worse than the usual bad day. Things at Home Depot—the manager's okay, but the assistant manager's a raging asshole. Anyway, I decided a workout might help. I'd bought these Kung Fu DVDs—"

"Kung Fu," the Lieutenant said.

Davis shrugged. "Seemed more interesting than running a treadmill."

Through a mouthful of McNugget, Han said, "Bruce Lee."

"Yeah," Davis said. "I put the first disc on. To start with, everything's fine. I'm taking it easy, staying well below the danger level. My back's starting to ache, the way it always does, but that's okay, I can live with it. As long as I keep the situation in low gear, I can continue with my tiger style."

"Did it help?" the Lieutenant asked.

"My worse-than-bad day? Not really. But it was something to do, you know?"

The Lieutenant nodded. Lee stared at the traffic edging up the road in front of the McDonald's. Han bit another McNugget.

"This time, there was no warning. My back's feeling like someone's stitching it with a hot needle, then I'm dropping out of heavy cloud cover. Below, a squat hill pushes up from dense jungle. A group of men are sitting around the top of the hill. They're wearing fatigues, carrying Kalashnikovs. I think I'm somewhere in South America: maybe these guys are FARQ; maybe they're some of Chavez's boys.

"I've been through the drill enough to know what's on the way: a ringside seat for blood and carnage. It's reached the point, when one of these incidents overtakes me, I don't freak out. The emotion that grips me is dread, sickness at what's coming. But this happens so fast, there isn't time for any of that. Instead, anger—the anger that usually shows up a couple of hours later, when I'm still trying to get the taste of blood out of my mouth, still trying to convince myself that I'm not the one who's so thirsty—for once, that anger arrives on time and loaded for bear. It's like the fire that's crackling on my back finds its way into my veins and ignites me.

"What's funny is, the anger makes my connection to the thing even more intense. The wind is pressing my face, rushing over my arms—my wings—I'm aware of currents in the air, places where it's thicker, thinner, and I twitch my nerves to adjust for it. There's one guy standing off from the rest, closer to the treeline, though not so much I—the thing won't be able to take him. I can practically see the route to him, a steep dive with a sharp turn at the very end that'll let the thing knife through him. He's sporting a bush hat, which he's pushed back on his head. His shirt's open, T-shirt dark with sweat. He's holding his weapon self-consciously, trying to looking like a ba-dass, and it's this, more than the smoothness of his skin, the couple of whiskers on his chin, that makes it clear he isn't even eighteen. It—I—we jackknife into the dive, and thirsty, Christ, thirsty isn't the word: this is dryness that reaches right through to your fucking soul. I've never understood what makes the thing tick—what *drives* it—so well.

"At the same time, the anger's still there. The closer we draw to the kid, the hotter it burns. We've reached the bottom of the dive and pulled up; we're streaking over the underbrush. The kid's completely oblivious to the fact that his bloody dismemberment is fifty feet away and closing fast. I'm so close to the thing, I can feel the way its fangs push against one another as they jut from its mouth. We're on top of the kid; the thing's preparing to retract its wings, slice him open, and drive its face into him. The kid is dead; he's dead and he just doesn't know it, yet.

"Only, it's like—I'm like—I don't even think, *No,* or *Stop,* or *Pull up.* It's more . . . I push; I shove against the thing I'm inside and its arms move. Its fucking arms jerk up as if someone's passed a current through them. Someone has—I have. I'm the current. The motion throws off the thing's strike, sends it wide. It flails at the kid as it flies past him, but he's out of reach. I can sense—the thing's completely confused. There's a clump of bushes straight ahead—*wham.*"

The Lieutenant had adopted his best you'd-better-not-be-bullshitting-me stare. He said, "I take it that severed the connection."

Davis shook his head. "No, sir. You would expect that—it's what would have happened in the past—but this time, it was like, I was so close to the thing, it was going to take something more to shake me loose."

"And?" the Lieutenant said.

Lee shoved his tray back, toppling his super-sized Dr. Pepper, whose lid popped off, splashing a wave of soda and ice cubes across the table. While Davis and the Lieutenant grabbed napkins, Lee stood and said, "What the fuck, Davis?"

"What?" Davis said.

"I said, What the fuck, asshole," Lee said. Several diners at nearby tables turned their heads toward him.

"Inside voices," the Lieutenant said. "Sit down."

"I don't think so," Lee said. "I don't have to listen to this shit." With that, he stalked away from the table, through the men and women swiftly returning their attentions to the meals in front of them, and out the side door.

"What the fuck?" Davis said, dropping his wad of soggy napkins on Lee's tray.

"That seems to be the question of the moment," the Lieutenant said.

"Sir—"

"Our friend and fellow is not having the best of months," the Lieutenant said. "In fact, he is not having the best of years. You remember the snafus with his disability checks."

"I thought that was taken care of."

"It was, but it was accompanied by the departure of Lee's wife and their two-year-old. Compared to what he was, Lee is vastly improved. In terms of the nuances of his emotional health, however, he has miles to go. The shit with his disability did not help; nor did spending all day home with a toddler who didn't recognize his father."

"He didn't—"

"No, but I gather it was a close thing. A generous percentage of the wedding flatware paid the price for Lee's inability to manage himself. In short order, the situation became too much for Shari, who called her father to come for her and Douglas."

"Bitch," Han said.

"Since then," the Lieutenant said, "Lee's situation has not improved. A visit to the local bar for a night of drinking alone ended with him in the drunk tank. Shari's been talking separation, possibly divorce, and while Lee tends to be a bit paranoid about the matter, there may be someone else involved, an old boyfriend. Those members of Lee's family who've visited him, called him, he has rebuffed in a fairly direct way. To top it all off, he's been subject to the same intermittent feast of blood as the rest of us."

"Oh," Davis said. "I had no—Lee doesn't talk to me—"

"Never mind. Finish your story."

"It's not a story."

"Sorry. Poor choice of words. Go on, please."

"All right," Davis said. "Okay. You have to understand, I was as surprised by all this as—well, as anyone. I couldn't believe I'd affected the thing. If it hadn't been so real, so like all the other times, I would have thought I was hallucinating, on some kind of wish-fulfillment trip. As it was, there I was as the thing picked itself up from the jungle floor. The anger—my anger—I guess it was still there, but . . . on hold.

"The second the thing was upright, someone shouted and the air was hot with bullets. Most of them shredded leaves, chipped bark, but a few of them tagged the thing's arm, its shoulder. Something was wrong: mixing in with its confusion, there was another emotion, something down the block from fear. I wasn't doing anything: I was still stunned by what I'd made happen. The thing jumped, and someone— maybe a couple of guys—tracked it, headed it off, hit it in I can't tell you how many places—it felt as if the thing had been punched a dozen times at once. It spun off course, slapped a tree, and went down, snapping branches on its way.

"Now it was pissed. Even before it picked itself up, the place it landed was being subject to intensive defoliation. A shot tore its ear. Its anger—if what I felt was fire, this was lava, thicker, slower-moving, hotter. It retreated, scuttled half a dozen trees deeper into the jungle. Whoever those guys were, they were professionals. They advanced on the spot where the thing fell and, when they saw it wasn't there anymore, they didn't rush in after it. Instead, they fell back to a defensive posture while one of them put in a call—for air support, I'm guessing.

"The thing was angry and hurt and the thirst—" Davis shook his head. He sipped his Coke. "What came next—I'm not sure I can describe it. There was this surge in my head—not the thing's head, this was my brain I'm talking about—and the thing was looking out of my eyes."

"It turned the tables on you," the Lieutenant said.

"Not exactly," Davis said. "I continued watching the soldiers maybe seventy-five feet in front of me, but I was . . . aware of the thing staring at the DVD still playing on the TV. It was as if the scene was on a screen just out of view." He shook his head. "I'm not describing it right.

"Anyway, that was when the connection broke."

Davis watched the Lieutenant evade an immediate response by taking a generous bite of his Double Quarter-Pounder with Cheese and chewing it with great care. Han swallowed and said, "Soldiers."

"What?"

"Soldiers," Han said.

Through his mouthful of burger, the Lieutenant said, "He wants to know what happened to the soldiers. Right?"

Han nodded.

"Beats the shit out of me," Davis said. "Maybe their air support showed up and bombed the fucker to hell. Maybe they evac'd out of there."

"But that isn't what you think," the Lieutenant said. "You think it got them."

"Yes, sir," Davis said. "The minute it was free of me, I think it had those poor bastards for lunch."

"It seems a bit much to hope otherwise, doesn't it?"

"Yes, sir, it does."

When the Lieutenant opted for another bite of his sandwich, Davis said, "Well?"

The Lieutenant answered by lifting his eyebrows. Han switched from McNuggets to fries.

"As I see it," Davis began. He stopped, paused, started again. "We know that the thing fucked with us in Fallujah, linked up with us. So far, this situation has only worked to our disadvantage: whenever one of us is in sufficient discomfort, the connection activates and dumps us behind the thing's eyes for somewhere in the vicinity of three to five minutes. With all due respect to Lee, this has not been beneficial to anyone's mental health.

"But what if—suppose we could duplicate what happened to me? Not just once, but over and over—even if only for ten or fifteen sec-

onds at a time—interfere with whatever it's doing, seriously fuck
with it."

"Then what?" the Lieutenant said. "We're a thorn in its side. So?"

"Sir," Davis said, "those soldiers hit it. Okay, yes, their fire wasn't
any more effective than ours was, but I'm willing to bet their percent-
ages were significantly higher. That's what me being on board in an—
enhanced way did to the thing. We wouldn't be a thorn—we'd be the
goddamned bayonet Han jammed in its ribs.

"Not that we should wait for someone else to take it down. I'm
proposing something more ambitious."

"All right."

"If we can disrupt the thing's routine—especially if we cut into its
feeding—it won't take very long for it to want to find us. Assuming
the second part of my experience—the thing has a look through our
eyes—if that happens again, we can arrange it so that we let it know
where we're going to be. We pick a location with a clearing where the
thing can land and surrounding tree cover where we can wait to ambush it. Before any of us goes to ruin the thing's day, he puts pictures,
maps, satellite photos of the spot on display, so that when the thing's
staring out of his eyes, that's what it sees. If the same images keep
showing up in front of it, it should get the point."

The Lieutenant took the rest of his meal to reply. Han offered no
comment. When the Lieutenant had settled into his chair after tilting
his tray into the garbage and stacking it on top of the can, he said, "I
don't know, Davis. There are an awful lot more ifs than I prefer to
hear in a plan. *If* we can access the thing the same way you did; *if* that
wasn't a fluke. *If* the thing does the reverse-vision stuff; *if* it understands what we're showing it. *If* we can find a way to kill it." He shook
his head.

"Granted," Davis said, "there's a lot we'd have to figure out, not
least how to put it down and keep it down. I have some ideas about
that, but nothing developed. It would be nice if we could control our
connection to the thing, too. I'm wondering if what activates the jump
is some chemical our bodies are releasing when they're under stress—
maybe adrenaline. If we had access to a supply of adrenaline, we could
experiment with doses—"

"You're really serious about this."

"What's the alternative?" Davis said. "Lee isn't the only one whose life is fucked, is he? How many more operations are you scheduled for, Han? Four? Five?"

"Four," Han said.

"And how're things in the meantime?"

Han did not answer.

"What about you, sir?" Davis said. "Oh sure, your wife and kids stuck around, but how do they act after you've had one of your fits, or spells, or whatever the fuck you call them? Do they rush right up to give Daddy a hug, or do they keep away from you, in case you might do something even worse? Weren't you coaching your son's soccer team? How's that working out for you? I bet it's a lot of fun every time the ref makes a lousy call."

"Enough, Davis."

"It isn't as if I'm in any better shape. I have to make sure I re-member to swallow a couple of tranquilizers before I go to work so I don't collapse in the middle of trying to help some customer load his fertilizer into his car. Okay, Rochelle had dumped me while I was away, but let me tell you how the dating scene is for a vet who's prone to seizures should things get a little too exciting. As for returning to college, earning my BS—maybe if I could have stopped worrying about how goddamned exposed I was walking from building to build-ing, I could've focused on some of what the professors were saying and not fucking had to withdraw.

"This isn't the magic bullet," Davis said. "It isn't going to make all the bad things go away. It's . . . it is what it fucking is."

"All right," the Lieutenant said. "I'm listening. Han—you listen-ing?"

"Listening," Han said.

X

4:11 A.M.

"So where do you think it came from?" Lee said.

"What do you mean?" Davis said. "We know where it comes from."

"No," Lee said, "I mean, before."

"Its secret origin," the Lieutenant said.

"Yeah," Lee said.

"How should I know?" Davis said.

"You're the man with the plan," Lee said. "Mr. Idea."

The Lieutenant said, "I take it you have a theory, Lee."

Lee glanced at the heap of coals that had been the fire. "Nah, not really."

"That sounds like a yes to me," the Lieutenant said.

"Yeah," Han said.

"Come on," Davis said. "What do you think?"

"Well," Lee said, then broke off, laughing. "No, no."

"Talk!" Davis said.

"You tell us your theory," the Lieutenant said, "I'll tell you mine."

"Okay, okay," Lee said, laughing. "All right. The way I see it, this vampire is, like, the advance for an invasion. It flies around in its pod, looking for suitable planets, and when it finds one it parks itself above the surface, calls its buddies, and waits for them to arrive."

"Not bad," the Lieutenant said.

"Hang on," Davis said. "What does it do for blood while it's Boldly Going Where No Vampire Has Gone Before?"

"I don't know," Lee said. "Maybe it has some stored in its coffin."

"That's an awful lot of blood," Davis said.

"Even in MRE form," the Lieutenant said.

"Maybe it has something in the coffin that makes blood for it."

"Then why would it leave to go hunting?" Davis said.

"It's in suspended animation," Lee said. "That's it. It doesn't wake up till it's arrived at a habitable planet."

"How does it know it's located one?" Davis said.

"Obviously," the Lieutenant said, "the coffin's equipped with some sophisticated tech."

"Thank you, sir," Lee said.

"Not at all," the Lieutenant said.

"I don't know," Davis said.

"What do you know?" Lee said.

"I told you—"

"Be real," Lee said. "You're telling me you haven't given five minutes to wondering how the vampire got to where it is?"

"I—"

"Yeah," Han said.

"I'm more concerned with the thing's future than I am with its past," Davis said, "but yes, I have wondered about where it came from. There's a lot of science I don't know, but I'm not sure about an alien being able to survive on human blood—about an alien needing human blood. It could be, I guess; it just seems a bit of a stretch."

"You're saying it came from here," the Lieutenant said.

"That's bullshit," Lee said.

"Why shouldn't it?" Davis said. "There's been life on Earth for something like three point seven *billion* years. Are you telling me this couldn't have developed?"

"Your logic's shaky," the Lieutenant said. "Just because something hasn't been disproved doesn't mean it's true."

"All I'm saying is, we don't know everything that's ever been alive on the planet."

"Point taken," the Lieutenant said, "but this thing lives above—well above the surface of the planet. How do you explain that?"

"Some kind of escape pod," Davis said. "I mean, you guys know about the asteroid, right? The one that's supposed to have wiped out the dinosaurs? Suppose this guy and his friends—suppose their city was directly in this asteroid's path? Maybe our thing was the only one who made it to the rockets on time? Or maybe it built this itself."

"Like Superman," Lee said, "only he's a vampire, and he doesn't leave Krypton, he just floats around it so he can snack on the other survivors."

"Sun," Han said.

"What?" Lee said.

"Yellow sun," Han said.

Davis said, "He means Superman needs a yellow sun for his powers. Krypton had a red sun, so he wouldn't have been able to do much snacking."

"Yeah, well, we have a yellow sun," Lee said, "so what's the problem?"

"Never mind."

"Or maybe you've figured out the real reason the dinosaurs went extinct," Lee said. "Vampires got them all."

"That's clever," Davis said. "You're very clever, Lee."

"What about you, sir?" Lee said.

"Me?" the Lieutenant said. "I'm afraid the scenario I've invented is much more lurid than either of yours. I incline to the view that the vampire is here as a punishment."

"For what?" Davis said.

"I haven't the faintest clue," the Lieutenant said. "What kind of crime does a monster commit? Maybe it stole someone else's victims. Maybe it killed another vampire. Whatever it did, it was placed in that coffin and sent out into space. Whether its fellows intended us as its final destination, or planned for it to drift endlessly, I can't say. But I wonder if its blood-drinking—that craving—might not be part of its punishment."

"How?" Lee said.

"Say the vampire's used to feeding on a substance like blood, only better, more nutritious, more satisfying. Part of the reason for sending it here is that all that will be available to it is this poor substitute that leaves it perpetually thirsty. Not only does it have to cross significant distances, expose itself to potential harm to feed, the best it can do will never be good enough."

"That," Lee said, "is fucked up."

"There's a reason they made me an officer," the Lieutenant said. He turned to Han. "What about you, Han? Any thoughts concerning the nature of our imminent guest?"

"Devil," Han said.

"Ah," the Lieutenant said.

"Which?" Lee asked. "A devil, or the Devil?"

Han shrugged.

XI

2005–2006

To start with, the Lieutenant called once a week, on a Saturday night. Davis could not help reflecting on what this said about the state of the man's life, his marriage, that he spent the peak hours of his weekend in a long-distance conversation with a former subordinate—as well as the commentary their calls offered on his own state of affairs, that not only was he always in his apartment for the Lieutenant's call, but that starting late Thursday, up to a day earlier if his week was especially shitty, he looked forward to it.

There was a rhythm, almost a ritual, to each call. The Lieutenant asked Davis how he'd been; he answered, "Fine, sir," and offered a précis of the last seven days at Home Depot, which tended to consist of a summary of his assistant manager's most egregious offenses. If he'd steered clear of Adams, he might list the titles of whatever movies he'd rented, along with one- or two-sentence reviews of each. Occasionally, he would narrate his latest failed date, recasting stilted frustration as comic misadventure. At the conclusion of his recitation, Davis would swat the Lieutenant's question back to him. The Lieutenant would answer, "Can't complain," and follow with a distillation of his week that focused on his dissatisfaction with his position at Stillwater, a defense contractor who had promised him a career as exciting as the one he'd left but delivered little more than lunches, dinners, and cocktail parties at which the Lieutenant was trotted out, he said, so everyone could admire his goddamned plastic leg and congratulate his employers on hiring him. At least the money was decent, and Barbara enjoyed the opportunity to dress up and go out to nicer places than he'd ever been able to afford. The Lieutenant did not speak about his children; although if asked, he would say that they were hanging in there. From time to time, he shared news of Lee, whom he called on Sunday and whose situation never seemed to improve that much, and Han, whose sister he e-mailed every Monday and who reported that her brother was making progress with his injuries; in fact, Han himself was starting to e-mail the Lieutenant.

This portion of their conversation, which Davis thought of as the Prelude, over, the real reason for the call—what Davis thought of as the SITREP—ensued. The Lieutenant, whose sentences hitherto had been loose, lazy, tightened his syntax as he quizzed Davis about the status of the Plan. In response, Davis kept his replies short, to the point. Have we settled on a location? the Lieutenant would ask. Yes sir, Davis would say, Thompson's Grove. That was the spot in the Catskills, the Lieutenant would say, south slope of Winger Mountain, about a half mile east of the principle trail to the summit. Exactly, sir, Davis would say. Research indicates the Mountain itself is among the least visited in the Catskill Preserve, and Thompson's Grove about the most obscure spot on it. The location is sufficiently removed from civilian populations not to place them in immediate jeopardy, yet still readily accessible by us. Good, good, the Lieutenant would say. I'll notify Lee and Han.

The SITREP finished, Davis and the Lieutenant would move to Coming Attractions: review their priorities for the week ahead, wish one another well, and hang up. As the months slid by and the Plan's more elaborate elements came into play—especially once Davis commenced his experiments dosing himself with adrenaline—the Lieutenant began adding the odd Wednesday night to his call schedule. After Davis had determined the proper amount for inducing a look through the Shadow's eyes—and after he'd succeeded in affecting the thing a second time, causing it to release its hold on a man Davis was reasonably sure was a Somali pirate—the Wednesday exchanges became part of their routine. Certainly, they helped Davis and the Lieutenant to coordinate their experiences interrupting the Shadow's routine with the reports coming in from Lee and Han, which arrived with increasing frequency once Lee and Han had found their adrenaline doses and were mastering the trick of interfering with the Shadow. However, in the moment immediately preceding their setting their respective phones down, Davis would be struck by the impression that the Lieutenant and he were on the verge of saying something else, something more—he couldn't say what, exactly, only that it would be significant in a way—in a different way from their usual conversation. It was how he'd felt in the days leading up to Fallujah, as if, with such momentous events roiling on the horizon, he should be speaking about important matters, meaningful things.

Twice, they came close to such an exchange. The first time followed a discussion of the armaments the Lieutenant had purchased at a recent gun show across the border in Pennsylvania. "God love the NRA," he'd said and listed the four Glock 21's's, sixteen extra clips, ten boxes of .45 ammunition, four AR-15's, sixteen extra high-capacity magazines for them, thirty boxes of 223 Remington ammo, and four USGI M7 bayonets.

"Jesus, sir," Davis had said when the Lieutenant was done. "That's a shitload of ordnance."

"I stopped at the grenade launcher," the Lieutenant said. "It seemed excessive."

"You do remember how much effect our guns had on the thing the last time . . ."

"Think of this as a supplement to the Plan. Even with one of us on board, once the thing shows up, it's going to be a threat. We know it's easier to hit when someone's messing with its controls, so let's exploit that. The more we can tag it, the more we can slow it down, improve our chances of using your secret weapon on it."

"Fair enough."

"Good. I'm glad you agree."

Davis was opening his mouth to suggest possible positions the four of them might take around the clearing when the Lieutenant said, "Davis."

"Sir?"

"Would you say you've had a good life? Scratch that—would you say you've had a satisfactory life?"

"I . . . I don't know. I guess so."

"I've been thinking about my father these past few days. It's the anniversary of his death, twenty-one years ago this Monday. He came here from Mexico City when he was sixteen, worked as a fruit picker for a couple of years, then fell into a job at a diner. He started bussing tables, talked his way into the kitchen, and became the principle cook for the night shift. That was how he met my mother: she was a waitress there. She was from Mexico, too, although the country— apparently, she thought my old man was some kind of city-slicker, not to be trusted by a virtuous girl. I guess she was right, because my older brother was born seven months after their wedding. But I came along two years after that, so I don't think that was the only reason for them tying the knot.

"He died when I was five, my father. An embolism burst in his brain. He was at work, just getting into the swing of things. The coroner said he was dead before he reached the floor. He was twenty-seven. What I wonder is, when he looked at his life, at everything he'd done, was it what he wanted? Even if it was different, was it enough?

"How many people do you suppose exit this world satisfied with what they've managed to accomplish in it, Davis? How many of our fellows slipped their mortal coils content with what their eighteen or twenty-one or twenty-seven years had meant?"

"There was the Mission," Davis said. "Ask them in public, and they'd laugh, offer some smartass remark, but talk to them one-on-one, and they'd tell you they believed in what we were doing, even if things could get pretty fucked up. I'm not sure if that would've been enough for Lugo, or Manfred—for anyone—but it would've counted for something."

"True," the Lieutenant said. "The question is, will something do?"

"I guess it has to."

Their second such conversation came two weeks before the weekend the four of them were scheduled to travel to upstate New York. They were reviewing the final draft of the Plan, which Davis thought must be something like the Plan version 22.0—although little had changed in the way of the principles since they'd finalized them a month earlier. Ten minutes before dawn, they would take up their positions in the trees around the clearing. If north was twelve o'clock, then Lee and Han would be at twelve—necessary because Han would be injecting himself at T minus one minute and would require protection—the Lieutenant would take two, and Davis three. The woods were reasonably thick: if they positioned themselves about ten feet in, then the Shadow would be unable to come in on top of them. If it wanted them, it would have to land, shift to foot, and that would be the cue for the three of them aiming their AR-15's to fire. In the meantime, Han would have snuck on board the Shadow and be preparing to jam it. As soon as he saw the opportunity, he would do his utmost to take the thing's legs out from under it, a maneuver he had been rehearsing for several weeks and become reasonably proficient at. The average time Han guesstimated he'd been able to knock the Shadow's legs out was fifteen seconds, though he had reached the vicinity of thirty once. This would be their window: the instant the thing's legs crumpled, two of them had to be up and on it, probably Davis and Lee since the Lieutenant wasn't placing any bets on his sprinter's start. One of them would draw the Shadow's notice, the other hit it with the secret weapon. If for any reason the first attacker failed, the second could engage if he saw the opportunity; otherwise, he would have to return to the woods, because Han's hold on the thing would be wearing off. Once the Lieutenant observed this, he would inject himself and they would begin round two. Round two was the same as round one except for the presumed lack of one man, just as round three counted on two of them being gone. Round four, the Lieutenant said, was him eating a bullet. By that point, there might not be anything he could do to stop the ugly son of a bitch drinking his blood, but that didn't mean he had to stay around for the event.

Davis knew they would recite the Plan again on Saturday, and then next Wednesday, and then the Saturday after that, and then the Wednesday two weeks from now. At the Quality Inn in Kingston, they would recite the Plan, and again as they drove into the Catskills, and yet again as they hiked up Winger Mountain. "Preparation," the Lieutenant had said in Iraq, "is what ensures you will fuck up only eighty percent of what you are trying to do." If the exact numbers sounded overly optimistic to Davis, he agreed with the general sentiment.

Without preamble, the Lieutenant said, "You know, Davis, when my older brother was twenty-four, he left his girlfriend for a married Russian émigrée six years his senior—whom he had met, ironically enough, through his ex, who had been tutoring Margarita, her husband, Sergei, and their four-year-old, Stasu, in English."

"No sir," Davis said, "I'm pretty sure you never told me this."

"You have to understand," the Lieutenant went on, "until this point, my brother, Alberto, had led a reasonably sedate and unimpressive life. Prior to this, the most daring thing he'd done was go out with Alexandra, the tutor, who was Jewish, which made our very Catholic mother very nervous. Yet here he was, packing his clothes and his books, emptying his meager bank account, and driving out of town with Margarita in the passenger's seat and Stasu in the back with all the stuff they couldn't squeeze in the trunk. They headed west, first to St. Louis for a couple of months, next to New Mexico for three years, and finally to Portland—actually, it's just outside Portland, but I can never remember the name of the town.

"She was a veterinarian, Margarita. With Alberto's help, she succeeded in having her credentials transferred over here. Has her own practice, these days, treats horses, cows, farm animals. Alberto helps her; he's her assistant and office manager. Sergei gave them custody of

Stasu; they have two more kids, girls, Helena and Catherine. Beautiful kids, my nieces.

"You have any brothers or sisters, Davis?"

"A younger brother, sir. He wants to be a priest."

"Really?"

"Yes, sir."

"Isn't that funny."

XII

5:53 A.M.

Lying on the ground he'd swept clear of rocks and branches, his rifle propped on a small log, the sky a red bowl overhead, Davis experienced a moment of complete and utter doubt. Not only did the course of action on which they had set out appear wildly implausible, but everything from the courtyard in Fallujah on acquired the sheen of the unreal, the delusional. An eight-foot-tall space vampire? Visions of soaring through the sky, of savaging scores of men, women, and children around the globe? Injecting himself with adrenaline, for Christ's sake? What was any of this but the world's biggest symptom, a massive phantasy his mind had conjured to escape a reality it couldn't bear? What had happened—what scene was the Shadow substituting for? Had they in fact found a trap in the courtyard, an IED that had shredded them in its fiery teeth? Was he lying in a hospital bed somewhere, his body ruined, his mind hopelessly crippled?

When the Shadow was standing in the clearing, swinging its narrow head from side to side, Davis felt something like relief. If this dark thing and its depravities were a hallucination, he could be true to it. The Shadow parted its fangs as if tasting the dawn. Davis tensed, prepared to find himself someplace else, subject to a clip from the thing's history, but the worst he felt was a sudden buzzing in his skull that reminded him of nothing so much as the old fuse box in his parents' basement. He adjusted his rifle and squeezed the trigger.

The air rang with gunfire. Davis thought his first burst caught the thing in the belly: he saw it step back, though that might have been due to either Lee or the Lieutenant, who had fired along with him. Almost too fast to follow, the Shadow jumped, a black scribble against the sky, but someone anticipated its leap and aimed ahead of it. At least one of the bullets connected; Davis saw the Shadow's right eye pucker. Stick-arms jerking, it fell at the edge of the treeline, ten feet in front of him. He shot at its head, its shoulders. Geysers of dirt marked his misses. The Shadow threw itself backwards, but collapsed where it landed.

"NOW!" the Lieutenant screamed.

Davis grabbed for his stake with his left hand as he dropped the ri-fle from his right. Almost before his fingers had closed on the weapon, he was on his feet and rushing into the clearing. To the right, Lee burst out of the trees, his stake held overhead in both hands, his mouth open in a bellow. In front of them, the Shadow was thrashing from side to side like the world's largest insect pinned through the middle. Its claws scythed grass, bushes. Davis saw that its right eye had indeed been hit, and partially collapsed. Lee was not slowing his charge. Davis sprinted to reach the Shadow at the same time.

Although the thing's legs were motionless, its claws were fast as ever. As Davis came abreast of it, jabbing at its head, its arm snapped in his direction. Pain razored up his left arm. Blood spattered the grass, the Shadow's head jerked toward him, and the momentary distraction this offered was, perhaps, what allowed Lee to tumble into a forward roll that dropped him under the Shadow's other claw and up again to drive his stake down into the base of its throat. Reaching for the cell-phone in his shirt pocket, Davis backpedaled. The thing's maw gaped as Lee held on to shove the weapon as far as it would go. The Shadow twisted and thrust its claws into Lee's collarbone and ribs. His eyes bulged and he released the stake. Davis had the cellphone in his hand. The Shadow tore its claw from Lee's chest and ripped him open. Davis pressed the three and hit SEND.

In the woods, there was a white flash and the *crump* of explosives detonating. A cloud of debris rushed between the trunks. The Shadow jolted as if a bolt of lightning had speared it.

"SHIT!" the Lieutenant was screaming. "SHIT!"

The Shadow was on its feet, Lee dangling from its left claw like a child's bedraggled plaything. Davis backpedaled. With its right claw, the Shadow reached for the stake jutting from its throat. Davis pressed the two and SEND.

He was knocked from his feet by the force of the blast, which shoved the air from his lungs and pushed sight and sound away from him. He was aware of the ground pressing against his back, a fine rain of particles pattering his skin, but his body was contracted around his chest, which could not bring in any air. Suffocating—he was suffocating. He tried to move his hands, his feet, but his extremities did not appear to be receiving his brain's instructions. Perhaps his hand-crafted bomb had accomplished what the Shadow could not.

What he could feel of the world was bleeding away.

XIII

2006

Although Lee wanted to wait for sunset, if not total darkness, a preference Davis shared, the Lieutenant insisted they shoulder their packs and start the trail up Winger Mountain while the sun would be broadcasting its light for another couple of hours. At the expressions on Lee and Davis's faces, he said, "Relax. The thing sweeps the Grove first thing in the morning. It's long gone, off feeding someplace."

The trail was not unpleasant. Had they been so inclined, its lower reaches were wide enough that they could have walked them two abreast. (They opted for single file, Lee taking point, Han next, the Lieutenant third, and Davis bringing up the rear. It spread the targets out.) The ground was matted with the leaves of the trees that flanked the trail and stationed the gradual slopes to either side. (While he had never been any good at keeping the names of such things straight, Davis had an idea the trees were a mix of maple and oak, the occasional white one a birch.) With their crowns full of leaves, the trees almost obscured the sky's blue emptiness. (All the same, Davis didn't look up any more than he could help.)

They reached the path to Thompson's Grove sooner than Davis had anticipated. A piece of wood weathered gray and nailed to a tree chest-high pointed right, to a narrower route that appeared overgrown a hundred yards or so in the distance. Lee withdrew the machete he had sheathed on his belt and struck the sign once, twice, until it flew off the tree into the forest.

"Hey," Davis said, "that's vandalism."

"Sue me," Lee said.

Once they were well into the greenery, the mosquitoes, which had ventured only the occasional scout so long as they kept to the trail, descended in clouds. "Damnit!" the Lieutenant said, slapping his cheek. "I used bugspray."

"Probably tastes like dessert topping to them, sir," Lee called. "Although, damn! at this rate, there won't be any blood left in us for Count Dracula."

Thompson's Grove was an irregular circle, forty feet across. Grass stood thigh-high. A few bushes punctuated the terrain. Davis could feel the sky hungry above them. Lee and Han walked the perimeter while he and the Lieutenant stayed near the trees. All their rifles were out. Lee and Han declared the area secure, but the four of them waited until the sun was finally down to clear the center of the Grove and build their fire.

Lee had been—Davis supposed the word was *off*, since they'd met in Kingston that morning. His eyes shone in his face, whose flesh seemed drawn around the bones. When Davis embraced him in the lobby of the Quality Inn, it had been like putting his arms around one of the support cables on a suspension bridge, something bracing an enormous weight. It might be the prospect of their upcoming encounter, although Davis suspected there was more to it. The Lieutenant's most recent report had been that Lee was continuing to struggle: Shari had won custody of Douglas, with whom Lee was permitted supervised visits every other Saturday. He'd enrolled at his local community college, but stopped attending classes after the first week. The Lieutenant wasn't sure he'd go so far as to call Lee an alcoholic, but there was no doubt the man liked his beer a good deal more than was healthy. After the wood was gathered and stacked, the fire kindled, the sandwiches Davis had prepared distributed, Lee cleared his throat and said, "I know the Lieutenant has an order he wants us to follow, but there's something I need to know about."

"All right," the Lieutenant said through a mouthful of turkey on rye, "ask away."

"It's the connection we have to the thing," Lee said. "Okay, so: we've got a direct line into its central nervous system. The right amount of adrenaline, and we can hijack it. Problem is, the link works both ways. At least, we know that, when the thing's angry, it can look out of our eyes. What if it can do more? What if it can do to us what we've done to it, take us over?"

"There's been no evidence of that," Davis said. "Don't you think, if it could do that, it would have by now?"

"Not necessarily," Lee said.

"Oh? Why not?"

"Why would it need to? We're trying to get its attention; it doesn't need to do anything to get ours."

"It's an unknown," the Lieutenant said. "It's conceivable the thing could assume control of whoever's hooked up to it and try to use him for support. I have to say, though, that even if it could possess one of us, I have a hard time imagining it doing so while the rest of us are trying to shorten its lifespan. To tell you the truth, should we succeed in killing it, I'd be more worried about it using the connection as a means of escape."

"Escape?" Davis said.

Lee said, "The Lieutenant means it leaves its body behind for one of ours."

"Could it do that?"

"I don't know," the Lieutenant said. "I only mention it as a worst-case scenario. Our ability to share its perceptions, to affect its actions, seems to suggest some degree of congruity between the thing and us. On the other hand, it is a considerable leap from there to its being able to inhabit us."

"Maybe that's how it makes more of itself," Lee said. "One dies, one's born."

"Phoenix," Han said.

"This is all pretty speculative," Davis said.

"Yes it is," the Lieutenant said. "Should the thing seize any of us, however, it will have been speculation well-spent."

"What do you propose, then, sir?" Davis said.

"Assuming any of us survives the morning," the Lieutenant said, "we will have to proceed with great caution." He held up his pistol.

XIV

6:42 A.M.

Davis opened his eyes to a hole in the sky. Round, black—for a moment, he had the impression the earth had gained a strange new satellite, or that some unimaginable catastrophe had blown an opening in the atmosphere, and then his vision adjusted and he realized that he was looking up into the barrel of the Lieutenant's Glock. The man himself half crouched beside Davis, his eyes narrowed. His lips moved, and Davis struggled to pick his words out of the white noise ringing in his ears.

"Davis," he said. "You there?"

"Yeah," Davis said. Something was burning; a charcoal reek stung his nostrils. His mouth tasted like ashes. He pushed himself up on his elbows. "Is it—"

"Whoa," the Lieutenant said, holding his free hand up like a traffic cop. "Take it easy, soldier. That was some blast."

"Did we—"

"We did."

"Yeah?"

"We blew it to Kingdom Come," the Lieutenant said. "No doubt there are pieces of it scattered here and there, but the majority of it is so much dust."

"Lee—"

"You saw what the thing did to him—although, stupid motherfucker, it serves him right, grabbing the wrong goddamned stake. Of all the stupid fucking . . ."

Davis swallowed. "Han?"

The Lieutenant shook his head.

Davis lay back. "Fuck."

"Never mind," the Lieutenant said. His pistol had not moved. "Shit happens. The question before us now is, Did it work? Are we well and truly rid of that thing, that fucking blood-drinking monster, or are we fooling ourselves? What do you say, Davis?"

"I . . ." His throat was dry. "Lee grabbed the wrong one?"

"He did."

"How is that possible?"

"I don't know," the Lieutenant said. "I do not fucking know."

"I specifically gave each of us—"

"I know; I watched you. In the excitement of the moment, Lee and Han must have mixed them up."

"Mixed . . ." Davis raised his hands to his forehead. Behind the Lieutenant, the sky was a blue chasm.

"Or could be, the confusion was deliberate."

"What?"

"Maybe they switched stakes on purpose."

"No."

"I don't think so, either, but we all know it wasn't much of a life for Han."

"That doesn't mean—"

"It doesn't."

"Jesus." Davis sat up.

The Lieutenant steadied his gun. "So?"

"I take it you're fine."

"As far as I've been able to determine, yes."

"Could the thing have had something to do with it?"

"The mix-up?"

"Made Han switch the stakes or something?"

"That presumes it knew what they were, which supposes it had been spying on us through Han's eyes for not a few hours, which assumes it comprehended us—our language, our technology—in excess of prior evidence."

"Yeah," Davis said. "Still."

"It was an accident," the Lieutenant said. "Let it go."

"What makes you so sure you're all right?"

"I've had no indications to the contrary. I appear in control of my own thoughts and actions. I'm aware of no alien presence crowding my mind. While I am thirsty, I have to desire to quench that thirst from one of your arteries."

"Would you be, though? Aware of the thing hiding in you?"

The Lieutenant shrugged. "Possibly not. You're taking a long time to answer my question; you know that."

"I don't know how I am," Davis said. "No, I can't feel the thing either, and no, I don't want to drink your blood. Is that enough?"

"Davis," the Lieutenant said, "I will do this. You need to understand that. You are as close to me as anyone, these days, and I will shoot you in the head if I deem it necessary. If I believed the thing were in me, I would turn this gun on myself without a second thought. Am I making myself clear? Let me know it's over, or let me finish it." The Lieutenant's face was flushed.

"All right," Davis said. He closed his eyes. "All right." He took a deep breath. Another.

When he opened his eyes, he said, "It's gone."

"You're positive."

"Yes, sir."

"You cannot be lying to me."

"I know. I'm not."

The end of the pistol wavered, and for a moment Davis was certain that the Lieutenant was unconvinced, that he was going to squeeze the trigger anyway. He wondered if he'd see the muzzle flash.

Then the pistol lowered and the Lieutenant said, "Good man." He holstered the gun and extended his hand. "Come on. There's a lot we have to do."

Davis caught the Lieutenant's hand and hauled himself to his feet. Behind the Lieutenant, he saw the charred place that had been the Shadow, Lee's torn and blackened form to one side of it. Further back, smoke continued to drift out of the spot in the trees where Han had lain. The Lieutenant turned and started walking toward the trees. He did not ask, and Davis did not tell him, what he had seen with his eyes closed. He wasn't sure how he could have said that the image behind his eyelids was the same as the image in front of them: the unending sky, blue, ravenous.

City of the Dog

I

I thought it was a dog. From the other side of the lot, that was what it most resembled: down on all fours; hair plastered to its pale, skeletal trunk by the rain that had us hurrying down the sidewalk; head drawn into a snout. It was injured—that much was clear. Even with the rain rinsing its leg, a jagged tear wept fresh blood that caught the headlights of the cars turning onto Central—that had caught my eye, caused me to slow.

Kaitlyn walked on a few paces before noticing that I had stopped at the edge of the lot where one of the thrift stores we'd plundered for cheap books and cassette tapes had burned to the ground the previous spring. (The space had been cleared soon thereafter, with conflicting reports of a Pizza Hut or Wendy's imminent, but as of mid-November it was still a gap in the row of tired buildings that lined this stretch of Central Ave.) Arms crossed over the oversized Army greatcoat that was some anonymous Soviet officer's contribution to her wardrobe, my girlfriend hurried back to me. "What is it?"

I pointed. "That dog looks like it's pretty hurt." I stepped onto the lot. The ground squelched under my foot.

"What are you doing?"

"I don't know. I just want to see if he's all right."

"Shouldn't you call the cops? I mean, it could be dangerous. Look at the size of it."

She was right. This was not one of your toy dogs; this was not even a standard-sized mutt. This animal was as large as a wolfhound—larger. It was big as Latka, my Uncle Karl and Aunt Belinda's German Shepherd, had appeared to me when I was seven and terrified of her, and more terrified still of her ability to smell my fear, which my cousins assured me would enrage her. For a moment, my palms were slick, and I felt a surge of lightness at the top of my chest. Then I set to walking across the lot.

Behind me, Kaitlyn made her exasperated noise. I could see her flapping her arms to either side, the way she did when she was annoyed with me.

Puddles sprawled across the lot. I leapt a particularly wide one and landed in a hole that plunged my foot into freezing water past the ankle. "Shit!" My sneaker, sock, the bottom of my jeans were soaked. There was no time to run back to the apartment to change. It appeared I'd be walking around the QE2 with one sopping sneaker for the rest of the night. I could hear Kaitlyn saying she'd *told* me to wear my boots.

The dog had not fled at my approach, not even when I dunked my foot. Watching me from the corner of its eye, it shuffled forward a couple of steps. The true size of the thing was remarkable; had it raised itself on its hind legs, it would have been as tall as I was. There was something about the way it walked, its hips high, its shoulders low, as if it were unused to this pose, that made the image of it standing oddly plausible. Big as the dog was, it didn't seem especially menacing. It was an assemblage of bones over which a deficit of skin had been stretched, so that I could distinguish each of the oddly shaped vertebrae that formed the arch of its spine. Its fur was pale, patchy; as far as I could see, its tail was gone. Its head was foreshortened, not the kind of elongated, vulpine look you expect with dogs bred big for hunting or fighting; although its ears were pointed, standing straight up, and ran a good part of the way down the side of its skull. I was less interested in its ears, however, than I was its teeth, and whether it was showing them to me. It continued to study me from one eye, but it appeared to be tolerating my presence well enough. Hands out and open in front of me, I stepped closer.

As I did, the thing's smell, diluted, no doubt, by the rain, rolled up into my nostrils. It was the thick, mineral odor of dirt, so dense I coughed and brought a hand to my mouth and nose. The taste of soil and clay coated my tongue. I coughed again, turned my head, and spat. "I hope you appreciate this," I said, wiping my mouth. I squinted at the wound on its leg.

A wide patch of the dog's thigh had been scraped clear of hair and skin, pink muscle laid bare. Broader than it was deep, it was the kind of injury that bleeds dramatically and seems to take forever to quiet. While I doubted it was life-threatening, I was sure it was painful. How the dog had come by this wound, I couldn't say. When we were kids, my younger brother had been famous for this sort of scrape, but those had been from wiping out on his bike in the school parking lot. Had this thing been dragged over a stretch of pavement, struck by a car, perhaps, and sent skidding across the road? Whatever the cause, I guessed the rain washing it was probably a good thing, cleaning away the worst debris. I bent for a closer inspection.

And was on my back, the dog's forepaws pressing my chest with irresistible force, its face inches from mine. There wasn't even time for me to be shocked by its speed. Its lips curled away from a rack of yellowed fangs, the canines easily as long as my index finger. Its breath was hot, rank, as if its tongue were rotten in its mouth. I wanted to gag, but didn't dare move. Rain spilled from the thing's cheeks, its jaw, in shining streams onto my neck, my chin. The dog was silent; no growl troubled its throat; but its eyes said that it was ready to tear my windpipe out. They were unlike any eyes I had looked into, irises so pale they might have been white surrounded by sclerae so dark they were practically black, full past the brim with—I wouldn't call it intelligence so much as a kind of undeniable *presence*.

As fast as it had put me down, the thing was gone, fled into the night and the rain. For a few seconds I stayed where I was, unsure if the dog were planning to return. Once it was clear the thing was not coming back, I pushed myself up from the sodden ground. "Terrific," I said. My wet sneaker was the least of my worries: it had been joined by jeans soaked through to my boxers; not to mention, my jacket had flipped up when I'd fallen, and the back of my shirt was drenched. "So much for the injured dog." Although doing so made me uncomfortably aware of the space between my shoulders, I turned around and plodded across the lot. This time, I didn't worry about the puddles.

That Kaitlyn was nowhere to be found, had not waited to witness my adventure with man's best friend, and most likely had proceeded to the club without me, was the sorry punchline to what had become an unfunny joke. Briefly, I entertained the idea that she might have run down the street in search of help, but a rapid walk the rest of the way to QE2 showed most shops closed, and the couple that were open empty of a short woman bundled into a long, green coat, her red hair tucked under a black beret. At the club's door, under the huge QE2 sign, I contemplated abandoning the night's plans and returning to my apartment on State Street, a trek that would insure any remaining dry spots on my person received their due saturation. I was sufficiently annoyed with Kaitlyn for the prospect of leaving her to wonder what had become of me to offer a certain appeal composed of roughly equal parts righteous indignation and self-pity. However, there had been a chance we might meet Chris here, and the possibility of her encountering him with me nowhere to be found sent me to the door to pay the cover.

Inside, a cloud of smoke hung low over the crowd, the din of whose combined conversation was sufficient to dull the Smithereens throbbing from the sound system. The club was more full than I would have expected for the main act that Wednesday, a performance poet named Marius Elliott who was accompanied by a five-piece rock band, guitars, bass, keyboards, drums, the whole thing. Marius, who favored a short black leather jacket and tight black jeans onstage, was an instructor at Columbia-Greene Community College, where he taught Freshman Writing. He was a lousy poet, and a lousy performer, too, but he was the friend of a friend I worked with, and the band was pretty good, enough so that they should have ditched him and found a frontman with more talent. This was Marius's second show at the QE2; I couldn't understand why the owner had booked him after hearing him the first time. While the club did feature poets, they tended toward the edgier end of the literary spectrum, in keeping with the place's reputation as the Capital District's leading showcase for up-and-coming post-punk bands. (That same friend from work had seen the Chili Peppers play there before they were red hot.) Marius wrote poems about eating breakfast alone, or walking his dog in the woods behind his apartment. Maybe the owner's tastes were more catholic than I knew; maybe he owed someone a favor.

In his low, melancholy voice, the Smithereens' lead told the room about the girl he dreamed of behind the wall of sleep. I couldn't see Kaitlyn. Given the dim light and number of people milling between the stage and bar, not to mention that Kaitlyn was hardly tall, there was no cause for my stomach to squeeze the way it did. Chris wasn't visible, either. Trying not to make too much of the coincidence, I pushed my way through to the bar, where I shouted for a Macallan I couldn't really afford, but that earned me a respectful nod from the bartender's shaven head.

The Scotch flaring on my tongue, I stepped away to begin a protracted circuit of the room in quest of my girlfriend. The crowd was a mix of what looked like Marius's community college students, their blue jeans and sweatshirts as good as uniforms, and the local poetry crowd, split between those affecting different shades of black and those whose brighter colors proclaimed their allegiance to some notion of sixties counter-culture. Here and there, an older man or woman in a professorial jacket struggled not to let the strain of trying to appear comfortable show; Marius's colleagues, I guessed, or professors from SUNY. The air was redolent with the odors of wet denim, cotton, and hair, of burning tobacco and pot, of beer, of sweat. I exchanged enough nods with enough faces I half recognized for me not to feel too alone, and traded a few sentences with a girl whose pretty face and hip-length blond hair I remembered but whose name eluded me. The Smithereens finished singing about blood and roses and were replaced by the Screaming Trees, their gravelly voiced lead uttering the praises of sweet oblivion.

At the end of forty-five minutes that took me to every spot in the club except the Ladies Room, and that left the Macallan a phantom in my glass, I was no closer to locating Kaitlyn. (Or Chris, for that matter, although I was ignoring this.) Once more at the bar, I set the empty glass on its surface and ordered another—a double, this round. A generous swallow of it was almost sufficient to quiet the panic uncoiling in my chest.

I was about to embark on another, rapid circuit of the crowd before the show began when I caught someone staring at me. Out of the corner of my eye, I thought the tall, pale figure was Chris, just arrived. I was so relieved to find him here that I couldn't help myself from smiling as I turned to greet him.

The man I saw was not Chris. He was at a guess two decades older, more, the far side of forty. Everything about his face was long, from the stretch of forehead between his shaggy black hair and shaggy black eyebrows, to the nose that ran from his watery eyes to his narrow mouth, to the lines that grooved the skin from his cheekbones to his jaw, from the edges of his nostrils to the edges of his thin lips. His skin was the color of watery milk, which the black leather jacket and black T-shirt he wore only emphasized. I want to say that, even for a poet, the guy looked unhealthy, but this was no poet. There are people—the mentally ill, the visionary—who emit cues, some subtle, some less so, that they are not traveling the same road as the rest of us. Standing five feet away from me doing nothing that I could see, this man radiated that sensation; it poured off him like a fever. The moment I had recognized he was not Chris, I had been preparing the usual excuse, "Sorry, thought you were someone else," or words close enough, but the apology died in my mouth, incinerated by the man's presence. The Screaming Trees were saying they'd heard it on the wing that I was going to die. I could not look away from the man's eyes. Their irises were so pale they might have been white, surrounded by sclerae so dark they were practically black. My heart smacked against my chest; my legs trembled madly, all the fear I should have felt lying pinned on my back in that empty lot finally caught up to me. With that thing's teeth at my neck, I hadn't fully grasped how perilous my position had been; now, I was acutely aware of my danger.

Two things happened almost simultaneously. The lights went down for the show, and Chris stood between the man and me, muttering, "Hello," unwrapping his scarf, and asking where Kaitlyn was. The pale man eclipsed, I looked away. When I returned my gaze to where he'd been standing, he was gone. Ignoring Chris's questions, I searched the people standing closest to us. The man was nowhere to be found. What remained of my drink was still in my hand. I finished it and headed to the bar as Marius Elliott and his band took the stage to a smattering of applause and a couple of screams. Chris followed close behind. I was almost grateful enough for him appearing to buy him a drink; instead, I had another double.

II

In the late summer of 1991, I moved to Albany. While I swore to my parents I was leaving Poughkeepsie to accept a position as senior bookseller at The Book Nook, an independent bookstore located near SUNY Albany's uptown campus—which was true; I had been offered the job—the actual reason I packed all my worldly belongings into my red Hyundai Excel and drove an hour and a half up the Hudson was Kaitlyn Bertolozzi. I believe my parents knew this.

Yet even then, the August morning I turned left up the on-ramp for the Taconic north and sped toward a freedom I had been increasingly desperate for the past four years of commuting to college—even as I pressed on the radio and heard the opening bass line of Golden Earring's "Twilight Zone," which I turned up until the steering wheel was thumping with it—even as the early-morning cloud cover split to views of blue sky—the sense of relief that weighted my foot on the gas pedal was alloyed with another emotion, with ambivalence.

At this point, Kaitlyn had been living in Albany for a little more than six months. After completing undergrad a semester early, she had moved north to begin a Master's in Teaching English to Speakers of Other Languages at the University Center. We had continued to speak to one another several times a week, and I had visited her as often as my school and work schedules permitted, which wasn't very much— once a month, if that. It was on the first of those visits, a couple of weeks after Kaitlyn had moved to the tiny apartment her parents had found her, that she introduced me to Christopher Garofalo.

He was not much taller than I was, but the thick, dark brown hair that rose up from his head gave the impression that he had a good few inches on me. His skin was sallow, except for an oblong scar that reached from over his left eyebrow into his hairline. When Kaitlyn and I met him at Bruegger's Bagels, his neck was swaddled in a scarf that he kept on the length of our lunch, despite the café's stifling heat. He shook my hand when he arrived and when he left, and each time his brown eyes sought out mine. In between, his conversation was sporadic and earnest. Kaitlyn and he had attended the same orientation session at the University for students starting mid-year. Chris was studying to be a geology teacher; after trying to find a living as part of a jazz band, he said, he had decided it was time for a career with more stability.

Once he had departed, I commented on his scarf, which I'd taken as the lingering affectation of a musician; whereupon my girlfriend told me that Chris wore the scarf to cover the scar from a tracheotomy. While my face flushed, she went on to say that he had been in a severe motorcycle accident several years ago, in his early twenties. He hadn't been wearing a helmet and should have been killed; as it was, he'd spent a week in a coma and had to have a steel plate set in his skull, which was the origin of the scar on his forehead. As a consequence of the trauma, he'd experienced intermittent seizures, which had required months of trial-and-error with different medications and combinations of medications to bring under some semblance of control. He was a sweet guy, Kaitlyn said, who was (understandably) self-conscious about the reminders of his accident. I muttered a platitude and changed the subject.

I wasn't especially concerned about my girlfriend having become friendly with another guy so soon; as long as I had known her, Kaitlyn had numbered more men than women among her friends, just as my circle of friends consisted largely of women. She had always had a weakness for what I called her strays, those people whose quirks of character tended to isolate them from the rest of the pack. Driving home that night, I was if anything reassured at a familiar pattern reasserting itself.

Three weeks to the day later, I listened on the phone as Kaitlyn, her voice hitching, told me she'd slept with Chris. While I'd made the same sort of confession to previous girlfriends, I'd never been on the receiving end of it before. I moved a long way away from myself, down a tunnel at one end of which was the thick yellow receiver pressed to my ear, full of Kaitlyn crying that she was sorry, while the other end plunged into blackness. Dark spots crowded my vision. I hung up on her sobs, then spent five minutes furiously pacing the bedroom that had shrunk to the size of a cage. Everything was wrong; a sinkhole had opened under me, dumping my carefully arranged future into muddy ruin. Before I knew what I was doing, the phone was in my hand and I was dialing Kaitlyn.

The next month was an ordeal of phone calls, two, three, four times a week. After the initial flourish of apologies and recriminations, we veered wildly between forced cheerfulness and poorly concealed resentment. Once Kaitlyn started to say that Chris was very upset about the entire situation, and I told her I wasn't interested in hearing about that fucking freak. Another time she complained that she was lonely, to which I replied that I was sure she could find company. Rather than slamming the receiver down, she cajoled me, told me not to be that way, she missed me and couldn't wait until she could see me. However, when I at last drove to see her one Thursday afternoon, Kaitlyn was reserved, almost formal. I wanted nothing more than to go straight to bed, to find in her naked body some measure of reassurance that we would recover from this. Kaitlyn demurred, repeatedly, until I left early, in an obvious huff.

Strangely, Kaitlyn's infidelity and its jagged aftermath only increased my desire to move to Albany. Those moments when regret and anger weren't gnawing at me, I told myself that, had I been there with her, this never would have happened. I could just about shift the blame for her sleeping with Chris onto us having been apart after so long so close together. There were times I could, not exactly pardon what Chris had done, but understand it. Underwriting my effort to reconcile myself to events was my desire to escape my home. As far as I could tell, my father and mother were no worse than any of my friends' parents—and, in one or two cases, they seemed significantly better—but I was past tired of having to be home by twelve and to call if I were going to be later, of having to play chauffeur to my mother and three younger siblings, of having to watch what I said lest my father and I begin an argument from which I inevitably backed off, because he had suffered a heart attack ten years earlier and I was deeply anxious not to be the cause of a second, fatal one. Although I was their oldest child, my parents had a much harder time easing their hold on me than they did with my siblings. My younger brother was already away at R.P.I., enrolled in their Bio-Med program, while my sisters enjoyed privileges I still dreamed of. When I had started at SUNY Huguenot, my father had assured me that, if I commuted to college the first year, I could move onto campus my sophomore year; during a subsequent disagreement, he insisted that the deal had been for me to remain home for two years, and then he and my mother would see about me living in a dorm. After that, I didn't raise the issue again, nor did he or my mother.

Albany/Kaitlyn was my opportunity to extricate myself from the life that seemed intent on maintaining my residence under the roof that had sheltered me for the last two decades. Every awkward conversation with Kaitlyn shook my hopes of leaving the bed whose end my feet hung over, while the arguments, aftershocks of that original revelation, that struck us shuddered my dream of Albany to rubble. That I went from the black mood that fell on me after Kaitlyn and I had concluded our latest brittle exchange, when I was convinced I would live and die in Poughkeepsie, to driving to my new apartment and job was a testament to almost brute determination. In the end, I had to leave my parents', which meant I had to do whatever was necessary to slice through the apron strings mummifying me, and if that included working through things with Kaitlyn—if it included making peace with Chris, accepting him as her friend—then that was what I would do.

Not only did I make peace with Chris, he was to be my roommate. What would have been impossible, inconceivable, a month before became first plausible and then my plan when I failed to find a place I could afford on my own, and the guy with whom Chris had previously been rooming abruptly moved out. Enough time had passed, I told myself. According to Kaitlyn, Chris was a night owl; he and I would hardly see each other. (I didn't dwell on how she knew this.) I decided I would stay there only until I could find another, better place, and then fuck you, Chris.

As it turned out, though, after more than a year, I was still in that apartment on State Street, in what I referred to as student-hell housing. Ours was the lower half of a two-story house wedged in among other two-story houses, the majority of them family residences that had been re-purposed for college students. My room was at the rear of the place, off the kitchen, and was entered through a kind of folding door more like what you'd find on a closet. Chris inhabited the front room, next to the combination living room–dining room; between us, there was an empty room opposite the bathroom. For reasons unclear to me, that room had remained unoccupied, though I didn't object to the extra distance from Chris. Kaitlyn had been right: he was up late into the night, sequestered in his room, which he did not invite me into and whose door—a single solid piece of wood some previous tenant had painted dark green—he kept closed. Probably the longest conversation I had with him had come when he'd showed me the basement, whose door, outside mine, was locked by a trio of deadbolts. The stairs down to it bowed perceptibly under my weight, the railing planted a splinter in the base of my thumb. A pair of bare bulbs threw yellow light against the cement walls, the dirt floor. The air was full of dust; I sneezed. Chris showed me the location of the fuse box, how to reset the fuses, the furnace and how to reset it. After I'd been through the procedures for both a couple of times, I pointed to the corner opposite us and said, "What's down there?"

Chris looked at the concrete circle, maybe two and a half feet in diameter, set into the basement floor. A heavy metal bar flaked with rust lay across it; through holes in either end of the bar, thick, heavily rusted chains ran to rings set into smaller pieces of concrete. He shrugged. "I'm not sure. The landlord told me it used to be a coal cellar, but that doesn't make any sense. Some kind of access to the sewers, maybe."

"In a private residence?"

"Yeah, you're right. I don't know."

When he wasn't in his room, Chris was at SUNY, either in class or at the library. Despite this, I saw him a good deal more than I would have wished, especially when Kaitlyn stayed over, which she did on weekends and occasional weeknights. I would be in the kitchen, preparing dinner, while Kaitlyn sat on the green and yellow couch in the living room, reading for one of her classes, and I would hear Chris's door creak open. By the time I carried Kaitlyn's plate through to the folding table that served as the dining room table, Chris would be leaning against the wall across from her, his arms crossed, talking with her about school. Although they stiffened perceptibly as I set Kaitlyn's plate down, they continued their conversation, until I asked Chris if he wanted to join us, there was plenty left, an offer he inevitably refused, politely, claiming he needed to return to his work. During the ensuing meal, Kaitlyn would maintain a constant stream of chatter to which I, preoccupied with what she and Chris had *actually* been discussing, would respond in monosyllables. If the phone rang and Chris happened to answer it, he would linger for a minute or two, talking in a low, pleasant murmur I couldn't decipher before calling to me that it was Kaitlyn. I knew they met for coffee at school every now and again, which seemed to translate into once a week.

Of course the situation was intolerable. Forgiving Chris—believing that what had occurred between him and Kaitlyn was in the past—accepting that they were still friends, but no more than that—all of it had been much easier when I was eighty miles removed from it, when it was a means to the end of me leaving home. As a fact of my daily life, it was a wound that would not heal, whose scab tore free whenever the two of them were in any kind of proximity, whenever Kaitlyn mentioned Chris, or (less frequently) vice versa. Had I known him before this, had we shared some measure of friendship, there might have been another basis on which I could have dealt with Chris. As it was, my principal picture of him was as the guy who had slept with my girlfriend. No matter that we might share the occasional joke, or that he might join Kaitlyn and me when we went to listen to music at local clubs and bars, and try to point out what the musicians were doing well, or even that he might cover my rent one month I needed to have work done on my car, I could not see past that image, and it tormented me. I was more than half convinced Kaitlyn wanted to return to him, and her protests that, if she had, she would have already, did little to persuade me otherwise.

One night, after I'd been in Albany six months, in the wake of a fierce argument that ended with Kaitlyn telling me she was tired of doing penance for a mistake she'd made a year ago, then slamming her apartment door in my face, and me speeding home down Western Avenue's wide expanse, I stood outside Chris's room, ready for a confrontation twelve months overdue. I hadn't bothered to remove my coat, and it seemed to weigh heavier, hotter. My chest was heaving, my hands balled into fists so tight my arms shook. The green door was at the far end of a dark tunnel. I could hear the frat boys who lived above us happily shouting back and forth to one another about a professor who was a real dick. I willed Chris to turn the doorknob, to open his door so that he would find me there and I could ask him what it had been like, if she'd pulled her shirt over her head, pushed down her jeans, or if he'd unhooked her bra, slid her panties to her ankles? Had she lain back on the bed, drawing him onto her, and had she uttered that deep groan when he'd slid all the way up into her? Had she told him to fuck her harder, and when she'd ridden him to that opening of her mouth and closing of her eyes, had she slid her hand between them to cup and squeeze his balls, bringing him to a sudden, thunder-

ous climax? A year's worth of scenes I'd kept from my mind's eye ca-
vorted in front of it: Kaitlyn recumbent on her bed, her bare body
painted crimson by the red light she'd installed in the bedside lamp;
Kaitlyn, lying on top of a hotel room table, wearing only the rings on
her fingers, her hands pulling her knees up and out; Kaitlyn with her
head hanging down, her arms out in front of her, hands pressed
against the shower wall, her legs straight and spread, soapy water sluic-
ing off her back, her ass. In all these visions and more, it was not I
who was pushing in and out of her, it was Chris—he had spliced himself into my memories, turned them into so much cheap porn. Worse,
the look I envisioned on Kaitlyn's face said, shouted that she was enjoying these attentions far more than any I'd ever paid her.

While I desperately wanted to cross the remaining distance to
Chris's door and smash my fists against it, kick it in, some inner mechanism would not permit me to take that first step. My jaw ached, I was
clenching my teeth so hard, but I could not convert that energy into
forward motion. If Chris appeared, then what would happen, would
happen. In the meantime, the best I could do was maintain my post.

Perhaps Kaitlyn had called to warn him, but Chris did not leave his
room that night. I stood trembling at his door for the better part of an
hour, after which I decided to wait for him on the living room couch. I
had not yet removed my coat, and I was sweltering. The couch was
soft. My lids began to droop. I yawned, then yawned again. The room
was growing harder to keep in focus. There was a noise—I thought I
heard something. The sound of feet, of many feet, seemed to be outside the front window—no, they were underneath me, in the basement. The next thing I knew, I was waking to early morning light. I
could have resumed my position outside Chris's door; instead, I retreated to my room. That was the closest I came to facing him.

Had a friend of mine related even part of the same story to me—
told me that his girlfriend had cheated on him, or that he couldn't stop
thinking about her betrayal, or that he was sharing an apartment with
the other guy—my advice would have been simple: leave. You're in a
no-win situation; get out of it. I was in possession of sufficient self-
knowledge to be aware of this, but was unable to attach that recognition to decisive action. In an obscure way I could perceive but not articulate, this failing was connected to my larger experience of Albany,

which had been, to say the least, disappointing. Two weeks into it, I had started having doubts about my job at the Book Nook; after a month, those doubts had solidified. Within two months of starting there, I was actively, though discreetly, searching for another position. However, with the economy mired in recession, jobs were scarce on the ground. None of the local bookstores were hiring full-time. I sank three hundred dollars into the services of a job placement company whose representative interviewed me by phone for an hour and produced a one-page résumé whose bland and scanty euphemisms failed to impress me, or any of the positions to which I sent it. I wasted an hour late one Tuesday sitting a test for an insurance position that the man who interviewed me told me I was unlikely to get because I didn't know anyone in the area, and so didn't have a list of people I could start selling to. (He was right: they didn't call me.) I lost an entire Saturday shadowing a traveling salesman as he drove to every beauty salon in and around Albany, hawking an assortment of cheap and gaudy plastic wares to middle-aged women whose faces had shown their suspicion the moment he hauled open their doors. That position I could have had if I'd wanted it, but the prospect was so depressing I returned to The Book Nook the following day. When I heard that their pay was surprisingly good and their benefits better, I seriously considered taking the exam that would allow me to apply for a job as a toll collector on the Thruway, going so far as to find out the dates on which and the locations where the test was being offered. But, unable to imagine telling my parents that I had left the job that at least appeared to have something to do with my undergraduate degree in English for one that required no degree at all—unwilling to face what such a change would reveal about my new life away from home—I never went. I continued to work at The Book Nook, using my employee discount to accumulate novels and short story collections I didn't read, and for which I soon ran out of space, so that I had to stack them on my floor, until my room became a kind of improvised labyrinth.

Nor did the wider world appear to be in any better shape. In addition to its reports on the faltering local and national economies, WAMC, the local public radio station, brought news of the disintegration of Yugoslavia into ethnic enclaves whose sole purpose appeared to be the annihilation of one another through the most savage means possible. The fall of the Berlin Wall, the breakup of the Soviet Union and end of the Cold War, which had promised brighter days, an end to the nuclear shadow under which I'd grown up, instead had admitted a host of hatreds and grievances kept at bay but not forgotten, and eager to have their bloody day. On EQX, the alternative station out of Vermont, U2 sang about the end of the world, and the melodramatic over-statement of those words seemed to summarize my time in Albany.

By that Wednesday night in November, when I fumbled open the door to the apartment and stumbled in, the Scotches I'd consumed at the QE2 not done with me yet, I had been living in a state of ill-defined dread for longer than I could say, months, at least. I had attempted discussing it with Kaitlyn over dinner the week before we went to see Marius, but the best I could manage was to say that it felt as if I were waiting for the other shoe to drop. "What other shoe?" Kaitlyn had said around a mouthful of dumpling. "The other shoe to what?"

I'd considered answering, "To you and Chris," but we'd been having a nice time, and I had been reluctant to spoil it. To be honest, though there was no doubt she and Chris were part of the equation, they weren't all of it: there were other integers involved whose values I could not identify. To reply "To everything" had seemed too much, so I'd said, "I don't know," and the conversation had moved on.

Yet when I saw that the apartment was dark, and a check of my room showed my bed empty, and a call to Kaitlyn's brought me her answering machine, I knew, with a certainty fueled by alcohol and that deep anxiety, that the other shoe had finally clunked on the floor.

III

For the next couple of days, I continued to dial Kaitlyn's number, leaving a series of messages that veered from blasé to reproachful to angry to conciliatory before cycling back to blasé. I swore that I was not going to her apartment, a vow I kept for almost three days, when I used my key to unlock her door Saturday night. I half expected the chain to be fastened, Kaitlyn to be inside (and not alone), but the door swung open on an empty room. The lights were off. "Kaitlyn?" I called. "Love?"

There was no answer. The apartment was little more than a studio with ambition; it took all of a minute for me to duck my head into the bedroom, the bathroom, to determine that Kaitlyn wasn't there. The answering machine's tally read thirty-one messages; I pressed Play and listened to my voice ascend and descend the emotional register. Mixed in among my messages were brief how-are-you's from Kaitlyn's mother, her younger brother, and Chris. When I recognized his voice, I tensed, but he had called to say he had missed her at the show the other night, as well as for coffee the next day, and he hoped everything was okay. After the last message—me, half an hour prior, trying for casual as I said that I was planning to stop by on my way home from work—I ran through the recordings a second time, searching for something, some clue in her mother's, her younger brother's words to where she had spent the last seventy-two hours. So far as I could hear, there was none. An hour's wait brought neither Kaitlyn nor any additional phone calls, so I left, locking the door behind me.

Two days later, I asked Chris to call Kaitlyn's parents. He was just in from a late-night library session; I had waited for him on the couch. He didn't notice me until he was about to open the door to his room. At my request, he stopped pulling off his gloves and said, "What?"

"I need you to call Kaitlyn's parents for me."

"Why?"

"I want to find out if she's there."

"What do you mean?"

"I haven't seen her since the other night at QE2."

"Maybe she's at her place." He stuffed his gloves in his jacket's pockets, unzipped it.

"I checked there."

"Maybe she didn't want to talk to you."

"No—I have a key. She isn't there. I don't think she has been since Wednesday."

"Of course you do," Chris muttered. "So where is she—at her parents, which is why you want me to call them. Why can't you do it?"

"I don't want to worry them."

Chris stared at me; I could practically hear him thinking, *Or look like the overly possessive boyfriend.* "It's late," he said. "I'm sure—"

"Please," I said. "Please. Look, I know—we—would you just do this for me, please?"

"Fine," he said, although the expression on his face said it was anything but. He hung his jacket on the doorknob and went to the phone.

Kaitlyn's father was still awake. Chris apologized for calling so late but said he was a friend of hers from high school who'd walked through his parents' front door this very minute—his flight had been delayed at O'Hare. He was only in town through tomorrow, and he was hoping to catch up with Kaitlyn, even see her. A pause. Oh, that was right, the last time they had talked, she had told him she was planning to go to Albany. Wow, he guessed it had been a while since they'd spoken. Could her father give him her address, or maybe her phone number? That would be great. Another pause. Chris thanked him, apologized again for the lateness of his call, and wished Kaitlyn's father a good night. "She isn't there," he said once he'd hung up.

"So I gathered."

"The number he gave me is the one for her apartment."

"Okay." I stood from the couch.

"I'm sure everything's all right. Maybe she went to visit a friend."

"Yeah," I said. "A friend."

"Hey—"

"Don't," I said. I started toward my room. "All because I stopped to help a fucking dog . . ."

"What?"

I stopped. "On the way to the club. There was this stray in that lot over on Central—you know, where the thrift store used to be. It looked like it was in rough shape, so I went to have a look at it—"

"What kind of dog?"

"I don't know, a big one. Huge, skinny, like a wolfhound or something."

Chris's brow lowered. "What color was it?"

"White, I guess. It was missing a lot of fur—no tail, either."

"Its face—did you see its eyes?"

"From about six inches away. Turned out, the thing wasn't that hurt, after all. Pinned me to the ground, stuck its face right in mine. Could've ripped my throat out."

"Its eyes . . ."

"This sounds strange, but its eyes were reversed: the whites were black, and the pupils were, well, they weren't white, exactly, but they were pale—"

"What happened with the dog? Were there any more?"

I shook my head. "It ran off. I don't know where to."

"There wasn't a man with it, was there?"

"Just the dog. What do you mean, a man? Do you know who owns that thing?"

"Nobody owns—never mind. You'd know this guy if you saw him: tall, black hair. He's white, I mean, really, like-a-ghost white. His face is lined, creased."

"Who is he?"

"Don't worry about it. If he wasn't—"

"He was at the club, afterwards. Right before you arrived."

"Are you sure?"

"I was about as far away from him as I am from you."

Now Chris's face was white. "What happened?"

"Nothing. One minute, he was standing there giving me the hee-bie-jeebies, the next—"

"Shit!" Chris grabbed his jacket from the doorknob. "Get your coat."

"Why?"

"Do you have a flashlight?"

"A flashlight?"

"Never mind, I have a spare." His jacket and gloves on, Chris shouted, "Move!"

"What are you—"

He crossed the room to me in three quick strides. "I know where Kaitlyn is."

"You do?"

He nodded. "I know where she is. I also know that she's in a very great deal of danger. I need you to get your coat, and I need you to get your car keys."

"Kaitlyn's in danger?"

"Yes."

"What—how do you know this?"

"I'll tell you in the car."

IV

For all that I had been residing in the city for over a year, my knowledge of Albany's geography was at best vague. Aside from a few landmarks such as the QE2 and the Empire State Plaza downtown, my mental map of the place showed a few blocks north and south of my apartment, and spots along the principle east-west avenues, Western, Washington, and Central. I had a better sense of the layout of Dobb's Ferry, Kaitlyn's hometown, to which I'd chauffeured her at least one weekend a month the past twelve. Chris told me to head downtown, to Henry Johnson. Once I'd scraped holes in the frost on the windshield and windows and set the heater blowing high, I steered us onto Washington and followed it to the junction with Western, but that was as far as I could go before I had to say, "Now what?"

Chris looked up from the canvas bag he was holding open on his lap while he riffled its contents. Whatever was in the bag clinked and rattled; the strong odor of grease filled the car. "Really?" he said. "You don't know how to get to Henry Johnson?"

"I'm not good with street names. I'm more of a visual person."

"Up ahead on the left—look familiar?"

"Actually, no."

"Well, that's where we're going."

"Well okay."

I turned off Western, passed over what I realized was a short bridge across a deep gully. "What's our destination?"

"A place called the Kennel. Heard of it?"

I hadn't.

"It's . . . you'll see when we get there."

We drove past shops whose shutters were down for the night, short brick buildings whose best days belonged to another century. Brownstones rode a steep side street. A man wearing a long winter coat and garbage bags taped to his feet pushed a shopping cart with an old television set canted in it along the sidewalk.

"How far is it?"

"I don't know the exact distance. It should take us about fifteen minutes."

"Enough time for you to tell me how you know Kaitlyn's at the Kennel."

"Not really. Not if you want the full story."

"I'll settle for the Cliff's Notes. Did you take her there?"

"No," he said, as if the suggestion were wildly inappropriate.

"Then how did she find out about it?"

"She didn't—she was brought there."

"Brought? As in, kidnapped?"

Chris nodded.

"How do you know this?"

"Because of the Keeper—the man you saw at the club."

"The scary guy with the weird eyes."

"You noticed his eyes."

"Same as the dog's."

"Yes."

"I don't . . . How do you know this guy, the what? the Keeper?"

"Ahead, there," Chris said, pointing, "keep to the left."

I did. The cluster of tall buildings that rose over Albany's downtown, the city's effort to imitate its larger sibling at the other end of the Hudson, were behind us, replaced by more modest structures, warehouses guarded by sagging fences, narrow two- and three-story brick buildings, a chrome-infused diner struggling to pretend the fifties were alive and well. As I drove through these precincts, I had the sense I was seeing the city as it really was, the secret face I had intuited after a year under its gaze. I said, "How do you know him?"

"He . . ." Chris grimaced. "I found out about him."

"What? Is he some kind of, I don't know, a criminal?"

"Not exactly. He's—he's someone who doesn't like to be known."

"Someone . . . All right, how did you find out about him?"

"Left. My accident—did I ever tell you about my accident? I didn't, did I?"

"Kaitlyn filled me in."

"She doesn't know the whole story. Nobody does. I didn't take a corner too fast: one of the *Ghûl* ran in front of me."

"The what? 'Hule'?"

"*Ghûl.* What you saw in that lot the other night."

"Is that the breed?"

Chris laughed. "Yes, that's the breed, all right. It was up towards Saratoga, on Route 9. I was heading home from band practice. It was late, and it was a New Moon, so it was especially dark. The next thing I knew, there was this animal in the road. My first thought was, *It's a wolf.* Then I thought, *That's ridiculous: there are no wolves around here. It must be a coyote.* But I had already seen this wasn't a coyote, either. Whatever it was, it looked awful, so thin it must be starving. I leaned to the left, to veer around it, and it moved in front of me. I tried to tilt the bike the other way, overcompensated, and put it down, hard."

In the distance, the enormous statue of Nipper, the RCA mascot, that crowned one of the buildings closer to the river cocked its head attentively.

"The accident itself, I don't remember. That's a blank. What I do remember is coming to in all kinds of pain and feeling something tugging on my sleeve. My sleeve—I'm sure you heard I wasn't wearing a helmet. I couldn't really see out of my left eye, but with my right, I saw the animal I'd tried to avoid with my right arm in its mouth. My legs were tangled up with the bike, which was a good thing, because this creature was trying to drag me off the road. If it hadn't been for the added weight, it would have succeeded. This wasn't any Lassie rescue, either: the look on its face—it was ravenous. It was going to kill and eat me, and not necessarily in that order.

"Every time the animal yanked my arm, bones ground together throughout my body. White lights burst in front of my eyes. I cried out, although my jaw was broken, which made it more of a moan. I tried to use my left arm to hit the creature, but I'd dislocated that shoulder. Its eyes—those same reversed eyes you looked into—regarded me the way you or I would a slice of prime rib. I've never been in as much pain as I was lying there; I've also never been as frightened as I was with that animal's teeth beginning to tear through the sleeve of my leather jacket and into the skin beneath. The worst of it was, the creature made absolutely no sound, no growl, nothing."

We passed beneath the Thruway, momentarily surrounded by the whine of tires on pavement.

"Talk about dumb luck, or Divine Providence: just as my legs are starting to ease out from the bike, an eighteen-wheeler rounds the corner. How the driver didn't roll right over me and the animal gripping my arm, I chalk up to his caffeine-enhanced reflexes. I thought that, if I were going to die, at least it wouldn't be as something's dinner. As it was, the truck's front bumper slowed to a stop right over my head. Had it been any other vehicle, my would-be consumer might have stood its ground. The truck, though, was too much for it, and it disappeared.

"When the doctors and cops—not to mention my mother—finally got around to asking me to relate the accident in as much detail as I could, none of them could credit a creature that wasn't a coyote that wasn't a wolf, which caused my crash and then tried to drag me away. I'd suffered severe head trauma, been comatose for five days—that must be where the story had come from. The wounds on my forearm were another result of the accident. Apparently, no one bothered to ask the truck driver what he'd seen.

"For a long time after that night, I wasn't in such great shape. Between the seizures and the different medications for the seizures, I spent weeks at a time in a kind of fog. Some of the meds made me want to sleep; some ruined my concentration; one made everything incredibly funny. But no matter what state I was in, no matter how strange or distant my surroundings seemed, I knew that that animal— that what it had done, what it had tried to do to me—was real."

To the left, the beige box of Albany Memorial Hospital slid by. I said, "Okay, I get that there's a connection between the thing that caused your accident and the one I ran into the other night. And I'm guessing this Keeper guy is involved, too. Maybe you could hurry up and get to the point?"

"I'm trying. Did you know that State Street used to be the site of one of the largest cemeteries in Albany?"

"No."

"Till almost the middle of the nineteenth century, when the bodies were relocated and the workers found the first tunnels."

"Tunnels?"

"Left again up here. Not too much farther."

To either side of us, trees jostled the shoulder. They opened briefly on the left to a lawn running up to shabby red brick apartments, then closed ranks again.

"So why are these tunnels so important?"

"That concrete slab in the basement, the one that's locked down? What if I told you that opens on a tunnel?"

"I'd still want to know what this has to do with where Kaitlyn is."

"Because she . . . when we . . . all right." He took a deep breath. "Even before my doctor found the right combination of anti-seizure meds, I was doing research. I probably know the name of every librarian between Albany and Saratoga. I've talked to anyone who knows anything about local history. I've spent weeks in the archives of the State Museum, the Albany Institute, and three private collections. I've filled four boxes worth of notebooks."

"And?"

"I've recognized connections no one's noticed before. There's an entire—you could call it a secret history, or shadow history, of this entire region, stretching back—you wouldn't believe me if I told you how far. I learned things . . ."

"What things?"

"It doesn't matter. What does is that, somehow, they found out about me."

"The Keeper and his friends."

"At first, I was sure they were coming for me. I put my affairs in order, had a long conversation with my mom that scared her half to death. Then, when they didn't arrive, I started to think that I might be safe, even that I might have been mistaken about them knowing about me."

"But you weren't. Not only were they aware of you, they were watching you, following you. They saw you with Kaitlyn. They figured . . ."

"Yeah."

My heart was pounding in my ears. A torrent of obscenities and reproaches threatened to pour out of my mouth. I choked them down, said, "Shouldn't we go to the cops? If you've gathered as much material on this Keeper as you say you have—"

"It's not like that. The cops wouldn't—if they did believe me, it wouldn't help Kaitlyn."

"I can't see why not. If this guy's holding Kaitlyn, a bunch of cops outside his front door should make him reconsider."

We had arrived at a T-junction. "Left or right?"

"Straight."

"Straight?" I squinted across the road in front of us, to a pair of brick columns that flanked the entrance to a narrow road. A plaque on the column to the right read ALBANY RURAL CEMETERY. I turned to Chris. "What the fuck?"

He withdrew his right hand from the bag on his lap, his fingers curled around the grip of a large automatic handgun whose muzzle he swung toward me. "Once this truck passes, we're going over there." He nodded at the brick columns.

The anger that had been foaming in my chest fell away to a trickle. I turned my gaze to the broad road in front of me, watched a moving van labor up it. The gun weighted the corner of my vision. I wanted to speak, to demand of Chris what the fuck he thought he was doing, but my tongue was dead in my mouth. Besides, I knew what he was doing. Once the van was out of sight, Chris waved the gun and I drove across into the cemetery.

Even in the dark, where I could only see what little my headlights brought to view, I was aware that the place was big, much bigger than any graveyard I'd been in back home. On both sides of the road, monuments raised themselves like the ruins of some lost civilization obsessed with its end. A quartet of Doric columns supporting a single beam gave way to a copper-green angel with arms and wings outstretched, which yielded to a gray Roman temple in miniature, which was replaced by a marble woman clutching a marble cross. Between the larger memorials, an assortment of headstones stood as if marking the routes of old streets. A few puddles spread among them. Tall trees, their branches bare with the season, loomed beside the road.

As we made our way further into the cemetery, Chris resumed talking. But the gun drew his words into the black circle of its mouth, allowing only random snippets to escape. At some point, he said, "Old Francis was the one who finally put it all together for me. He'd found an Annex to the Kennel during a day-job digging graves. A pair of them came for him that night, and if there hadn't been a couple of decent-sized rocks to hand, they would have had him. But he'd played the Minor Leagues years before, and his right arm remembered how to throw. Even so, he hopped a freight going west and stayed out there for a long time." At another point he said, "You have no idea. When the first hunters crossed the land bridge to America, the *Ghûl* trailed them." At still another moment he said, "Something they do to the meat." That Chris had not dismounted his hobby-horse was clear.

All I could think about was what was going to happen to me once he told me to stop the car. He wouldn't shoot me in it—that would leave too much evidence. Better to walk me someplace else, dispose of me, and ditch the car over in Troy. He didn't want to leave me out in the open, though. Maybe an open grave, shovel in enough dirt to conceal the body? Too dicey: a strong rain could expose his handiwork. One of the mausoleums we passed? Much more likely, especially if you knew the family no longer used it. When he said, "All right: we're here," in front of an elaborate marble porch set into a low hill, I felt an odd surge of satisfaction.

I had the idea this might be my time to act, but Chris had me turn off the engine, leaving on the headlights, and hand him the keys. He exited the car and circled around the front to my side, the automatic pointed at me throughout. Standing far enough away that I couldn't slam my door against him, he urged me out of the car. I wanted—at least, I contemplated refusing him, declaring that if he were going to shoot me, he would have to do it here, I wasn't going to make this any easier for him. I could hear myself defiant, but his shouted, "Now!" brought me out in front of him without a word.

"Over there," he said, pointing the gun at the mausoleum. "It should be open."

That sentence, everything it implied, revived my voice. "Is this where you took Kaitlyn?" I said as I walked toward the door.

"What?"

"I've been trying to figure out how you did it. Did you meet her at the club and whisk her out here? What—did you have a cab waiting? A rental? I can't quite work out the timing of it. Maybe you brought her somewhere else first? Some place to hold her until you could take her here?"

"You haven't heard a single thing I've been saying, have you?"

"Were you afraid I'd discover it was you? Or was this always your plan, kill the girl you couldn't have and the guy she wouldn't leave?"

"You asshole," Chris said. "I'm doing this for Kaitlyn."

That Kaitlyn might be unharmed, might be in league with Chris, was a possibility I had excluded the second it had occurred to me as I drove into the cemetery, and that I had kept from consideration as we'd wound deeper into its grounds. There would be no reason for her to resort to such an extreme measure; if she wanted to be with Chris, she could be with him. She already had. All the same, his statement was a punch in the gut; my words quavered as I said, "Sure—you tell yourself that."

"Shut up."

"Or what—you'll shoot me?"

"Just open the door."

The mausoleum's entrance was a tall stone rectangle set back between a quartet of pillars that supported a foreshortened portico. One the front of the portico, the name UPTON was bordered by dogs capering on their hind legs. Behind me, there was a click, and a wide circle of light centered on the door. There was no latch that I could see. I put out my right hand and pushed the cold stone. The door swung in easily, spilling the beam of Chris's flashlight inside. The heavy odor of soil packed with clay rode the yellow light out to us. I glanced over my shoulder, but Chris had been reduced to a blinding glare. His voice said, "Go in."

Inside, the mausoleum was considerably smaller than the grandiosity of its exterior would have led you to expect. A pair of stone vaults occupied most of the floor, only a narrow aisle between them. The flashlight roamed over the vaults; according to the lids, Beloved Husband and Father Howard rested to my left, while Devoted Wife and Mother Caitlin took her repose on the right. (The woman's name registered immediately.) Under each name, a relief showed a nude woman reclining on her left side, curled around by a brood of young dogs, a pair of which nursed at her breasts. Beyond the stone cases, the mausoleum was a wall of black. The air seemed slightly warmer than it was outside.

With a clatter, the light tilted up to the ceiling. Chris said, "I put the flashlight on the end of the vault to your left. I want you to take two steps backwards—slowly—reach out, and pick it up." I nodded. "And if you try to blind me with the light, I'll shoot."

When I was holding the bulky flashlight, I directed its beam at the back of the mausoleum. A rounded doorway opened in the center of a wall on which the head of an enormous dog had been painted in colors dulled by dust and time. Eyes whose white pupils and black sclerae were the size of serving plates glared down at us. The dog's mouth was wide, the door positioned at the top of its throat. A click, and a second light joined mine. "In there," Chris said.

"I was wondering where you were going to do it."

"Shut up."

I stepped through the doorway into a wide, dark space. I swept the light around, saw packed dirt above, below, to either side, darkness ahead. There was easily enough room for me and Chris and a few more besides, though the gray sides appeared to close in in the distance. The air was warmer still, the earth smell cloying. Chris's light traced the contours of the walls, their arch into the ceiling. It appeared we were at one end of a sizable tunnel. "All right," Chris said.

"Where's Kaitlyn?"

"Shut up."

"Aren't you going to let me see her?"

"Shut up."

"Oh, I get it. This is supposed to be the icing on the cake, isn't it? You bring me to the place you killed my girlfriend, but you shoot me without allowing me to see her."

I turned into the glare of Chris's flashlight, which jerked up to my eyes. I didn't care. Tears streaming down my cheeks, I said, "Jesus Christ: what kind of a sick fuck are you?"

Chris stepped forward, his arm extended, and pressed the automatic against my chest. My eyes dazzled, I couldn't see so much as feel the solid steel pushing against my sternum. The odor of soil and clay was interrupted by that of grease and metal, of the eight inches of gun ready to bridge me out of this life. Between clenched teeth, Chris said, "You really are a stupid shit."

"Fuck you."

The pressure on my chest eased, and I thought, *This is it. He's going to shoot me in the head.* My mouth filled with the taste of, not so much regret as sour pique that this was the manner in which my life had reached its conclusion, beneath the surface of the city of my disappointment, murdered by the broken psychotic who'd spoiled my relationship and fractured what should have been the start of my new life. *It's only a moment,* I thought, *then you'll be with Kaitlyn.* But I didn't believe that. I would be dead, part of the blackness, and that was the most I had to look forward to.

"Here you are."

Not for an instant did I mistake this voice for Chris's. It wasn't only that it was behind me—the instrument itself was unlike any I'd heard, rich and cold, as if the lower depths of the tunnel in whose mouth we stood had been given speech. Ignoring Chris, I spun, my light revealing him, the white man with the shaggy black hair and seamed face who'd held me with his strange eyes in QE2, the man Chris had dubbed the Keeper. He'd exchanged his black leather jacket for a black trenchcoat in whose pockets his hands rested. Chris's flashlight found that long face, deepened the shadows in its creases. The man did not blink.

Chris said, "You know why I've come."

"Yes?"

"I'm here to offer a trade."

"What do you offer?"

"Him."

"What?" I looked over my shoulder. Chris still held the automatic pointed at me.

"Shut up."

"You're going to trade me for Kaitlyn?"

"Shut up."

"So whatever this guy and his friends—you think—this is your solution?"

"Shut up."

"Jesus! You're even worse than I thought."

"This'll be the best thing you've ever done," Chris said. "I've lived with you long enough to know. It's the best thing you could ever do for her."

I opened my mouth to answer, but the Keeper coughed, and our attentions returned to him. He said, "For?"

"The woman you took six days past."

"A woman?"

"Damn you!" Chris shouted. "You know who I'm talking about, so can we cut the coy routine? In the names of Circë, Cybele, and Atys, in the name of Diana, Mother of Hounds, I offer this man's life for that of the woman you took and hold."

"Let us ask the Hounds," the man said. From the darkness behind him, a trio of the same creatures I'd crossed a vacant lot to help on a rainy night emerged into the glow of our flashlights and slunk toward me. Big as that thing had been, these were bigger, the first and largest as tall at the shoulder as my chin, its companions level with my heart. Each was as skeletally thin as that first one, each patched with the same pale fur. At the sight of them, my mind tilted, all my mental furniture sliding to one side. Everything Chris had said in the past hour tumbled together. Inclining their heads in my direction, the Hounds walked lazily around me, silent except for the scrape of their claws on the tunnel floor. Their white skin slid against their bones, and I thought that I had never seen creatures so frail and so deadly. The leader kept its considerable jaws closed, but its companions left theirs open, one exposing its fangs in a kind of sneer, the other licking its lips with a liver-colored tongue. Their combined reek, dirt underscored with decay, as if they'd been rolling in the remains of the cemetery's more recent residents, threatened to gag me. I concentrated on breathing through my mouth and remaining calm, on not being afraid, or not that afraid, on not noticing the stains on the things' teeth, on not wondering whether they'd go for my throat or my arms first, on not permitting the panic that was desperate to send me screaming from this place as fast as my legs would carry me from crossing the boundary from emotion to action. The trio completed their circuit of me and returned to the Keeper, assuming positions around him.

"The Hounds are unimpressed."

I could have fainted with relief.

"What do you mean?" Chris said. "In what way is this not a fair trade?"

"The Hounds have their reasons."

"This is bullshit!"

"Do you offer anything else?"

"What I've offered is enough."

The man shrugged, turning away.

"Wait!" Chris said. "There are boxes—in my room, there are four boxes full of the information I've collected about you. Return the woman, and they're yours, all of them."

The man hesitated, as if weighing Chris's proposal. Then, "No," he said, and began to walk back down the tunnel, the things accompanying him.

"Wait!" Chris said. "Stop!"

The man ignored him. Already, he and his companions were at the edge of the flashlight's reach.

"Me!" Chris shouted. "Goddamn you, I offer myself! Is that acceptable to the Hounds?"

The four figures halted. The Keeper said, "Freely made?"

"Yes," Chris said. "A life for a life."

"A life for a life." The man's face, as he revolved toward us, was ghastly with pleasure. "Acceptable."

"What a surprise."

"Leave the light—and the weapon."

Chris's flashlight clicked off. The clatter of it hitting the floor was followed by the thud of the automatic. His shoes scuffed the floor and he was stepping past me. He stopped and looked at me, his eyes wild with what lay ahead. He said, "Aren't you going to stop me? Aren't you going to insist you be the one they take for Kaitlyn?"

"No."

He almost smiled. "You never deserved her."

I had no answer for that.

When he was even with them, the Hounds surrounded him. From the tensity of their postures, the curl of their lips from their teeth, I half expected them to savage him right there. The straightening of Chris's posture said he was anticipating something similar. The Keeper bent his head toward Chris. "It's what you really wanted," he said, nodding at the blackness. One of the smaller things nudged him forward with its head, and the four of them faded down into the dark. For a time, the shuffle of Chris's feet, the scrape of the things' claws, told their progress, then those sounds faded to silence.

His gaze directed after Chris, the Keeper said, "Leave. What's left of him won't be too happy to learn the life he's bartered for was yours."

I didn't argue, didn't ask *What about Kaitlyn?* I obeyed the man's command and fled that place without another word. In my headlong rush through the mausoleum proper, I ran my left hip into the corner of Howard Upton's vault so hard I gasped and stumbled against his wife's, but although the pain threatened to steal my breath, the image of what might be stepping into the mausoleum after me propelled me forward, out the still-open entrance.

My car was where we'd left it, its headlights undimmed. I fumbled for my wallet and the spare key I kept in the pocket behind my license. As I lowered myself into the driver's seat, my hip screaming in protest, I kept checking the door to the mausoleum, which remained ajar and in which I continued to think I saw shadowy forms about to emerge. The car started immediately, and in my haste to escape the way I'd come I backed into a tall tombstone, which cracked at the base and toppled backwards. I didn't care; I shifted into first and sped out of the cemetery, stealing glances in the rearview mirror all the way to my apartment.

V

Despite the bruise on my hip, the increased pain and difficulty moving that sent me to the emergency room the next day with a story about colliding with a doorstep, to learn after an X-ray that I had chipped the bone, I half expected Chris to walk in the front door as usual the following night. It wasn't that I doubted what had happened—I was in too much discomfort—it was more that I couldn't believe its finality. Not until another week had passed, and the landlord appeared wanting to know where Chris and his rent were (to which I replied that I hadn't seen him for days), did the fact of his . . . I didn't have the word for it: his sacrifice? his abduction? his departure? Call it what you would, only when I was standing at the open door to his room, which was Spartan as a monk's cell, watching the landlord riffle through Chris's desk, did the permanence of his fate settle on me.

The week after that brought a concerned call from Kaitlyn's parents, asking if I'd seen their daughter (to which I replied that I hadn't had any contact with her for weeks). This began a chain of events whose next link was her father driving to Albany to ask a number of people, including me, the last time they'd seen Kaitlyn. Within a couple of days, the police were involved. They interviewed me twice, the first time in a reasonably friendly way, when I was no more than the con-

cerned boyfriend, the second time in a more confrontational and extended session, occasioned by the detective's putting together my dis-
closure that Kaitlyn and Chris had been briefly involved with the fact
that both of those people had gone missing in reasonably close proximity to each other. There wasn't any substantial evidence against me,
but I had no doubt Detective Calasso was certain I knew more than I
was saying. Kaitlyn's mother shared his suspicion, and during a long
phone call before Christmas she attempted to convince me to tell her
what I knew. I insisted that, sorry as I was to have to say it, I didn't
know what had happened to Kaitlyn. I supposed this was literally true.

Not that I hadn't dwelt on the matter each and every day since I'd
awakened fully dressed on my futon, my hip pounding, a trial of muddy footprints showing my path from the front door to the refrigerator,
the top of which served as a nominal liquor cabinet, to my room,
where the bottle of Johnny Walker Black that had plunged me into unconsciousness leaned against my pillows. That Kaitlyn should be at the
far end of that dark tunnel, surrounded by those things, the Hounds,
the *Ghûl*, was unbelievable, impossible. Yet a second stop at her
apartment failed to reveal any change from my previous visit. I sat on
the edge of her bed, the lights out, my head fuzzy from the painkiller
I'd taken for my hip, and struggled to invent alternative scenarios to
the one Chris had narrated. Kaitlyn had met another guy—she was in
the midst of an extended fling, a romantic adventure that had carried
her out of Albany to Cancun, or Bermuda. She'd suffered a breakdown
and had herself committed. She'd undergone a spiritual awakening and
joined a convent. But try as I did to embrace them, each invention
sounded more unreal than the last, no more than another opiate-
facilitated fantasy.

I weighed going after her, myself, returning to the mausoleum
suitably armed and equipped and braving the tunnel to retrieve her. I
even went so far as to browse a gun store on Route 9, only to discover
that the weapons I judged necessary if I were to stand any kind of
chance—a shotgun, a minimum of three pistols, boxes of ammunition
for each—cost vastly more than my bookstore salary would allow. Trying to buy guns on the street was not a realistic option: I had no idea
where to go, how to open any such transaction. On a couple of occasions I found myself driving north through the city, retracing the path

Chris and I had followed to the cemetery. When I realized what I was doing, I turned onto the nearest side street and headed back toward my apartment. Some nights I unlocked the deadbolts on the basement door and descended the stairs to stand staring down at the cement circle sunk in the floor. The chains securing the bar across it looked rusted right through; with a little effort, I ought to be able to break them, heave the cover up, and . . . I made sure to lock the basement door behind me.

On the morning of February 2, 1993, as the sun was casting its light across the apartment's front window, I stuffed every piece of clothing I owned, all my toiletries, whatever food was in the cupboards over the sink, into a green duffel bag that I struggled out the front door, down the front steps, and through my Hyundai's hatchback. The apartment's door was wide open, the place full of my possessions, but I started the engine, threw the car into gear, and fled Albany. I didn't return home to my parents; I didn't head north or west, either. I wanted the shore, the sea, someplace where the earth was not so deep, so I sped east, along I-90, toward what I thought would be the safety of Cape Cod. I didn't stop for bathroom breaks; I didn't stop until Albany was a ghost in my rearview mirror and the Atlantic a grey sheet spread in front of me.

All the way to Provincetown, while I pressed the gas pedal as near the floor as I could and maintain control of the car, I kept the radio at full volume, tuned to whatever hard rock station broadcast the clearest. Highway to Hell bled into Paranoid became Lock Up the Wolves. Although the doors, the dash thrummed with a bass line that changed only slightly from song to song, and my ears protested another shrieking singer, guitar, none of it was enough to drown out the sound that had drawn me from my bed the previous night and rushed me to the basement door, hands shaking as I unsnapped the deadbolts and turned the doorknob. Some kind of loud noise, a crash, and then Kaitlyn—I had heard her voice echoing below me, calling my name in that low, sing-song tone she used when she wanted to have sex. I had thought I was in a dream, but her words had led me up out of sleep, until the realization that I was awake and still hearing her had sent me from my room, kicking over several stacks of books on the way. The door open, I switched on the light and saw, at the foot of the stairs, shielding her eyes against the sudden brightness, Kaitlyn, returned to me at last.

At the sight of her there—the emotion that transfixed me was some variety of *I knew it.* I knew she hadn't really vanished, knew she wasn't lost under the earth. She was wearing the oversized army great-coat, which was streaked with mud. Her feet were bare and filthy. Her skin was more than pale, as if her time underground had bleached it. Her hair was tangled, clotted with dirt, her mouth flaked with something brown.

I was on the verge of running down the stairs to her when she lowered her hand from her eyes and I saw the white centers, the black sclerae. A wave of dizziness threatened to topple me headlong down the stairs. Kaitlyn smiled at my hesitation, reached over, and pulled open her coat. Underneath, she was naked, her white, white flesh smeared with dirt and clay. She called to me again. "Here I aaa-mmm," she half sang. "Didn't you miss me? Don't you wanna come play with me?"

A bolt of longing, of desire sudden and intense, pierced me. God help me, I did want her. My Eurydice: I wanted to bury myself in her, and who cared if her eyes were changed, if her flesh bore evidence of activities I did not want to dwell on? I might have—might have crossed the dozen pieces of wood that separated the life to which I clung from that which had forced itself on me, surrender myself to sweet oblivion, had a large, bony shape not stumbled into view behind Kaitlyn. Of the *Ghûl* I had seen previously, none had given so profound an impression of being unaccustomed to walking on all fours. It held its head up too high, as if unused to the position. Its weird eyes were rheumy, its gums raw where its lips drew back from them. It curled around Kaitlyn from behind, dragging its muzzle across her hip before nuzzling between her thighs. She sighed deeply. Eyes lidded, lips parted, she extended her hand toward me while the other pressed the *Ghûl*'s head forward.

The thing pulled away long enough to give me a sidelong glance, and it was that gesture that sent me scrambling backwards, grabbing for the door and slamming it shut, throwing myself against it as I snapped the deadbolts. It kept me there while I listened to the stairs creak under the combined weights of Kaitlyn and her companion, who settled themselves on the opposite side of the door so that she could murmur tender obscenities to me while the *Ghûl*'s claws worried the wood. They left with the dawn. Once I was sure they were gone, I ran into my room and began frantically packing.

If the far end of Cape Cod was not as secure a redoubt as I might have thought, hoped, if Martha's Vineyard and Nantucket proved no more isolated, they were preferable to Albany, whose single, outsized skyscraper was an enormous cenotaph marking a necropolis of whose true depths its inhabitants remained unaware. I fled them, over the miles of road and ocean; I am still fleeing them, down the long passage that joins *now* to *then*. That flight has defined my life, is its individual failure and the larger failures of the age in sum. I see the two of them still, down there in the dark, where their wanderings take them along sewers, up into the basements of houses full of sleeping families, under roads and rivers, to familiar cemeteries. Kaitlyn has grown more lean, her hair long. She has traded in her old greatcoat for a newer trench-coat. The *Ghûl* lopes along beside her, nimble on its feet. It too has become more lean. The scar over its left eye remains.

The Shallows

"Il faut cultiver notre jardin."—Voltaire, *Candide*

"I could call you Gus," Ransom said.

The crab's legs, blue and cream, clattered against one another. It did not hoist itself from its place in the sink, though, which meant it was listening to him. Maybe. Staring out the dining room window, his daily mug of instant coffee steaming on the table in front of him, he said, "That was supposed to be my son's name. Augustus. It was his great-grandfather's name, his mother's father's father. The old man was dying while Heather was pregnant. We . . . I, really, was struck by the symmetry: one life ending, another beginning. It seemed a duty, our duty, to make sure the name wasn't lost, to carry it forward into a new generation. I didn't know old Gus, not really; as far as I can remember, I met him exactly once, at a party at Heather's parents' a couple of years before we were married."

The great curtain of pale light that rippled thirty yards from his house stilled. Although he had long since given up trying to work out the pattern of its changes, Ransom glanced at his watch. 2:02 P.M., he was reasonably sure. The vast rectangle that occupied the space where his neighbor's green-sided house had stood, as well as everything to either side of it, dimmed, then filled with the rich blue of the tropical ocean, the paler blue of the tropical sky. Waves chased one another toward Ransom, their long swells broken by the backs of fish, sharks, whales, all rushing in the same direction as the waves, away from a spot where the surface of the ocean heaved in a way that reminded Ransom of a pot of water approaching the boil.

(Tilting his head back, Matt had said, *How far up do you think it goes? I don't know,* Ransom had answered. Twenty feet in front of them, the sheet of light that had descended an hour before, draping their view of

173

the Pattersons' house and everything beyond it, belled, as if swept by a breeze. *This is connected to what's been happening at the poles, isn't it?* Matt had squinted to see through the dull glare. *I don't know*, Ransom had said, *maybe. Do you think the Pattersons are okay?* Matt had asked. *I hope so*, Ransom had said. He'd doubted it.)

He looked at the clumps of creamer speckling the surface of the coffee, miniature icebergs. "Gus couldn't have been that old. He'd married young, and Heather's father, Rudy, had married young, and Heather was twenty-four or -five . . . call him sixty-five, sixty-six, tops. To look at him, though, you would have placed him a good ten, fifteen years closer to the grave. Old . . . granted, I was younger, then, and from a distance of four decades, mid-sixty seemed a lot older than it does twenty years on. But even factoring in the callowness of youth, Gus was not in good shape. I doubt he'd ever been what you'd consider tall, but he was stooped, as if his head were being drawn down into his chest. Thin, frail: although the day was hot, he wore a long-sleeved checked shirt buttoned to the throat and a pair of navy chinos. His head . . . his hair was thinning, but what there was of it was long, and it floated around his head like the crest of some ancient bird. His nose supported a pair of horn-rimmed glasses whose lenses were white with scratches; I couldn't understand how he could see through them, or maybe that was the point. Whether he was eating from the paper plate Heather's uncle brought him or just sitting there, old Gus's lips kept moving, his tongue edging out and retreating."

The coffee was cool enough to drink. Over the rim of the mug, he watched the entire ocean churning with such force that whatever of its inhabitants had not reached safety were flung against one another. Mixed among their flailing forms were parts of creatures Ransom could not identify, a forest of black needles, a mass of rubbery pink tubes, the crested dome of what might have been a head the size of a bus.

He lowered the mug. "By the time I parked my car, Gus was seated near the garage. Heather took me by the hand and led me over to him. Those white lenses raised in my direction as she crouched beside his chair and introduced me as her boyfriend. Gus extended his right hand, which I took in mine. Hard . . . his palm, the undersides of his fingers, were rough with calluses, the yield of a lifetime as a mechanic. I tried to hold his hand gently . . . politely, I guess, but although his arm trembled, there was plenty of strength left in his fingers, which closed on mine like a trap springing shut. He said something, *Pleased to meet you, you've got a special girl, here,* words to that effect. I wasn't paying attention; I was busy with the vice tightening around my fingers, with my bones grinding against one another. Once he'd delivered his pleasantries, Gus held onto my hand a moment longer, then the lenses dropped, the fingers relaxed, and my hand was my own again. Heather kissed him on the cheek, and we went to have a look at the food. My fingers ached on and off for the rest of the day."

At the center of the heaving ocean, something forced its way up through the waves. The peak of an undersea mountain, rising to the sun: that was still Ransom's first impression. Niagaras poured off black rock. His mind struggled to catch up with what stood revealed, to find suitable comparisons for it, even as more of it pushed the water aside. Some kind of structure—structures: domes, columns, walls—a city, an Atlantis finding the sun, again. No—the shapes were off: the domes bulged, the columns bent, the walls curved, in ways that conformed to no architectural style—that made no sense. A natural formation, then, a quirk of geology. No—already, the hypothesis was untenable: there was too much evidence of intentionality in the shapes draped with seaweed, heaped with fish brought suffocating into the air. As the rest of the island left the ocean, filling the view before Ransom to the point it threatened to burst out of the curtain, the appearance of an enormous monolith in the foreground, its surface incised with pictographs, settled the matter. This huge jumble of forms, some of which appeared to contradict one another, to intersect in ways the eye could not untangle, to occupy almost the same space at the same time, was deliberate.

Ransom slid his chair back from the table and stood. The crab's legs dinged on the stainless steel sink. Picking up his mug, he turned away from the window. "That was the extent of my interactions with Gus. To be honest, what I knew of him, what Heather had told me, I didn't much care for. He was what I guess you'd call a functioning alcoholic, although the way he functioned . . . he was a whiskey-drinker, Jack Daniel's, Jim Bean, Maker's Mark, that end of the shelf. I can't claim a lot of experience, but from what I've seen, sour mash shortcuts to your mean, your nasty side. That was the case with Gus, at least. It wasn't so much that he used his hands—he did, and I gather the hearing in Rudy's left ear was the worse for it—no, the whiskey unlocked the cage that held all of Gus's resentment, his bitterness, his jealousy. Apparently, when he was younger, Rudy's little brother, Jan, had liked helping their mother in the kitchen. He'd been something of a baker, Jan; Rudy claimed he made the best chocolate cake you ever tasted, frosted it with buttercream. His mother used to let him out of working with his father in the garage or around the yard so he could assist her with the meals. None of the other kids—there were six of them—was too thrilled at there being one less of them to dilute their father's attention, especially when they saw Gus's lips tighten as he realized Jan had stayed inside again.

"Anyway, this one night, Gus wandered into the house after spending the better part of the evening in the garage. He passed most of the hours after he returned from work fixing his friends' and acquaintances' cars, Hank Williams on the transistor radio, Jack Daniel's in one of the kids' juice glasses. In he comes, wiping the grease off his hands with a dishtowel, and what should greet his eyes when he peers into the refrigerator in search of a little supper but the golden top of the cherry pie Jan made for the church bake sale the next day? Gus loves cherry pie. Without a second thought, he lifts the pie from the top shelf of the fridge and deposits it on the kitchen table. He digs his clasp-knife out of his pants pocket, opens it, and cuts himself a generous slice. He doesn't bother with a fork; instead, he shoves his fingers under the crust and lifts the piece straight to his mouth. It's so tasty, he helps himself to a second, larger serving before he's finished the first. In his eagerness, he slices through the pie tin to the table. He doesn't care; he leaves the knife stuck where it is and uses his other hand to free the piece.

"That's how Jan finds him when he walks into the kitchen for a glass of milk, a wedge of cherry pie in one hand, red syrup and yellow crumbs smeared on his other hand, his mouth and chin. By this age—Jan's around twelve, thirteen—the boy has long since learned that the safest way, the only way, to meet the outrages that accompany his father's drinking is calmly, impassively. Give him the excuse to garnish his injury with insult, and he'll take it.

"And yet, this is exactly what Jan does. He can't help himself, maybe. He lets his response to the sight of Gus standing with his mouth stuffed with half-chewed pie flash across his face. It's all the provocation his father requires. *What?* he says, crumbs spraying from his mouth.

"*Nothing,* Jan says, but he's too late. Gus drops the slice he's hold- ing to the floor, scoops the rest of the pie from the tin with his free hand, and slaps that to the floor as well. He raises one foot and stamps on the mess he's made, spreading it across the linoleum. Jan knows enough to remain where he is. Gus brings his shoe down on the ruin of Jan's efforts twice more, then wipes his hands on his pants, frees his knife from the table, and folds it closed. As he returns it to his pocket, he tells Jan that if he wants to be a little faggot and wear an apron in the kitchen, that's his concern, but he'd best keep his little faggot mouth shut when there's a man around, particularly when that man's his father. Does Jan understand him?

"*Yes, pa,* Jan says.

"*Then take your little faggot ass off to bed,* Gus says.

"What happened next," Ransom said, "wasn't a surprise; in fact, it was depressingly predictable." He walked into the kitchen, deposited his mug on the counter. "That was the end of Jan's time in the kitchen. He wasn't the first one outside to help his father, but he wasn't the last, either, and he worked hard. The morning of his eighteenth birth- day, he enlisted in the Marines; within a couple of months he was on patrol in Vietnam. He was cited for bravery on several occasions; I think he may have been awarded a medal. One afternoon, when his squad stopped for a rest, he was shot through the head by a sniper. He'd removed his helmet . . . to tell the truth, I'm not sure why he had his helmet off. He survived, but it goes without saying, he was never the same. His problems . . . he had trouble moving, coordinating his arms and legs. His speech was slurred; he couldn't remember the names of familiar objects, activities; he forgot something the second after you said it to him. There was no way he could live on his own. His mother wanted Jan to move back home, but Gus refused, said there was no way he was going to be saddled with an idiot who hadn't known enough to keep his damn helmet on. Which didn't stop him from accepting the drinks he was bought when Jan visited and Gus pa- raded him at the V.F.W."

Behind him, a pair of doors would be opening on the front of a squat stone box near the island's peak. The structure, whose rough ex-

terior suggested a child's drawing of a Greek temple, must be the size
of a cathedral, yet it was dwarfed by what squeezed out of its open
doors. While Ransom continued to have trouble with the sheer size of
the thing, which seemed as if it must break a textbook's worth of physical laws, he was more bothered by its speed. There should have been
no way, he was certain, for something of that mass to move that quickly. Given the thing's appearance, the tumult of coils wreathing its head,
the scales shimmering on its arms, its legs, the wings that unfolded into
great translucent fans whose edges were not quite in focus, its speed
was hardly the most obvious detail on which to focus, but for Ransom,
the dearth of time between the first hint of the thing's shadow on the
doors and its heaving off the ground on a hurricane-blast of its wings
confirmed the extent to which the world had changed.

(*What was that?* Matt had screamed, his eyes wide. *Was that real? Is
that happening?* Ransom had been unable to speak, his tongue dead in
his mouth.)

Like so many cranes raising and lowering, the cluster of smaller
limbs that rose from the center of the crab's back was opening and
closing. Ransom said, "I know: if the guy was such a shit, why pass his
name on to my son?" He shrugged. "When I was younger—at that
point in my life, the idea of the past . . . of a family's past, of continuity
between the present and that past, was very important to me. By the
time Heather was pregnant, the worst of Gus's offenses was years
gone by. If you wanted, I suppose you could say that he was paying for
his previous excesses. He hadn't taken notice of his diabetes for decades. If the toes on his right foot hadn't turned black, then started to
smell, I doubt he ever would have returned to the doctor. Although . .
. what that visit brought him was the emergency amputation of his
toes, followed by the removal of his foot a couple of weeks later. The
surgeon wanted to take his leg, said the only way to beat the gangrene
that was eating Gus was to leap ahead of it. Gus refused, declared he
could see where he was headed, and he wasn't going to be jointed like
a chicken on the way. There was no arguing with him. His regular doctor prescribed some heavy-duty antibiotics for him, but I'm not sure
he had the script filled.

"When he returned home, everyone said it was to die—which it
was, of course, but I think we all expected him to be gone in a matter

of days. He hung on, though, for one week, and the next, and the one after that. Heather and her mother visited him. I was at work. She said the house smelled like spoiled meat; it was so bad, she couldn't stay in for more than a couple of minutes, barely long enough to stand beside Gus's bed and kiss his cheek. His lips moved, but she couldn't understand him. She spent the rest of the visit outside, in her mother's truck, listening to the radio."

Ransom glanced out the window. The huge sheet of light rippled like an aurora, the image of the island and its cargo gone. He said, "Gus died the week after Heather's visit. To tell the truth, I half expected him to last until the baby arrived. Heather went to the wake and the funeral; I had to work. As it turned out, we settled on Matthew— Matt, instead."

His break was over. Ransom exited the kitchen, turned down the hallway to the front door. On the walls to either side of him, photos of himself and his family, his son, smiled at photographers' prompts years forgotten. He peered out one of the narrow windows that flanked the door. The rocking chair he'd left on the front porch in a quixotic gesture stood motionless. Across the street, the charred mound that sat inside the burned-out remains of his neighbor's house appeared quiet. Ransom reached for the six-foot pole that leaned against the corner opposite him. Careful to check that the butcher knife duct-taped to the top was secure, he gripped the improvised spear near the tape and unlocked the door. Leveling the weapon, he stepped back as the door swung in.

In two months of maintaining the ritual every time he opened any of the doors into the house, Ransom had yet to be met by anything. The precaution was one on which his son had insisted; the day of his departure north, Matt had pledged Ransom to maintaining it. With no intention of doing so, Ransom had agreed, only to find himself repeating the familiar motions the next time he was about to venture out to the garden. Now here he was, jabbing the end of the spear through the doorway to draw movement, waiting a count of ten, then advancing one slow step at a time, careful not to miss anything dangling from the underside of the porch roof. Once he was satisfied that the porch was clear, that nothing was lurking in the bush to its right, he called over his shoulder, "I'm on my way to check the garden, if you'd like to join me."

A chorus of ringing announced the crab's extricating itself from the sink. Legs clicking on the wood floors like so many tap shoes, it hurried along the hall and out beside him. Keeping the spear straight ahead, he reached back for one of the canvas bags piled inside the door, then pulled the door shut. The crab raced down the stairs and to the right, around the strip of lawn in front of the house. Watching its long legs spindle made the coffee churn at the back of his throat. He followed it off the porch.

Although he told himself that he had no desire to stare at the remnants of his neighbor Adam's house—it was a distraction; it was ghoulish; it was not good for his mental health—Ransom was unable to keep his eyes from it. All that was left of the structure were fire-blackened fragments of the walls that had stood at the house's northeast and southwest corners. Had Ransom not spent ten years living across the road from the white, two-story colonial whose lawn had been chronically overgrown—to the point that he and Heather had spoken of it as their own little piece of the rain forest—he could not have guessed the details of the building the fire had consumed. While he was no expert at such matters, he had been surprised that the flames had taken so much of Adam's house; even without the fire department to douse it, Ransom had the sense that the blaze should not have consumed this much of it. No doubt, the extent of the destruction owed something to the architects of the shape the house's destruction had revealed.

(*There's something in Adam's house,* Matt had said. The eyes of the ten men and woman crowded around the kitchen table did not look at him. *They've been there since before . . . everything. Before the Fracture. I've heard them moving around outside, in the trees. We have to do something about them.*)

About a month after they had moved into their house, some ten years ago, Ransom had discovered a wasps' nest clinging to a light on the far side of the garage. Had it been only himself, even himself and Heather, living there, he would have been tempted to live and let live. However, with an eight-year-old factored into the equation, one whose curiosity was recorded in the constellations of scars up his arms and down his legs, there was no choice. Ransom called the exterminator, and the next day the nest was still. He waited the three days the woman recommended, then removed the nest by unscrewing the frosted glass jar to which it was anchored. He estimated the side stoop the sunniest part of the property; he placed the nest there to dry out. His decision had not pleased Heather, who was concerned at poison-resistant wasps emerging enraged at the attack on their home, but after a week's watch brought no super-wasps, he considered it reasonable to examine it with Matt. It was the first time he had been this near to a nest, and he had been fascinated by it, the gray, papery material that covered it in strips wound up and to the right. Slicing it across the equator had disclosed a matrix of cells, a little less than half of them chambering larvae, and a host of motionless wasps. Every detail of the nest, he was aware, owed itself to some physiological necessity, evolutionary advantage, but he'd found it difficult to shake the impression that he was observing the result of an alien intelligence, an alien aesthetics, at work.

That same sensation, taken to a power of ten, gripped him at the sight of the structure that had hidden inside Adam's house. Its shape reminded him of that long-ago wasps' nest, only inverted, an irregular dome composed not of gray pulp but a porous substance whose texture suggested sponge. Where it was not charred black, its surface was dark umber. Unlike the house in which it had grown up, Ransom thought that the fire that had scoured this dwelling should have inflicted more damage on it, collapsed it. In spots, the reddish surface of the mound had cracked to reveal a darker substance beneath, something that trembled in the light like mercury. Perhaps this was the reason the place was still standing. What had been the overgrown yard was dirt baked and burnt brittle by the succession of fires. At half a dozen points around the yard, the large shells of what might have been lobsters—had each of those lobsters stood the size of a small pony—lay broken, split wide, the handles of axes, shovels, picks spouting from them.

(Matt had been so excited, his cheeks flushed in that way that made his eyes glow. The left sleeve of his leather jacket, of the sweatshirt underneath it, had been sliced open, the skin below cut from wrist to shoulder by a claw the size of a tennis racket. He hadn't cared, had barely noticed as Ransom had washed the wound, inspected it for any of the fluid [blood?] that had spattered the jacket, and wrapped it in gauze. Outside, whoops and hollers of celebration had filled the morning air. *You should have come with us,* Matt had said, the remark less a reproach and more an expression of regret for a missed opportunity. *My plan worked. They never saw us coming. You should have been there.* Despite the anxiety that had yet to drain from him, pride had swelled Ransom's chest. Maybe everything wasn't lost. Maybe his son . . . *Yes, well,* Ransom had said, *someone has to be around to pick up the pieces.*)

Ransom continued around the front lawn to what they had called the side yard, a wide slope of grass that stretched from the road up to the treeline of the rise behind the house. If the wreckage across the street was difficult to ignore, what lay beyond the edge of the yard compelled his attention. Everything that had extended north of the house: his next door neighbor Dan's red house and barn, the volunteer fire station across from it, the houses that had continued on up both sides of the road to Wiltwyck, was gone, as was the very ground on which it all had been built. As far ahead as Ransom could see, to either side, the earth had been scraped to bare rock, the dull surface of which bore hundred-yard gouges. Somewhere beyond his ability to guesstimate, planes of light like the one on the other side of his house occulted the horizon. Ransom could not decide how many there were. Some days he thought at least four, staggered one behind the other; others he was certain there was only the one whose undulations produced the illusion of more. Far off as the aurora(e) was, its sheer size made the figures that occasionally filled it visible. These he found it easier to disregard, especially when, as today, they were familiar: a quartet of tall stones at the top of a rounded mountain, one apparently fallen over, the remaining three set at irregular distances from one another, enough to suggest that their proximity might be no more than a fluke of geology; from within the arrangement, as if stepping down into it, an eye the size of a barn door peered and began to push out of. Instead, he focused on the garden into which he, Matt, and a few of his neighbors had tilled the side yard.

While Ransom judged the crab capable of leaping the dry moat and clambering up the wire fence around the garden, it preferred to wait for him to set the plank over the trench, cross it, and unlock the front gate. Only then would it scuttle around him, up the rows of carrots and broccoli, the tomatoes caged in their conical frames, stopping on its rounds to inspect a leaf here, a stalk there, tilting its shell forward so that one of the limbs centered in its back could extend and take the object of its scrutiny in its claw. In general, Ransom attributed the crab's study to simple curiosity, but there were moments he fancied that, prior to its arrival in his front yard the morning after Matt's departure, in whatever strange place it had called home, the crab had tended a garden of its own.

Latching but not locking the gate behind him, Ransom said, "What about Bruce? That was what we called our dog . . . the only dog we ever had. Heather picked out the name. She was a huge Springsteen fan. The dog didn't look like a Bruce, not in the slightest. He was some kind of weird mix, Great Dane and greyhound, something like that. His body . . . it was as if the front of one dog had been sewed to the back of another. He had this enormous head—heavy jowls, brow, huge jaws—and these thick front legs, attached to a skinny trunk, back legs like pipe cleaners. His tail—I don't know where that came from. It was so long it hung down almost to his feet. I kept expecting him to tip over, fall on his face. I wanted to call him Butch, that or something classical, Cerberus. Heather and Matt overruled me. Matt was all in favor of calling him Super Destroyer, or Fire Teeth, but Heather and I vetoed those. Somehow, this meant she got the final decision, and Bruce it was."

The beer traps next to the lettuce were full of the large red slugs that had appeared in the last week. One near the top was still moving, swimming lazily around the PBR, the vent along its back expanding and contracting like a mouth attempting to speak. The traps could wait another day before emptying; he would have to remember to bring another can of beer with him tomorrow. He said, "Heather found the dog wandering in the road out front. He was in pretty rough shape: his coat was caked with dirt, rubbed raw in places; he was so thin, you could've used his ribs as a toast rack. Heather was a sucker for any kind of hard case; she said it was why she'd gone out with me in the first place. Very funny, right? By the time Matt stepped off the school bus, she'd lured the dog inside with a plateful of chicken scraps (which he devoured), coaxed him into the downstairs shower (after which, she said, he looked positively skeletal), and heaped a couple of old blankets into a bed for him. She tried to convince him to lie down there, and he did subject the blankets to extensive sniffing, but he refused to allow Heather out of his sight. She was . . . at that point, she tired easily—to

be honest, it was pretty remarkable that she'd been able to do everything she had—so she went out to the front porch to rest on the rocking chair and wait for Matt's bus. When she did, the dog—Bruce, I
might as well call him that; she'd already settled on the name—Bruce
insisted on accompanying her. He plopped down beside her and remained there until Matt climbed the front steps. I would have been
worried . . . concerned about how Bruce would react to Matt, whether
he'd be jealous of Heather, that kind of thing. Not my wife: when Matt
reached the top of the stairs, the dog stood, but that was all. Heather
didn't have to speak to him, let alone grab his collar."

The lettuces weren't ready to pick, nor were the cabbages or broccoli. A few tomatoes, however, were sufficiently red to merit plucking
from the plants and dropping into the canvas bag. The crab was roam-
ing the top of the garden, where they'd planted Dan's apple trees. Ransom glanced over the last of the tomatoes, checked the frames. "That
collar," he said. "It was the first thing I noticed about the dog. Okay,
maybe not the first, but it wasn't too long before it caught my eye.
This was after Matt had met me in the driveway with the news that we
had a guest. The look on his face . . . he had always been a moody
kid—Heather and I used to ask one another, *How's the weather in Matts-
ville?*—and adolescence, its spiking hormones, had not improved his
temperament. In all fairness, Heather being sick didn't help matters
any. This night, though, he was positively beaming, vibrating with
nervous energy. When I saw him running up to the car, my heart
jumped. I couldn't conceive any reason for him to rush out the side
door that wasn't bad: at the very best, an argument with his mother
over some school-related issue; at the very worst, another ambulance
ride to the hospital for Heather."

A blue centipede the size of his hand trundled across the dirt in
front of him. He considered spearing it, couldn't remember if it con-
trolled any of the other species in the garden. Better to err on the side
of caution—even now. He stepped over it, moved on to the beans. He
said, "Matt refused to answer any of my questions; all he would say was,
You'll see. It had been a long day at work; my patience was frayed to a
couple of threads and they weren't looking any too strong. I was on the
verge of snapping at him, telling him to cut the crap, grow up, but
something, that grin, maybe, made me hold my tongue. And once I was

inside, there was Heather sitting on the couch, the dog sprawled out beside her, his head in her lap. He didn't so much as open an eye to me.

"For the life of me, I could not figure out how Heather had gotten him. I assumed she had been to the pound, but we owned only the one car, which I'd had at work all day. She took the longest time telling me where the dog had come from. I had to keep guessing, and didn't Matt think that was the funniest thing ever? It was kind of funny . . . my explanations grew increasingly bizarre, fanciful. Someone had delivered the dog in a steamer trunk. Heather had discovered him living in one of the trees out front. He'd been packed away in the attic. I think she and Matt wanted to hear my next story."

Ransom had forgotten the name of the beans they had planted. Not green beans: these grew in dark purple, although Dan had assured him that they turned green once you cooked them. The beans had come in big, which Dan had predicted: each was easily six, seven inches long. Of the twenty-five or thirty that were ready to pick, however, four had split at the bottom, burst by jellied, inky coils that hung down as long again as the bean. The ends of the coils raised toward him, unfolding petals lined with tiny teeth.

"Shit." He stepped back, lowering the spear. The coils swayed from side to side, their petals opening further. He studied their stalks. All four sprang from the same plant. He swept the blade of the spear through the beans dangling from the plants to either side of the affected one. They dinged faintly on the metal. The rest of the crop appeared untouched; that was something. He adjusted the canvas bag onto his shoulder. Taking the spear in both hands, he set the edge of the blade against the middle plant's stem. His first cut drew viscous green liquid and the smell of spoiled eggs. While he sawed, the coils whipped this way and that, and another three beans shook frantically. The stem severed, he used the spear to loosen the plant from its wire supports, then to carry it to the compost pile at the top of the garden, in the corner opposite the apple trees. There was lighter fluid left in the bottle beside the fence; the dark coils continued to writhe as he sprayed them with it. The plant was too green to burn well, but Ransom reckoned the application of fire to it, however briefly, couldn't hurt. He reached in his shirt pocket for the matches. The lighter fluid flared with a satisfying *whump*.

The crab was circling the apple trees. Eyes on the leaves curling in the flames, Ransom said, "By the time Heather finally told me how Bruce had arrived at the house, I'd been won over. Honestly, within a couple of minutes of watching her sitting there with the dog, I was ready for him to move in. Not because I was such a great dog person—I'd grown up with cats, and if I'd been inclined to adopt a pet, a kitten would have been my first choice. Heather was the one who'd been raised with a houseful of dogs. No, what decided me in Bruce's favor was Heather, her . . . demeanor, I suppose. You could see it in the way she was seated. She didn't look as if she were holding herself as still as possible, as if someone were pressing a knife against the small of her back. She wasn't relaxed—that would be an overstatement—but she was calmer.

"The change in Matt didn't hurt, either." Ransom squeezed another jet of lighter fluid onto the fire, which leapt up in response. The coils thrashed as if trying to tear themselves free of the plant. "How long had that boy wanted a dog . . . By now, we'd settled into a routine with Heather's meds, her doctors' visits—it had settled onto us, more like. I think we knew . . . I wouldn't say we had given up hope; Heather's latest tests had returned better than expected results. But we—the three of us were in a place we had been in for a long time and didn't know when we were going to get out of. A dog was refreshing, new."

With liquid pops, the four coils burst one after the other. The trio of suspect beans followed close behind. "That collar, though . . ." Bringing the lighter fluid with him, Ransom left the fire for the spot where the affected plant had been rooted. Emerald fluid thick as honey topped the stump, slid down its sides in slow fingers. He should dig it out, he knew, and probably the plants to either side of it, for good measure, but without the protection of a pair of gloves he was reluctant to expose his bare skin to it. He reversed the spear and drove its point into the stump. Leaving the blade in, he twisted the handle around to widen the cut, then poured lighter fluid into and around it. He wasn't about to risk dropping a match over here, but he guessed the accelerant should, at a minimum, prove sufficiently toxic to hinder the plant from regrowing until he could return suitably protected and with a shovel.

There was still the question of whether to harvest the plants to either side. Fresh vegetables would be nice, but prudence was the rule of

ther side. Fresh vegetables would be nice, but prudence was the rule of the day. Before they'd set out for the polar city with Matt, his neighbors had moved their various stores to his basement, for safe keeping; it wasn't as if he were going to run out of canned food anytime soon. Ransom withdrew the spear and returned to the compost, where the fire had not yet subsided. Its business with the apple trees completed, the crab crouched at a safe remove from the flames. Ransom said, "It was a new collar, this blue, fibrous stuff, and there was a round metal tag hanging from it. The tag was incised with a name, 'Noble,' and a number to call in case this dog was found. It was a Wiltwyck number. I said, *What about the owner? Shouldn't we call them?*

"Heather must have been preparing her answer all day, from the moment she read the tag. *Do you see the condition this animal is in?* she said. *Either his owner is dead, or they don't deserve him.* As far as Heather was concerned, that was that. I didn't argue, but shortly thereafter I unbuckled the collar and threw it in a drawer in the laundry room. Given Bruce's state, I didn't imagine his owner would be sorry to find him gone, but you never know.

"For five days Bruce lived with us. We took turns walking him. Matt actually woke up half an hour early to take him out for his morning stroll, then Heather gave him a shorter walk around lunchtime, then I took him for another long wander before bed. The dog tolerated me well enough, but he loved Matt, who couldn't spend enough time with him. And Heather . . . except for his walks, he couldn't bear to be away from her; even when we had passed a slow half-hour making our way up Main Street, Bruce diligently investigating the borders of the lawns on the way, there would come a moment he would decide it was time to return to Heather, and he would leave whatever he'd had his nose in and turn home, tugging me along behind him. Once we were inside and I had his leash off, he would bolt for wherever Heather was—usually in bed, asleep—and settle next to her."

He snapped the lighter fluid's cap shut and replaced it beside the fence. The crab sidled away along the rows of carrots and potatoes on the other side of the beans and tomatoes. Ransom watched it examine the feathery green tops of the carrots, prod the potato blossoms. It would be another couple of weeks until they were ready to unearth, though after what had happened to the beans, a quick check was in or-

walking up the street the same way his dog had. William Harrow: that was the way he introduced himself. It was a Saturday. I was cooking brunch; Matt was watching TV; Heather was sitting on the front porch, reading. Of course, Bruce was with her. September was a couple of weeks old, but summer was slow in leaving. The sky was clear, the air was warm, and I was thinking that maybe I'd load the four of us into the car and drive up to the Reservoir for an afternoon out."

On the far side of the house, the near curtain of light, on which he had watched the sunken island rise for the twentieth, the thirtieth time, settled, dimmed. With the slow spiral of food coloring dropped into water, dark pink and burnt orange spread across its upper reaches, a gaudy sunset display that was as close as the actual sky came to night anymore. A broad concrete rectangle took up the image's lower half. At its other end, the plane was bordered by four giant steel and glass boxes, each one open at the top. To the right, a single skyscraper was crowned by an enormous shape whose margins hung over and partway down its upper stories. Something about the form, a handful of scattered details, suggested an impossibly large toad.

The first time Ransom had viewed this particular scene, a couple of weeks after Matt and their neighbors had embarked north, a couple of days after he had awakened to the greater part of Main Street and its houses gone, scoured to gray rock, he had not recognized its location. *The polar city?* Only once it was over and he was seated on the couch, unable to process what he had been shown, did he think, *That was Albany. The Empire State Plaza. Those weren't boxes: they were the bases of the office buildings that stood there. Fifty miles. That's as far as they got.*

He was close enough to the house for its silhouette to block most of the three figures who ran onto the bottom of the screen, one to collapse onto his hands and knees, another to drop his shotgun and tug a revolver out of his belt, the third to use his good hand to drag the blade of his hatchet against his jeans' leg. The crab paid no more attention to the aurora's display than it ever did; it was occupied in withdrawing one of the red slugs from a beer trap. Ransom cleared his throat. "Heather said she never noticed William Harrow until his work boots were clomping on the front stairs. She looked up from her book, and there was this guy climbing to meet her. He must have been around our age, which is to say, late thirties. Tall, thin, not especially remarkable looking one way or the other. Beard, mustache . . . when I saw the guy, he struck me as guarded; to be fair, that could have been because he and Heather were already pretty far into a heated exchange. At the sound of the guy's feet on the stairs, Bruce had stood; by the time I joined the conversation, the dog was trembling.

"The first words out of Harrow's mouth were, *That's my dog.* Maybe things would have proceeded along a different course . . . maybe we could have reached, I don't know, some kind of agreement with the guy, if Heather hadn't said, *Oh? Prove it.* Because he did; he said, *Noble, sit,* and Bruce did exactly that. *There you go,* Harrow said. I might have argued that that didn't prove anything, that we ourselves had trained the dog to sit, and it was the command he was responding to, not the name; but Heather saw no point in ducking the issue. She said, *Do you know what shape this animal was in when we found him? Were you responsible for that?* and the mercury plummeted.

"Matt came for me in the kitchen. He said, *Mom's arguing with some guy. I think he might be Bruce's owner.*

"*All right,* I said, *hold on.* I turned off the burners under the scrambled eggs and home fries. As I was untying my apron, Matt said, *Is he gonna take Bruce with him?*

"*Of course not,* I said.

"But I could see . . . as soon as I understood the situation, I knew Bruce's time with us was over, felt the same lightness high in the chest I'd known sitting in the doctor's office with Heather a year and half before, which seems to be my body's reaction to bad news. It was . . . when Matt—when I . . ."

From either end of the plaza, from between two of the truncated buildings on its far side, what might have been torrents of black water rushed onto and over the concrete. There was no way for the streams to have been water: each would have required a hose the width of a train, pumps the size of houses, a score of workers to operate it, but the way they surged toward the trio occluded by the house suggested a river set loose from its banks and given free rein to speed across the land. The color of spent motor oil, they moved so fast that the objects studding their lengths were almost impossible to distinguish; after his initial viewing, it took Ransom another two before he realized that they were eyes, that each black tumult was the setting for a host of eyes,

eyes of all sizes, shapes, and colors, eyes defining strange constellations. He had no similar trouble identifying the mouths into which the streams opened, tunnels gated by great cracked and jagged teeth.

Ransom said, "Heather's approach . . . you might say that she combined shame with the threat of legal action. Harrow was impervious to both. As far as he was concerned, the dog looked fine, and he was the registered owner, so there was nothing to be worried about. *Of course he looks good,* Heather said, *he's been getting fed!*

"If the dog had been in such awful shape, Harrow wanted to know, then how had he come all the way from his home up here? That didn't sound like a trip an animal as severely abused as Heather was claiming could make.

"He was trying to get as far away as he could, she said. Had he been in better condition, he probably wouldn't have stopped here.

"This was getting us nowhere—had gotten us nowhere. *Look,* I said. *Mr. Harrow. My family and I have become awfully attached to this dog. I understand that you've probably spent quite a bit on him. I would be willing to re-imburse you for that, in addition to whatever you think is fair for the dog.* Here I was, pretty much offering the guy a blank check. Money, right? It may be the root of all evil, but it's solved more than a few problems.

"William Harrow, though . . . he refused my offer straightaway. Maybe he thought I was patronizing him. Maybe he was trying to prove a point. I didn't know what else to do. We could have stood our ground, insisted we were keeping Bruce, but if he had the law on his side, then we would only be delaying the inevitable. He could call the cops on us, the prospect of which made me queasy. As for escalating the situation, trying to get tough with him, intimidate him . . . that wasn't me. I mean, really."

With the house in the way, Ransom didn't have to watch as the trio of dark torrents converged on the trio of men. He didn't have to see the man who had not risen from his hands and knees scooped into a mouth that did not close so much as constrict. He didn't have to see the man with the pistol empty it into the teeth that bit him in half. And he did not have to watch again as the third figure—he should call him a man; he had earned it—sidestepped the bite aimed at him and slashed a groove in the rubbery skin that caused the behemoth to veer away from him. He did not have to see the hatchet, raised for a second strike, spin off into the air, along with the hand that gripped it and most of the accompanying arm, as the mouth that had taken the man with the pistol sliced away the rest of the third man. Ransom did not have to see any of it.

(At the last moment, even though Ransom had sworn to himself he wouldn't, he had pleaded with Matt not to leave. *You could help me with the garden,* he had said. *You'll manage,* Matt had answered. *Who will I talk to?* Ransom had asked. *Who will I tell things to? Write it all down,* Matt had said, *for when we get back.* His throat tight with dread, Ransom had said, *You don't know what they'll do to you.* Matt had not argued with him.)

Its rounds of the garden completed, the crab was waiting at the gate. Ransom prodded the top of a carrot with the blunt end of the spear. "I want to say," he said, "that, had Heather been in better health, she would have gone toe-to-toe with Harrow herself . . . weak as she was, she was ready to take a swing at him. To be on the safe side, I stepped between them. *All right,* I said. *If that's what you want to do, then I guess there isn't any more to say.* I gestured at Bruce, who had returned to his feet. From his jeans pocket, Harrow withdrew another blue collar and a short lead. Bruce saw them, and it was as if he understood what had happened. The holiday was over; it was back to the place he'd tried to escape from. Head lowered, he crossed the porch to Harrow.

"I don't know if Harrow intended to say anything else, but Heather did. Before he started down the stairs with Bruce, Heather said, *Just remember, William Harrow: I know your name. It won't be difficult finding out where you live, where you're taking that dog. I'm making it my duty to watch you—I'm going to watch you like a hawk, and the first hint I see that you aren't treating that dog right, I am going to bring the cops down on you like a hammer. You look at me and tell me I'm lying.*

"He did look at her. His lip trembled; I was sure he was going to speak, answer her threat with one of his own . . . warn her that he shot trespassers, something like that, but he left without another word.

"Of course Heather went inside to track down his address right away. He lived off Main Street, on Farrell Drive, a cul-de-sac about a quarter of a mile that way." Ransom nodded toward the stone expanse. "Heather was all for walking up there after him, as was Matt, who had eavesdropped on our confrontation with Harrow from inside the front door. The expression on his face . . . It was all I could do to persuade the two of them that chasing Harrow would only antagonize him, which wouldn't be good for Bruce, would it? They agreed to wait a day, during which time neither spoke to me more than was absolutely necessary. As it turned out, though, Heather was feeling worse the next day, and then the day after that was Monday and I had work and Matt had school, so it wasn't until Monday evening that we were able to visit Farrell Drive. To be honest, I didn't think there'd be anything for us to see.

"I was wrong. William Harrow lived in a raised ranch set back about fifty yards from the road, at the top of a slight hill. Ten feet into his lawn, there was a cage, a wood frame walled and ceilinged with heavy wire mesh. It was maybe six feet high by twelve feet long by six feet deep. There was a large doghouse at one end with a food and water dish beside it. The whole thing . . . everything was brand new. The serial numbers stenciled on the wood beams were dark and distinct; the mesh was bright; the doghouse—the doghouse was made out of some kind of heavy plastic, and it was shiny. Lying half in the doghouse was Bruce, who, when he heard us pull up, raised his head, then the rest of himself, and trotted over to the side of the cage, his tongue hanging out, his tail wagging.

"Heather and Matt were desperate to rush out of the car, but none of us could avoid the signs, also new, that lined the edge of the property: NO TRESPASSING, day-glo orange on a black background. Matt was all for ignoring them, a sentiment for which Heather had not a little sympathy. But—and I tried to explain this to the two of them— if we were going to have any hope of freeing Bruce, we had to be above reproach. If there were a record of Harrow having called the police on us, it would make our reporting him to the cops appear so much payback. Neither of them was happy, but they had to agree, what I was saying made sense.

"All the same, the second we were back home, Heather had the phone in her hand. The cop she talked to was pretty agreeable, although she cautioned Heather that as long as the dog wasn't being obviously maltreated, there wasn't anything that could be done. The cop agreed to drive along Farrell the next time she was on patrol, and Heather thanked her for the offer. When she hung up the phone, though, her face showed how satisfied she was with our local law enforcement."

Beyond the house, the scene at the Empire State Plaza had faded to pale light. Finished checking the carrots and potatoes, Ransom crossed to the gate. The crab backed up to allow him to unlatch and swing it in. As the crab hurried out, he gave the garden a final look-over, searching for anything he might have missed. Although he did not linger on the apple trees, they appeared quiet.

On the way back around the yard, the crab kept pace with him. Ransom said, "For the next month, Heather walked to Farrell Drive once a day, twice when she was well enough. During that time, Bruce did not leave his cage. Sometimes, she would find him racing around the place, growling. Other times, he would be leaping up against one wall of the pen and using it to flip himself over. As often as not, he would be lying half in the doghouse, his head on his paws. That she could tell—and believe you me, she studied that dog, his cage, as if his life depended on it (which, as far as she was concerned, it did)—Harrow kept the pen tidy and Bruce's dishes full. While she was careful not to set foot on the property, she stood beside it for half an hour, forty-five minutes, an hour. One afternoon, she left our house after lunch and did not return till dinner. When Bruce heard her footsteps, he would stop whatever he was doing, run to the nearest corner of the cage, and stand there wagging his tail. He would voice a series of low barks that Heather said sounded as if he were telling her something, updating the situation. *No change. Still here.*

"She saw Harrow only once. It was during the third-to-last visit she made to Bruce. After a few minutes of standing at the edge of the road, talking to the dog, she noticed a figure in the ranch's doorway. She tensed, ready for him to storm out to her, but he remained where he was. So did Heather. If this guy thought he could scare her, he had another thing coming. Although she wasn't feeling well, she maintained her post for an hour, as did Harrow. When she turned home, he didn't move. The strange thing was, she said to me that night, that the look on his face . . . granted, he wasn't exactly close to her, and she hadn't wanted him to catch her staring at him, but she was pretty sure he'd looked profoundly unhappy."

The crab scrambled up the stairs to the porch. His foot on the lowest step, Ransom paused. "Then Heather was back in the hospital, and Matt and I had other things on our minds beside Bruce. Afterwards . . . not long, actually, I think it was the day before the funeral, I drove by William Harrow's house, and there was the cage, still there, and Bruce, still in it. For a second, I was as angry as I'd ever been; I wanted nothing more than to stomp the gas to the floor and crash into that thing, and if Bruce were killed in the process, so be it. Let Harrow emerge from his house, and I would give him the beating I should have that September morning.

"I didn't, though. The emotion passed, and I kept on driving."

Ransom climbed the rest of the stairs. At the top, he said, "Matt used to say to me, *Who wants to stay in the shallows their whole life?* It was his little dig at his mother and me, at the life we'd chosen. Most of the time, I left his question rhetorical, but when he asked it that afternoon, I answered him; I said, *There are sharks in the shallows, too.* He didn't know what to make of that. Neither did I." Ransom went to say something more, hesitated, decided against it. He opened the door to the house, let the crab run in, followed. The door shut behind them with a solid *thunk*.

At the top of the garden, dangling from the boughs of the apple trees there, the fruit that had ripened into a score, two, of red replicas of Matt's face, his eyes squeezed shut, his mouth stretched in a scream of unbearable pain, swung in a sudden breeze.

The Revel

1. The Chase

Every Werewolf story—these days, at least—features a chase. This one is no exception.

Indeed, it may well be that the chase has become the heart of the story, its true heart, and not the scene of transformation, which, while certainly spectacular, cinematic, the opportunity for all manner of verbal pyrotechnics, is light on meaning. The change to wolf, the face opening into snout, the fingers erupting into claws, the voice rushing the register from scream to howl, is about the animal within, and, at this point in our post-Darwinian history, how new or shocking is this?—whereas the chase is about predator and prey, and so about power, and so about matters more subtle and problematic. Most likely we will, and should, identify with the prey, find the predator a figure of fear. Most likely.

It may help to imagine the chase—whose narrative purpose is to draw you into the story immediately—projected on a movie screen. So much of contemporary horror fiction references film either as a substitute for written precedents or as inspiration for elaborately gruesome descriptions that such a suggestion should not seem surprising. You will want to imagine yourself in a darkened theater, probably with a date or a friend (since who goes to a horror movie alone?). Perhaps you have a tub of popcorn, perhaps a box of Sour Patch Kids, perhaps you find food at the theater distracting and annoying. When the screen lights, the first thing you are aware of is motion, is a pair of blurred legs racing forward. You hear breath panting, feet rustling dead leaves and cracking dead branches. As the camera switches to a long shot, you see that we are in a forest, one in upstate New York if you are able to determine such matters—if not, the forest will look more or less familiar, depending on your location—and that it is late autumn. If you are the kind of person to be struck by such details, you may notice that the bare trunks, the occasional evergreen, have been photographed in such a way as to suggest a maze through which the man who owns the running legs is careening. At this distance, you can obtain a better view of him, as he bolts from left to right across the screen, almost tripping on a root. He is white, of average height, medium build, possibly mid- to late thirties although it is hard to be sure, dressed in green camou- flage pants, shirt, and baseball cap, brown boots, and a bright orange hunting vest. He does not appear to be carrying a gun of any kind. In the third shot, a close up of his face, you see that it is plain, undistin- guished by anything more than the terror distorting it.

There is more, much more, that you could know about this man, the facts of an entire life. (Obviously, you would not have access to this in the opening scenes of a film.) For example, you could know that he is a graduate of Harvard University, at which he obtained his MBA and his wife. You could know that his older brother, Donald, first took him hunting when he was fourteen; it had to be Donald be- cause their father had been killed the year before in a train wreck in Arizona (decapitated). You could know that, before he left to go hunt- ing this morning, he changed his infant son's sodden diaper and found the pungent smell oddly endearing. You could know that he likes country music, that he enjoys bacon, egg, and cheese on a hard roll, that he has season tickets for the Yankees that he does not use as much as he would like. You could know something very bad about him—that when he was fifteen, he crushed the skull of a neighbor's Doberman with a baseball bat; you could know something very good about him—that recently he has contributed half the cost of a new daycare center at his church (Methodist). You could know all this but it is, in a sense, irrelevant. It's not irrelevant to him, of course, or to the people in his life, but it's of little matter to us, the audience. He is the sacrifice: he is here to be murdered, and rather horrifically at that, for our interest. His death begins the Revel. Certainly, there have been oth- ers before him, as we will find out later on, but he is the first we en- counter, and the spilling of his blood consecrates the story's opening.

It would be possible to cut between the man's running legs and another set of legs, between his wide blue eyes and a pair of yellow eyes. Depending on the subsequent portrait of the Werewolf we mean

to paint, we might dip into his consciousness at the outset, an effort
also more easily realized in prose than on film. We might describe the
copper blood on his tongue and lips, the sharp tang of the man's fear
in his nostrils, the joyful surge of his muscles as he runs smoothly and
well across the forest floor. Yet such details seem to give away too
much too soon, as overly heavy-handed soundtrack music, rather than
heightening tension, tends to relieve it. For the moment, then, let us
keep the Werewolf off stage; for now, let him be that clash of leaves
that draws ever closer.

Perhaps the man is talking as he runs, a half-sobbing chain of
sound that includes numerous *Please God*s and a few *Oh Jesus*es and a
number of indistinguishable words. Perhaps he says something like,
"My kids, God, please, my kids," perhaps, "Blood, oh Jesus, blood." If
we want, we can flash back to the scene of carnage from which he is
fleeing, to a ribcage laid open and scarlet wet, trees splashed with vis-
cera, but again, there will be time for that later, and most likely, the
man is trying very hard not to think of that, because if he did, he might
find himself too afraid to run. Instead, he is trying to think of the red
pickup truck that he drove out here four hours ago and that cannot be
much further. In fact, there it is, at the foot of the hill he has crested.

Now comes the cruel part of the story—the first cruel part, anyway—and that is that the man is going to be killed, at last, within sight
of escape and freedom. At this point, we do not know if such cruelty is
deliberate on the part of the Werewolf, or an accident of fate, simply
the point at which the predator brings down the prey. It is what you
are expecting, your heart pounding despite yourself: you know the man
is going to be caught and killed by what is racing up behind him; the
only real question is, How exactly is it going to happen? Will he fumble
open the door to the truck, throw himself inside, slam the door behind
him, thumb the lock, and collapse across the front seat, panting furiously, only to have the windshield crash in on him? Or will he even
make it that far?

In this case, he will not make it inside the truck, because as he is
running down the hill toward it—half falling would be more accurate,
his boots kicking up great scuffs of dirt and leaves—he is jamming his
hand in the right front pocket of his pants, attempting to locate his
keys, which do not seem to be there. His effort continues as he sprints

the space between the foot of the hill and the truck, his cap, which has been ever more perilously perched atop his head, finally flying free, revealing a head of dark brown hair. He does not stop at the truck so much as slam into it, the loud thud jarring. He continues to shove his hand into his right, then his left pants pocket, his breath coming faster, his lips releasing a steady stream of "Oh come on" and "Oh God, come on," while in the background the sound of the Werewolf's pursuit, as it tops the hill, bounds down it, and surges toward the truck, is steadily louder.

You will not see the Werewolf leap on the man and in one fluid motion tear out his throat. You will listen to it. What you will see is shot from underneath the truck. You watch the man's boots, faced toward the truck at first then turning as something you cannot distinguish rushes closer. You hear the man's scream, and a growl that becomes a roar, and the sharp sound of teeth ripping out a large chunk of meat. The scream halts. The boots wobble, then sway to the left as the man, already a corpse, topples to the ground.

This is the beginning. Should we mention that the man's keys were in the left breast pocket of his bright orange hunting vest, tucked there by him because it had a button flap and so would keep them secure? This is just the kind of ironic detail that horror narratives love, isn't it? No doubt the irony has its effect, but no doubt, too, such occurrences validate the secret sense we have—perhaps it is more a secret fear—that such little things as what pocket you put your keys in are what make the difference between life and death, and not such big things as your faith in God or your lack thereof. The narrative to come will embrace this savage irony, take it to its breast, to the extent that it will be tempting to read the Werewolf as the incarnation of this trope. But it isn't, is it?

2. The Setting (A): The Village

Here we are with the Chief of Police as he's driving along Main Street on his way to work. Slideshow, in rapid succession: shopping plazas, traffic light, animal hospital, traffic light, Indian restaurant, insurance agent, houses, churches (Episcopal and Methodist), gas station, bus station, florist, Chinese restaurant, bank, bars, barber, deli, boutiques, bookstores, Greek restaurant, record store, traffic light, bar, bank, police station, bridge (across the Svartkill), Frenchman's Mountain (a long ridge stubbled with bare trees that walls the near horizon).

Of course the village he's driving through is based on a real place, so much so that it might be more honest to call it the name that marks it on the map of upstate New York. You have wondered—who hasn't?—to what extent the places you meet in stories and novels are tied to real locations. The answer is: more closely than you think. (The same is true of the people in them.) Nonetheless, we wish to preserve some freedom of movement, so that should we need the police station to be on the western edge of the village, as opposed to the center of downtown, we will be able to have it there. Let's call this place Huguenot, which should be an obvious enough clue to anyone who lives in or around the actual village to its true identity—but please, hold it loosely in mind.

Interesting, isn't it? how it has to be a village. It does seem as if much of horror fiction takes place in small communities, doesn't it? Of course there are exceptions: you can name one or two or ten narratives that contradict such an assertion, but consider the vast tide that fulfills it. Horror thrives in community, and what embodies community better than a village? Large enough to contain a number and variety of people, yet small enough for the majority of them to know one another, the village is the place where the threat to one can be felt by all. Perhaps there's a certain amount of nostalgia, too, in horror's love for the village, a longing for a kind of ideal community we don't experience anymore. Or perhaps not.

3. The Setting (B): The Forest

Imagine tall trees stretching back into gloom on every side of you. It is not important that you have much arboreal expertise: if you do, picture oak, maple, the occasional birch; if not, picture your generic tree. The majority of trees in this area are deciduous, and thus autumn-bare, but a few evergreens jostle for elbow room. The ground is a jigsaw of yellow, brown, red, and orange leaves. Huguenot, like so many other American settlements, was built within the great forest that once blanketed the North American continent, a blanket whose edges have steadily been pushed back, even as more houses, more buildings, have been constructed within the forest, in quest of the privacy that is supposed to be a mark of personal wealth and success. But the forest has not gone so far away as we might suppose. There are still groups of trees scattered throughout the village, and you do not have to drive very far—ten minutes, fifteen depending on the direction you choose—before you find one of the forest's fingers.

It may be that you think of the forest as little more than an abstraction; it may be that you are one of the people who believe in the forest as a pristine natural paradise, Robert Frost's woods so lovely, dark, and deep. If either of these is the case, take your car on one of those ten- or fifteen-minute drives, until you arrive at one of the digits the forest pokes into the world. Park your car. Leave your cellphone, your Blackberry, your iPod in the glove compartment. Lock the car. Be sure you put your keys someplace safe—someplace you can get to them quickly should the need arise—and walk out into the trees.

Don't stop after ten or fifteen minutes: keep going for an hour, two, until you are deep in a place you have not seen before. Feel free, should you like, to lean against a tree, sit on a log—mind it isn't rotten, though. Now, here, feel how far away you are from everyone and everything you know, feel to what distance your life—which is to say, the routines you inhabit—has receded. Look at the trees around you. They almost seem to form a maze, don't they? Feel how exposed you are. Something could be watching you, couldn't it? It sounds silly to say, yes, but something out behind one of these trees could be watching you. Try not to jump when you hear that crashing in the undergrowth. Most likely, it's a pair of squirrels chasing each other, or a fawn still clumsy. Do you think you can find your way back to your car? You did walk in a straight line, didn't you? What direction was that from? Something could be watching you, couldn't it? Can you feel the hairs on the back of your neck prickling? They really do that, you know.

What would you do if a tall, pale man in a soiled black suit stepped from behind one of the trees? What would you do when you saw that his eyes were yellow? Would you bolt? No one would blame you if you did. You would find, though, that an hour is a long time to walk, and the woods are perhaps not so friendly as you had thought. Branches tug at your feet as you run over them; tree limbs whip your face and arms. You might find that everything looks the same, that you cannot find the route that brought you here. A look behind—do you dare risk a look behind? You know what you hear: growling (which makes you think of that dog you were so afraid of as a child), tree limbs snapping as something large barrels through them. It does not matter where you put your car keys, does it? because like our friend at the beginning of this story, you aren't going to have the chance to use them; you will not come close to finding your car. As you feel your pursuer closing in on you, you might as well scream, vent your rage and fear and frustration, empty your lungs. There is a deep laugh, the kind of laugh a big dog or a bear might make if such things could laugh, and then a lightning bolt of pain scores your neck as a massive paw strikes it open, almost separating your head from your body, which falls dead on the leaf-strewn ground. Your vision bursts white, and that is all you know. What remains of you will be found the following day, when the police chief is realizing that something very bad, an unprecedented bad, is on his hands.

The woods are dark and deep. Lovely?

4. The Characters (A): The Police Chief

Tall, six foot three, but more than height, he gives the impression of size, as his weight pushes the red needle on his bathroom scale ever further from two hundred and fifty pounds and ever closer to three hundred. His doctor has told him to slim down, which he fully intends, but he can still bench as much as he could in the Navy, experiences no shortness of breath or chest pains, and finds it difficult to accept that his health has been or in any way might be impaired by what he estimates a few extra pounds. His hands and feet are almost abnormally large, so much so that it is difficult for him to find shoes that fit in any of the local stores, and his face is similarly large. His eyes are blue and liquid, his cheeks crisscrossed by red nets of capillaries, his nose narrow and close to his face. He wears his hair crewcut short. If he does not look particularly friendly, neither does he look particularly hostile; the principle impression he gives is of wariness.

He has held his position for the last half-dozen years, and he prides himself on knowing all Main Street's merchants, and all the town's clergy, by name. It is true that he knows not a few of them from various infractions of the law, ranging from Bill Getz—owner of Pete's Corner Pub—passing out in the middle of Main Street at four on a Saturday morning after sampling a bit too much of the thirty-year-old Armagnac a friend brought him from the south of France, to Judy Lavalle—former manager of the White Orchid boutique—stabbing her husband in the leg with a packing knife after she uncovered his affair with her assistant manager.

The Police Chief has an almost surprisingly forgiving attitude toward such faults. This is because he believes that, at root, human beings are hopelessly corrupt, depraved, every one of us always ready to cross some law or code of behavior should the opportunity present itself. The Police Chief does not understand why humanity is this way; he just knows it is. He is rarely surprised by any of the crimes, small or large, to which he is called on to respond. That is about to change.

Is it necessary to say that the Police Chief is the narrative's representative of order? In a horror narrative, it is rare for there not to be such a figure, either institutionally sanctioned or self-appointed. Such a character embodies the social structure(s) under assault from the monster. Close to the center of the story's events, s/he has access to all manner of information, as a result of which s/he serves as a kind of guide through the narrative's winding corridors. (This figure may also have ready access to all manner of weaponry, the benefits of which are not to be underestimated.)

Nowadays, it is common enough to show this character flawed—perhaps to express our continuing unease with the powers that regulate our lives, our suspicion that the institutions attacked by the monster were already rotting; or perhaps in the interest of heightening narrative tension. In case the Police Chief's sour view of humanity is not sufficient instance of this, it may help to know that, two years ago, in his official capacity, he systematically harassed Harold Stonger, former bartender at Dionysus bar and grill, over the course of three months, to the point that Stonger attempted suicide by opening his wrists with a box cutter. The Police Chief's reason for doing so was a car accident involving his then-eighteen-year-old daughter, Chloe, who had used a fake ID to consume four margaritas before sliding behind the wheel of her 1990 Volvo. It was not the first time Chloe had used this ID, which was of almost professional quality. The accident her drinking led to consisted in her driving her car off the road and into a small tree at a relatively slow speed; although the consequences at home were severe, Chloe walked away from her car unharmed. Nonetheless, the Police Chief made it his personal mission to allow Harry Stonger no peace. Persistent and involved traffic stops, several raids on Dionysus leading to one sizable fine, a handful of visits to Stonger's apartment, left the man no doubt that the Police Chief wanted him gone from Huguenot. In all fairness to the Police Chief, he in no way encouraged Stonger to open his wrists, though when he learned of it he could only express his disappointment that the EMTs had not arrived at Stonger's apartment a little later.

5. The Characters (B): Barbara Dinasha

Proprietor of the Dippie Hippie mostly used clothing store on Main Street, she is in her mid-forties, her long hair more gray than blond. Currently she lives in the small apartment over her store, where she sits at a black table next to the bay window that overlooks Main Street. She wears a white terrycloth robe over a peach cotton nightdress. There is a mug of coffee on the table, beside a yellow legal pad on which Barbara draws the man whose face has filled her dreams every night for the past two weeks. She uses a blue ballpoint pen whose scratch on the paper is the only sound aside from Barbara's breathing.

Barbara has resided in the apartment since last winter, when she moved there after having left her husband of fourteen years and their eight-year-old son, for reasons of which no one was sure but everyone had an opinion. Her husband—as yet, they remain legally separated, and when he has been drinking too much at Pete's Corner Pub, Tom Dinasha still expresses hope of an eventual reconciliation—is a carpenter and handyman and well liked, as is her precocious son, Brian, who is a star pitcher in the local Little League; but since Barbara draws most of her clientele from the SUNY college, her consequent dip in popularity with the village's permanent residents has not appreciably decreased her store's business.

Barbara likes the college students: she herself attended the State University twenty-five years before, which was how she came to Huguenot from Northport, Long Island. She majored in Studio Art before dropping out to spend the next seven years of her life on the Grateful Dead tour, which was not inconsistent with the reasons that had brought her upstate in the first place, namely, a desire to be at the school whose reputation was for maintaining the spirit and behavior of the sixties, in which Barbara was just old enough to regret not having been able to participate.

At a diner in Carbondale, Illinois, she met her future husband, who, as it happened, was a lifelong resident of Huguenot who was hitchhiking cross-country to see the Dead in St. Louis. They spent six months on the Dead tour, then returned to Huguenot, where Tom learned carpentry from his father, and they lived together in an old barn that he gradually rebuilt into a house. Tom Dinasha became a fixture in Huguenot, first as the guy you could call on when your regular guy couldn't make it, then as your regular guy. Barbara remained his elusive and somewhat aloof companion, observed taking the occasional art course at the college, but otherwise keeping to herself until a modest inheritance arrived after her father's death and she decided to open the Dippie Hippie. By that time, a year had passed since she had found herself pregnant and she and Tom had married because, as each said to her and his close friends and relations, neither of them was brave enough not to. At the wedding, Barbara's father had been well enough to give his daughter away; in six months, the cancer that had eaten one lung would have finished the rest of him. (Barbara's mother left the house when Barbara was fourteen, and she has not heard from or about her since.)

She doesn't care for the Chief of Police, who, from her interactions with him over the years, especially since opening the store, she has come to view as slow-moving, dull-witted, provincial, and bigoted. She knows he sees her as little more than an aging, would-be hippie who likely burned out what little there was of her mind to begin with years ago. (She does not know, but would not be surprised to learn, that he also suspects her of moving some kind of drug, probably pot but possibly something harder, through her store. While he has only entered the Dippie Hippie once, when it opened, to wish Barbara well in her enterprise, he and his officers make it a point both to watch it and to make Barbara aware that they are watching it.)

This morning, though she has seen his car pass down Main Street on its way to the station, the Police Chief is far from her concern. She is thinking about her dreams—dream might be the better word, since it has been substantially the same thing every night: she and a tall, pale man wearing a soiled black suit walking side by side in the woods, somewhere, she knows with dream-certainty, on Frenchman's Mountain (not that she has spent much time there). The man speaks to her, and this is where the variation in the dream occurs: every night, he says something different. One night, it was, "Do you know that Doors song?" Another, it was, "But you haven't told them, have you?" A third time, he said, "I could help you." She cannot remember all his utterances, although she has the sense that they tend to fall into one of two camps: either "Break on through, Barbara, break on through," or "Let me help you. All you have to do is say yes." Once he has spoken his piece, they stop and he turns to face her, extending his right hand in a gesture so familiar that she takes it without thinking. It feels strange, like holding a wet wire brush; looking down, she sees that his hand with its slender fingers has become a large paw, covered in bristly fur and soaked in bright red blood, which dribbles over her skin. She starts to look up at the man, is on the verge of seeing something, something crowds the top of her vision, when she sits upright in bed, awake.

Barbara does not believe in this man/monster as having any objective existence. Despite the fear, the weirdness, occasioned by the recurrence of him in her dreams, she understands him to be no more than the manifestation of a subconscious feeling that has become lodged—temporarily, she had thought—in the theater of her unconscious. This emotion is guilt, its source her leaving her son.

Needless to say, we know better, don't we? In a horror story, dreams, hunches, instincts—those parts of our lives we file under the headings of the Irrational, or the Atavistic—are keys with which the narrative presents its characters. Those who accept those keys fit them to the locks of the doors in front of them, find their way through to the next part of the maze; those who let them drop to the floor will live long enough to regret their mistake. Of course, part of the function of these elements is to add to the sense of unease the story wishes to evoke in the reader by appealing to her or his own experience of them. In addition: 1) they move the narrative along; 2) they're an economical way of introducing or incorporating the more fantastic elements of the story into it; and 3) they form part of the springboard from which the protagonist(s) will take the leap into whatever impossible explanation is required for the horrors confronting them. In the end, the narrative will go beyond merely invoking this side of experience; it will validate it, privilege it, as if to say that it is in everything we do our best to suppress, to trivialize, that survival lies.

Barbara is our anchor; she is the character who stands for the rest of the village inhabitants. Unlike the Police Chief, the Werewolf, you, Barbara cannot go everywhere, see everything. As the Revel continues and the narrative veers from extravagance to extravagance, she stays in place, refusing the madness of the dance.

6. The Characters (C): The Werewolf

What about the Werewolf, then?

To be frank, it's a dilemma. While it remains offstage, no more than a shadow cast across its victims, the monster is a blank, an empty space you fill with your fears, with whatever chases you from sleep and makes you sit bolt upright in bed at four in the morning, heart banging. At the moment, the Werewolf is your Werewolf; it is whatever you have conjured from hearing that word and reading about his depredations. (Might we go so far as to say that, right now, the Werewolf is you? [No, no, of course not.])

That won't do, though, will it? You would like a photograph of him, wouldn't you? over which you might linger. You would like to examine his face closely, pore over each and every detail of it, attempt to match what is outside to what is inside. Are you familiar with phrenology? It was a nineteenth-century science that tried to ascertain personality characteristics through mapping the shape of the skull. You laugh at such an idea—we all do—but how far away from it are we, truly? We search the newspaper and magazine pictures of the perpetrators of whatever outrage currently confronts us, desperate for a clue to their motivation in the set of their eyes, the curve of their mouths, the tilt of their heads. We stare at ourselves in mirrors, trying to see what it is in the mystery of our faces that makes us fail the way we do.

You would like a picture: will a drawing suffice? Three drawings, actually: that's what Barbara Dinasha has produced on her legal pad.

Her work is rough, but there is a sureness to it that makes you wonder what would have become of her had she remained in the college's art program. The first shows the man's head: squarish, its features sharply angled, so much so that it might remind you of a piece of Cubist sculpture. In her dreams, the man has impressed her as made of edges, as if his face had been struck from a block of flint by quick blows from a hammer. The hair is lank, parted on the right side; Barbara has shaded it with her pen, seeing the blue ink as dark brown that does not appear to have been washed in the last two or three days. She has dotted the square jaw to indicate the dark stubble traversing it. The nose is broad and flat; the lips full and the mouth wide; the eyes wide and dark—brown, Barbara thinks, although they may be black.

Her second sketch is of the man's hands, which are distinguished by long, thin fingers and particularly the ring fingers, which stretch longer than the middle fingers. Fine hair covers the back of the hands out along to the ends of the fingers. The edges of the nails are ragged, dirty.

Barbara's final drawing is of the man in whole, a slender figure dressed in a dark suit and white dress shirt open at the collar. Like the others, it sufficiently resembles the man from her dreams that, were the police pursuing him—as they are, though they do not know it—they could no worse than show these drawings to men and women on the street, post copies of them in conspicuous places. Barbara, however, is as unsatisfied with this one as she is the two others. In part, her discontent arises from the limitations of her medium. There is no way for her to render the man's voice, which lingers in her ears as if he had whispered there a moment ago. It is deep, more so even than her father's, and he sang bass for the church choir, and it possesses a calm authority that she would find appropriate to a surgeon. The remainder of Barbara's discontent is rooted in her inability to reproduce the feeling the man leaves in her. Were she to take up her pen once more and add a pair of goat horns to his head and a goatee his chin, bedeck him with a barbed tail and pitchfork, and surround him with a corona of flames, the effect, while exaggerated and cartoonish, would more closely approximate that he has on her.

Something more? Something more definite? How about this: there's an old man, Mr. Dock, the former head librarian of the village library, who has retired to his bungalow halfway out to Frenchman's Mountain. Were you to show him Barbara Dinasha's sketches, his brow would contract, he would remove his glasses for a cleaning from a handkerchief, then inspect the drawings again. Unable to deny his recognition, he might tell you about a young man who left Huguenot to study medicine up in Albany when he, Mr. Dock, was thirteen, some seventy years gone. Alphonse Sweet came of the Quebecois who moved into the region at the end of the nineteenth century; a bright lad, though cruel, terribly cruel. He didn't return, Alphonse—killed, it was said, up in some sort of ghost town in Western Canada under dubious circumstances. He was buried there. No, Mr. Dock doesn't know what Alphonse was doing there.

(Oh—and hungry: the Werewolf is always hungry.)

7. The Characters (D): You

Yes, you're part of this. Do you even need to ask? You leap from character to character, a voyeur rifling through home movies of the most intimate sort:

—You're the Police Chief receiving the call that Ed Cook, the County ME, has been found dead in the doorway to his apartment. Rubbing the sleep from your eyes, you listen to Shelley Jacobson struggling to keep her voice calm as she says that Ed had been torn open, there was blood all over the place, and while they aren't sure, it looks as if certain . . . parts have been removed from the body. Bile burning at the back of your throat, you say, Let me guess: kidneys, part of the liver, and the tongue. That's right, Jacobson says, the emotion in her words momentarily overwhelmed by her surprise. You don't tell her that the same selection had been removed from each of the hunters found on Frenchman's Mountain, that Ed Cook had phoned you to discuss this last night. Looks like we've got a gourmand on our hands, he'd said, almost his final words to you. You don't repeat his attempt at witticism; instead, you tell Shelley that you'll be right there and hang up.

—You're Barbara Dinasha, opening the latest letter from the oncologist, skimming his most recent plea to you to return for treatment; even if the cancer isn't curable, there's a decent chance that treatment could earn you another three months, possibly more. You remember your doctor telling you that your constant tiredness wasn't chronic fatigue: it was your body exhausting itself on the invader that already had colonized most of it. You're not that far away from the overwhelming panic that rose in you as you left the doctor's office, that manifested itself in the desire to run, to escape, to leave the life you had and keep moving until nothing familiar remained—within a week, it was this impulse that would take you from your home and family to the apartment over the store, a flight that solved nothing, simplified nothing, that only made the situation of your dying worse. By the time you understood that you needed to talk to Tom, to Brian, things had reached the point that you could not see a way to do so. You drop the letter into the trash and, for an instant, hear a voice saying, "I could help you, Barbara. All you have to do is ask."

—You're each and every one of the Werewolf's victims. You're the quartet of hunters sitting around their early morning fire, fighting the chill air with a flask of Talisker, your rifles propped against the logs you're sitting on, less concerned with firing those guns than with maintaining an annual tradition fifteen years old, a kind of secular retreat, and if one of you should by luck take down a prize buck, that would be nice, but it's not essential. You're the single mother out for a morning jog who's decided to take one of the paths on the Mountain, even though it's hunting season and your mother has warned you about the idiots out who can't tell the difference between a woman and a deer. You're the ME, wishing you felt one-tenth as calm as you did your best to sound to the Police Chief, glad that at least you spoke with him before you opened the bottle of gin chilling in your freezer, which you already know will do nothing to dilute the images of those four men's remains—and never has that euphemism been so accurate—but which may help to still the shaking that has seized your hands since you drew to the end of the final autopsy. You're a pair of dancers leaving The Blue Belle out on Route 299, discussing whether to drive into the village for a drink at Peter's Corner Pub because, although it's close to two, Pete's will still be open, and the two of you are wound tight from too many cigarettes and too many lap dances for too many freaks, who seem to have been drawn from their caves, their mother's basements, by the last few days' carnage. You're the chef, sous-chef, and waitress in early to the Toreador on Main Street to assemble salads, start soups, and decide on the day's specials, the three of you unable to discuss much besides the killer who has chosen Huguenot as his theater, and about whom a host of rumors, most centered on what he's taken from the bodies of those he's butchered, are in heavy circulation.

—You might even be the Werewolf himself, which the hunters experience as something enormous, dark, snarling, that leaps into their midst and lays one of them open before any has registered its presence. For the single mother out on the mountain trail, the Werewolf is first the tall, pale man whose black suit is soaked with the blood of the man in whose exposed insides he's rooting around, and then he's something else, something she knows the moment she pivots away from she has no chance of outrunning, but maybe she can call for help before it's too late. For the ME, the Werewolf is a tall, pale man in a soiled black suit standing outside his apartment door, who, when he grins, shows a mouth with many too many teeth. For the dancers, the Werewolf is a rising growl in the backseat of the car. For the staff of Toreador, the Werewolf is a roar and shape too big for their narrow kitchen.

8. Some Headlines (In Lieu of Successive Descriptions of, Essentially, the Same Thing)

HUNTERS KILLED: Four Men Found Murdered on Frenchman's Mountain; Woman Who Notified Police Missing.

CORONER MURDERED: Was Working On Slain Hunters; Police Chief Refuses to Rule Out Connection to Previous Crime.

DANCERS MISSING: Were Seen Leaving The Blue Belle Two Nights Ago; Car Found Abandoned and Bloody.

RESTAURANT MASSACRE: Staff at Local Café Victims of Horrific Crime.

HUGUENOT HORROR: Upstate New York Town Terrorized by Savage Murder Spree; Twelve Confirmed Dead, Additional Deaths Feared; Residents Panicked; Local and State Police Baffled.

9. A Small Town in the North

Where does he come from, the Werewolf? What drew Alphonse Sweet (it's he: no need to play coy) to that ghost town in Western Canada? What did he find there? Why did he leave his studies at Albany in the first place? What was he looking for?

The answers lie on the other side of an experience that the monster himself cannot articulate; when he tries to bridge it to them, he sees images sparse and stark.

> White. Whiteness. The town,
> Distant on the tundra.
> Words on white paper.
>
> Two rows of buildings,
> The town sits on the plain, lonely
> Even of ghosts.
>
> Wind whistles up Main
> Street. Empty windows return
> No reflections.
>
> Snow breaks underfoot.
> Wooden planks groan, protesting
> The wind's attention.
>
> Flurries cloud the air.
> At the heart of swirling snow,
> Five figures standing.
>
> Heavy fur robes drape
> Bodies. Carved animal masks
> Substitute for faces.
>
> A plea, an offer,
> A withered hand extended,
> Taken. Whiteness. White.

10. Trees Painted on Plywood Walls

For Barbara, the narrative's climax begins with a crash that jolts her from a (blessedly) dreamless sleep. Eyes wide, heart thwacking against her sternum, she sits up in bed, a single question, *What was that?* flashing in her mind in great neon blue letters. She does not know the answer. Was it a lamp? She doesn't think so. This sound was not the dull clang of metal echoing off a hardwood floor: it was brittle, the sharp crack of glass breaking—one of her windows, maybe, or the full-length mirror hung sideways in the living room to give the space the illusion of increased size. Is there an intruder in her apartment? She listens for the floor creaking under the weight of an intruder's sneaker, but hears nothing.

Barbara throws back her bed's heavy quilt and rises from it, stooping to take the heavy flashlight she keeps under the bed in case of a blackout. The flashlight has a nylon loop at its end to slip around your wrist; Barbara does so, gripping the flashlight close to the end because she does not want it for illumination: she wants it for a weapon. Should there be anyone prowling her apartment, be he sociopath or drunken fratboy, she intends to beat him senseless first and ask questions later. She does not feel self-conscious or melodramatic in the least. Nor does she recognize her response to the noise within the context of a horror narrative as ill-advised, if not a mistake of the fatal variety; Barbara doesn't care for horror stories—though no doubt she would know the scene she is in if you pointed it out to her.

She slides across the floor to the door, where she listens while counting to two hundred, time enough for any intruder to think that the noise her heard from her bedroom was nothing more than her turning over in her sleep. She leans her head out of the doorway far enough for her to see down the short hallway to the living room. The living room appears to be empty. She cannot see all of it from here, however, so, flexing her fingers on the flashlight and raising it, Barbara steps from her bedroom and crosses the distance to the living room, more calm than she would have predicted had you asked her to imagine herself in such a scene, yet still apprehensive lest one of the boards in the hall floor creak and betray her. None do. She halts at the threshold to the living room and tilts forward, peering from side to side. She still cannot see every last bit of the living room, but it appears empty; neither does she observe evidence of broken glass, either from the windows or the mirror on the wall. Taking a breath, Barbara steps into the room.

No one is there. Having established this fact through a series of quick glances, Barbara verifies it by turning in a slow circle, flashlight held at the ready. The room is empty of anyone save herself; nor have its contents been disturbed. Whatever she heard must have come from outside. Relaxing her grip on the flashlight, Barbara walks to the bay window and surveys Main Street. It's quiet. A group of college kids, most of them underage, no doubt, stands in front of Pete's Corner Pub, smoking and talking—given the presence of the killer, an exercise in collective bravado. A state police car cruises up the street, drawing glances from the kids. It would appear that none of the plate glass windows opening into the shops along Main Street has been smashed. Barbara steps back and, with one more look around the living room, exits it.

She is at the doorway to her bedroom, which is to say, she has walked a short distance in a short time (though it has been time enough for her to wonder if the noise she heard was a vivid dream [not that she knows anything about those]), when there is another crack, louder than the first, the same crash of shattering glass, without a doubt from the living room. Barbara jumps, then turns and runs back into the living room, flashlight firmly in hand.

This time, she sees immediately that the mirror has fallen completely from its frame, which contains only darkness. "Shit," she says, crouching to search for pieces of glass, which, she thinks, it's a wonder didn't slice her foot.

Although there are no lights on in Barbara's apartment except for the nightlight in her bathroom, there is enough light streaming in through the front window for her to be able to see around the living room surprisingly well. As she slides her hand over the floor, that light dims, as if someone had his hand on a dial and turned it all the way to zero. It's like the descriptions Barbara has read of losing consciousness: everything goes black; the only difference is that Barbara maintains awareness as the room vanishes around her. She is not afraid, only confused, wondering what has happened; some type of power outage, she supposes, which reminds her of her flashlight, whose switch she locates and slides on.

She is no longer in her living room. A corridor stretches in front of and behind her, its walls unstained plywood, its ceiling somewhere in the darkness overhead. Her apartment's hardwood floor has been replaced by gray concrete. The plywood walls are decorated with trees painted in black, white, and gray, some thick, some thin, as if trying to suggest perspective. They have all been painted with branches bare. Looking at them, Barbara thinks of her dreams, of standing with the tall pale man in the woods on Frenchman's Mountain. Barbara points the flashlight from walls to floor, from floor to ceiling (undistinguishable), from ceiling to walls, from walls to ceiling, from ceiling to floor, unable to understand what she is seeing, the part of her brain that processes information jammed. The mundaneness of her surroundings only adds to her confusion. Were she to find herself transported to an alien jungle teeming with wailing blue flowers, slithering pink vines, a six-legged green beast with a mouth of curving fangs creeping toward her, the landscape and its inhabitants would be consistent with the strangeness of the shift; the weirdness of this move, however, strains against the ordinariness of her slapdash surroundings, the kind of thing you might expect at a low-budget haunted house at Halloween. Walls, floor, walls, ceiling, floor, walls, walls, walls: she jerks the flashlight from one to the other frantically, as if one of the surfaces is going to surrender the secret of what has happened to her. She drags her free hand through her hair, hoping the pain of her fingers tearing through its tangles will yank her out of this place and back to reality. But all the pain does is to confirm the concrete cold beneath her, the painted trees shining on the coarse walls.

Barbara switches off the flashlight, plunging herself into darkness once more. She counts to ten, then turns the flashlight back on. When she does, she is again faced with the plywood walls and their arboreal decorations; this time, though, the sight of those walls prompts her to action. Perhaps a failsafe switch has been thrown somewhere in the depths of her brain; perhaps the neurons that had stalled have been bypassed. Barbara stands and approaches the wall to her right. It is solid—braced, it seems, from the other side. Letting the flashlight dangle, she tries with both hands to move it, with no more luck. Annoyance prickles her skin, causes her to mutter, "What is this?" There is as much reason to walk forward as back, so Barbara starts walking forward. As she does, she sees a white light shining in the distance ahead. Thinking it might be the flashlight reflecting on a window or mirror, she slides the switch to off. When the light continues to shine, Barbara switches the flashlight on and hurries toward it. She keeps the beam on the floor in front of her, but the glow is strong enough for her to be able to see the walls on either side of her. The trees painted on them appear to writhe as she passes them; a trick of the light, she is sure.

As she moves ahead, Barbara notices that the corridor branches off on either side of her at irregular intervals. While she wonders where those branchings lead, she does not linger at any of them. Should this light in front of her be a disappointment, there will be time for her to return to them. It occurs to her that she is walking through a giant maze—being led through it, more like—and then she hears something. It is difficult to say what it is: it is one of those sounds that is so low, so soft, that you are not sure you even heard it in the first place; you are not sure it was not your mind whispering to you. If there is someone in the room with you, you will say, "Excuse me?" and the other person will look up from their book and say, "I didn't say anything." Barbara stops walking, and the sound appears to halt as well. Maybe it was only her feet echoing off the concrete and plywood. There it is again, faintly, a sound, a sound like, a sound like someone weeping, like someone at the hiccoughing end of hours of unrelenting crying. It seems to be coming from the other side of the wall to her right; how far back from it, Barbara cannot guess. Could it be another person, someone else trapped in here with her? What else could it be? Barbara takes a deep breath and calls out, "Hello! Is there anyone there? Can anyone hear me? Hello! I'm over here! Can you hear me? Hello?" Her voice slaps flat against the plywood. She looks at the wall, which is painted with a series of spectral white trees that remind her of birches. There is no answer. The weeping fades. Barbara repeats her call, receives no answer, tries a third time. When she judges she has waited a sufficient time for a reply and has had none, she continues toward the light. She does not hear the sound of weeping any more.

Before long, Barbara sees that the light in front of her is a single lightbulb, dangling at one end of a cord running into the darkness overhead. It marks the end of the corridor: a third wall connects those to either side of her, blocking her way. A single black tree, squat, enormous, its branches spreading out like a web of nerves, decorates the surface. Barbara's pace slows as a combination of anger and unease seizes her legs. She is on the verge of turning around when she notices what appears to be the outline of a door set in the wall, at the heart of the tree. Directing the flashlight's beam at it, she sees that there is a door: there is the doorknob; there are the hinges. With her luck, she thinks, it'll be locked.

She is wrong. When she grips the doorknob and turns it, the door swings open easily. Stepping through it, she finds herself in a large dark space, at the far end of which a man sits at a table, lit by a source she cannot identify. When Barbara sees the man, her pulse quickens, sweeping the anger and unease from her. From her place at the door, she calls, "Hello? Hello?" and walks toward him.

"Barbara, welcome!" the man says.

11. A Cabin in the Woods

For the Police Chief, the narrative's climax begins on Frenchman's Mountain, to which he has driven this afternoon in order to revisit the site of the first murder—well, the first victim he discovered, when he pulled his cruiser up behind the dusty black pickup parked well back from the road up and over Frenchman's Mountain in a makeshift lot favored mainly by occasional hunters. In twenty years on the job, the Police Chief can count on his fingers the number of cases he's worked that have stymied him the way this one has, left him feeling he's playing perpetual catch-up. Of all the unpleasant sensations that attend his job, this is the one he likes the least; in fact, he detests it. Things are bad enough that were the State Troopers, or even the Feds, who appeared yesterday, to untangle this mess, he could not only live with it, but be happy about it. As things stand, though, the smug attitudes the State Troopers brought with them melted away at the sight of the first group of victims; nor have they had any more success stopping, let alone catching, the killer than the Police Chief and his staff. For the first time, he actually feels a certain solidarity with the men and women he generally considers his rivals. Should things continue the way they have been, he expects even the Feds will seem more human.

However, the Police Chief doesn't intend to let the situation progress any further, so he's driven out here, to revisit the scene of that first discovery. He's parked at one end of a dirt road that curves away from Route 299. To his right, the ground is straight for about fifty feet, then rises in a steep hill down which the marks of the first victim's run remain visible. To his left, the ground dips to a line of trees that stretches around in front of him and climbs the side of the hill. Directly ahead of him is the spot where the hunter's boots and jeans were visible sprawled beside the truck over which the rest of him had been splashed. The ground remains dark from the blood that soaked into it.

Despite his belief in humanity's innate depravity, the Police Chief has been shocked by what he has witnessed this last week. Like listening to a talk in a language he only partly understands, his mind cannot process everything it has taken in. He has not felt afraid so much as amazed, as if he has voyaged to a strange new country whose people follow customs utterly alien to him. Before now, the worst thing he had seen had occurred when he was in the Navy and serving on the flight deck of the Intrepid. In a moment of fatal carelessness, a sailor walked into the spinning propeller of an airplane. That had been worse than bad, but it had been an accident. The savagery of this past week reeks of intention, but an intention neither the Police Chief nor any one of his fellows has been able to see to the bottom of. It's the kind of over-the-top behavior you find in Hollywood melodramas, not daily life. And yet, here they are.

As a rule, the Police Chief is not afraid of the woods. Over the course of his life he has spent a good deal of time in them, and he possesses the confidence that comes with experience; in addition, he is sufficiently large that most things he might encounter in the woods of upstate New York have the good sense to avoid him, and any that do not, he has more than a fair chance of being able to handle, and well at that. (The handgun riding his hip doesn't hurt his confidence.) Now, though, he feels a finger of fear tickle the base of his spine as he realizes that he is being watched. The forest is quiet, so much so that his breathing, the leaves crackling under his shoes, sound loud as thunderclaps. With the certainty of religious revelation, he knows that the killer, the monster behind the murders of twelve men and women, is standing about halfway up the hill to his right, just far enough back in the woods to prevent him from being seen. He is watching the Police

Chief's actions with a keen and rapacious intelligence, a savage humor.
Were the Police Chief's sense of the killer's location a shade more definite, he could draw his gun and do his best to validate that hunch.
Since it isn't, there is nothing for him to do but sprint in that direction,
certain that, by the time he arrives at the man's position, he will long
since have been reabsorbed by the trees.

As his quadriceps and calves burn with the effort of propelling
him up the hill, as his hand grips the butt of his pistol, ready to haul it
from its holster, the Police Chief realizes that the killer is not moving,
that he can feel the man's gaze on him still, a spotlight illuminating him
as his feet push off soil that slides away beneath them. He knows that
it can't be this simple, that the killer isn't just waiting for the Police
Chief to take him in, that either he's ready to bolt or this is a trap, but
if the killer will wait until the Police Chief reaches the top of this hill—
if he judges there's no way this big a man could catch him, the Police
Chief is ready to put that conceit to the test. If the man has laid some
sort of trap, the Police Chief is ready to try that, too.

He gains the top of the hill and keeps going, pushes himself not to
slacken, to slow. His lungs are bellows full of fiery air. Ahead and to
the right, about fifteen feet into the trees, is that . . .? A tall figure re-
gards his approach, its shadowed face broken by a bright grin, and the
Police Chief's gun is out and in his hand. Now the killer turns, but it's
too late, even as he breaks into a run, the Police Chief is too close for
him to escape. He considers dropping to a firing crouch, but there are
too many trees, not to mention the possibility—though faint—of a
random civilian out for a walk. It's no matter: the sight of the tall man
running has sent a tide of adrenaline through the Police Chief, and the
prospect of closing his hands on this maniac fills his pounding heart
with fierce joy.

The killer leads the Police Chief along a trail so faint as to be non-
existent, cutting right, left, right, left, and left again. Leaves crash,
sticks snap, the occasional stone shoots away from the toe of the Police Chief's boot. One misstep and he's down with a broken ankle, but
he doesn't slow his pace. As the killer turns right, down a short rise,
then left along a dry stream bed, the Police Chief stays on him. When
he dodges right over a large mound and along another trail barely
there, the Police Chief draws closer to him. He does not recognize the

place to which he has been led. Rows of evergreens zigzag away like the walls of so many hallways. The air is full of the Christmas smell of pine. In front of the killer, a line of evergreens lock branches in a dark green wall.

Without breaking stride, the tall man plunges into the trees. The Police Chief follows. For a long moment, he can see nothing. Branches whip his face; he raises his forearms and lowers his head. The trees extend deeper than he had anticipated. He can hear the killer pushing through trees mere feet ahead of him. If the man wants to ambush him, coming out from this thicket offers a perfect opportunity: a second to gain your bearings, and then turn your attention on your pursuer. Guarding his face with his free hand, the Police Chief lowers his gun.

Events are moving too quickly for the Police Chief to articulate what he expects on the other side of these evergreens. Were it possible to slow time, he might say that he judges it most likely that the killer will be on the move once more; however, he would not be surprised to find the man standing off to one side or the other, a knife or hatchet in his upraised hand. Whatever he expects, it is not what confronts him as he bursts free of the trees at last. It is a cabin, the kind of slope-roofed box hunters use to insure they're in proper position as the sun is on the rise. The entire structure sits a foot or so off the ground, raised by concrete blocks to discourage pests and keep seasonal flood-water out. Its walls are maybe ten feet to a side; the largest one holds a wide window. To the left of the window a door hangs open.

Gun in front of him, the Police Chief circles the back of the cabin. It wouldn't do for the killer to slip out a back door while the Police Chief frets a possible ambush at the front. A quick duck to the ground to glance up under the cabin confirms the front door as the only entrance. The Police Chief pauses his survey as he approaches the front wall and its large window. No doubt the killer can hear him rustling the leaves out here, but sound can play tricks on you; no need to assist the man with a clear view of him. Stepping close to the cabin, the Police Chief lowers himself and eases around it, well below the bottom of the window. In front of him, the open door blocks his view of the cabin's interior. The Police Chief has a vision of the killer standing in the doorway, a loaded shotgun in his hands. Or worse, a bomb, something that will reduce the two of them to burnt blood and carbon.

Never mind, he thinks as he creeps around the door. As long as the killing stops, never mind.

A glance shows the doorway empty, the edge of what might be a couch on the right. The Police Chief's best guess: the killer is hiding behind the couch, using it for cover. The Police Chief is reasonably certain his gun will find that couch little of an obstacle. He releases the safety, clears the door. In the floor, gun to the right. On the count of three. THREE!

12. Six Drawings Hung in a Coffeehouse

At last, the height of the Revel, the moment the characters gather to enact the story's culmination. Here exposition, explanation, digression, flashback, analysis, have ceased their usefulness; here we have reached the point of the pure image. How many such images does it take to convey a story's climactic actions? Two, four? How about six?

You may want to imagine these as large drawings, each one done on paper eleven inches wide by fourteen inches long. They're mounted on black cardboard that presumably intends to frame them, but each one has been placed slightly askew—apparently in error, since the misplacement adds nothing to each picture—and it's hard not to be annoyed by this. The pictures have been executed in pencil traced with pen and ink, colored in places with dabs of watercolor. Their style: if you know about such things, you will recognize the debt they owe to the early work of Bernie Wrightson, who illustrated the original *Swamp Thing* comic books; the figures display the same rubbery fleshiness that distinguishes Wrightson's drawing from this time, the same feeling of texture.

This is not the kind of display you are likely to find in your local museum, unless you live near one of those institutions that prides itself on surfing the cutting edge. You are more likely to encounter these images at your neighborhood coffee shop, whether corporate or independent, alongside samples of other local art. To see them—to study them—you will have to lean over other patrons at their undersized tables, drawing the irritated glances of couples clasping hands over their lattes, businessmen flourishing their copies of the *Wall Street Journal* like personal banners. Ignore them.

In the first drawing, Barbara Dinasha, her back to you, stands in front of an unfinished wooden table at which sits a man with the head of a beast. She is wearing a long-sleeved nightdress that descends past her knees; the man has on a soiled black suit and a white dress shirt whose top button is open. Although Barbara's face is not visible, the stiffness of her back, her arms close to her sides, indicate tension; while his face is visible, it is harder to read the expression on the man's animal features, which could be described as those of a wolf but which also suggest both a bull and a goat. Barbara's peach nightdress commands the center of the picture; to either side of the beast-headed man, blue-white semi-abstractions suggest open mouths.

The second drawing shows a hand cradling an apple. Its fingers are slender, their joints slightly enlarged, the thick nails that end them jagged, dirty. Fine hair covers the skin, thickens toward the wrist that extends from a white cuff. The apple is the apotheosis of the fruit: large, perfectly proportioned, its skin shining. The reflection of Barbara Dinasha's face curves over the right side of the apple, foreshortened and distorted by the angle from which the artist has chosen to portray it, but the expression on her features appears to hover somewhere between horror and surprise. Dull yellow, the fingernails are the only color in this piece.

For the third drawing, the artist has turned the paper lengthwise. The Police Chief, in profile from the waist up, is at the left hand edge of the picture. Together, his gun at hip level, his left hand outstretched, his eyes narrowed, suggest a man walking in little light. Behind him runs a wooden wall, the swirling grain of which composes figures twisting upwards, their mouths exaggerated screams. On the wall, a line of trees has been graffitied. Tall, thin, their branches bare, they would be easy to confuse with the writhing forms were it not for the fact that they have been painted. Gray, white, and black, they seem to recede into the paper.

Also done lengthwise, the fourth drawing is the most involved; perhaps this is why the artist has chosen to leave it in black and white. Set in the same space as the first, its left side is taken up by the man with the beast's head. He is in motion, his left leg up and bent, his left foot on the wooden table, his arms out and slightly forward. His suit strains against his arms, his legs. Its fabric looks more ragged, worn, almost hairy. Lips peeled back from a forest of curved fangs, the beast mouth is open in a snarl you can almost hear. Above, behind the man, the air is turbulent, a chaos of swirls, as if full of something that is expressing itself through this figure. In the center of the picture, Barbara Dinasha is diving to the floor, her eyes shut, her mouth taut, her hands over her head. It is as if she is trying to leap free of the scene in which she has found herself. The picture's right shows the Police Chief, his right arm straight out, braced with his left, his index finger already tightened on the trigger of his gun, which is just about to erupt with fire and noise. Lips drawn back from his teeth, the Police Chief's face is bright with rage. Above, behind him, the air is still, empty.

A single color, a deep, almost luminous red, splashes across the fifth drawing as if some terrific act of violence has burst across it. It's blood, an explosion of it, on the left side of which is the right shoulder of the man with the beast's head, and on the right side of which is the top of his right arm. His back is to you, the coat that looks even more rough, hairy, pierced by three holes surrounded by starbursts of blood. The beast head is thrown back, the eye you can see wide with pain, the mouth gasping at the wound being done to it. Behind him, the Police Chief leans forward and to his left, the pose of a man putting all his force into a throw. His eyes are shaded by the brim of his hat, but his mouth is open, his teeth clenched. Study the drawing and you will discern the fingers of his right hand gripping the right hand of the man with the beast's head.

Drawn from the floor of this space looking up, the final picture shows Barbara Dinasha to the left, leaning against the unfinished wooden table with her right arm. Her nightgown, her hair, are wet with blood. She is not looking at the Police Chief, who stands on the right, bent slightly at the waist, still holding the hand of the man with the beast's head's right arm, the torn end of which rests in a pool of blood on the floor. The arm is sinewy, covered in thick, coarse hair. The Police Chief's uniform is also stained with blood. His eyes do not register Barbara; like hers, they are focused on the object in the drawing's foreground, in its left-hand corner: an apple, only the right side of which is in view. It is impossible to tell whether the apple's skin is undisturbed, or if the white of its flesh shows through a bite. The artist has painted the apple pale green-going-to-red, but that isn't what causes you to linger on this drawing, ignoring the customers shaking their newspapers at you, edging past you with weighted *Excuse me*s—no, it's the reflection the artist has suggested on the apple's shining skin. It's you.

At first, you aren't sure—actually, you are sure, almost before you realize what you're seeing, but there's no way it could be you, is there? A double-check of the artist's name confirms that you do not know him. Yet there you are; it isn't some quality of the paint making it a mirror. You're in there with Barbara and the Police Chief. And the man with the beast's head, too: he must be in there, even though you can't see him. Well, his body must be. The expression on your face is difficult to read. Is it curiosity? Eagerness? Hunger?

June, 1987. Hitchhiking. Mr. Norris.

Once, when he was eight, Laird had asked his father about hitchhiking.

"Boy," his father had said to him, "you do not hitchhike."

"You did," he'd answered.

"Times were different, then. Now . . ."

"What if I don't have a choice? What if it's an emergency?"

"You can call for help on the radio."

"What if the radio's broken?"

"Holmes's cabin's four miles due east. You should be able to make that in half an hour, easy."

"You have to cross the river to get there. What if it's flooded?"

His father had sighed, deeply, and the boy had felt the first stirrings of nervousness. "Why can't you let this be?"

He'd looked away. "I just want to know. In case there's an emergency."

After a moment during which he could feel the weight of his father's gaze resting on him, the old man had said, "All right. If the radio's broken, and the river's in flood, and whatever else I can't imagine has left you with no choice but to hitchhike, then you wait and you watch. You pick a car with a family in it, a dad, a mom, couple of kids. You should be okay that way. You do not wave at a police car; you see a police car coming, you walk along like you're on a Sunday stroll. And you do not, you absolutely do not, flag down a car or a truck with a single driver. No way, uh-uh. You're better off staying with whatever disaster it is than getting in a car with some strange guy."

He'd wanted to ask his father why he had to avoid solo drivers, what was so bad about them, but he'd sensed his father at the end of his patience, and had let the question go unasked.

Now, nine years later, his head still spinning from whatever had been in the cloth Mr. Norris had pressed to his face, his arms and legs useless, Laird thought, *Right you were, Dad.*

Ten feet in front of him, the man who had offered him a ride on the outskirts of Big Delta had the trunk of his car propped open and was bent over inside it. To either side of him within the gaping space, Laird could see what looked like bricks, stacked in rough mounds. Ballast, he supposed, for bad weather; a car as old as this one would need all the help it could get once the weather soured. His worn tweed jacket riding up the back of his white shirt, Mr. Norris stretched for something deep in the trunk. He was whistling: "I'm On the Top of the World." Head still down, he withdrew a pair of squat candles, one of which he set on each of the brick mounds.

Pretty much the moment the car door had slammed shut, Mr. Norris had offered one soft hand in welcome and declared himself an accountant, retired early to see these grand United States while he was still able to enjoy them. Never settled down, Mr. Norris had continued while his cathedral of a car had rolled along the Alaska Highway. Just . . . never happened. Used to think it was a failing on his part, but now that he'd left his job behind, there was no one holding him back, no one telling him he couldn't drive cross country if that was what he felt like doing for the next year. He'd gone on like that for a while, describing the spots he'd visited in the bland enthusiasm of a travel brochure: the White House, the St. Louis Arch, the Grand Canyon. The man hadn't seemed an accountant; he'd projected none of the crispness, the precision you would expect from someone who'd spent his adult years managing people's money. His threadbare tweed jacket, his wrinkled shirt and trousers, had marked him as a member of a less prestigious profession, an assistant manager who'd never advanced. Even the itinerary that had continued to spill out of his mouth had sounded forced—rehearsed, lines in a monologue he'd written for himself. If a little peculiar, Laird had judged it none of his business. Plenty of people came to Alaska looking to reinvent themselves, leave the calamities of their old lives behind and become something else, something new. So Mr. Norris wanted to be a retired accountant: let him be a retired accountant.

He'd seen the white handkerchief in the man's right hand, but hadn't registered it as a threat. The recitation of place names pouring out of Mr. Norris's mouth had numbed him, somehow, so that even when the cloth had pressed against his nose and mouth, it had taken him an almost shocking amount of time to process what was happening, and then it had been too late.

There was a couple hundred dollars in his bag, the proceeds of a month's assorted odd jobs for an old woman whose cataracted sight had contracted her world to the first floor of her bungalow. Laird hoped that might be enough for Mr. Norris, but he doubted it. When the man withdrew from the trunk of his car and turned to him, the roll of duct tape in his left hand and the length of knife in his right confirmed that doubt.

Laird had his own blade tucked down the back of his jeans, a KA-BAR he'd bought off an old trucker in his cups who claimed it had seen him safely out of the Chosin Reservoir. As yet, Mr. Norris had not discovered it, but if he intended to truss Laird up (and especially if he had any designs on, say, removing Laird's jeans), then he'd find the knife and that would be that. The adrenaline surging through his blood felt as if it were burning up whatever had soaked that handkerchief, but not fast enough. There was no point in calling for help: for one thing, his tongue was as sluggish as the rest of him; for another, the evergreens clustered around them were a clear indication Mr. Norris had left the highway in favor of a more secluded location. He waited until Mr. Norris was crossing the distance between them to say, "Wait."

The man had not realized he'd regained consciousness. His whistle died on his lips, and he stopped in his tracks, which put him slightly beyond the reach of Laird's right boot. His brows lowered in consternation.

"If it's money . . ." Laird started.

"It isn't money," the man said.

"You can't—"

"Oh yes I can," Mr. Norris said; although his words lacked the confidence it would have required to make them sound truly threatening. However many times he'd done this before, Laird guessed, his victims had been unconscious. He said, "Why?"

"You wouldn't—"

"Does it have to do with that?" He shook his head at the trunk, its brick piles with their candles.

The look that passed over Mr. Norris's face was equal parts fear and admiration. "Maybe you would understand," he said. "Although," he added through a half-laugh, "I'm not sure I do." He lowered himself into a crouch. "This car," he said, "it's not a car. Well, of course it is, but it's also something else. It's an instrument, like a pen. Yes, a pen. The earth is its paper. I'm using it—I'm like the hand that uses it to write a sentence. Only, in this case, it's not so much a sentence I'm writing as a word—a kind of word—a word that's also a hole in the paper—and what comes through the hole. I know, it's all very confusing.

"Anyhow, a pen needs ink, or what good is it? A pen that's doing this kind of work requires special ink. I don't suppose I have to tell you what that is, do I?"

Laird said nothing.

"I didn't think so," Mr. Norris said. "What I've done is, I've tinkered with the floor of the trunk, so that, once I have a fresh source of ink in there, and I've made the requisite . . . openings, the ink can spill out in a uniform stream that's fine enough not to attract the notice of any of the authorities. You would be amazed at how far I can travel, how much penmanship I can complete, before I have to stop and look for a new source.

"I'll tell you one more thing, and then I'm going to have to resume my work. *I'm very close to being done.* I'm not sure if you'll be quite enough for what remains, but I can't imagine I'll need even all of another young man or woman after you. I can't tell you . . . Can you feel it?" Mr. Norris swept his arms around him, almost upsetting his balance. "I'm no longer alone; I haven't been for some time, now. The Word's attendants, its supplicants . . . As I've drawn nearer to the end of my task, I've had glimpses of them—not enough to say what I've seen with any certainty, just that they're present, all around me."

As if in reply, the branches of the evergreens around them clashed in a sudden breeze, and Laird thought the spaces between them darkened. There wasn't time to worry about that, though; if he were going to make a move, this was the time. He concentrated on his right foot, on throwing himself forward and lashing out as hard as he could, connecting the toe of his workboot with Mr. Norris's face, or, better, his throat. He didn't see much point to a prayer, so he went ahead with the kick.

His leg failed him. Instead of crushing Mr. Norris's nose or collapsing his windpipe, it made it no higher than his left knee. The man yelped and, his eyes wide with shock and pain, toppled onto his ass. Forcing himself to move, Laird turned on his side, grabbing for the KA-BAR and catching its hilt on the first try. He rolled back, bringing the knife up to meet what he was sure would be the downward stroke of Mr. Norris's blade, but the man had dropped his knife and was struggling to his feet. The roll of tape was still in his other hand. Laird lunged for him, but his legs hadn't regained sufficient strength, and he fell, slashing wildly as he went. He heard a scream, then was on his face. The scream continued as he strained to push himself to his feet. Finally, he had to settle for flipping himself onto his back, the knife up in the best guard he could manage.

He need not have worried. Mr. Norris was on his knees in front of the open trunk. The backs of his trousers, the skin and meat beneath them, had been sliced open, skin and fabric bright with blood. Laird's swipe had hamstrung him. He supposed he was not out of danger, yet, but he found the continuous scream climbing from the man's mouth oddly reassuring.

By the time his legs were steady enough to stand on, Mr. Norris's scream had faded to a drone. He'd wiped the KA-BAR clean on the grass; now, the knife held point up in front of him, Laird circled around Mr. Norris until he came to the front passenger door. It was open. He reached in for his bag and saw as he did so that the key was still in the ignition. For half an instant, he contemplated taking the car, before rejecting the idea. That was what he needed, to be pulled over driving a stolen car whose trunk was a forensic scientist's nightmare of swirled bloodstains. Even had he been willing to chance it, his gorge rose at the prospect of sitting surrounded by this thing, this rolling abattoir.

That left the question of what to do with Mr. Norris. Ten minutes ago, fighting for his life, he would have had no trouble opening the man from nave to chops with his knife. The battle over, though, the man bested, crippled, killing him became a more problematic affair. Not that Laird saw anything wrong in dragging the KA-BAR across Mr. Norris's throat, but he might be able to provide the police with information about the people he'd bled to death in the trunk of his car, and that might mean something to family members still hoping for news of their son or daughter. The man had not changed his position; afraid, no doubt, of further pain; and Laird did not figure him for much of a flight risk. All the same, he dipped back into the car, shoved his knife among the wires tangled under the steering wheel, and did what damage he could.

A single path, more an indentation in the underbrush, led out of the clearing. The sun hadn't moved too much in the sky, so he probably wasn't that far a walk from Big Delta. Maintaining a wide space between himself and the back of the car, Laird made for the exit. He did not hold his knife at the ready, but neither did he return it to its place under the back of his jeans.

As he passed the trunk, Mr. Norris stopped moaning. The KA-BAR raised, Laird stopped and turned to him. The man's face was white as flour. "Where are you going?" he said.

"Back to Big Delta."

"You can't do that! You can't leave me here!"

"Don't worry, you're not gonna bleed to death. Not before the cops get here, at least. It doesn't look like I hit any arteries."

"That's—they're coming! Do you understand me? They're coming!"

"I know: I'm going to fetch them."

"Not the police, you stupid hick. The attendants. The supplicants. They're all around us, and they won't be able to resist the blood . . ."

Laird had some smart reply ready for the man, but movement on the far side of the car stilled his tongue. He looked in that direction, toward where the evergreens were thickest, where it was darker than it should have been this time in the afternoon. The trees shifted with a breeze he didn't feel, and then he saw it wasn't the trees moving, it was what was between the trees, the tall, spindly things he had mistaken for their shadows. For a moment, he watched them stepping forward, raising legs that were much too thin too high, a comedian's parody of walking quietly, and then he was running as fast as he could in the other direction, out of the clearing along the path that wound across a great meadow.

He tripped, caught his foot, and went into a forward roll from which he emerged up and running. Somewhere behind him, he was aware of a terrible sound, but he did not let that stop him. His chest was a bellows full of white-hot air. His arms and legs were knots of pain. He kept running until he reached the highway, until he was nearly run down by a UPS driver. He took the ride the man offered him and did not once look back at the way he'd come.

He did not tell anyone about Mr. Norris, or any of it.

Mother of Stone

I

No one who was present for any of it will say much, at least, not over the phone. In some cases, this appears due to embarrassment at the nature of the events, not to mention concern over their possible effects on business. One or two show what might be genuine unease, even fear, but it is difficult to judge their authenticity. They might be playing their parts as they feel the rumors demand. The Episcopal priest seems genuinely confused by her share of the narrative, but Episcopalians aren't much for clarity in these kinds of matters, are they?

Lawrence Schmidt, now the Wynkoop Inn's sole owner and proprietor, fails to answer two weeks' worth of e-mail and, when you finally have him on your cell, balks at saying more than that, while he was deeply saddened by Mrs. Torino's death, he doesn't feel it appropriate to indulge any of the . . . *gossip* that has accumulated around that terrible event. When you ask if this means that there was nothing out of the ordinary, unusual, in the weeks leading up to the car accident that decapitated nine-months' pregnant Rachel Torino—nothing related to a statue that had been unearthed on the Inn's grounds earlier that month—Lawrence answers that those are exactly the kinds of rumors he has no desire to feed. Your question about what is supposed to have taken place afterwards—you can think of no other word to describe it than the exorcism, or attempted exorcism, of that statue—provokes the man to something like anger. What is it you think you're playing at? he demands. He thought you said you were a college professor, a scholar, not a staff writer for the *Weekly World News*. Although you assure him of the legitimacy of your intentions and your credentials, it is obvious the conversation has reached its terminus. There seems little point in asking about Margaret Garrick, his former business partner, who dropped out of sight immediately after the accident and has not been seen since, so you thank Lawrence for his time.

Yvonne Fisher, who was a waitress in the Inn's dining room, hangs up on you before you have finished explaining the reason for your call. Unsure if the disconnection was deliberate, you redial her number, only to have her Fuck Off confirm that she did hang up on you in the first place. Christina Henderson, another waitress, at least hears you out, but insists that she will not discuss anything over the phone. If you're in the neighborhood, get in touch and she'll see. As for the Reverend Maria Au Claire: once the parish secretary puts your second call to her through, the Episcopal priest spends most of her time parsing her words. Yes, there was an . . . she supposes you could call it an event some years ago. No, she wouldn't describe it as super-natural so much as preternatural; though she's open to the possibility it was some variety of mass hysteria. That said, *something* happened. For all the attention she devotes to worrying over her language, the Rever-end conveys very little in the way of actual information and concludes the conversation by stating that she has an appointment waiting. No, she answers, she won't talk to you again on the phone.

Your attempts at discussing the circumstances surrounding Rachel Torino's death with those who reported it for the local newspapers fare little better. Naomi Glass, who covered the accident for the *Wilt-wyck Daily Freeman,* claims no awareness, let alone knowledge, of the kind of events to which you allude, and, she assures you, she's always kept her ear pretty close to the ground. Nor can Jacqueline Pitlor, who writes for the *Middletown Times-Herald Record,* or Heidi Lima, of the *Poughkeepsie Journal,* add anything definitive to what they already have written; although Heidi Lima is willing to share a rumor—off the re-cord, of course—that the reason for Margaret Garrick's disappearance is that, shortly after the accident, she suffered a complete breakdown, which necessitated her immediate and continuing hospitalization. Pretty Gothic, she says, wouldn't you agree?

II

If you are to research the relation between the online stories about the statue that was excavated and put on display at the Wynkoop Inn and actual events, a discussion of which will form a chapter in the book you have proposed on Internet narratives (what you have christened electronic folklore)—in which one academic press has expressed qualified interest—it would appear you will have to leave your apartment in Garden City, rent the least-expensive car available, and drive two hours north, to Ulster County. While no doubt booking a room at the Inn for a couple of nights would be useful, the weight of such an accommodation is more than your strongest credit card can support, so instead you arrange to stay at the Great Republic Motel, whose website promises lodgings as grand as its name at a price you can afford. To stretch your budget as far as you can, you reserve for a Tuesday, because although fall has only just started to siphon the green from the leaves, the weekends already see an upturn in residents of the City seeking their Autumn Experience, and the motel's Friday-through-Monday rates reflect this.

You pass the five days before you depart finishing the latest grading for the five sections of Freshman Writing you are dragging through the process of writing a research paper. The focus of your classes is Haunting and Possession, which you had thought would be entertaining enough for both the students and you, but by the fiftieth essay discussing the film adaptation of *The Exorcist* as an expression of parental anxieties over rebellious children, even the prospect of researching an actual instance of the ritual has lost some of its appeal. However, the tenure your book will earn you is sufficient to seat you at your computer after the day's comments have been delivered, sifting the online archives of the *Wiltwyck Daily Freeman,* the *Middletown Times-Herald Record,* and the *Poughkeepsie Journal* for further information on the car accident that occurred on Main Street of the town of Stonington ten years ago, in 1998. (You had just completed your doctoral coursework at Tufts and were putting together a committee for your dissertation. While fraying at the edges, the pattern at the center of your marriage was still recognizable.) The Middletown paper's coverage was most extensive, with one day's article addressing the accident, the next day's the life of Rachel Torino. From this second article, you learn that Rachel Torino, née Follet, was a graduate of SUNY Huguenot, a returning student who had recently completed her degree in elementary education. You also learn that her husband, James, emerged unscathed from the crash that claimed his wife. A photograph of the couple accompanies the second piece. It shows a short woman with long hair and long bangs smiling widely as she wraps her arms around a man with a broad chest and short, curly hair. Perhaps because it is late and you are tired, you weigh contacting James Torino, e-mailing or phoning him, before rejecting the idea as too much. Even academic research should know some kind of ethical boundaries. You print the photo of the Torinos and slip it into the manila folder in which you keep material relevant to this chapter.

III

On a bright Tuesday morning in early October, you take the train to the rental place, hand your credit card to a young woman with a high ponytail and square glasses whom you almost recognize as a former student, sign and initial the rental agreement in a half-dozen places, and receive the keys to your car. It is a GEO Metro that shade of teal that was popular in the early nineteen-nineties. The sight of it prompts an unexpected spasm of nostalgia in the pit of your stomach. For the first half of 2007, the last great love of your life drove a car like this from Baltimore to Garden City and back again on I-95. You place your overnight bag in the nominal back seat, your briefcase in the front passenger seat, and slot the key in the ignition.

Your trip across town to pick up I-87 goes faster than you had anticipated, and before long you have crossed the Hudson and are speeding through the hills and mountains that shoulder up north of the City. It never has ceased to amaze you that such apparent wilderness, such remoteness and solitude, exist so close to New York's concrete and steel regularity. As you maneuver the Metro around the high mass of one eighteen-wheeler after another, you recall your first trip to the Hudson Valley. Reassuring yourself that it was only for a year or two, until a better job appeared, you had accepted the position at Queens Community College and immediately been deluged with the preparations for five classes, not to mention arranging the move from Boston to New York. Your marriage was . . . by then, it was beyond frayed; it was almost completely undone. During a weekend conference in Quebec City, you had spent the night with a graduate student from Oxford, and although the two of you had not actually had sex, it was a sufficient betrayal for you to feel the need to confess it to your husband upon your return. He had no equivalent trespass with which to wound you, though he angrily declared that he had visited the local strip club twice. That he would accompany you out of Boston was a matter of some doubt. However, when the time came for you to travel to New York to survey prospective apartments, he surprised you by suggesting he could join you, share the driving. (You had your own car, then, a battered Honda Civic.) As it turned out, he drove all the way there and all the way back. You filled two frantic days crisscrossing the City, viewing a total of nineteen apartments. At the beginning of the third day, you selected the place in Garden City, which, though a fifth-floor walk-up, offered more space for (slightly) less money. Your husband appeared happy with the choice—with everything; indeed, it was his suggestion that the two of you take a drive, do a bit of exploring, which led you along the Hudson past Peekskill, to the town of Garrison, across the river from West Point's gray walls. You shared a late lunch at a café and passed a pleasant hour walking the town's sidewalks before returning to the car to head for Boston. Those three days had been lighter than any in your recent past, as if the burden of your combined missteps had been, not so much lifted as shifted, set to the side; although you did not subscribe to any belief in the magical power of a change of scene, as the two of you sped east that night you wondered if perhaps a new place might mean a new chance. For a few days after you were back in Boston, that seemed the case. When your husband proposed that he remain in the old apartment after you had started your new job—in hopes of receiving a better offer for it than you so far had—the idea had sounded reasonable, even responsible. No doubt your suspicions should have been raised by his insistence that you move only your things; though on your more generous days, of which this is one, you can almost credit his motivation as (mostly) practical.

In the years since your marriage's unraveling, you have ventured the Hudson Valley a handful of times, usually in the company of your present lover. Once you rode the Trailways bus to Huguenot—whose exit you must take and which is suddenly ahead on the right—for a conference at the SUNY campus there. In a classroom whose five beige walls were each a different length, you delivered a paper on Sara Gran's *Come Closer* to an audience of two undergraduates and one of the conference organizers. Afterwards, you spent a couple of hours at one of the local bars in conversation with a writer whose name you cannot remember about the role of horror stories in contemporary culture. You promised to look up his books as soon as you returned home. You did not.

Traffic on Huguenot's Main Street is light. After having kept the speedometer just shy of eighty for the last two hours, you have to concentrate on driving in what feels like slow motion. As far as you can remember, with the exception of a few cosmetic changes, such as a new Japanese noodle restaurant, the town is roughly the same as it was during your last visit, two years ago. You pass through Huguenot quickly and, within the space of another twenty-five minutes spent driving over the ridge that defines the horizon behind the town, are on Route 209 heading into Stonington.

IV

Of course you've seen pictures of the Wynkoop Inn online: you've printed a quartet of the best ones, studied them. But the image of a thing is no substitute for the thing itself, and as you pass the Inn on your right your foot relaxes on the gas. Set at the top of a slight rise, the building is a stone box whose size recalls its previous life as a mansion. Its front is traversed by a shallow porch upon which a pair of rocking chairs guards a large wooden door. To either side, a trio of windows flanks the door. Above the porch, a half-dozen dormer windows protrude from the great slope of the Dutch roof. Red, yellow, and white flowers fill spiral beds on the front lawn.

Rachel Torino must have died right around where you are now. Gooseflesh raises the skin on your forearms—an adolescent response, surely, yet there is a second when you can almost hear the scream of tires losing their grip on the road. A honk from the car behind you hurries you forward.

V

To reach the Grand Republic Motel, you turn left at the major intersection in the center of Stonington. In the near distance, the Catskills rise rounded. The motel is a mile along on the right, its white strip of rooms bordered by green pastures from which chocolate brown cows watch you steer into the parking lot. A short, plump woman whose head is capped by tight, metallic curls takes her time checking you in, peppering the process with questions about you, the reasons for your trip. Although you can't help feeling you're trending toward paranoia, you lie, telling her you're a writer taking a few days off from your latest novel. When this prompts the woman to proclaim herself a great reader, and ask what you write, you gamble on horror fiction, which pays off in the distaste that curdles her expression. Before you can stop yourself, you say that your current project concerns a young academic who visits a small town to investigate reports of an evil statue. Either the woman has no idea what you are referring to or she is remarkably self-controlled—an interpretation of the blankness of her features that seems to take your paranoia into the realm of outright mental illness. You thank her, collect your key and the guide to the region she offers you, and exit her office.

The room you have reserved is clean, the double bed inviting after the drive up, which has left you more drained than you anticipated, your shoulders and neck tight with fatigue. However, the clock is ticking, so you settle for a quick wash and head out. You noticed a bagel place at the turn-off for the motel, to which you go for a plain bagel with tuna salad and a review of the circumstances surrounding the unearthing of the mysterious statue.

VI

That said statue was dug up near the Inn's north wall, no one disputes. Work was under way to expand the Inn's outdoor facilities; the plan was for a side exit that would open to a large patio area suitable for wedding receptions and similar occasions. The soil in this region is notoriously damp, a consequence of its high clay content. This complicated the use of the generous lawn around the Inn. A patio, while not as lovely as manicured green grass, was judged a necessary evil. After marking off the area with Margaret Garrick, who appears to have been in charge of such matters, the groundskeeper set to work with his shovel.

This man, Stephen Holland, is still employed tending the Inn's grounds. You find him in one of the outbuildings behind the Inn, wiping the grass shavings from a riding mower. His sweeping gut, the collar of flesh under his chin, give the impression that his size is all surplus, yet the breadth of his shoulders, the thickness of his biceps, his forearms, indicate that there is more substance to him. In a voice whose accent draws a line between him and the south shore of Long Island, he asks, Something I can help you with? when his eye catches you standing in the doorway.

There is no evading it: you must tell him the reason you have parked the Metro in the small lot beside the Inn and walked back here. You say that you are researching the statue that was excavated on the Inn's grounds in 1998. Lawrence Schmidt has refused to talk to you, and you've been unable to locate Margaret Garrick, so that's brought you to Stephen, who you understand held the actual shovel.

You a reporter? Stephen Holland asks.

Professor, you say, assistant professor in the English department at Queens Community College.

That so? What do you teach?

Freshman writing, mostly, although you get to teach a class in myth and folklore, which is your specialty.

Is that why you're interested in the statue, some kind of modern myth thing?

Actually, yes, you say, unable to keep the surprise from your voice. You're working on a book on Internet narratives—on what you're calling electronic folklore. These are stories you find online that purport to be true but often wander a considerable distance from their source material. A lot of the time, these stories wind up adapting elements of other popular narratives.

Uh huh. This one's what? *The Exorcist?*

You nod. The escalating events, the pair of clergy called in to deal with the matter . . .

One hand rubbing his beard, Stephen Holland studies you, then says, All right. If you can keep up with him as he performs his duties, he'll answer your questions. There's only one thing he won't talk about, and that's what happened to Mrs. Garrick. She was the one who hired him when he first came up here, thirty years ago, took a chance on him, and she always did right by him. He figures he owes her that much.

Of course, you say. Would he mind telling you about unearthing the statue? Does he remember the details?

Sure, he says, he remembers that. He removes a rake from the wall to his left and walks out of the shed. You follow him. He'd spent the early part of the morning drive a shovel into ground that was thick as a fuckin brick. Already, he was regretting telling Mrs. Garrick that they didn't need to hire a backhoe, he'd have the place cleared out in a day. It had rained the previous day—thunder and lightning, torrential rain—and the soil was saturated, a goddam swamp. There were clouds of mosquitoes the size of fuckin vampire bats; his arms looked like he had the chicken pox. He was digging next to the Inn, because he thought that maybe the soil might be a little less dense over there, which it seemed like it was, and then the shovel hit something.

Right from the start, Stephen states, he knew it wasn't just a rock. He has stopped at the rear of the lawn, where grass surrenders to trees. He turns the rake over and begins to gather the grass he has mown. Usually, he says, there's a machine that does this—you know, an attachment for the tractor. Like a big garbage bag.

You nod. What happened to it?

It broke, Stephen says, and he hasn't gotten around to fixing it, yet. It's all right: in case you haven't noticed—he slaps his expansive gut—he kind of needs the exercise.

You smile.

Okay, he says, where was he?

The statue—

Yeah. The sound was all wrong for a rock—more high-pitched, almost grainy, if you get what he means. He withdrew the shovel and slid it into the soil slowly, even gently. There was something there, all right, and as he repeated his searching, he saw that whatever was buried there was a good couple-three feet at least. Margaret saw what he was up to and came out to ask him what was going on. He told her he'd hit something under the ground. Like a pipe? she asked. Uh-uh, he said. I think maybe it's a statue.

Isn't that funny? Stephen says. It could've been a pipe, some kind of ceramic, or it could've been part of an old building, or something left over from the Inn's past, of which there's more than enough, but no, he was pretty sure it was a statue.

Margaret Garrick fetched a shovel from the shed and started to help him—whatever else you could say about her, she was always willing to pitch in and lend a hand. Together, they dug around the object's margins, then, at Margaret's suggestion, they traded their shovels for garden trowels and spent the next hour clearing thick earth from what was, in fact, a statue. When Stephen realized what it portrayed, he took a step back and, although he hadn't seen the inside of a church since his confirmation, crossed himself. Not irreverently, he said, Jesus Christ. Mrs. Garrick's response was more measured: she sat back on her heels, resting her elbows on her knees, and said, Hmmmm.

VII

The expression on Stephen Holland's face says that his memory of the statue is undimmed. In answer to your question, he says that he doesn't have any photos of the thing. At the request of Reverend Au Claire, any and all pictures of it in the Inn's possession were gathered and burned. There had been plans to include a photo of the statue in the new brochure for the Inn, but the brochure had not progressed beyond the draft stage, and those drafts were consigned to the fire that Stephen lit in one of the stone barbecues behind the Inn.

You have searched online, but the most that has turned up is a series of images posted in early 2007 of figures excavated on the Greek island of Keros. Forty-five hundred years old, the apparent products of the Cycladic culture that preceded Hellenic civilization, these statues are starkly geometric, inverted triangles with undersized circles for heads. Bulges midway down their fronts apparently represent pregnancy; the archeologists who unearthed these figures speculate that they are images of the mother-goddess whose worship was supplanted by that of Zeus and his offspring. Every single one of the statues excavated was broken, possibly as a gesture of contempt by adherents of the newer gods.

The simple abstraction of the Keros statues suggests the contemporary as much as the ancient; in this regard, they are the opposite of the three feet of marble Stephen Holland and Margaret Garrick exposed. The sole surviving image of it—a color photograph paper-clipped to a manila envelope in the file cabinet of an art history professor you will visit shortly—shows a work whose realism of form and detail suggests the apex of the Classical Greeks, or of their Renaissance Italian children. The figure is that of a woman, her bare feet on a plain round base. She is wearing a long, sleeveless dress that suggests a toga but that would not look out of place against a number of backdrops. Her plump arms are bent at the elbows, her hands crossed over a belly that swells with a child ready to make its entry into the world. The piece is more than competently sculpted; there is a touch of real art in the stretch of the dress's fabric over the woman's midriff, the thickness of her ankles, the veins raised on the tops of her feet. It is that artistry that lends the statue's other detail so much power. It is headless, deliberately so: the neck shows a cross-section of bone, throat, muscle, blood vessels.

That fuckin thing, Stephen Holland says. Who the fuck carves a statue like that?

VIII

This same question occurred to Margaret Garrick, who, after helping Stephen to wrestle the sculpture out of its hole and hosing it clean of the remaining dirt, returned to her office at the rear of the Inn and phoned the art department at Penrose College, across the Hudson in Poughkeepsie. Margaret had met Janet Naida at the Stonington Library the previous winter, when the professor had given a talk on the significance of Stonington and its historic Main Street to the work of Annabel Ferris, a sculptor whose 1981 death in a car crash truncated a career of some promise. (Apparently, Ferris was decapitated just up the road from the spot where Rachel Torino died, a coincidence that makes the hairs on the back of your neck bristle.) According to Stephen, the professor drove over the next day and spent about an hour examining the statue—including, he says, photographing it—only to tell Margaret that a) it wasn't Annabel Ferris's work and b) she couldn't say whose work it was. He gathers that Professor Naida did some more digging, so to speak, after she left, but as far as he knows, she didn't find anything.

He has gathered the grass clippings into a sizable mound that he uses his rake to drive across the yard toward a plot of earth surrounded by a high fence—the vegetable garden, he explains. He'll add this to the compost.

Right, you say. Did he have anything more to do with the statue? Did he see anything?

Nah. Stephen shakes his head. He mounted it in the dining room—Mrs. Garrick was talking about bringing in a professional, but Stephen told her to save her money. It was a more complicated job than he'd anticipated—he swears, nothing connected to that fuckin thing was easy. He had his doubts about putting the statue where people were eating—really, is that what you want to look at while you're having your dinner? But Margaret insisted, the same way she insisted the thing had to go up in the northwest corner, even though the wall there was all pipe and wires. It turned what should have been an afternoon's job into a day and a half of running back and forth to the hardware store. He had to jury-rig this support . . . anyway, that was the extent of his involvement with the statue, until the very end, after that woman died. He was the one who took it down from the wall and drove it over to Holy Redeemer.

What was that like?

Weird. Stephen opens a gate at one end of the vegetable garden, sweeps the pile of cut grass onto a larger heap there.

You wait.

Stephen combs the grass over the compost. When he is satisfied, he closes the garden gate and sets off for the shed. Once he has hung the rake on the wall and washed and dried his hands and face in a small sink, he says, For a couple-three days, things around here had been *off.* He was friends with Julian, the chef—well, not exactly friends, the guy could be a real douche, but when a big delivery arrived for the kitchen, Stephen didn't mind helping him move things around, and sometimes he'd bum a cigarette off Julian—the point is, Julian had told him some crazy shit that was supposed to have happened with the statue.

What kind of stuff?

Bizarre stuff, Stephen says. You planning on talking to any of the girls who were working in the dining room?

Yes, you say, Christina Henderson.

Then she can tell you what she saw up close and personal, Stephen says. Suffice it to say, everyone was on edge. There was this feeling in the air—okay, don't go turning this into some kind of Psychic Friends bullshit, but it was like the air was—it was like you could almost hear something, or as if you'd just heard something, and your ears were still ringing with the sound.

What sound was that?

A scream, Stephen says, a woman's scream. And then the accident happened—Jesus, God. Mrs. Garrick was . . . It was Larry, actually, Larry Schmidt who sought him out to say they were sending the statue over to Holy Redeemer, and was there any way he could impose on Stephen . . . ?

What did he say?

He said sure, Stephen says.

Wasn't he nervous?

Not really, he says. Maybe a little. He isn't sure what he was. Freaked out, he supposes. It was like, first they'd found this fuckin statue, then all this weird shit happens, then this woman, this pregnant woman, winds up the same as the statue, and right in front of the Inn. Yeah, it was probably coincidence, or mass hysteria, or all of the above, but there are times when coincidence feels like something else, you know? As if you're seeing into the way the world really works, underneath all the science and logic and shit. Whatever—he was only too happy to take the statue someplace else. Hell, if Larry'd asked him to dump the thing in the Hudson, he'd have been happy to do so.

The Inn was pretty much deserted. After the strangeness of the last few days, the guests had decided to seek their accommodations elsewhere. The dining room was dark—with the police and firemen out front . . . there hadn't seemed much point in opening it. None of the girls had come in; Julian had been there for a little while, but he was long gone. Larry was at the front desk, but that was mostly because he didn't have anywhere else to be. He'd offered to help Stephen move the statue, but Stephen had declined. He could just imagine the damned thing dropping on Larry's foot.

There's something about a big empty space, Stephen says. It's not the same thing as being outside, in the middle of a field or something. You stand inside it, and you can feel it, the way it holds emptiness inside itself. Know what I mean?

Do you? You nod.

The statue was where it was supposed to be; there was nothing strange about it—beyond the obvious. Stephen had a hand truck with him. He wrestled the sculpture off its perch and lowered it onto the truck. The fuckin thing felt even heavier than it had when he'd hoisted it up there, but that was probably his imagination. Tore the hell out of his back, though. Would've given him the perfect excuse to drop the damned thing, smash it to pieces.

Why didn't he?

He shrugs. Larry had told him it was Margaret who wanted the statue moved to the church. So that was what he did. He carted it out of the Inn, loaded it onto his pickup—more trouble for his back—and drove it the mile and a half to Holy Redeemer. He didn't use Main Street: that wouldn't have been—that wouldn't have been right. Instead, he took the access road. If you drive along beside the outbuildings, you'll find an old road that cuts through the woods over to 213. It isn't more than a couple of ruts in the dirt; a good rain and it's a fuckin bog. That was the route Stephen chose. It's a short ride, he says, but it felt like a fuckin eternity. The moon was—it wasn't full, that would've been too much, but it wasn't far off, and the sky was full of clouds racing across it. One minute, the line of grass in front of him, the rows of trees to either side, would be lit white, the next, the whole scene would fade from view, until all that was left was the stretch of road picked out by his headlights. As the darkness thickened, he drove more slowly: because he was being cautious, he told himself, which was bullshit. He'd taken this road enough times and his truck was big enough that, if he'd wanted to race it, he could have, pitch-blackness or not. It was   clouds would slide off the moon, and the trees, the grass, would solidify around him, and it all looked different, the tree trunks covered in faces, the grass full of shadows that didn't belong to anything. He had this intense sensation of being watched, Stephen says. Even when his surroundings disappeared again, he could feel something, something keeping track of him. He was never so happy to see a church as he was when he finally pulled up in front of Holy Redeemer.

And? you ask. What happened next?

That's as much as he knows. He unloaded the statue, brought it into the basement, the what-do-you-call-it, undercroft, and that was him.

He hasn't heard anything?

He's heard a ton of shit, Stephen says, most of it exactly that, shit. You'll have to speak to Reverend Au Claire about what came next.

IX

Stephen Holland's refusal does not surprise you. You thank him for his time and help and ask if he would be willing to talk to you again, in case you need to check anything with him.

Yeah, sure, he says, and wishes you luck on the rest of your mission.

Back in the Metro, you scribble into your notebook for half an hour, until your hand has cramped with writing so much, so fast. (Why don't you use a tape recorder? your ex-husband once asked you, the question a guise for yet another accusation of your continuing unreasonableness. Though you knew the answer wouldn't matter, you said, Because some people hold back if they know they're being taped. Besides, I have a great memory.) Once the pain has lessened, you call information on your cell. Penrose College's main number brings you into contact with a pleasant woman who connects you to Professor Janet Naida's extension. You are expecting the professor's voicemail and have composed a brief message asking her to call you back, but Janet Naida herself answers the phone. You can imagine how you sound, tripping over your tongue, despite which, you manage to convey to Professor Naida that you are researching the statue about which Margaret Garrick called her ten years ago, and you were hoping you might speak to her about it. The professor sounds genuinely surprised by the subject of your call, and while she insists that she is extremely busy, consents to a brief interview—her word—in an hour and a half, between classes. Do you know where her office is?

You do not. To be honest, you're not sure what the best route to Penrose is.

Professor Naida provides you with detailed directions that take you from the Wynkoop Inn, over the Wiltwyck-Rhinecliff Bridge, and down the east shore of the Hudson with a minimum of difficulty; in fact, the most challenging part of your journey is navigating the parking lots of Penrose College in search of the strip of blacktop set aside for visitors. Your quest leads you among the college's Gothic-revival buildings, its wide green lawns, its students diligently dressed to deny their affluence, and though you know it should not, the sight of all this calls to mind the utilitarian box where you teach, low-budget construction pretending to be Frank Lloyd Wright, its cramped patches of grass, its students dressed to the aspirations pop culture has bestowed on them. The taste that fills your mouth grows more bitter as you walk the hall to Professor Naida's office, past flyers advertising lectures, concerts, readings. The professor answers her door, and the black pantsuit-pink blouse combination she is wearing—obviously purchased at one of the boutiques that dot the streets around Penrose—makes your own gray slacks and white blouse—on sale at J. C. Penney—seem like jeans and a T-shirt.

X

Professor Naida confines her blond hair in a tight bun whose severity is matched by the sharp lines of her high cheekbones and almost vulpine jaw. She welcomes you into her high-ceilinged office much as you expect she would a student come for a conference, directing you to a wooden chair while seating herself in a large leather armchair positioned beside the room's single tall window. To her right, a table that resembles an overly ambitious stool supports a hardcover copy of her book on Annabel Ferris (which, she tells you, was the principal source for the film starring Gwyneth Paltrow), and a small sculpture of the artist's head (which, she volunteers, is only a copy of the artist's last self-portrait; although, she adds, she saw and briefly held the original during her consultant work for the film).

After you have thanked her for agreeing to speak to you, but before you can pose your first question, Professor Naida declares that she should start by telling you that she does not know what artist carved the statue that was hauled out of the earth at the Wynkoop Inn. When she agreed to drive over to inspect the piece, she already was ninety-nine percent certain that it had nothing to do with Annabel Ferris. Anna, as the professor calls her, rarely worked at anything so (comparatively) large; though not strictly speaking a miniaturist, her preference was for the intimate. Her more substantial sculptures could be counted on one hand without need of all its digits, and since those pieces were accounted for, the chances of this new statue being a hitherto undocumented work were so slender as to be almost nil. But Anna had lived the last decade of her life less than a mile from the spot where the sculpture had been discovered, and almost nil was not the same as nil, and this was what put Professor Naida behind the wheel of her Saab for a trip across the river. She can't deny it: the professor hoped that she might be the one to identify a hitherto unknown piece by her favorite artist.

From the moment she saw it, though, Professor Naida knew the statue was not one of Anna's. To begin with, the technique was wrong. While Anna's style has been described as a return to realism, it is a realism that is very much aware of the abstract movements that preceded it. Anna was not afraid to bend in the direction of the abstract, the geometric, if doing so would strengthen the work at hand. In comparison, whoever had sculpted this statue acted as if the developments of the last hundred-plus years had not happened. It was the style of a good deal of religious, i.e. Catholic, work, in which the need for recognition of the figure being represented outweighs aesthetic considerations. Nonetheless, the professor must admit, the skill on display in this piece was of a higher level—a significantly higher level—than much of what you find in your local church.

Yes, she was disappointed; how could she not be? The more she studied the statue, the more the evidence that it was not Anna's work accumulated. In addition to the matter of style, there was that of subject. Anna favored representations of herself and, somewhat later, her infant son. While the last two of her larger sculptures were of herself in the closing months of pregnancy, they showed her dressed in sweatpants and a T-shirt, hair up, seated cross-legged in one, on a chair in the other. Anna's life frequently had been violent, starting with abuse at the hands of her father and continuing with abuse at the hands of her first agent/lover, but she kept her art free of it. When she entered the studio, Professor Naida says, Anna deliberately left that part of her life at the door. For her, art was a place of calm. That was absolutely essential to her vision. The kind of savagery you find in Margaret Garrick's statue is completely out of keeping with Anna's work. She will admit, though, to being struck by a coincidence: Anna's final series of self-portraits possess the approximate dimensions to have served as the sculpture's head. The angle at which she ended the neck of her second-to-last self-portrait is uncannily close to that of the statue.

But coincidence is not evidence of conspiracy. The final nail in the coffin, so to speak, was the statue's material. Throughout her life, Anna struggled for money; predictably, it wasn't until after her death that her art began to attract the kind of attention—critical and financial—that would have allowed her to sculpt with the quality of materials she longed for. The block of marble from which the headless pregnant woman was carved was about as fine a grade as you could buy; the professor is reasonably certain it's Parian marble, which comes from a Greek island and would have been hopelessly beyond Anna's budget.

Just to be sure, though, Professor Naida re-opened her archive of Anna's personal writing and searched for anything that might hint at a connection between her and the statue. There are large gaps in the record of Anna's life—especially when she was working, she tended to ignore her correspondence and skimp on her journal entries. This was the case at the time of her death, when she was engaged in her last series of self-portraits. A week before she was killed, Anna mentioned dreaming of the Mother, but it was common for her mother to appear in Anna's dreams, particularly when she was creating. Had Rodney Siece been alive, the professor might have contacted him—he was her second agent, and with her during the last days of her life. In fact, he was in the car with her when she was killed; he emerged from the accident unhurt. Unfortunately, Rodney was dead. After Anna's demise, Rodney, obviously traumatized by the experience, took to alcohol and Valium in generous doses. Within six months, he, too, was gone.

When you have the chance to ask Professor Naida if she has any thoughts, speculations, as to who might have been responsible for the statue, she shakes her head and admits that she investigated possible answers to that question. To reduce long days in the library to a single sentence, she learned nothing. None of Annabel Ferris's contemporaries who were associated with this part of New York—Brandner, Fox, Hall—had worked in this style, so the professor expanded her search, looking as far back as the eighteen-eighties, only to reach another dead end. While the area has seen more than its fair share of artists, some lifelong residents, others passing through, none produced anything remotely like this. For a short time, Professor Naida was intrigued by a minor detail from local history: during the nineteen-teens, when the Ashokan Reservoir was being constructed a few miles from the Inn, Italian stonemasons were brought in for some of the work on the dam and other structures. Apparently, the employment paid well, enough to afford a piece of fine marble, and if one of those workers had decided to settle in Stonington . . . The problem was, she could locate no record of any such figure, which you would assume there would have to have been had he turned out other pieces with the skill of this one. Apparently, though, whoever carved this statue laid down his hammer and chisel after completing it. Why he buried it next to the Inn, she cannot say. It strikes her as a gesture of renunciation, Prospero destroying his books.

While you are not certain what significance to ascribe to the statue's burying, the professor's interpretation immediately strikes you as wrong. You bury what is precious, treasure or the loved dead. You might consign to the earth that which you fear. If you are renouncing something, wouldn't you want the act to be more definitive? Wouldn't you smash the statue, make sure there was nothing left of it? However, you do not argue the point with Professor Naida, who has risen from her chair and turned to a file cabinet behind her. Apparently, your interview/lecture is done. Standing, you thank the professor for her time. She has withdrawn a manila folder from the drawer she has opened. Here, she says, she has something for you. She crosses the office, holding out the folder. A photograph has been paper-clipped to it. There is a color copy of the picture beneath it, to which the professor says you are welcome.

XI

Despite all the discussion that has been devoted to it, the mental image of it you have constructed, the sight of the actual statue startles you, causes you to breathe in sharply, as if you've stepped out into a sub-zero day with no jacket on. Thanking Professor Naida again, you slide the copy from under the original and insert it into your notebook, which feels heavier for the addition.

For a moment, you consider asking the professor if she has heard anything of the events subsequent to her visit. In her office, though, with its tall bookcases, its framed photographs of her with Gwyneth Paltrow, its arts-and-crafts desk, such questions seem glorified gossip. You thank Professor Naida a third time, and depart.

XII

Since you are on the other side of the Hudson, you flip through your notebook to Christina Henderson's number. Before you have finished re-introducing yourself to her, Christina says that she remembers you and yeah, she remembers she said she'd talk to you if you were around. She's at work—she manages a restaurant called Archipelago—but the doors won't open for a couple of hours, so if you can come right now, she supposes she can take a break for a little while. She gives you directions to the side street in Rhinebeck where the restaurant is located, and after a hurried ten minutes writing down the high points of your conversation with Professor Naida, you are on your way back up Route 9.

XIII

Archipelago is a low building at the end of a short, narrow road. Christina Henderson meets you at its front door dressed in a white silk blouse and black slacks. A pair of steep high heels makes her even taller than she already is. The *chignon* into which she has drawn the dark curls of her hair gives her a youthful air at odds with the bags under her eyes and the lines incised on her forehead. Though holding open the restaurant door, Christina asks you if you would mind speaking with her while she takes her cigarette break. Even as you say, Of course, she pushes past you, on her way to the rear of the building. There, a single chair to which some wit has taped a sign reading SMOKERS HELL sits beside a plastic bucket full of sand from which the ends of a carton's worth of cigarettes protrude. From the right pocket of her slacks, Christina fishes a cigarette, which she ignites with the lighter she withdraws from her left pocket. She is not one of those smokers whose first draw causes her shoulders to relax, her posture to ease; instead, she hugs her free arm across herself, looks off into the trees behind the restaurant, and asks what it is you want to know.

When you say you're researching the statue, she says she didn't think anything of it. Yvonne—one of the other girls—was a wreck from the start, completely freaked out by the thing, but as far as Christina was concerned, it was an old statue, and old statues usually looked like that. The Venus de Milo, right? Granted, those statues lost their arms or whatever through the passage of time, whereas this headless woman started that way, but you understand what she's saying, right?

In reply to your nod, Christina says that things went wrong almost immediately. The first couple of nights, it was small stuff: Yvonne dropped an entire tray; Jo—the other girl—spilled someone's soup in their lap; Christina lost her grip on two successive bottles of wine. None of it was anything that didn't happen once in a while, but for all of it to occur so close together felt . . . weird.

After that, the situation sped downhill. Several customers seated near the statue heard a baby crying, faintly but persistently, and after listening to the sound for anywhere from five to twenty minutes, waved one of the waitresses over and suggested, with varying degrees of good humor, that someone needed to attend to that child. One pair of diners, a flashy young couple up from the City, announced that this place was costing them far too much to have their dinner spoiled by a kid whose mother couldn't look after it and insisted that the Inn pick up the tab for a meal at another, quieter establishment.

You ask what response they received. Christina says she was all for telling them to take a flying fuck at a rolling donut, but Mrs. Garrick worked something out with them.

Were there any children at the Inn?

Christina shakes her head. It wasn't unheard of for parents to bring their kids to the Inn, but they tended to be older, at least five or six. Unless there was a wedding or other big celebration, in which case you might see an influx of babies. And no, there weren't any weddings going on when the complaints started to roll in.

What did she do?

The end of her cigarette flares. The first couple of times, she says, none of us knew what the diners were talking about, so we smiled, and nodded, and reassured them someone would take care of it. The customer's always right, you know? It seemed to satisfy them—most of them.

Did any of you hear anything?

Yvonne—at least, she said she did, Christina says, the tone of her voice a clear indication of her opinion of Yvonne's claims. At night, after the dining room had closed and the three of us were sitting around with Julian, the chef, sharing a bottle of wine, this far-away expression would come over Yvonne's face—Christina imitates it: eyes focused on the distance, face slack, mouth contracted. She'd wait until the rest of us noticed she'd stopped talking, and then she'd ask if we heard it. Christina's voice becomes breathy as she says, Oh, poor little thing. You want your mama, don't you? Where is she? She puts her cigarette to her mouth. Honestly.

Was that all?

Christina blows a jet of smoke. Not hardly. The crying continued—more importantly, the complaints about the crying continued, until Christina spoke to Mrs. Garrick. Whether she made the connection to the statue, Christina can't say; although, really, how could she not? There was a vent in the floor near the statue; Margaret convinced herself that that was the source of the sound everyone was hearing. She had Stephen Holland close it, and as far as she was concerned, that was that.

Was it?

Customers stopped complaining, Christina says, but that may have had as much to do with the fact that she and the other girls avoided seating them near the statue. Not to mention, word had gotten around, and some diners requested tables away from it.

You ask if anyone left because of what they heard, or heard of. Christina says, No, not then. So long as the freaky stuff was confined to that part of the Inn, customers were more curious than anything.

Maybe not curious enough to want to sit next to the statue, but enough to get a charge out of being in the same room as it. You know how people are. Anyway, a couple of days after the vent was shut, the statue bled.

Bled?

During Saturday dinner. The dining room was packed. She had seated a couple beside the statue. She had to; there was no room. They were young and didn't seem to mind. After Christina set their main courses in front of them, before she could ask if they needed anything else and express her hope that they would enjoy their meal, there was a noise—like a balloon losing its air—and something sprayed all over Christina and the couple. For a moment, she couldn't see, because whatever it was had gotten in her eyes. She wiped them, and her fingers came away red. There was red all over the place: her blouse, the table, the meals, the diners. And the smell, like raw steak. Christina was still trying to understand what had just happened when the man at the table raised one hand to his mouth and pointed to the statue with the other. She turned and saw the blood bubbling out of the statue's neck like water from a water fountain. Above it, the ceiling and wall were dripping red from the jet of blood that had hissed up from the statue. While Christina watched the blood spilling over the marble neck slow from a torrent to a stream, the woman at the table turned around and, seeing the statue, let loose a scream like you hear in a cheesy horror movie. That did it—the diners nearest the statue, who'd been holding their collective breaths at the spectacle unfolding next to them, bolted from the dining room. In turn, their flight cleared the rest of the place. One woman, a doctor, came over to help, only to retreat when she saw the scene up close.

Christina stabs out her cigarette, consults her watch, decides she has time for another. The first customers won't show up for an hour and a half, she says, though she really should wrap this up. There are things she still has to do.

You understand, you say. But you have to ask what happened after that . . . incident.

Everybody left, Christina says, immediately correcting herself, Well, not everybody. Maybe half the people who were present at dinner had checked out by morning. The rest were gone within a couple of days, after they met *her*.

Her?

She doesn't know what to call her. The woman from the statue. Its subject.

XIV

The first ones to see her were a pair of lawyers up from the City—early middle-age, total power couple. They didn't arrive till the morning after the mess in the dining room, so they had no clue what they'd checked into. Christina had been up past midnight helping Margaret Garrick to wipe blood off the statue, the wall, the ceiling; to clear the tables of their plates, their cups, their silverware; to gather the tablecloths into two piles, one for those with the usual stains, another for those spattered and smeared with blood; to mop the floor. In gratitude, Margaret had given her the next day off, which meant she wasn't there when—

You're sorry, but you have to interrupt. How, you ask, did Margaret respond to blood pouring out of the statue she had unearthed?

Christina pauses. When she speaks, it is in measured tones. Margaret wasn't in the dining room while all hell was breaking loose; although she isn't sure, Christina thinks she was in her office. By the time the screams and shouts brought her running, there was a crowd of upset guests to deal with, which she spent the next couple of hours doing. Where a complimentary bottle of wine from the cellar would soothe jangled nerves, Yvonne or Jo ran to fetch and deliver it with an opener and a pair of glasses. Where wine was insufficient, Margaret offered what she could, from a meal at one of the other restaurants on Main Street to a full refund with her sincerest apology. She managed to hold onto about half the guests, which Christina thought wasn't too bad, considering the circumstances. Anyway, when she walked into the dining room to survey the damage, you could see how drawn her face was. She stared at the statue for a long time. Christina was waiting for her to say something, to ask for her version of events. What she said, though, when she did speak, was, Let's clean up.

That was it?

That was it. You could tell she had a million questions—you could feel her dying to ask them. But if she did, if she heard what Christina had to say, then whatever explanation she had provided the guests, whatever rationalization, would snap, leaving Margaret to confront something outrageous, impossible. She didn't ask, and Christina, who was trying to wrap her mind around what she'd seen, didn't offer. Instead, they made small talk about the weather, gossiped about the guests, the other staff. It was just as well. If she'd described the blood rushing from the statue's neck down its body, she would have started screaming, herself.

XV

Back to the Vanderhoffs—that was the couple's name, the first ones who saw *her*. They had booked the Suffolk room (all the Inn's rooms were named after New York counties). To reach this one, you climbed the stairs to the second floor, turned right at the top, and walked down the hall to where it T-junctioned the narrow corridor that crossed the front of the house. There, you turned left. At the end of the corridor, there was a door on your left. You opened it, walked a short hallway, and the door to Suffolk was on your left. The night they arrived, the Vanderhoffs were on their way out to dinner—the Inn's dining room hadn't reopened yet—and as they stood outside their door, fiddling with the lock, they noticed something at the other end of the hall. Although the sky wasn't completely dark, the hall's only window was heavily draped, so that the space was dim, thick with shadows. At first, Mrs. Vanderhoff thought it was a trick of the light, but Mr. Vanderhoff agreed that there was something or someone there. She was on the verge of calling hello when the figure slid forward—that was the way they described it, she slid toward them—and they saw that it was missing its head.

For a moment, they were frozen, watching the headless woman gain more definition as she moved closer to the window's weak light, and then Mr. Vanderhoff was jamming a key into the door lock, unable to understand why it refused to fit until he realized it was the key to his Acura and began searching his pants for the room key, which he'd had in his hand a second ago. Mrs. Vanderhoff was looking at the open wound of the woman's neck, the blood that stenciled her skin and snaked the neckline of her pale, sleeveless dress. Mr. Vanderhoff couldn't find the key. Mrs. Vanderhoff was telling him to hurry, hurry up, for Christ's sake, hurry up, she's almost here, which the woman was, she had passed in front of the window, she was ten feet away from them, less. They could hear something, a high-pitched sound neither could identify. Mr. Vanderhoff still couldn't find the key. Mrs. Vanderhoff had backed up against him, was pressing herself into him. The woman was an arm's length away. Mrs. Vanderhoff could see the ruin of the woman's neck, the way her dress belled out around the great curve of her belly. Mr. Vanderhoff was cursing, a litany of fucks. The woman was right beside them. A fine mist of blood filled the air. Mrs. Vanderhoff closed her eyes as it sprayed her face, the hands she raised to shield herself; Mr. Vanderhoff felt it haze the back of his neck. His fingers closed on the little metal outline of Suffolk County to which the room key was chained; he yanked it from his pocket so hard the rest of its contents rained on the carpet. Mrs. Vanderhoff had turned her head to the side, her hands continuing to present what defense they could to the cloud of blood. The key shunked in; Mr. Vanderhoff threw open the door; Mrs. Vanderhoff's feet caught his and they fell into the room. Her elbow drove into his side, and he was momentarily without breath. Mrs. Vanderhoff scrambled away from where he lay gasping to the other side of the bed. Mr. Vanderhoff was aware of something wet falling on his cheek, his forehead, but by the time he forced himself to focus on the doorway, it was empty.

XVI

Despite her insistence that she must return to work, Christina has lit a third cigarette. I know, she says, how could I possibly know all this, right?

You nod.

They told me themselves, she says. Although she was not in the least inclined to return to it, she had decided to come into the Inn that evening, after all. Turned out she liked the prospect of staying alone in her apartment to dwell on what she'd witnessed even less than returning to the scene of the crime, so to speak. With the dining room closed, there wouldn't be much for her to do, but maybe Julian could use help with the kitchen maintenance stuff. It took her a while to get ready, which meant that she walked into the Inn just as the Vanderhoffs were walking out. Christina recognized the pair and smiled at them, because even though the guy gave off a creepy, I'm-undressing-you-with-my-eyes vibe, they were good tippers, and as long as his hands didn't try to follow his eyes, she could fake niceness. But this time, the two of them looked . . .

Like they'd seen a ghost?

Shellshocked, Christina says. Traumatized. As if they'd been in the middle of a horrible accident.

You stare at her. That's an interesting choice of words.

She starts to ask what you mean, then her cheeks redden. Jesus. She plunges her cigarette into the sandbucket, stands. She's sorry, but this has taken too long as it is . . .

Wait, you say, stepping in front of her. What happened with the Vanderhoffs?

Christina stops. They told me, she says. Standing in the front hall, spots of blood visible on their hair, their ears where they'd missed with the washcloth, the couple opened their mouths and the story came pouring out. Christina was almost as surprised by the intimacy of their tone as she was by what they were saying. Once they were finished, they took the bags they hadn't bothered setting down out the front door and did not return.

Had they told anyone else?

They told everybody else, Christina says, everyone they met, from Margaret Garrick to Yvonne to a couple checking in. It was like each new person set the counter back to zero.

How did Margaret Garrick react?

You have to understand, it wasn't only the Vanderhoffs telling their tale of terror to her: it was pretty much all the guests left at the Inn. She—the woman, the headless woman—appeared throughout the Inn, in the halls, in the rooms, in one old guy's bathroom. Christina thinks the Vanderhoffs were the first, but the question's academic. Within a couple of hours of their departure, the rest of the Inn was empty.

XVII

What about, you begin, but Christina shakes her head and says, No, she isn't going to talk about . . . the next day. She's sorry, but she's said as much as she's comfortable with and anyway—moving around you—her break is over.

You half run to keep up with her. As her hand is about to close on the handle to the restaurant's front door, you say, Did you see her? Did the woman appear to you?

The handle in her grip, her arm tensed, Christina hesitates, considering the tips of her shoes for one-Mississippi, two-Mississippi, three-Mississippi before letting her arm drop and turning to you. Her face unreadable, she crosses her arms. You are unsure if she intends her expression to be your answer and are on the verge of thanking her for her time, when she says, That night—the night everyone left. In the dining room. She'd been in the kitchen for the last couple of hours with Julian, who didn't really need her help but had put her to work, anyway, checking their stocks, fetching what they were low on from the pantry, preparing more of the house salad dressing, the cinnamon-apple ice cream, emptying a bottle of red one oversized glass at a time. He wasn't much of a talker, Julian, and he had not objected when Christina switched on the tiny transistor radio he kept on the counter next to the refrigerator. The reception was terrible; the only station that would come in clearly was the public radio station out of Wiltwyck. Christina wasn't the biggest fan of public radio, but they were playing classic jazz—not that experimental stuff: Louis Armstrong and Ella Fitzgerald. The blat of Louis's trumpet rolled off the steel countertops, while Ella's girlish voice found the kitchen's high ceiling and corners. It was almost enough to make Christina cheerful, as if the blood that had sprayed from the statue had been a waking dream, the Vanderhoffs' story an elaborate joke.

Except . . . she'd had this feeling. She couldn't say since when. Maybe she'd awakened with it that morning. Or maybe it had been there after the blood in the dining room. Or maybe, the more aware of it she became, the more she realized it had been there for some time, now, ever since Margaret and Stephen Holland had exposed the statue. Whatever—it was as if she were on the verge—it was like in the movies, when they show something terrible happening, yes, an accident, there's a second immediately before one car smashes into another when all the sound seems to get sucked out of the air and what you have is this pause, this negative space that you can hear. That was what she was feeling as she pushed open the kitchen door and stepped into the dining room, balancing a tray of freshly cleaned water glasses for the three tables at the back of the room. The glasses already on the tables weren't that bad—they were fine, really, but replacing them was one more way to keep busy.

It took until she was halfway through the second table, which was the big round one, eight settings, for Christina to notice *her*. She looked up, and there the headless woman was, seated at one of the small tables along the south wall, her back to Christina. There was blood everywhere: running down the chair, her neck, spreading across the back of her white dress, sprayed up the wall, puddled on the dishes in front of her, at the bottom of her water glass, weighting the purple and yellow flowers leaning from the vase at the table's center. As soon as Christina saw her, she could smell her, her blood, the red reek of it, like biting tinfoil. There was more—there was something on her plate, a scarlet mound that Christina knew the moment she laid her eyes on she did not want to see any clearer but that she could not stop her feet from carrying her toward. She couldn't understand what she was looking at—her brain refused the task—and then her brain had no choice, because she was standing next to the woman, staring down at the table, and she saw—there was—the—

Christina's hand is over her mouth, her eyes liquid with tears. When you ask her what she saw, she shakes her head, turns, and is inside Archipelago, whose door whunks as she locks it behind her.

Almost as surprised by her action as by her narrative, you approach the door. Its smoky panes reveal little of the space beyond, a bench, perhaps, at right angles to a coat rack. You search the walls to either side of the door for a bell, buzzer, but find nothing. You consider tapping on the glass, but can't decide if that would be pushing things too far. Sudden motion on the other side of the door, a pair of legs striding toward you, trousers, men's shoes, hurries you back, toward the parking lot. You feel but cannot actually see someone watching you from the front door as you duck into the Metro. Although desperate to open your notebook and begin writing, you decide it will be more prudent to do so away from the restaurant.

XVIII

As it turns out, the first quiet place you find is the parking lot of the McDonald's into which you pull once you have crossed over the Wiltwyck-Rhinecliff Bridge (which, you suppose, from this direction should be the Rhinecliff-Wiltwyck Bridge). A quick trip to the drive-through window brings you a fish sandwich, large fries, and a small Coke, not your preferred dinner menu, but sufficient to satisfy the hunger that has overtaken you on the drive back from Archipelago. Sandwich in one hand, pen in the other, notebook balanced on your knees, you record everything you can of your conversation with Christina Henderson.

Once you have finished your notes and your meal, you page through your notebook until you arrive at the number for Holy Redeemer Episcopal Church. It is not too late; perhaps you can fit a meeting with Reverend Au Claire into your day. Somewhat to your surprise, the Reverend answers the office phone at the church herself. Her tone is pleasant enough until you identify yourself, when her words lose several degrees of warmth. Yes, she says, she remembers you, and she would expect you to have remembered her telling you that she had said everything she was going to.

On the phone, you say.

Excuse me?

The Reverend's exact words were that she had said as much as she could on the phone, you remind her. You're here to speak to her in person. Currently, you're sitting in the parking lot of the McDonald's next to the Wiltwyck Mall. If the Reverend would like, you can stop over tonight.

No, Reverend Au Claire says, she meets with the parish book club in an hour.

Tomorrow?

The priest sighs.

You can come over first thing in the morning—

In the afternoon, she says. One o'clock.

That would be fine, you say. Thank you.

XIX

On the drive back to Stonington, you decide to stop at the town library, the site of Professor Naida's long-ago lecture. Located a few hundred yards up and across Main Street from the Wynkoop Inn, the library is a more modest structure, one of the stone houses favored by the Dutch settlers of this area, to which has been added a pair of extensions, a long room at the rear, and a shorter room on the left. The main entrance is to the right, at the end of a short flagstone walk bordered by flowerbeds crowded with tall white and purple plants. Past a bulletin-board quilted with flyers for community activities and organizations, the check-out desk stretches along the wall to your right. Seated behind it, a young woman with strong features and a head of long, thick brown hair leans over a book from whose pages she does not look up until you are standing in front of her and clear your throat. Still focused on whatever scene they have been reading, her large brown eyes take a moment to register you. When they do, she shakes her head and apologizes, explaining that she was caught up in this book.

That's all right, you say. What book is it?

In answer, the young woman tilts the volume up so that you can see the cover: *A Good and Happy Child*. I've never read this before, she says.

How is it? you ask.

Pretty wild. She bookmarks her page and closes the novel. What can she help you with?

You're wondering what the library has in the way of local history.

Like, the town, or do you mean the county?

The town, you say.

Honestly, the librarian says, we don't have much. There are a couple of books on the state history shelf that mention Stonington, but they don't say very much, only that the town was founded by Huguenots who moved to the other side of Frenchman's Mountain to get away from the English. The library has a selection of local newspapers from the 1890s—someone donated them a few years ago. What is it you're trying to find out about?

There was a statue that was on display at the Wynkoop Inn about ten years ago—you're researching that.

The librarian's eyes widen. You mean the Bloody Mother?

You aren't sure, you say. This was a statue of a pregnant woman—

Who's headless, right?

That's right. Has she seen it?

No, the librarian says, she was in middle school when the statue was up. One of her friends' older sisters worked at the Inn, and she told them stories—

Is that so? Does she mind you asking what those stories were?

Crazy stuff. The statue was supposed to have bled, especially if a pregnant woman was standing next to it. Apparently, this one woman went into labor right there, and when the baby was born, it had a red ring all the way around its neck. And of course, there was the woman who was killed on Main Street. She was, like, super-pregnant, and she was in a car accident that cut her head clean off, right in front of the Inn. The story goes that, if you stand in front of a mirror in a darkened room and say Bloody Mother three times, she'll appear behind you.

The woman who was killed, or the statue? Or the woman the statue was carved of?

Huh, the librarian says. She always assumed it was the woman who died on Main Street, but now that you mention it, she's not sure.

What was supposed to happen to you if you saw her?

She doesn't know, the librarian says, adding that she never asked. The prospect of seeing that figure behind her seemed terrible enough on its own. Maybe you died of fright.

There were other stories, too, the librarian says. Urban legends, right? Except this place isn't so urban. Every year, on the anniversary of the accident that killed that woman, a trail of bloody footprints appears in front of the Wynkoop Inn, all the way from the spot on the road where it happened to the front door. They don't fade out or anything; they have to be washed away. She hasn't seen them, herself, but she knows a girl who worked there and saw them two years in a row. The librarian's also known people who claim to have seen a headless woman standing by the side of the road when they drove past the Inn late at night—one guy even swore she appeared in the back seat of his car—but that sounds pretty crazy. As if the rest of it doesn't, she laughs.

Pretty crazy, you say.

XX

A brief inspection of the state history shelf confirms the librarian's prediction as to the relevance of its materials. On your way back out, the librarian waves you over and, as you approach the front desk, holds out a sheet of paper to you. This is Constance Braddon's number, she says. Mrs. Braddon's the town historian. She might know something about the statue.

You thank her. There is another number written below the historian's. You point to it. What's this one?

The librarian blushes. That's mine, she says. In case you want to talk or anything.

XXI

From the library's parking lot, you call Constance Braddon's number. As you expected, the town historian says that it is too late for her to see you, tonight, but if you can stop over first thing tomorrow morning, she can spare you an hour. Your appointment with her set, you consider the number written below hers. Your first and so far only relationship with a woman took place three years ago, when what you had thought was a friendly drink at a local bar with a woman from payroll ended in a tangle of sweaty sheets on her bed. You had long considered yourself cosmopolitan in matters of sexuality, but nonetheless were somewhat surprised at how comfortable you were with the whole thing. Concerned to minimize gossip, the two of you were discreet to a fault, which stoked the intensity of the affair. Perhaps that was why it burned out as quickly as it did. In three months, she was declaring your relationship over, and while you sometimes ached for the physical side of it, there hadn't been enough else between the two of you for you to feel all that upset. Although your subsequent lovers have been men, you have not closed off the possibility of another woman should the right one appear. Is that what this is? Has the entire purpose of your trip been nothing more than an excuse for you to meet the next great love of your life? It's a romantic notion, but so what? At the very least, calling the number might lay the groundwork for a future relationship.

In the end, though, you close your phone and start the car. As one of your old boyfriends used to say, Sex makes you late for class, not to mention for early-morning appointments with the town historian. You fold the paper and tuck it in amongst your notes. There is nothing to stop you calling the librarian once you're home. Even if you don't, it is nice to have felt desire stirring in you, to have known yourself the cause of desire in another.

XXII

In your room at the Great Republic Motel, you switch on your laptop and connect to the motel's wi-fi. You are tired—what you think of as grown-up tired, the fatigue that attaches to you over the course of the day and weighs you down at the end of it. Nonetheless, you connect to Google and type Annabel Ferris's name into the search bar. It takes 0.12 seconds for the search engine to return approximately 420,000 responses. Wikipedia leads the way, followed by the official site for the Gwyneth Paltrow film and the site for Janet Naida's book on Ferris. Below the top responses, a half-dozen thumbnail pictures line up under the heading, "Images of Annabel Ferris." The first and fourth are of Ferris in profile, her head craned forward. The second and third show Gwyneth Paltrow staring off to the left, her lips parted, her hair hanging in the chop that seemed to draw as much commentary as her performance. The last two photos are close-ups of marble faces. You click on the image furthest to the right, which opens a window showing the marble portrait of a woman's head in three-quarter profile. The large, rounded nose and the chin, jutting forward slightly as if the lower teeth are overlapping the upper, mark the face as Annabel Ferris's; the subscript to the picture identifies it as her Self-Portrait #3. You've seen this piece before. As part of your preparations for this trip, you sought all images of all of Ferris's sculpture. This time, it isn't only that you notice the sharp angle at which the base of the neck has been cut—not an exact match for the headless statue, but not too far off it—but that you're struck by the style in which the self-portrait was executed, something approaching classical Greek or Roman, the hair lying close to the head in tight ringlets, the features serene, the eyes blanks.

XXIII

After the day you've had, the stories you've heard, your dreams should be full of headless women, ghostly voices delivering cryptic warnings about the Bloody Mother. If they are, their contents are not substantial enough either to disturb your sleep or to remain with you the next morning, when you roll over to check the room's digital clock and realize you've overslept and are on the verge of being late for your appointment with the town historian. That you are able to shower, rush through a coffee and bagel at the corner bagel shop, and pull into the historian's driveway only five minutes behind schedule must count as some variety of minor miracle. The house you hurry toward is a modest two-story Colonial whose white siding is speckled green with mold, an appropriate-looking residence for the caretaker of local memory. As you clump up the front stairs, Constance Braddon opens the front door.

Petite, her dark brown hair streaked with gray, the town historian wears a navy skirt, white blouse, and navy sweater unbuttoned at top and bottom. A pair of reading glasses magnifies her eyes behind clouds of scratches. You're here, she says.

Yes, you say, unsure if five minutes' tardiness is sufficient to warrant an apology. Already, though, she has turned and is leading you into the house. There is something vaguely maternal about her; you would not be surprised if she offered you a cup of tea, a biscuit. But she does not mention water, let alone anything hot.

Mrs. Braddon, as she introduces herself, confesses to a certain curiosity concerning the sculpture's origin; although, she adds, she is as interested in its having been buried. While she sweeps heaps of paper to one side so that she can seat you at the scuffed dining room table where she says she does her real work—the upstairs office is more for storage—Mrs. Braddon asks you if you are familiar with the practice of burying a statue of St. Joseph in the yard of a house you wish to sell? It comes from the Catholics, the Italian Catholics, to be specific, so it may have as much to do with Italian culture as Catholic tradition. You know the story about the founding of Rome, yes? Not Romulus and Remus, no, the story about the workmen digging the foundations of the city who unearthed a bloody head—a sculpture, you understand, of a man's head. (Does Virgil mention it?) The workers were concerned the head might be a bad omen, a perfectly reasonable concern, until someone—Mrs. Braddon can't remember his name—declared the bloody sculpture a good omen, and that appears to have satisfied everyone. Considering Roman history, though, perhaps those workers' fears were justified.

You clear your throat and ask Mrs. Braddon her opinion of Professor Naida's theory that the statue was buried as an act of renunciation on the part of its maker. Mrs. Braddon nods and says that, while this is hardly her area of expertise—she's an amateur historian, not a psychologist—this seems an awfully elaborate way to give something up. Of course, such elaborateness could be the point, to underscore the significance of what's being renounced. All the same, it strikes her that you might bury a statue of someone if the person herself were unavailable: if the body had been lost at sea, say, or if you were separated from her by a great distance. You might employ such a substitute to help yourself grieve; though the statue's missing head raises certain questions, she knows. While this might be the way in which the sculpture's original died, why would the artist choose to represent her this way? Usually, we portray the beloved dead in a more idealized fashion, at least more completely, which raises the possibility that this model was not-so-beloved, after all, that the piece might have been . . . call it an act of aggression. If this were the case, then interring it could be a sign of changed sentiments on the part of the artist. On the other hand, burial has been used as a sign of contempt, out of sight, out of mind and all that. Were the sculpture intended as a hostile gesture, burying it could have been a way to pile insult on top of injury.

However, Mrs. Braddon says, this is more speculation than she cares to indulge in. Are there any matters of fact she can assist you with?

You ask the historian if she knows about anything . . . unusual taking place at the Inn after the statue was put on display.

Know? She shakes her head. During the two weeks the sculpture was up at the Inn, she was aware of several disturbances there. Stonington is a small enough community that news travels its circuit in the matter of a day, particularly if it's bad. From conversation with the ladies at the library when she stopped in to borrow a book, as well as from a brief exchange with a friend of Margaret Garrick's on line at Shop Rite, Mrs. Braddon understood that something odd was occur-

ring at the Inn, but none of the people with whom she spoke could offer more than bland assertions spiced with strange details, and their
stories tended to trip up one another. Someone had been served a
bowl of blood instead of their soup became someone had flung a pan
of blood at the wall became someone had cut himself with a steak
knife and bled all over their meal and table. Whatever happened had
done so in proximity to the statue, which no one cared for. People had
seen things—in the halls, the rooms—that had frightened not a few of
them right out of the Inn. A man had run out of the front door, his
shirt decorated with what appeared to be blood—or so one of the li-
brarians had heard from her cousin who was driving past as the man
emerged. You see? Mrs. Braddon says.

Nodding, you ask what she thinks happened, why there were these
disturbances at the Inn.

Here she is back to speculating, Mrs. Braddon says. There have
been reports of strange goings-on at the Wynkoop Inn for as long as
it's been open; albeit the majority of those center on the Schenker
brothers. They were the last owners of the place when it was a private
residence. Twins, Casper and Isaac. Their father couldn't decide which
of them to leave the family home to, so he played King Solomon and
split it between them, which pleased neither brother. Things soured to
the point that each claimed possession of half the house, and they built
a wall right down the middle of the place. Casper started a rumor that
Isaac was practicing black magic on his side of the wall.

Was there any evidence that he was? you ask.

Oh, there were plenty of odd folks who came calling on Isaac, but
he was something of a scholar of ancient languages. No one found any
Satanic altars after his death, if that's what you mean. More likely than
not, it was his brother looking to get at him. Mrs. Braddon laughs. She
doesn't know if you have any children, yourself, but if you do . . .

You do not.

In any event, she says, there have been sightings of one or the other
brother for years, all of them reasonably benign. The brothers were
striking fellows: tall, thin as rails—the story goes that Isaac tried to grow
a beard, but it never amounted to much. Usually, whichever brother it is
is wearing a top hat and long coat and walking along what used to be his
side of the wall. People have been frightened *of* them, but not *by* them.

What took place over that fortnight, though, there's no precedent
for—at least, none that Mrs. Braddon is aware of. It was as if the Inn
were seized by a form of mass hysteria. Certainly, the statue didn't help
matters any. Mrs. Braddon was invited to view it by Margaret Garrick,
who hoped she might succeed where Professor Naida had failed and
slot the piece into a history. This was a couple of days before the
statue was mounted in the dining room. Margaret had it covered in the
back shed. The instant the sheet slithered off and Mrs. Braddon realized what she was looking at, she said, Dear Jesus—not as an oath, you
understand, but a prayer. You haven't seen the sculpture, have you?

Professor Naida showed you a picture of it, you say.

That doesn't compare, Mrs. Braddon states. The thing itself was—
it was as if you were looking at a real woman, nine months pregnant, in
the second, the millisecond, after something, some incredible violence,
has severed her head from her neck, before she has completely understood what she has just been subject to. It was as if you were witnessing her death overtaking her. Honestly, she can't imagine what Margaret was thinking, putting up that statue in the dining room. She would
have been better donating it to the County Historical Society, or the
Art Center at Penrose, or she could have tried selling it to a collector.
The historian half smiles. It appears she's leapt from speculation right
into—what?—psychic impressions? That said, while it's a testament to
the artist's skill, she cannot pretend the sculpture did not disturb her.
Especially if the guests at the Inn had been privy to any talk of ghostly
occurrences, it would have been no surprise if their attention had
gravitated to that statue.

Really, though—it isn't as if Mrs. Braddon spoke with, let alone
properly interviewed, any of the people who were at the Inn at the
time. She supposes she might have, if it hadn't struck her as so . . . sen-
sationalistic. But then that terrible accident happened, and Margaret—
well. For all that—at least, for the accident, Mrs. Braddon recom-
mends you speak to Jacqueline Wright. She was the state trooper who
was first on the scene. In fact, if memory serves, she was half a dozen
cars back, so she practically saw it all take place. Trooper Wright, she
thinks, is still stationed at the barracks on Route 209, toward Wiltwyck.

And Margaret Garrick?

That poor woman, Mrs. Braddon says, and politely declines to be drawn any further. She stands and you, understanding the sign, follow suit. Before she can move around the table to escort you to the door, you say you have one more question. Of course, the historian says.

You've read that, after the accident, the statue was . . . exorcised. Or that an exorcism of it was attempted.

Reverend Au Claire, Mrs. Braddon says. She took to do with the sculpture after—afterwards. She assumes Margaret asked her to do so, since she was a member of her congregation. The Reverend is at Holy Redeemer, off 209 past the shopping center. You want to talk to her.

Hasn't Mrs. Braddon heard—

This is as much as she is willing to say, Mrs. Braddon says, as much hearsay as she cares to trade in. She may not have her Ph.D., but she won't be party to perpetuating gossip and superstition.

You apologize, stating that it isn't your intention to spread either gossip or superstition, you're only trying to verify what did and did not take place, but Mrs. Braddon leads you to the front door and stands half-behind it as you exit her home. You wish that you could think of something to say to her, some parting statement that would reaffirm the integrity of your project, put her in her place, but nothing comes to mind, so you have to settle for a Thank You that she does not answer.

XXIV

Since your interview with Constance Braddon has ended early, you return to the Great Republic Motel and pack your overnight bag. The phone book on the room's desk lists the number of the New York State Police barracks on Route 209. A call to them reveals that this is Trooper Wright's day off. The man you speak to is unwilling to give you the trooper's home number, but consents to take down a detailed message for her. While you are walking to the front office to check out, your cell chirps, and when you answer it, a woman's voice says, This is Jackie Wright.

The state trooper is almost surprisingly willing to meet with you, offering to drive in right now if that's convenient. It isn't, you say, but maybe in a couple of hours? You have an appointment at one; could you get together at three, three-thirty someplace?

She can do that. There's a Dunkin' Donuts in the shopping plaza on 209. At the risk of conforming to popular stereotypes, why doesn't she see you there?

That would be fine, you say. You describe yourself to her, she to you, and you thank her for her willingness to talk to you.

Don't thank me yet, she says, you haven't heard what she has to say.

XXV

The woman behind the counter at the bagel shop is starting to recognize you, though not enough to attempt conversation with you as you sit eating your tuna salad bagel and reviewing your notes. Lunch completed, you head for Holy Redeemer Church, early for that next appointment. The Reverend Au Claire greets you at the front door to the rectory, a tall, narrow house with a steep, peaked roof that contrasts sharply with the low, angular church with which it shares a parking lot. The priest is not as old as you expect her to be. The slender woman who directs you into the sitting room to your left cannot be much past forty. Although her black shirt rises to a black collar with a white notch, you have a difficult time picturing the Reverend performing an exorcism (about which, it must be admitted, your principal source of imagery is the famous movie). A quartet of blue padded chairs arranged around a low coffee table occupies the center of the sitting room. You select the closest one on the left, which places you opposite a picture of Jesus executed in the flat, gilded style of an Eastern Orthodox icon. Reverend Au Claire lowers herself into the chair across from you, folding her hands as she does.

When she does not speak, you clear your throat and thank her for seeing you under such short notice. This earns you a nod. You hesitate, waiting for the Reverend to speak, to offer a comment, a question. She does not. You explain that you are working on a book on what you call electronic legends. These are stories you find on the Internet that claim to be fact but frequently stray a considerable distance from their source material, in the process incorporating elements from all kinds of other narratives, from folklore to film.

Reverend Au Claire nods again. The skin around her large, brown eyes is plum, stained by insufficient sleep.

You first encountered a reference to the statue at the Wynkoop

Inn while checking through the contents of a website devoted to cataloguing reports of exorcisms. In addition to listings by country, state, city, and year, the site featured a miscellaneous category that included stories of the ritual performed on pets, houses, and a variety of items including a hairdryer, a clock radio, and a chainsaw. As the Reverend can imagine, upon closer inspection, the overwhelming majority of these narratives failed to withstand much scrutiny.

There was one, however—the report of a statue that had been associated with the death of an expectant mother in a car accident, and which subsequently had received the combined attentions of a rabbi and an Episcopal priest—that proved more durable. Although the website located the event only in upstate New York, you found another page that identified the town as Stonington. A call to the local synagogue turned up Rabbi Singer two years in his grave, but offered the unexpected benefit of connecting you to Mrs. Barbara Cohen, secretary to the current and previous rabbis. While refusing to say anything for the record, informally, Mrs. Cohen confirmed the former rabbi's involvement in what she referred to as That Business With The Statue. Not that she was present for any of it, herself, but everyone had known things weren't right over at the Inn ever since they'd put that horrible thing on display. There were all kinds of stories flying around, and then, when that poor mother was killed in that car crash . . .

Together with the responses to your subsequent inquiries from such people as Lawrence Schmidt, Mrs. Cohen's remarks seemed strong evidence that this was an event worth investigating. Since your arrival here, your conversations with Stephen Holland and especially Christina Henderson have solidified your conviction that something truly strange—truly uncanny—took place a decade ago.

And, Reverend Au Claire says, you would like her to supply the dramatic climax to the tale, compose a scene that would do Hollywood proud.

No, no, you say, that isn't it at all.

It's all right, the Reverend says, though the tone of her voice makes you wonder. It's understandable. So often, God seems not just reserved, but withdrawn, in hiding. It makes sense that people would be intrigued by stories that promise to show Him acting in a very direct and dramatic manner.

Does that mean she participated in something direct and dramatic?

The Reverend almost smiles. Dramatic, she says. As for direct . . .
She shakes her head.

You don't understand.

Since your last call, the Reverend says, she's thought about what
she might say to you. Christina—Hanson?

Henderson.

Henderson. She was at the Inn?

She was a waitress in the dining room.

If she's told you what she saw, the Reverend says, then you have
some notion of what Phil Singer and she had heard.

Was that what convinced the two of them to exorcise the statue?

She had the statue brought into the church because Margaret Garrick was one of her parishioners, and something of a friend. Following
the accident, Margaret was beyond distraught—really, she was on the
verge of a complete breakdown. She came to the rectory asking for
help, and as a result of their conversation, the Reverend agreed to accept the statue temporarily. Stephen Holland drove it over in his
pickup; she had him place it in the undercroft. That night . . . she had
been up late talking with Trooper Wright. Have you spoken to her?

Not yet, you say. Later today.

The trooper was the first one on the scene, and was understandably
shaken by it. She knew nothing about the statue, but she had seen . . .

Yes?

The Reverend will let her tell you, herself, should she choose to. In
any event, it was well after two by the time she turned off her bedside
lamp. Her eyes couldn't have been closed more than five minutes
when she heard the screams.

Screams?

At first, because she had been so close to sleep—had had one foot
in unconsciousness—she hadn't been sure if the sound had forced its
way out of her dreams. Even after the screaming continued, she wasn't
certain. There was a quality to it, as if she were experiencing a memory,
but one so overwhelming it felt as if it were real. Nonetheless, she
threw off her bedclothes and unlocked the door to her room. The
screaming sounded as if it were coming from inside the rectory, which
was a distinct possibility. The Reverend used to leave the front door to

the residence unlocked, in case one of her parishioners found herself or himself in sudden need of a place to stay. It was not a policy she advertised outside of her congregation, and even to them she mentioned it only in passing, and at that point only one of them had taken her up on her offer. With the rectory accessible, there was the possibility that someone with whom she was not familiar might let himself in, and while she believed that refuge should be available to all who sought it, there was a reason she kept her bedroom door locked. As she ducked her head in and out of the other upstairs rooms, then started downstairs, it occurred to her that she probably would feel slightly more secure were she gripping a baseball bat, or one of the golf clubs an Episcopal priest is supposed to treasure. What a sight that would make, she thought. A blessing, or a beating?

But there was no woman on the first floor, either. Yes, she was certain the person whose throat was pouring forth these screams was a woman. The Reverend checked the rectory's nominal basement and found it empty, as was the lawn surrounding the house. She could not understand how the screaming had not drawn the attention of any of the neighbors. She crossed to the church, threw open the door, and was met by darkness. She assumed some well-meaning soul had turned off the vestibule's light, but when she ran her hand over the wall to find the switch, she felt not brick, but rough stone. The difference was such a surprise that she jerked her hand back as if she'd been burned. The air inside the church, usually still and dry, even dusty, was moving, damp, freighted with a rich, metallic smell that made her want to spit. All the while, her ears rang with the screaming, which did not stop when she panicked and fled the church, running back to the rectory and bolting the door behind her. Not until she was on the phone with Phil Singer did the screaming cease, all at once, as if a radio had been clicked off.

What, you ask, made her call the rabbi?

Phil had been—she supposes you could call him her spiritual advisor—since shortly after she'd met him. She's not sure what your religious sentiments are . . .

You shrug.

Fair enough, she says, you are an academic. A more . . . traditionally minded person of faith—her mother, say—might have found the idea of an Episcopal priest seeking advice on matters of religion from a rabbi, even one as eclectic and charming as Phil, unusual. From the moment the Reverend had met him, though, she'd been in complete and utter sympathy with him. Not that there was anything inappropriate in their friendship. He was an older man, enough so to have served in Korea and had a substantial career as an anthropologist before abandoning that life to study at Hebrew Union. If anything, she supposes, he served as a kind of father-figure for her. He was a small man, delicate, with sharp features and bright eyes that were almost black. He favored good clothes, but seemed unwilling to accept the wear that the years had made to his frame, with the result that his jackets hung on him like drapes, his trousers had to be cinched tight around his waist. The only article of clothing that truly fit him was the cream-colored fedora he affected around town. When she dialed his number, the Reverend had no idea if he would answer, but he picked up on the first ring, as if he'd been waiting for her call. He listened to her barely coherent recitation of the night's events and said he would be right over.

In the twenty minutes or so it took him to arrive, the Reverend brewed a pot of strong coffee and dressed. She considered returning to the church, but decided to wait for Phil. He showed up wearing a plaid shirt and jeans, the only time she'd seen him dressed so casually; the fedora, however, was in place. He cradled a stack of books, which he carried into the kitchen and lowered onto the table. There were four of them, oversized volumes that reminded her of her family Bible, an enormous book in which the record of her family's major events—births, deaths, christenings, marriages—had been recorded. These were no Bibles. Their plain covers were cracked and worn with age, the edges foxed. Gray swoops and swirls marked the path Phil's cuff had swept through the dust on them. He spread the books across the table, and she saw that one of them, not the thickest, was bound with a thick leather strap and a large metal lock.

Phil, she said, what is all this?

Information, he said. The screaming has stopped?

Yes, she said, thinking, Isn't it obvious?

He nodded. That's good. Is that coffee fresh?

XXVI

Over a mug of steaming black coffee, Phil Singer reminded the Reverend that he had not always been a rabbi.

Yes, she said.

From his youth, he said, he had been fascinated by myth. His parents were not especially observant. They kept the high holy days, but more as a way of maintaining their cultural identity than as a sign of faith. They were intellectuals: Marx and Freud were as much a part of the household as Moses or David. They believed in exposing their son to the widest possible range of traditions, and in letting him pursue his interests. Aside from a break to experience the joys of shooting at and being shot at by Red Chinese soldiers, this he did, right up to a doctorate from Columbia and a professorship at Indiana.

None of this was news to the Reverend, but when she went to say so, Phil held up his hand and continued speaking. He was obsessed, he said, with what lay before the beginning, the figures, the stories, the traditions that preceded the earliest records. You could catch glimpses of their contours, hints of their history, in the texts, the art, the customs that had come after. Though he was unconvinced by Graves's *White Goddess,* he responded to the impulse behind it. His summers he spent in Europe and the Middle East, starting his investigations at the margins and moving steadily inward, until he was standing outside a ramshackle hut in what was then the southwest Union of Soviet Socialist Republics, what has since regained the name of Azerbaijan. How happy his parents would have been to have seen their boy visiting the Workers' Paradise. Phil snorted. The U.S.S.R. was many things, but a paradise it was not.

The woman he had traveled so far—and, not to be immodest, at some risk—to talk to was old, that age past old age, when a certain kind of person comes to seem a part of the landscape, a rock or tree carved into an approximation of the human. Her eyes were yellow with cataracts, her gums long empty of teeth, her scalp home to only a few wisps of colorless hair. With one exception, her clothes were plain, drab, three sweaters buttoned over a shapeless dress underneath. The exception was a royal blue scarf the woman wore around her head as a kind of shawl. It was cheap, polyester, mass-produced in some factory who-knew-where, but it wrapped around her like a mark of royalty. Phil had been told, he didn't say by whom, to bow deeply to her and hold out the offerings the same nameless advisor had recommended: three cartons of Benson and Hedges cigarettes and a bottle of good cognac. The woman grunted and shuffled back into her cottage. She did not close the door behind her, which Phil gambled was a sign he could follow her. His wager paid off, and for the rest of that summer and several to come he learned from her.

By now, the Reverend was completely lost. What? she asked. What did this woman teach you that was so important, you have to tell me about it now?

What she passed on, Phil said. You're familiar with the Indo-Europeans, yes? The fellows whose language grew into so many others? Their gods, their traditions did the same, spread into new countries and adapted to fit the surroundings. We've been able to reconstruct some of it by working backwards from what we know, inferring the features of the parent from the similarities among her children's features. This woman, though, she had the stories, the customs, as they had been, before they migrated across the continent. Most anthropologists, himself included, would have placed them anywhere from nine to eleven thousand years in the past. They would have been wrong. What fell from this woman's lips was older, so much older. When the last ice sheets had started their crawl down from the north, this knowledge was old, that mother-tongue the latest in a long line to convey it. He learned everything the old woman had to teach him, and by the time she was finished, he had made the acquaintance of other men and women who were willing to build on her education.

It was bad, Phil said. He was bad. Maybe there are things man was not meant to know, maybe there are not, but there are things this man was not meant to know. The theory, you see, was accompanied by a praxis whose results were—he would say incredible, but after what the Reverend had described to him, maybe not so much. It wasn't important. What he studied consumed everything in his life. His position at the university, his friends, God help him, his family: it took all of them—or he should say, he gave all of them to it, willingly. Nor was that enough. The body of knowledge he had embraced would not be satisfied until it had devoured him, too, scooped what was *him* out of his body the way you spoon the seed out of a ripe avocado and filled the hollow with itself, leaving him nothing but a vessel for passing it on to whoever tracked him to whatever hovel he'd retreated to, the only trace that would remain of him the type of liquor he would require for his tuition. If there was to be any hope for him holding onto his self, he had to abandon the path he had been on for decades— break his staff and bury his books, so to speak. He must try to walk in a new direction, which led him back to the faith of his fathers, and from there, to the rabbinate.

XXVII

You have to understand, the Reverend says, Phil Singer was among the kindest, calmest, *sanest* people she knew. The clergy are—they're no different from their congregations, really. Some are full of the Spirit, to put it diplomatically, and some are more measured in their faith. Some lose their belief altogether. She supposes it goes without saying that one of the surest ways to test your faith is to become a minister of it. It isn't so much the big things, the diseases and disasters—those you're ready for; you expect them to challenge your faith. No, what grinds you down are the little things, the hundred daily failings you witness in yourself and in others, the pettiness, the spite, the jealousy, the dull, stupid meanness in people. When you start, you know you aren't going to be working any miracles, but you imagine there will be a kind of nobility to the calling you've answered, a kind of austere beauty. Sooner than you'd like, that image is replaced by another, of yourself as a department manager in a spiritual big-box, where the customers are shopping for the maximum of salvation at the deepest discount they can find. The temptation to—not despair so much as permanent discouragement, can feel overwhelming.

Phil, though, never showed the slightest sign of that. He was a pragmatist without being a pessimist. The Reverend knew that he'd been married and had grown children and grandchildren with whom he maintained an uneasy correspondence, but she attributed their estrangement to Phil's split from their mother/grandmother. He'd been quite open about his responsibility for the disintegration of his marriage, if a bit vague as to the exact circumstances. The Reverend had assumed an affair, alcoholism, one of the usual mid-life obstacles, not . . . she wasn't sure what Phil had described to her. Membership in some kind of cult? Already the day had gone from terrible to frightening; now it appeared to be moving again, from frightening to she couldn't say what. She wanted to tell Phil to hold on a minute, to stop, go outside, come in a second time, and start all over. But he had finished his coffee, rinsed the mug and set it on the dishrack, and was turning to the books he'd placed on the table.

XXVIII

The books, Phil said, he didn't exactly bury. He put them in a trunk, chained and padlocked the trunk, and kept it in a safe place. These last five years, that had been in the middle of a heap of junk in the basement. The best spot to hide something is in plain sight, yes? The books couldn't be burned—they could, but that—it was better for them not to be destroyed. He couldn't give them away; he could not be responsible for placing them into someone else's hands. Eventually, he knew, he would have to come up with a plan for their disposition—perhaps the Vatican's Black Library would accept them.

In any event, it seemed they were going to prove useful, now. For the last week, he had been hearing some very unusual rumors concerning a statue that had been put on display at the Wynkoop Inn. He'd been spending more and more time in his basement, pretending to fiddle with this or that while eyeing the trunk. He remembered, Phil said. He had done everything in his power to put the knowledge out of his mind, but what he had learned was seared into his memory. The second Barbara Cohen told him that the sculpture mounted on the Inn's dining room wall was of a headless woman big with child, he had recognized the Mother of Stone.

Who? the Reverend said.

The Romans called her the *magna mater,* the great mother, Phil said. They borrowed her from the Greeks, who conflated her with Gaia, their Mother Earth. The Greeks had her from Phrygia, in Asia Minor, where she was known as Cybele, the Mother of the Mountain. She is very ancient, and very terrible. He had opened one of the books and was turning onionskin pages. *Les mystères du ver,* he said, nodding at the volume. The Reverend did not recognize the title. Here, Phil said, pointing to a passage. Drawing near, the Reverend saw a block of dense black script beneath what looked like a woodprint of a headless pregnant woman, done in a style that suggested the medieval. She could not decipher the language or, for that matter, the precise characters in which the text was written; it resembled what she'd seen of Gothic, but not enough for her make anything of it. Phil, however, was sliding his index finger across the rows of text, his lips moving soundlessly.

This Cybele, he said at last, was served by ten priestesses. Once each generation, those priestesses who could would get themselves with child, in order to draw the Mother—that is one of her names— into themselves and so bring her to a new generation. For the Mother ever longed for a greater closeness to her children. Yes, yes. Rituals, more rituals—ah. But the—you could call him the Sky Father—had grown jealous of the Mother, who, in some versions of the story, was his mother, too. Therefore, he devised a trap for her. When her priestesses met for her worship, he sent his followers into her grotto. They slew the guards and laid their hands on the priestesses, whom they carried to the top of a high mountain. There they put the priestesses to death, cutting the heads from their bodies and hanging those bodies by their feet, so that all the blood ran out of them into the ground. As they did this, the Sky Father's followers spoke secret words he had given them. In this way did the Sky Father and his party bind the Mother to the mountain.

That isn't all, Phil said. It never is. There were no priestesses left, but there were still those who were loyal to the Mother. They hunted the ones who had defiled the Mother's grotto and profaned her servants and took revenge on them. Then they offered themselves as a new sacred order, the men making themselves more like women to be pleasing to the Mother.

What, the Reverend said, were they cross-dressing?

And self-castrating, Phil said. The problem was, their deity had been overthrown, confined in a way none of them knew how to undo. They could maintain some of the forms of her worship, but what had animated those rituals had been placed beyond them. Until one fellow had an idea. If the Mother were locked in stone, then she might be brought forth through stone, through representations of her carved from the very rock of the mountain that held her. Most of these statues conformed to the prototypical image of a fertility goddess: undersized head, oversized breasts, enormous hips, tiny feet. It appears they served their purpose. But another fellow—quite possibly the same one who'd hit on carving the Mother's image, though Phil didn't think so—believed that, if the Mother were to be portrayed, it should be with the violence that had been inflicted upon her. There is something almost uniquely powerful about the spectacle of the suffering god, isn't there?

These statues, Phil said, were a mistake. The Mother had demanded her fair share of blood—as was the case with so many deities, it was the preferred way to slake her thirst—but always within the context of her worship. The sculptures this nameless artist struck from the rock—it was as if, in giving form to the savagery that had been visited upon her, he had provided an egress for the anger and pain that act had aroused. Blood ran from the statues as if they were alive, and blood ran from those around them, especially women carrying children. In short order, the statues were taken down and buried, secret words said over them in order to subdue the Mother's wrath in them.

The information concerning what these images could do proved more difficult to suppress. Down through the millennia, new sculptures of the Mother have been carved, some as an aid to worship, others as a means of study, still others as a weapon. One of the popes—the Borgia, Alexander VI—commissioned a statue of the Mother that he had presented to a hated rival under the guise of a peace offering. By the time the man suspected the gift, the tiled floors of his villa were running with blood. In fact, Phil said, he wondered if this sculpture sitting under the Reverend's church might be the same one. There was a somewhat . . . odd character who came to these parts around the turn of the twentieth century. He lived in a big house that stood where the reservoir is now. From what he understood, a number of unusual items were noted in the man's possession.

Wait, the Reverend said. Just—wait. All you need to do is carve this particular image and you'll unleash—blood? death?

It's a little more involved than that, Phil said. He had closed the book he'd been reading from and turned his attention to the volume whose covers were locked shut. Unless you have a piece of the mountain where the Mother was bound and possess the skill to work its material, you must employ certain procedures in order to bring the Mother forth from your sculpture.

Certain procedures? the Reverend said. Like what? sacrificing a virgin?

No, Phil said. It is important that she is not a virgin. She should be expecting a child, the closer to her delivery, the better.

XXIX

Had you asked her, the Reverend says, if God were active in the world, she would have answered that she believed He was, but His movements tended to be subtle, often hard to detect. If you had followed up that question by asking her about the host of obvious, even garish miracles recorded throughout the Bible, in the lives of the saints, she would have replied that those were other times. Were she being particularly candid, she would have added that many of the miraculous events described in Scripture probably had perfectly natural explanations—what was important was the attribution of those events to a loving God. And were you one of her close friends—Phil Singer, say—she would have confided in you that she judged many of the supernatural occurrences incorporated into the biblical narratives to be outright myth—not a lie, you understand, but a figurative means of expressing a truth.

Now here she was, listening to her good friend tell her that she was in the midst of a myth, that she was in one of the older biblical stories, when the God of the Israelites was only one deity contending with a pantheon of rivals. Not to mention disclosing a tradition of what sounded like black magic, which would be ludicrous if it hadn't involved apparent human sacrifice. Stop, she wanted to say. This was everything about religion she couldn't stand: the sin, the superstition, the violence.

But Phil had removed a key from his jeans and unlocked the fourth book. He opened its cover, and the kitchen light dimmed. Darkness filled the air in swirling motes, like a storm of ash. The Reverend crossed herself and raised her hands to shield herself from them, but the black flakes swept through her flesh as if they weren't there. Phil, she said.

He was barely visible, the center of a storm of darkness. He had picked up another of the books and was holding it out to her. If you would, he said. She took the volume, which was far and away the thickest of the four. Its cover was plain except for a small design at its center: a slender ring broken at about seven o'clock. From amongst its pages, a ream of other sheets of paper protruded. It will be simpler, Phil said, if you start at the back and work your way forward—it should be a dozen or so pages from the end.

What, the Reverend asked, was she looking for?

She would know it, Phil answered, when she saw it.

She did. The book was a kind of journal-cum-scrapbook, its pages crowded with writing in various shades of blue, black, green, and red, some passages running parallel to one another, others looping one around the other, still others squeezing into margins. Photographs and postcards, some black and white, others full color, all of different locations, had been slotted between the sheets; while maps, newspaper clippings, mimeographs, photocopies, and computer printouts had been paper-clipped, taped, and stapled to the pages. The Reverend recognized pictures of the cathedral at Chartres, an inscription of a labyrinth on a gray rock, a painting of two rows of stylized figures racing their chariots toward each other, framed by lines of Hindi. Eleven pages in, a sheaf of photocopies unfolded and she found herself reading the Anglican Communion's Major Rite of Exorcism. This is supposed to be in the Bishop's Book, she said.

It was, Phil said. The Bishop of Edinburgh's, to be precise.

But, she said, it's the Bishop's Book. It's not supposed to be opened to just anyone.

Everything you've seen—you're seeing, Phil said, and you want to obsess over the Bishop's Book? Fine. He had known the Bishop. Lovely man. He permitted that copy to be made. Satisfied?

This, she said, you want me to perform an exorcism?

He wanted her to perform that rite, yes.

But, the Reverend said, there are procedures for this sort of thing. Someone's supposed to perform an official investigation, and the bishop is supposed to give approval, and the priest who undertakes the exorcism is supposed to be more mature, experienced . . . And anyway, what exactly is it that needs exorcising? The ghost of a murdered goddess?

More or less, Phil said. We are trying to push the wrath that has found its way out of the statue back inside it.

For which you need an Anglican rite?

For which he needed her belief in that rite.

What was he going to be doing, she said, reciting Psalm 91 and blowing the Shofar?

He would be saying some words it was probably best she didn't listen to too closely.

XXX

She can't say it was unbelievable, the Reverend says, because there was Phil, surrounded by pieces of blackness, as if all the letters on all the pages of the book he'd unlocked had risen into a whirlwind of ink—not to mention the screaming she'd heard, and whatever had happened to the interior of the church, and everything that had occurred with the headless statue, the report of which she had ascribed to Margaret Garrick's hysteria over the death at her front door, but which at this point appeared largely true. Nor can she call it insane, because there was a certain kind of logic—no, that isn't the right word. There was a consistency to what was unfolding around her that made it sound more than plausible—it sounded compelling. What it was was unbearable. She, who spent her days visiting the ailing members of her graying congregation in their beds at the local hospitals, who passed her nights worrying over the decline in Sunday's collection amount, whose excuse for a diversion was mediating a dispute between a ninety-two-year-old widow and her fifty-nine-year-old son about her ability to operate a motor vehicle safely: she was being summoned to battle with supernatural agencies. The coffee she had swallowed churned in her stomach. Her hands shook; her knees trembled the way they had before her first high school dance.

Without waiting for her answer, Phil Singer was heading for the front door. Hang on, the Reverend said, there were some things she needed to gather.

XXXI

Darkness trailing behind him like a ragged cape, Phil led the way to the church, the Reverend doing her best not to trip over her feet as she scanned the Major Rite. At the entrance to Holy Redeemer, Phil stopped and said, If you'd like to begin.

You've seen the movies, the Reverend says, *The Exorcist* and its imitators. You have an idea of what came next: the Sign of the Cross, the opening prayers, the reading from the Gospels. If there's anything that would surprise you about the actual rite, it's how much longer everything takes. Throughout, Phil remained silent, until she withdrew the vial of holy water from her pocket, popped the top with her thumb, and splashed the church door. As she was pronouncing her latest Amen, he uttered a word, a single syllable. The sound started somewhere deep in Phil's throat, then on its way out collapsed into itself, so that what emerged was barely distinguishable from a bark. She couldn't guess at the language that counted such a word among its vocabulary. Speaking it appeared to lend Phil a certain energy: he stood straighter, his eyes shining, all trace of middle-of-the-night fatigue gone. Shall we? he asked, and opened the door and strode inside.

XXXII

The interior of the church was still dark, the air still restless, damp, laden with a thick, meaty smell. Does it sound odd if she admits that the first emotion she felt confronting that cool blackness was relief? She had not hallucinated, had not encouraged Phil to his revelations personal and historical for a fantasy. Right away, though, her relief was swallowed by dread so strong it made her stomach twist. She snapped on the flashlight she'd brought with her and continued her part of the exorcism.

Actually, she says, that isn't true, not exactly. Before she proceeded with the rite, she swept the flashlight's beam around her.

You wait, then say, And?

It wasn't a very powerful light, the Reverend says. Ten feet out, it faded almost to nothing.

But—

But the church had . . . changed, she says. It had . . . reduced, sim-plified. As far as she could tell, she and Phil were standing at the en-trance to a sizable cave. The ground in front of them sloped down at a gradual angle. She waited for Phil to begin descending it. When he did not, she resumed the rite.

At the conclusion of the next reading from the Gospels, Phil gave voice to a second, guttural word. It might have been the same one he'd spoken outside the church; she wasn't sure. The sound of it scraped against her ears, seemed to thicken the motes of darkness swirling around her friend. The flashlight flickered. Can you read as you walk? Phil said.

Yes, she said.

Then follow me, he said, and proceed with the ritual. He started down the slope into the cave.

XXXIII

They walked, the Reverend says, for a long time. The floor leveled, which made it somewhat easier for her to carry on reciting the exor-cism. A couple of steps ahead of her, Phil was bursting with energy, as if he were barely restraining himself from breaking into a run. The blackness surrounding him shone like fresh ink spilled on a page. She did her best to concentrate on the words of the rite, but she kept see-ing things at the edges of her vision. The glow of her flashlight seemed to pick out faces in the rock under her feet, shadows that didn't belong to anything. She had the most intense sensation of being watched, the Reverend says, and you can be sure, a woman who preaches to a con-gregation of a hundred-plus knows about being looked at. Out in the darkness around them, she could feel something, somethings, keeping track of them.

She was still reading when they arrived at the statue. Phil stopped short, and she almost collided with him. Right away, the Reverend says, she understood where they were—she could see a figure at the very top of her vision—but she did not lift her eyes from the page un-til she had delivered her Amen and Phil coughed another, or maybe it was the same, word. Then she pointed her flashlight at the form before them.

You haven't seen the statue, have you? the Reverend says. No, that's ridiculous—how could you? She had the photos of it burned, afterwards. It was awful. Not only was the subject disturbing, to say the least, but the style, the skill with which it had been rendered made it monstrous, obscene. It was intolerable to look at, yet she could not keep her eyes from it. Her flashlight flared on something at its base: blood, a shallow pool encircling the sculpture, fed, she saw, by a network of narrow streams winding out of the darkness. She traced the flashlight's beam along the nearest line of blood to the foot of a shadowed form. Not shadowy, the Reverend says, shadowed. She played the light up the figure, but it remained obscure, as if it were behind a curtain. Despite this, she could detect the swell of its belly, the space where its head should have been. She swept the flashlight in an arc and saw the other tributaries descending from the feet of the other occluded forms, each with a rounded belly and headless neck. Their collective blood was the red reek clouding the air.

Phil, she said.

Go on, please, Marie, he said.

This time, when she resumed the exorcism, Phil spoke, too, in more of what she had christened the Black Speech of Mordor. Do you know Tolkien?

You do.

The Reverend nods. Because she was focused on the rite, she heard it as background noise, an unpleasant sequence of snarls, coughs, and cries that sounded like nothing meant to be produced by a human throat. There was an irregular rhythm to his sentences that intersected the up and down of hers at odd moments, so that it was almost as if they were speaking halves of a single word. The language— the Black Speech—clawed at her ears, as if each syllable were covered in barbs; she had the sense that, were she not intent on the pages balanced on her hand, her ears would be bleeding.

The statue appeared to be fading, along with the pool of blood, the shadowed company, as if it had all been projected onto a large screen and the bulb in the projector were being turned down, in order that she could see what the screen had concealed. She was looking into a small, squarish room, possibly a bedroom, although there was no bed within it, only a tall wooden crate set lengthwise near the middle. At one end of the box, the statue lay atop a heap of old blankets and sheets. The walls, painted pale green, had been chalked with symbols, as had the ceiling and floor. The Reverend couldn't identify most of them. She picked out a scattering of Greek characters, what she was reasonably sure were Arabic letters, but aside from the broken circle she'd seen on the cover of the book she was holding, the rest were unfamiliar: circles bisected by straight lines bisected by short, wavy lines; a long, gradual curve like a smile; what might have been a cup or a chalice. To her right, the door to the room swung inwards, and a man led a woman into it. Both were wearing togas, but they were more the improvised arrangement of a white sheet and a pair of safety pins common to amateur productions of Shakespeare or fraternity parties than historically accurate clothing. The man was young, pale, and thin, his chin fringed by black hair aspiring to a beard. The woman was equally young, though with better color and a fuller form, one grown large with pregnancy. The tilt of the woman's head, the wander of her eyes, suggested that she was under the influence of some substance, a suggestion that was borne out by the ease with which the young man lowered her to and positioned her on the wooden crate, making it a kind of couch for her. She lay placidly, with her head at the statue-end of the box, while the young man said things the Reverend could not hear. He seemed to be reassuring her as he crouched on the other side of the box, searching for something on the floor with his hands. Once he found it, he stood slowly, so as not to disturb the woman, who was staring intently at one of the symbols on the ceiling. She did not see the huge Bowie knife shining in his right hand. Even when he raised it over his head and swung it down into her bare throat, the Reverend could almost believe the woman never saw her death descending.

She understood that what she was witnessing was a kind of vision. That did not make it any easier to watch. Sharp as the knife appeared, the young man's arm was not up to the task, and while the blood vented out of the wound he'd inflicted, the woman was able to raise her hands enough for him to have to hold them away with his free hand while he hacked at her throat a second and a third time. Her head severed, he pushed it off the box onto the floor, dropped the knife, and moved along the corpse, from which blood continued to spill. Catching it under the back and hips, he hoisted the body, tilting the neck down to help the blood continue its exit. Its destination was, of course, the sculpture, whose white limbs drank in the blood that splashed them. As he struggled to hold the corpse up, the young man's lips moved quickly. When he could support it no longer, he let the body crash onto the crate and sat down heavily beside it. His arms, his chest, his face were spotted and streaked red; he pulled the toga from the corpse and wiped himself with it. After he regained his strength, the young man stood, approached the statue, which looked much less blood-drenched than it should have, and picked it up. His arms straining with the weight, he hurriedly carried the statue out of the room. He did not return.

The Reverend continued with the exorcism, the words to which seemed to be losing their sense, blending with Phil's Black Speech into a third thing altogether. She heard herself saying Amen, and In the Name of the Father, and of the Son, and of the Holy Spirit, and Let us pray, but she was finding it difficult to maintain the larger sense of what she was reading. The bloody tableau before her dimmed to darkness, swallowed by whatever memory had displayed it, and in the space it had occupied, the Reverend saw a faint shape whose outline suggested the statue, returned to view.

It was not. At what might have been the far end of a long tunnel stood a woman. She, too, was dressed in a white toga, but the gather and folds of it showed it to be no costume. The distance made it difficult for the Reverend to distinguish the woman's features with any certainty, but she had the impression of a regal, even haughty, cast to them. The woman was enormously pregnant, and she carried the swell of her belly proudly. There are some Christian theologians, the Reverend says, who have suggested the usefulness of re-conceptualizing the Trinity in female terms, as Mother, Daughter, Spirit. If you had told her the woman she was seeing was the Mother in that schema, she would have accepted it. This was creation made manifest.

And then the woman's throat split open, spilling blood down her front. The top of her toga went from scarlet to crimson as the blood soaked into and spread across the fabric, slicking it to her body. Her hands grabbed her belly, whose surface convulsed as the child inside responded in panic to the violence done its mother. Blood streamed from her throat, from her mouth, from her legs. Her toga was sopping, almost black. Blood spattered and puddled and pooled at her feet. Her face twisted, with pain, or sorrow, or rage, the Reverend could not say. Eyes full of tears, voice rasping, she gave all her attention to proceeding with the rite.

The next time she dared glance up, the woman was gone, her place taken by the statue, which was no longer situated in a pool of blood, guarded by the shadowed ranks of the murdered. The Reverend went on with the rite. She was not sure when she noticed that Phil was no longer uttering the Black Speech; she had the sense that he had ceased some time ago, but could not pinpoint the exact moment. She stole a look at him and was startled to see his mouth set in a smile so wide it was as much a grimace. She pronounced another Amen and he remained silent. She pushed on with the remainder of the rite. Her mouth was dry, her lips chapped. It felt as if she had been speaking all night. She recited the Lord's Prayer, traced the Sign of the Cross in the air, read another passage from the Gospels. She invoked the aid of a host of angels and saints. She sprinkled the rest of her holy water. She shifted Phil's book from one hand to the other and back again. Around her, the air steadily filled with light. She invoked the Trinity one more time. She delivered her final Amen.

In the silence that followed, she raised her eyes from the book and found herself and Phil standing in the undercroft, its high windows glowing with the dawn. She closed the book and took in the walls hung with the felt banners the Sunday school kids had assembled, the pamphlet table by the door with its red-and-white-checked cloth, the folding tables and chairs stacked below the large window into the kitchen. In the center of the water-stained carpet was the statue, no less awful than before, but perhaps slightly less intimidating.

Phil Singer's mouth had relaxed from its rictus grin; he, too, had closed and lowered his book. The storm of blackness that had encircled him was gone. The energy that had radiated from him was gone, too; if anything, he looked older than he had when he'd arrived a few hours ago. He turned his gaze away from the sculpture and said he would bring his car to the back door. He thought it would be easier for them to transport the statue to it via that route. Also, there was less chance of anyone seeing them that way.

The Reverend nodded but did not say anything, though she passed

Phil's book back to him. She waited in the undercroft while he took his books and fetched his Accord, and she helped him to carry the sculpture past the kitchen and bathrooms and out the back door, and to wrestle it into his trunk. The back of his car sagged with the weight. Throughout, the Reverend remained silent. Only when the trunk had thunked shut did she say, Phil, what happened here?

You and I—but mostly you—prevented something bad from becoming worse, he said.

So it worked? she said. The rite, the exorcism, was a success?

As much as such things can be, he said.

What does that mean?

It means you should get some sleep and not worry about anything, he said.

There was one more question she wanted to ask him, the Reverend says, but she couldn't bring herself to frame it, not after what they'd just finished, after what had occasioned it in the first place. But as she stood watching Phil turn out of the church parking lot, the image of the woman at the end of that long tunnel, her throat parting to spill her blood over her distended belly, rose in her memory. The expression on her face . . .

XXXIV

A check of your watch reveals that you are out of time with the Reverend Au Claire. If you intend to keep your appointment with Trooper Wright, you must leave now. This is not a problem: the priest appears to have reached the end of her story. Enough questions to keep the two of you here the rest of the afternoon compete for your tongue. You settle on asking what became of the statue.

She presumes Phil reburied it, the Reverend says. Of course, the next time she saw him, that was the first thing she said to him, but he would offer no more than that it was in a safe place. His house was a few miles from town, as you're going over the mountain toward Huguenot. It sat on a little bit of property; she presumes he dug a hole somewhere out there and dropped the sculpture into it. To be honest, after Phil passed away a couple of years ago and a few of his friends took it upon themselves to clean out his house, she half expected one of them to bump into it in his basement, covered with an old blanket.

No one did, though.

And the exorcism? you say. It was effective? No more appearances by the headless woman?

There have been rumors aplenty, the Reverend says. Most of them undoubtedly the product of overactive imaginations colliding with well-handled gossip, facilitated by alcohol.

But, you say, she feels she succeeded.

The Reverend smiles, as if at a private joke.

You have another meeting that you're just about to be late for, you say, prompting the priest to rise from her chair, but you would very much appreciate it if you could speak with Revered Au Claire for a little while later on, maybe after your next interview is finished?

She's sorry, the priest says, but no, she's said all she has to say.

But—

You don't want to be late for your appointment, she says, do you?

XXXV

There is nothing you can do. You thank the Reverend for her time and her candor, neither of which she appears too happy to have granted you so much of, and rush out the rectory's front door. The plaza in which the Dunkin' Donuts at which you've agreed to meet Jacqueline Wright is slotted is a literal two-minute drive from the church, but you speed there, anyway, afraid that the trooper will have taken your delay for a cancellation and left already. You wish you could spare five minutes to write down the highlights of your interview with the Reverend Au Claire, but you dare not be any later. As you step out of the Metro, you survey the parking lot for the roof rack of a police cruiser. When you fail to find one, your heart sinks. You are on the verge of unlocking the door you just locked when you remember that this is the trooper's day off, so she will have driven here in whatever vehicle she owns.

Inside the Dunkin' Donuts, you are greeted by a woman seated at one of the tables by the front window. She rises to shake your hand, a tall woman whose figure is not quite ample enough to qualify as stout. Her grip is firm. You thank Jacqueline Wright for waiting for you and apologize for your lateness: your last interview ran long. It's all right, the trooper says, she's been enjoying a coffee and a blueberry muffin. Do you want something?

A coffee would be nice, you admit, if she wouldn't mind giving you another minute. Maybe you could get her something while you're at the counter, another muffin, perhaps? She declines, leaving you to fetch a large coffee with extra milk from a woman who looks too old to be working the cash register at a Dunkin' Donuts. You wonder if she's the owner. Coffee in hand, you return to the front of the shop and take up your seat opposite Jacqueline.

You were talking to someone else about the accident? she says.

Peeling back the tab on the lid to your cup, you nod. As you told her on the phone, you're researching the circumstances surrounding Rachel Torino's death ten years ago. There have been reports of . . . unusual events in the weeks leading up to the accident that took her life, all of them connected to a statue that was unearthed on the grounds of the Wynkoop Inn. You've spoken to Stephen Holland about it, and Christina Henderson, as well as an art history professor at Penrose College and Constance Braddon. Before you came here, you were talking to the Reverend Au Claire.

Sounds like you've been busy, the trooper says.

Very, you say. You're trying to be thorough.

Which is why you contacted her.

Exactly. Mrs. Braddon suggested it, actually.

Did Constance tell you that she saw the accident happen?

She thought you had, you say.

Jacqueline nods. Her large green eyes seem open almost too wide. She was seven cars behind, on her way back to the barracks. Needless to say, she didn't witness the poor woman's death, but she saw the truck lose control. It was one of those trucks that carries sheets of glass, you know, tilted on its sides. Traffic was stopped on the trooper's side of the road—a delivery van waiting to make a left turn further ahead, which it couldn't do because the cars going the other way were traveling at a steady clip. The glass truck was part of that moving traffic. About ten yards in front of the car in which the woman—

Rachel Torino.

Right, Rachel Torino—about ten yards from where she and her

husband were sitting, the front left tire of the glass truck blew out. The trooper heard it: it sounded like an explosion. The truck dipped and swerved to its left. The driver overcorrected to his right, and as he did, the pickup following him crashed into his back. From what she understands, it took the forensics guys a couple of weeks to work everything out, the forces, the angles, the velocities, that kind of stuff. Practically speaking, what resulted was one of the tall sheets of glass on the back of the truck coming loose, falling onto the very front of the Torinos' car, and shattering. One of the pieces—only one, that was all it took—was large enough to smash through the passenger's side of the windshield and sever Rachel's head.

That's . . . pretty remarkable, you say.

The forensics crew claimed it wasn't even a one in a million thing. It was more like a one in a billion occurrence. Jacqueline takes a sip from her coffee.

That must have been difficult to see.

It was a goddamned nightmare, she says. Once she understood what had taken place in front of her, she flipped on her car's lights and steered onto the shoulder. There were already people out of their cars and moving in the direction of the Torinos' car when she threw her cruiser into Park. Fortunately, she'd had the foresight to call in the accident before she exited her car, because once she did, the first person she met was the husband—

James.

James, yeah—he was walking toward her. He was covered in blood, so much that, at first, she thought he'd been injured, until she saw what he was cradling in his arms. His wife's eyes were open, her expression one of slight surprise, as if the baby within her had dealt her an especially sharp kick. Just tell me she's going to be okay, he was saying. She's expecting our first child. Just tell me she's going to be okay.

Jesus, you say.

Yeah, Jacqueline says. His mind had collapsed, you know?

You nod.

She shakes her head. Such a shame. It's hard to imagine anyone getting over that. It—she had a difficult time with it herself. While you're in the Academy, they show you photos of accident victims—

pretty graphic stuff—but they're only pictures. This wasn't her first traffic fatality, but it was worse than anything she'd seen before. The EMTs who showed up were pretty rattled by it, too. After she turned James Torino over to them, she did what she could to chase the spectators away from the car and the . . . rest of his wife's remains. She recognized Margaret Garrick among them—she must have come running down the front steps of the Inn—and though she noticed the look of horror on the woman's face, the trooper didn't note it as particularly remarkable. Everybody was horrified, herself included. She knows she shouldn't, but she can't help thinking that, if she had been more attentive, she might have picked up on the signs Mrs. Garrick must have been giving off.

Signs?

That she was going to cut her throat.

What?

From what she understands, Jacqueline says, the woman had been under a tremendous amount of stress, all of it related to the statue you mentioned. It sounds like some kind of mass hysteria to her, but its effects on Mrs. Garrick were real enough. Early the morning after the accident—about four A.M.—the call came in that there had been some kind of incident at the Wynkoop Inn involving a knife, and at least one person was injured. Funny, the trooper says, she wasn't supposed to be on duty, especially after what she'd seen the previous day. But she'd already agreed to cover a colleague's shift, and the barracks was short-handed, so her C.O. didn't have much choice in the matter. It was fine with her. She preferred being out on patrol to sitting at home, dwelling on what she'd seen. Anyway, she'd stopped in to speak to Reverend Au Claire for a little while, which had satisfied her C.O. for the moment.

To tell the truth, though, she'd passed those late hours driving back and forth on the stretch of 209 where the accident had happened, so maybe she wasn't as okay as she told herself she was. It meant that, when dispatch put out the news about the Inn, she was right there to respond to it. Mrs. Garrick was lucky she was. She'd cut herself pretty deep—grabbed one of the butcher knives in the kitchen and sawed her neck open. There was a waitress with her. She did what she could to stanch the flow of blood, which wasn't enough, really, but then Jacqueline arrived, and then the EMTs came hot on her heels. Apparently, it was touch and go for a while there—Mrs. Garrick had done more damage to herself than you would have thought possible—but she survived; although she couldn't speak anymore, had damaged her voicebox. The trooper understands that, as soon as she was well enough to be moved, she was transferred to a private psychiatric facility.

That—you were present for all that, you say. It must have been surreal.

It was, Jacqueline says. Later on, she needed to take some sick leave, to sort out what had happened. Well, not what had happened, but its effect on her.

Of course, you say.

After the EMTs arrived at the Inn, there was an incident that made her aware of how much she'd been traumatized by the last day's incidents. She takes another sip from her coffee.

You wait.

She had identified the knife the moment she entered the kitchen, the trooper says. Mrs. Garrick had dropped it beside her, and the waitress had kicked it aside. While there was no doubt in Jacqueline's mind about what had taken place in here, proper procedure had to be followed. So as soon as the EMTs had come bustling into the kitchen and she'd told them what she knew and backed out of the way, she set about securing the evidence, i.e. the knife. She carried a pair of rubber gloves in her pocket for such an eventuality. She snapped them on, bent beside the knife, and picked it up by the end of its handle. It was huge, a prop from a horror movie. Blood slid down to the tip of the blade and dribbled onto the floor. She held it up for inspection and, reflected in the knife's stainless steel, saw something—saw someone.

Someone?

Jacqueline Wright takes a deep breath and releases it with the name: Rachel Torino. Her head was missing, and she was wearing a white, like a white dress, but she was pregnant, so the trooper had no doubt of her identity. She was standing behind where the EMTs were working furiously over Mrs. Garrick, tearing open packets of bandages, drawing something into a syringe, maintaining steady chatter. Jacqueline turned, and there was no one, no headless ghost, inclining the ruin of her neck toward the EMTs and their patient. Out of the corner of her eye, something moved. She pivoted to the right, and there, reflected on the polished metal of the refrigerator door, she saw the ghost again, standing this time, with her back to the trooper, once more leaning over the EMTs. She seemed so solid; Jacqueline could clearly see the places where the blood had run from her neck and plastered the dress to her skin. When the trooper moved her head, though, the floor between her and the EMTs was vacant. She stepped away from the refrigerator, and suddenly she saw the ghost everywhere: curving around the side of a soup pot on the stove; cupped in the bowl of a serving spoon; multiplied in rows of wine glasses. She was suspended in a window; she wavered in a water jug; she was upside down in the tiling on the floor. No matter where Jacqueline found her, she was oriented in the same direction, toward where Margaret Garrick lay, having tried and failed to join her, to become like her. When you thought about it, she had done a remarkable job. It wouldn't take much more to complete what she'd begun.

The EMT was talking for at least a minute before his words started to make sense to her. Jackie? she heard him saying. Is everything all right? Are you feeling okay? She couldn't understand why he was asking her these questions, or why he was standing, his hands held out in front of him, as if to ward her off or grab her, until she followed the line of his gaze and saw the knife clenched in her hand, her grip so tight, the blade was shaking.

XXXVI

Naturally, she says, she placed the knife down on the nearest countertop and exited the kitchen posthaste.

Naturally, you say. You have recognized the stare with which the trooper has been regarding you for the duration of your conversation: it is the bright look of someone taking powerful psychiatric medications. Your experience is not sufficient for you to identify the exact class of drug, but you have dealt with enough students being treated for mental health disorders to feel that some measure of caution is in order. You don't know what circumstances have brought her to this point in her life—it's entirely possible that it's completely unrelated to the narrative she is relating to you—but it would not do to raise any memories that would complicate her condition. If you haven't already. You clear your throat and ask, Was that your last encounter with the ghost?

More or less. She shrugs. There were times she'd think she saw something, but it never turned out to be anything. She knows there are all kinds of stories about the ghost, local legends, but she never experienced anything like that.

You are on the verge of winding the interview down, thanking Jacqueline for her time and telling her that you have to think about the drive back home, when she says, All this—everything she went through—kind of messed her up. For the longest time—she's talking years—she had these moments where she'd find herself looking at the knives in her kitchen. She has one of those wooden blocks with slots for all the different knives you might use in your cooking. Some-times—not too often, but often enough to be a problem—she would slide the butcher knife from its space and stand staring at it. Her knife wasn't as high-end as the one Margaret Garrick had turned on herself. That one had been a single edge so sharp you could see it; this one was serrated, albeit finely. She wasn't sure which would cut better. Granted, the knife at the Inn was restaurant-grade, hers a condo-warming pre-sent purchased at J. C. Penney, but with a strong enough arm behind it, she would bet her knife could make it at least as far as Mrs. Gar-rick's, if not further. When she would have these . . . episodes, it was like she could almost hear something, a scream, coming from deep in-side the blade's mirrored surface. She couldn't decide if the scream were of pain, or anger, fury.

It was not a good time, Jacqueline says. There were—well, there were a lot of things going on—going wrong in her life. In the end, she got some help, and things started to improve. One thing her therapist told her, though, was that dwelling on this kind of stuff tends to draw it closer to you. She doesn't want to freak you out or anything, but she feels like she has to tell you to be careful.

XXXVII

Your conversation with Jacqueline Wright concluded, you opt to re-main at Dunkin' Donuts and start work on recording as much of your last two interviews as you can retrieve from your memory. Thinking of it as the toll you're paying for the extra time you intend to stay here, you purchase another coffee with extra milk and a coffee roll, and settle down to work with your notebook and your pen.

XXXVIII

A third coffee and two trips to the toilet later, you have transcribed as much of your interviews with Marie Au Claire and Jacqueline Wright as you can recall. Your writing hand has gone beyond painful to numb, your lower back has tightened into a clench that has sent you rummaging your purse for the bottle of ibuprofen you carry for such contingencies. You shake out your hand, crack your knuckles, lean back in your chair. Outside the front window, night has faded the cars in the parking lot to the same dull color. You pick up the pen to put it away and cannot resist jotting a final few questions: What is the significance of the broken ring design on the cover of the book Phil Singer gave to Marie Au Claire? Personal emblem, or (oc)cult symbol? Is there a connection between the young man Marie Au Claire reported seeing in her vision and Isaac Schenker? Are there any records of Isaac engaging in unusual behavior? What ritual did Phil Singer perform? What are the other rites of exorcism, aside from Christian and Jewish? Do any involve speaking in another language? Why did Annabel Ferris carve her self-portraits to fit the statue's neck?

XXXIX

After a frugal dinner at the pizza place across the parking lot from the Dunkin' Donuts—an order of garlic knots, a plain slice, and a Coke—you return to the rental car. There is enough gas left in its undersized tank to return you over the mountains to Huguenot, where you remember several gas stations on the approach to the Thruway entrance. Traffic is light, and you make the left out of the lot without difficulty. In the dark, your route, hardly familiar, seems strange, the turns you must make coming too soon or not soon enough, the roads you follow full of sudden curves you take too fast. Under normal conditions, you would have a white-knuckle grip on the steering wheel, your eyes glued to the road, sweat trickling down the small of your back, but these are not normal circumstances. You have been handed not another chapter for the study you are writing, but another book altogether. While it incorporates electronic legends—and thus can be linked to the book you'll finish as soon as possible—this work gathers local history, mass hysteria, and fringe religious practices under its purview. Though you have to be careful not to put your cart before your horse, it could be the kind of academic work whose appeal extends to a broader audience, that levers its author out of her community college job into a position at a four-year university, that makes her money.

In front of you, the road climbs steeply. The car's engine whines as you force it up the mountain's slope. It has been a long time since you've felt this pure excitement about a project. Your dissertation, perhaps? After having lived your life for—for years, really, as if it were being told to you, as if you were a character being pushed through it by a middling writer's inexpert hand, suddenly, finally, you are on the verge of moving from second- to first-person, of taking on the telling of your life. You wonder if you can start writing this book as you're bringing the other one to a close.

The car crests the top of the slope. Now the road drops as dramatically as it rose, hooking sharply to the left a hundred yards below, in front of a block of exposed rockface. To your right, standing on the nominal shoulder, a figure flashes past, your headlights flaring on the white dress she wears. You whip your head around to verify what you think you saw, the great, rounded belly, the red wound across her throat, but she's gone, and anyway, the brake pedal has sunk all the way to the floor, and the car is gathering speed, hurtling toward the bare mountain. Surely, though, surely, the face you saw above that bloody line wasn't yours?

Story Notes

I think it was sometime in the fall of 1977 that CBS broadcast a one-hour special on the making of the original *Star Wars*. Fascinated to learn the assortment of techniques and tricks by which the movie's visual effects had been accomplished, I was captivated. I've been that way with most things—especially most things art-related—for as long as I can remember. Whether documentary specials on Willis O'Brien and Ray Harryhausen, or *How to Draw Comics the Marvel Way,* or Stephen King's story notes to *Skeleton Crew,* I love learning about what lies behind the artworks I enjoy. Undoubtedly, it's not unrelated to my own creative aspirations.

All of which is to say that, if you're the kind of reader who feels the same way about such things as do I, here are some story notes. If not, no hard feelings.

"Kids": To begin with, a *jeu d'esprit.* This story came to be because, at the Boskone science fiction and fantasy convention in 2008, a number of his fellow writers realized that horror critic and (far too) occasional horror writer Jack M. Haringa had the dubious distinction of having been included in the novels of several of his friends, pretty much so he could be murdered, and that by zombie children. It's that kind of community, yes. A number of us thought it would be funny to select a day in the near future on which we would post to our blogs short stories (and the occasional poem) in which we also would kill Jack—zombie children optional. Jack knew nothing of our plans, and was suitably disturbed when the varied reports of his demise began to appear on the blog pages of those he had considered his colleagues, even friends. My goals were twofold: to honor the tradition of having Jack consumed by zombie children, and to do so in a way that paid heed to his day job as English teacher at a private school and to the man's vast erudition. It strikes me that the scene of a group of monsters falling on a hapless individual is one of the archetypal moments in a certain sub-set of the modern horror novel, what I guess you might call the horde narrative. I'm not sure who originated it. (Bradbury? Matheson? King? Undoubtedly, Jack knows.) To his credit, Jack took the whole kill-him-in-your-blog project in the passive-aggressive spirit in which it was in-tended, and even agreed to allow the entries to be collected in a slender book, *Jack Haringa Must Die!*, the proceeds from which went to support the Shirley Jackson Awards. Thus does the recognition of literary ex-cellence benefit from Jack's horrible death(s).

"How the Day Runs Down": In the late 1990s, I began to write a monologue in the voice of the Stage Manager from Thornton Wilder's *Our Town*. Its subject: zombies. I don't know why I did this. Possibly, it was because I had read and seen Wilder's play performed a number of times during my high school years. To be frank, I'd never cared for it that much, but I found the voice of the stage manager surprisingly easy to imitate, and the conceit of having his placid town overrun by the living dead struck me as more funny than it probably should have. I actually got quite far with the thing before being lured away by other projects. Fast forward about a decade, and my friend, the talented young editor John Joseph Adams, e-mailed me that he was putting to-gether a reprint anthology of the best zombie stories from the last few decades. "That's funny," I replied, "I started a zombie story, once . . ." John urged me to finish it for his anthology, and I said I would. The piece was always intended to be written in play format—if for no other reason than that it was a response to another play—but this time, I de-cided I would parallel Wilder's play more closely than I had my first attempt. For one thing, I would include brief scenes showing daily life in the aftermath of the zombie apocalypse. For another, I would focus on a young woman's story as a way to lens my story's thematic con-cerns. Of course the fourth wall would be broken, but I wanted to go further still, moving select bits of the action out among the (at this point, hypothetical) audience. Not to mention, I intended to have the Stage Manager, himself, affected by what was erupting around him, which seemed to me among the most effective ways I could indicate the depth and dimensions of the crisis facing the story's characters.

John was happy with the story—as was Gordon Van Gelder, who published it pretty much simultaneously in the *Magazine of Fantasy & Science Fiction*—and readers were happy with his *The Living Dead*, which was the best-selling anthology with which I've (so far) been involved. No doubt, the book benefitted from the momentum that had been generated by David Wellington's *Monster* trilogy and Max Brooks's *World War Z,* as well as the general cultural ascendancy of the zombie. (Or what should more properly be called the post-Romero zombie, I suppose.)

With "Kids," this story was my try at the figure of the post-Romero zombie. If there's any continuity between the collection you're holding in your hands and the one that preceded it (*Mr. Gaunt and Other Uneasy Encounters*), it's been my ongoing desire to make my way through the tropes and traditions of the horror field—as well as a desire to see what happens when you bring those tropes into contact with narrative techniques drawn from the length and breadth of literary history. (Which, to be sure, is nothing new in horror: it's what writers from H. P. Lovecraft to Peter Straub have done before me.) To be honest, I don't find this version of the zombie all that interesting. Unless, like David Wellington, you're going to play with the parameters of the monster, the zombie strikes me as not much more than a glorified plot device, one that could be replaced by any other mass threat. I'm tempted to say that these stories represent the limit of my engagement with the zombie, but there is another idea I have in mind . . .

Oh—and one more thing: given the popularity of the post-Romero zombie, it was perhaps inevitable that a story about these creatures written as a play would make its way to an actual stage. The first time this happened was at the 2010 Boskone, when a number of people associated with the Shirley Jackson Awards did a dramatic reading of roughly the first half of the story. The second and more substantial staging of the piece was done by Nicu's Spoon theater in Manhattan during July of 2011, under the direction of Stephanie Barton-Farcas, who brought together a fine cast of veterans and newcomers in a production that I thoroughly enjoyed. Having anything I'd written performed in a real theater by real actors was not something I'd ever anticipated, and I'd be lying if I said the experience didn't make an impression on me. Another story to work on . . .

"Technicolor": The first time I met famous editor Ellen Datlow, at the 2003 Readercon, she asked me, "When are you going to send me a story?" Talk about flattered: from that moment, it was my goal to do exactly this. I started a piece for her *Inferno* anthology, but it grew and took too long. (Come to think of it, I have to finish that story, too.) At the 2007 Readercon, Ellen invited me to a new project, an anthology of stories inspired by the work of Edgar Allan Poe—*not,* she hastened to make clear, pastiches, but stories that drew on Poe for inspiration while going their own way. I said yes on the spot, and named the story to which I wanted to respond: "The Masque of the Red Death." Together with "Ligeia," it's my favorite of Poe's stories, both for the luxuriousness of its prose and the mystery of its setting, the strange abbey where Prince Prospero and the rest of his court flee in a vain attempt to escape the plague ravaging his kingdom.

I've pondered that abbey for a long time, since at least my freshman year of college, when my Honors English class read a selection of Poe's stories and, as part of our discussion of "The Masque," were asked by our professor to interpret the significance of the progression of colors through the abbey's rooms. One by one, the class gave its answers, our professor crowding the blackboard with our readings. When he was done, just as the class session was almost over, we asked him what the colors meant. "I have no idea," he said cheerfully. As you might imagine, this was not the most satisfying of answers; although it may have been among the most productive, since later I would write a lengthy paper for another class in which I'd address the significance of the abbey, and then later still, I'd tackle the subject in this story for Ellen. Not to mention the times in-between when I'd taught it . . .

From the start, I knew the story would be written in the form of a lecture. As such, it represents my continuing engagement with academia as both a subject of and source of ideas and models for my fiction. In between the stories in my previous collection and this one, I wrote and published my first novel, *House of Windows,* another academic story that I had thought might have exhausted my interest in this type of story. However, as the story I named "Technicolor" and the original piece that ends this book showed, I was wrong. Given how much of a role academia has played and continues to play in my life, I suppose it's not much of a surprise that I should keep returning to it. Certainly, it was a pleasure to write in my lecturer's arch voice. It was also a pleasure to invent Prosper Vauglais and his mysterious green book, a hoax in which I was sufficiently successful to cause at least one librarian to ask me where they could find additional information concerning it. Indeed, this was typical of the story: the further into it I went, the more I found myself engaging of Poe, his biography, his literary modes, and especially his stories: "Ligeia," most obviously, but also "The Cask of Amontillado." I submitted the story right at the deadline, and was pleased to have Ellen accept it for the anthology, a pleasure which only increased when I read the finished book, *Poe: 19 New Tales Inspired by Edgar Allan Poe.* I'm proud of every book I've been part of, but the stories in this one struck a particular chord with me. While I've been connected to H. P. Lovecraft—both as critic of his fiction and fiction writer responding to it—it's with Poe that I have and feel the oldest, deepest connection. (Which must extend back at least to Mrs. Lovelock, my seventh grade English teacher, playing the class a record of "The Tell-Tale Heart" at Halloween.) "Technicolor" was the most successful story I'd published up that point: Ellen took it for the second volume of her *Best Horror of the Year,* and it was reprinted by Rich Horton in his year's best, too. Thank heavens for unanswered questions of literary interpretation.

"The Wide, Carnivorous Sky": In the fall of 2008, John Joseph Adams told me that he was editing a new reprint anthology, this one having to do with vampires. I immediately promised to write him another original story. This proved to be more of a challenge than I had anticipated. Unlike had happened with "How the Day Runs Down," this time, I had no partially written original to recreate. There was an idea I'd been kicking around after my wife and I had visited the south of France in 2002, about a monster that was vulnerable not to light, but darkness, but that was going to be a debased god of some sort, not a vampire. I had it in mind that I wanted to invert what had become the monster's predominant qualities: cultured, charming, darkly romantic. My vampire would be animal, savage, relentless, and I thought that the reversals I was planning might expand to include changing its fear of dawn to a fear of dusk. I tend to associate vampires with closed, even claustrophobic places, so I decided this one would be a creature of vast, open spaces. I had run across the phrase "the wide, carnivorous sky" somewhere on the Internet and had jotted it down on a scrap of paper; the words conjured for me the nightmare visions Philip K. Dick is supposed to have experienced of a face as big as the sky looking down at him. I toyed with the idea of the sky itself as the monster, but couldn't make that work. Then, one morning, I had the TV on, tuned to one of the morning talk shows like *Live! With Regis and Kelly* (don't judge me), and the guest of the moment was a man who was a veteran of the Iraq war. He was on to talk about a charity with which he was involved that helped wounded soldiers resuming their lives in the U.S. In the course of his interview, this man talked about the circumstances of his own wounding, which involved the Humvee in which he was riding striking an IED. The resulting explosion left him pinned on his back by part of his vehicle, staring up at the sky.

With that detail, I had my story. I wrote the opening sections fairly quickly, while my younger son and I accompanied my wife on a trip to San Francisco for the 2008 meeting of the Modern Language Association. The dialogue—the dynamic—among the characters emerged almost fully formed. The precise details of their encounter with the vampire, as well as the exact nature of that creature, took much longer to work out. That was due in no small part to my desire to get right as much of my character's experience as soldiers and then as casualties as I could. I knew that these guys had encountered the creature during the second battle for Fallujah, so I spent a good deal of time researching the facts of that battle, and of the train of events set rolling when a soldier is wounded in battle. Since I had imagined my vampire taking advantage of the chaos of combat to take its bloody meal, I thought it likely would seek out other places of conflict, too, which led me into more research on places like Darfur. I don't want to claim this story as something it's not, but it does represent my continuing desire to incorporate the events of the contemporary world into my fiction. The further I went into the narrative, the more somber I found myself growing at the realization that, even without the war in Iraq, there was a surfeit of opportunities for my monster to feed.

While I've never been as attentive to deadlines as a writer of my relative lack of stature should, I went way past the limit on this one, largely because I couldn't find quite the right ending. In particular, I was concerned that the story's closing scene, with the two survivors facing one another, unsure if the monster might be living on in/as one of them, too closely resembled the end of John Carpenter's remake of *The Thing*. I actually went so far as to discuss the matter with John Adams over the phone, and with his reassurances, went with the ending I had planned—then e-mailed him a slightly revised one two days after that. The patience of a saint, that man.

"City of the Dog": This was the second story I wrote for another anthology Ellen Datlow was putting together. The book was to feature new stories inspired by H. P. Lovecraft, to be a kind of thematic sequel to *Poe*. As with the previous volume, Ellen did not want pastiches; as she put it, "No tentacles." I promptly broke this rule by writing a story that was more full of tentacles than a tank of octopi. To what I like to think of as her credit, Ellen did not reject the story out of hand—but she did admit that it was more, well, tentacular than she preferred, and said that she wanted to hold on to it to see what else came in in the meantime. In response, I withdrew that story from submission and declared that I would write another one, *sans* tentacles. Even as I had been writing that first story, I had been thinking that, one of these days, I should try to do something with another of Lovecraft's favorite monsters, the ghoul. Confronted with the sudden prospect of having to complete a new story for Ellen, I decided to plunge ahead with the ghoul. My treatment of the monster was influenced in no small part by Caitlín R. Kiernan's re-imagining of it in her fine novel, *Low Red Moon;* though my ghouls are somewhat less decadent than hers. I had been thinking of setting a story in Albany, where I spent two miserable years in the early 1990s, for some time; I knew it would concern a character whose life was falling apart, and who would see a monstrous face looking up at him from a drain opening. (This image undoubtedly was rooted in the climax of T. E. D. Klein's brilliant "Children of the Kingdom.") At one event or another, I had discussed my unhappy experience of New York State's capital with Ellen, who told me that her own time there as a student at SUNY had left her with similar associations. It was a short leap to placing the ghoul into—or under—Albany. Perhaps because the setting evoked such a strong response in me, more explicit autobiography appeared in this story than is usually the

case for me. In this regard, it's not unlike "Laocoön," the original novella in my previous collection; in both cases, a kind of lacerating self-
exploration runs alongside the story's more fantastic elements. The
story ran longer than the first one I'd written for the Lovecraft project,
and this, combined with my not finishing it until very close to the
deadline, kept it out of what became *Lovecraft Unbound.* I was sorry not
to make it into the book, but Gordon Van Gelder took the story for
the *Magazine of Fantasy & Science Fiction,* and then Ellen herself took it
to reprint in the third volume of her *Best Horror of the Year.* So the story
I'd written for Ellen Datlow wound up in one of her books, after all,
just not the one I'd planned on.

(As for that first story: I eventually revised it and placed it with a
book of stories S. T. Joshi was editing, *Black Wings II.* More on that in
the notes to my next collection.)

"The Revel": An editor I met at the World Fantasy Convention in San
Jose in 2009 contacted me a couple of months after the convention
was over to ask me to contribute a story to an anthology he was putting together around the theme of werewolves and shapeshifters. His
request sent me back to the story I'd begun in the summer of 1999,
when my wife and I first started seeing one another. At the time, it had
been maybe another decade since I'd written anything that could be
construed as out-and-out horror fiction; though I'd continued to read
in the genre sporadically. (Now, I see that all the writing I'd done over
those ten years—a long novel, a short novel, a novella, a couple of
novelettes, a handful of stories—had mapped an emotional terrain of
dread, loss, and absence: in other words, that I was already within the
horror field without realizing it.) My wife was completing her dissertation on Jack Kerouac's *Dr. Sax* and *Visions of Cody,* and in our conversations about what Kerouac had achieved in those books—especially
Dr. Sax—Fiona told me that he had considered the popular culture of
his youth a suitable vehicle for literary expression. For reasons that
may have been no more complicated than that the time was right for
me to hear it, this struck me with the force of revelation. Within a matter of weeks, I had plunged headlong into a new story, one that was
both a story about a werewolf and a story about werewolf (and horror)
stories in general. I wrote it by longhand while Fiona worked at her

computer, the two of us stopping every now and again so she could take a break and I could read to her what I'd written. She was encouraging, and her comments were smart, exactly the combination I needed. For the remainder of that summer and on and off over the year that followed, I added to the story, which left the vicinity of story pretty quickly and steamed through novelette, novella, and kept going. Eventually, I put it aside, first to write nonfiction (research papers, essays, reviews), and then to work on the other horror stories it had made it possible for me to write. I didn't forget about it; sometimes, I imagined I'd return to it for my third or fourth novel, when I'd achieved enough credibility as a writer for readers to give a crazy experimental work a chance.

When the opportunity to write a story for this anthology arose, though, I thought of that unfinished narrative, and decided it would be worth it to see if I couldn't carve the mass of prose I'd produced into a story. (Okay, a novelette.) Interestingly, this led to the piece becoming more experimental in places, as I tried to figure out how to fit pages and pages of my werewolf's depravities, not to mention his history, into a smaller space than I'd originally planned. From the moment I'd written that first sentence, all those years ago—which remained the same in this version—I had known that this werewolf was not going to be a figure of sympathy—no Lon Chaney, Jr. here, or the protagonist of Thomas Tessier's fine *The Nightwalker.* This was not just going to be the kind of willing werewolf Stephen King had portrayed in *The Cycle of the Werewolf,* this was going to be one of the great beasts, something more akin to Grendel or his mother. (The primal monsters John Byrne had employed during his run on the first *Alpha Flight* comic series were in my mind, too.) In terms of metafictional ploys, I went further than I had before or since, and when it came time to give the story a title, I followed Laird Barron's lead and stole a term from *The Darkening Garden,* John Clute's lexicon of critical terms to describe what happens in horror narratives. For Clute, revel is the moment in the typical horror story when everything flies apart, which seemed to fit what I was trying to do too well to pass up.

As it turned out, I was a couple of days past the deadline for the anthology. I submitted the story, anyway, but received no acknowledgment from the editor. After about a week of utter silence, I sent the story to Gordon Van Gelder, who bought and published it very quickly. To my surprise and pleasure, Ellen Datlow took the story for the same volume of *The Best Horror of the Year* in which "City of the Dog" was already included. Talk about gobsmacked: I couldn't believe my good fortune. I dedicate all my stories to my wife, but it was particularly nice to have one that derived from the very first thing I'd written for her honored in such a way.

"The Shallows": The inspiration for this story dates back to the 2001 Necronomicon convention held in Providence, Rhode Island. This was my first trip to what was the last of these events. One of the panels at the convention dealt with new additions to the Cthulhu Mythos—what I suppose you might call pastiches. Writer and editor Darrell Schweitzer was on this panel, and during the discussion he opined that most Lovecraft pastiches were a waste of time, since, he went on, they added nothing substantial to Lovecraft's vision. That said, Darrell suggested that there might be one more kind of Lovecraftian story to write, and that was the account of what happens after Cthulhu and his friends return to take control of the Earth. Such a story, Darrell said, would need to focus on what the remaining humans were doing to keep human, which he supposed would consist in small gestures, habits, rituals.

His idea stuck with me, and if I never went so far as to commit such a story to paper, I turned the idea for it over in my mind every now and again. When I received an invitation from Darrell to submit a story to an anthology he was editing in which the stories were set following Cthulhu's victory, I already had a general sense of the story's shape: a man maintaining his daily routines in the face of a radically fractured world. The first image I had for the piece was of a tiny cottage situated on a great stone shelf, the middle and further distance obscured by huge clouds of light. Along with that image came a title, "The Shallows," which I knew referred to a part of this altered Earth where the cataclysmic changes wrought by the Lovecraftian apocalypse would be at a minimum. I imagined the person who lived in this cottage watching groups of people and other things coming and going out of the clouds of light, the depths. The problem with this plot, though, was that I couldn't believe that the creatures passing by wouldn't knock on the cottage door, and once they did, there was no way my protagonist would be able to survive them. I discussed the matter with Laird Barron over the course of a couple of phone calls, and it was during these that I hit upon having my protagonist telling stories about the life that was as a means of keeping it alive. I thought there might be some kind of creature accompanying him—not a grand, cosmic monstrosity, but something smaller, more domestic, that wouldn't be a threat and that could serve as an audience for his stories. I pictured the creature as a kind of spider crab; Laird suggested it might be related to the beetles in his story, "The Forest," who inherit the Earth in the future and who attempt to preserve the relics of human civilization. I liked the idea of the spider crab as a kind of organic technology sent to record one of the few surviving human's memories. In the same way, I liked those memories, which were more of the "dirty realism" of Raymond Carver than the cosmic horror of Lovecraft, but whose narratives couldn't help refracting their surrounding context. As I write this, my older son, Nick, is completing his training as an officer for the Baltimore City PD, and I suppose the story's treatment of Ransom's relationship with Matt reflects my own experience of being father to a son eager to embrace adulthood. Beyond that, the story of Bruce the dog has some basis in my family's experience: the first house that Fiona and I rented was across and up the street from an old farmhouse whose owners kept a dog in a similar cage to the one Bruce winds up in. We used to watch the poor animal, bored silly, running around in there, chasing its tail. Fiona went so far as to walk over and ask the owners if they'd mind if she took the dog for a walk, but they refused. It seemed obvious that they'd found the dog more work than they could handle but, rather than admit their error and try to find another family for him, had chosen to persist in their mistake. They fed the dog, kept the cage clean, and from what I could tell, drove him out of his mind. I have to admit, in a lot of ways, I'm not particularly enamored of Lovecraftian pastiche. There are moments, though, when it allows you access to a kind of emotional resonance that it's hard to beat. When *Cthulhu's Reign* appeared in 2011, it met with significantly less critical response than I felt its contents deserved, and while I was grateful to have "The Shallows" reprinted by Ross Lockhart in his *Book of Cthulhu,* I'd encourage anyone interested to seek out the earlier volume.

"June, 1987. Hitchhiking. Mr. Norris": Another *jeu d'esprit,* this time at the expense of my great good friend, Laird Barron. I consider myself fortunate in counting among my friends and acquaintances a good number of the better writers of my generation (a list that has to include Paul Tremblay, Sarah Langan, Michael Cisco, Simon Strantzas, Ian Rogers, Richard Gavin, Stephen Graham Jones, Nathan Ballingrud, Glen Hirshberg, and Nick Mamatas), but it's with Laird that I feel the most fundamental connection, to the point that I've often referred to him as the other younger brother I never had. Which is somewhat odd, given that our personal histories are so radically different. We connected over our writing—in fact, it was Gordon Van Gelder who, the month after my first story appeared in the *Magazine of Fantasy & Science Fiction,* e-mailed me to say that I should check out the current issue of the magazine, because there was a story in it by another new writer he thought I would appreciate. I did appreciate "Shiva, Open Your Eye," and Laird's subsequent stories in *F&SF* and Ellen Datlow's late lamented SCIFICTION, and when I wrote to Laird, it was a terribly formal, even mannered, e-mail expressing my admiration for his work. That admiration has never faded: I've written appreciations of his stories, reviews of his books, and fully expect to do so, again. What I respected—what I responded to in his fiction, and still do, is the tremendous integrity he brings to it. Laird takes the material of horror seriously—which isn't to say there's no room for either irony or out-and-out comedy in his fiction, but the joke is never on the reader. It's an approach I believe we share, and while our friendship has expanded to take in such shared interests as martial arts, Japanese movies, and *Archer,* it remains rooted in our shared love of the horror field. So a couple of years ago, when the bottom dropped out of Laird's life and he found himself in a bad place, it was inevitable that I would think of horror as a way to cheer him up. Specifically, in an echo of the "Jack Haringa" project, I contacted the writers I knew and who knew Laird with the proposal that, on a given day, we should post on our blogs excerpts from the Secret Life of Laird Barron. The response was overwhelmingly positive, and on the day appointed, Laird discovered that some of his more outré adventures had not gone unnoticed. There wasn't a bad entry in the bunch, but I'd be remiss if I didn't call attention to Kurt Dinan's, which photoshopped Laird into any number of famous photos to tell the story of his involvement in the testing of a longevity drug. I knew I was going to treat Laird's younger years, and his encounter with a situation straight out of one of his own stories. It's kind of a shame—as of this writing, those pieces remain uncollected. But they did cheer Laird up, so mission accomplished, there.

"Mother of Stone": By this point in these notes, you'll have noticed how many of these stories came from invitations to contribute to themed anthologies—whose deadlines I sometimes missed, or whose editors sometimes rejected me. This story, which is original to this collection, had its beginning in another such invitation, to an anthology Ellen Datlow and Nick Mamatas were coediting on the topic of local ghost stories retold. Living in the Hudson Valley, I had my pick of some pretty choice legends: Sleepy Hollow's about an hour away, and there's more that could be done with that old Hessian, the Headless Horseman. As it so happened, though, I'd recently been handed an even more local ghost story by a friend with whom Fiona and I were having dinner. This friend had been a server at a local restaurant on whose grounds the statue of a headless pregnant woman had been excavated—after which, a car accident had claimed the life of the restaurant's owner, who was driving a convertible and was decapitated. Because of this, and other, weird occurrences our friend wouldn't discuss, a Catholic priest and a Methodist minister were brought in to perform an exorcism on the statue, after which, it was reburied. That was all our friend wanted to say—in fact, it was her husband who'd urged her to share the story with us in the first place. Of course I tried to research the events our friend had described, and, predictably, could find nothing. What I'd heard, though, was more than enough to build a story around, and this, I set out to do. From the start, I knew that the piece would be written in second person—mostly because I wanted to see what would happen if I told it this fashion. I figured it would place the reader in the story in an interesting way; only much later did it occur to me that this could also represent the protagonist's feeling alienated from her life. I knew as well that the story would be relayed through multiple narrators folded into the protagonist's interview process and that it would be an example of the exorcism narrative. I got down to writing. The story grew. And grew. And grew. It grew to the point it was going to be too long for Ellen and Nick's anthology, and then it stopped growing, which is to say, right at the point my protagonist sat down for her interview with the Reverend Au Claire, on the verge of the account of the actual exorcism, the story stalled. I had read and watched the film adaptation of *The Exorcist*, which is pretty much the touchstone for these kinds of narratives. I was familiar with literary exorcisms such as those attempted by the protagonists of Stephen King's "The Mangler" and Sara Gran's *Come Closer*, as well as cinematic varieties like *The Exorcism of Emily Rose*. I was aware that, in many ways, the story I was writing was following the pattern established by those narratives: weird events escalating in intensity and severity, until the clergy are called in. Fair enough, but I wanted the exorcism itself to be something of a departure. The deadline for the anthology came and went without a solution presenting itself. I put the story aside and moved onto other projects. Every now and again, I returned to it, usually to flesh out one of the sections I'd already written. When I assembled this collection of stories, I decided to finish what I had taken to calling the statue story and include it as the book's original. That, I figured, would give me the push I needed to work out the scene that was, in many ways, the heart of the story. It did, though I trespassed on the good graces of S. T. Joshi and Derrick Hussey (my editor and publisher, respectively) much more than, in good conscience, I should have. The story that resulted employs a number of devices that are at or near the heart of my work: the academic life and its pursuits; a local setting and history; the use of multiple voices; a concern with the persistence of trauma at levels ranging from the personal to the metaphysical. It's a good way to end this book.

Afterword:
Note Found in a Glenfiddich Bottle

Where do you get your ideas?
   Don't ask questions like that!

We were seated at the Langan kitchen table, John and I. This was a late, late night deep in the lonesome October. I'd recently made the trip from Tok Junction, Alaska, to Rifton, New York, in my '98 Chevy pickup. A storm had followed me and now it shook the house and made the low lights flicker.

   I wasn't headed back the way I'd come anytime soon. Hadn't seen the old boy since the previous winter, so we had a lot of catching up to do. We discussed my arduous transcontinental trek, dogs, karate, and a bunch of stuff I can't recall. Eventually, the conversation turned to literature. A few weeks prior, he'd mailed me a draft of his latest manuscript, *The Wide, Carnivorous Sky*. Man, I've been reading horror and dark fantasy since I was a kid, yet those stories of John's creeped me out like nothing I've seen since old school scribes such as T. E. D. Klein and Karl Edward Wagner. It seemed the big eccentric bastard was truly coming into his own.

   But that's not what was on his mind.

   He poured me another shot of Glenfiddich and looked me in the eye and said, "That broken ring doohickey you use in your Old Leech stories . . . you got that from me."

   "Hmm. Can't recall. I just figured it was a gift from my muse."

   "I'm your muse, you sonofabitch!"

   "Why is it you sound so much like Jeff Ford when you're mad?"

   "Anyway, it's mine. The broken ring symbol appeared in 'On Skua Island' back in 2001."

   Okay, that struck a chord. "Hm, guess I appropriated the hell out of that thing, eh?" I chuckled and had another drink. He'd sold that tale to the *Magazine of Fantasy & Science Fiction*. His first pro sale, in fact. My own had come along within a few weeks and to the same publication. We admired each other's work, began corresponding, and struck up a friendship, which ultimately led to my liberating his broken ring description and deploying it in a few of my own cosmic horror yarns.

"Sorry to be touchy," John said. "A colleague of mine at SUNY New Paltz did quite a bit of research into the matter, you see. That's where *I* originally came up with the idea. You remember Bob Shaw?"

"Cracked some tomes of quaint and forgotten lore, did he?"

John folded his spectacles and put them in his shirt pocket. He didn't smile. "My anthropologist friend claimed to have seen that symbol three times. Once, in the Shetlands as a pictogram in a sea cave. Another time carved into the wall of cellar of a medieval church in Provence. And last year when he took his family camping in the Adirondacks. That one was some kind of weird fossil embedded in a cliff face. In all three cases there were little shrines set up with offerings. Recent, too."

"What kind of offerings?"

He shrugged. "Bob didn't say. He became very secretive toward the end. Thank the gods I got some of our conversations on tape."

"Toward the end? Something happen to him?"

"Nah," John said and drained his booze. "He's been missing for a few months."

Later that night I woke and looked out the window. There was John in his pajamas standing just beyond the lamppost glow on the other side of the street at the edge of the woods. His clothes fluttered in the wind and his hair stood on end. He waved his arms as if conducting a symphony. I glanced away, then back again, and he was gone, just like in every ghost story you've ever read.

Early the next morning we strolled around the neighborhood, tossing fallen branches into the bushes. It was cold and wet. Mist clung to the shrubbery.

"'Mother of Stone' is a very disturbing tale," I said by way of an icebreaker. I'd suffered a nightmare featuring John's new manuscript.

Headless fertility goddesses spewing blood from either end, me crashing my truck into a ravine, burning alive in unholy fire, and that sort of thing. "So, uh, is it based on a true story too?" I was kidding, a little.

"Completely fabricated," John said. "C'mon, give me some credit for an original idea."

"Even a blind hog finds an acorn every now and again. Dude, seriously, that's a crazy story. Gave me bad dreams."

"Nope, I wove it from whole cloth. Well except for the bit about the headless statue."

"What the fuck, over?"

"I heard the story at a faculty party. There's an abandoned church along Route 32. Developers dug up the property a couple of years ago. Weirdness ensued. An associate of mine in the department decided to investigate, maybe do a paper . . ."

"What the hell is that?" I pointed to a cedar a few yards off the road. Someone had nailed a goat skull into the trunk at eye level.

"Oh. Oh! That was here when we bought the place."

"Who was the owner, a hillbilly satanist? Good grief, I didn't see shit this trippy in Backwater, Alaska."

"I think the fellow was a landscaper. By the way, I've meant to ask you about Alaska . . ."

"You gonna take it down? Probably gives your wife the willies." It gave *me* the willies, that was for sure.

"We kind of like it," John said.

"You guys like it," I said.

"Yeah. Want some pancakes? I'll make us some pancakes."

I was in the middle of my second stack when it occurred to me to ask, "That professor friend of yours ever write a paper on the headless statue?"

John shook his head sadly. "She died in a car accident. I got her notes, though. Couldn't have written my story without them."

That Langan just keeps getting better and better! That's what the publishers and editors and critics say. The choir has it right, too. I've known the guy for more than a decade and while he was always excellent, there's a certain hard-bitten maturity to his latter work that lends it a transcendental quality. Yeah, he's gotten better, all right.

Problem is, he's also gotten weirder and weirder. He skips assigned panels at conventions, or shows up three sheets to the wind and bellicose as all hell. He writes cryptic entries on his blog and incoherent diatribes to industry rags like *Locus* and *Publishers Weekly*. He blows off his teaching gig at the university and vanishes for days at a stretch, rambling through the Catskills, subsisting on roots, berries, and the occasional hapless squirrel.

I didn't give it much thought at first. Artists are an eccentric bunch—and horror authors? Egad. Nah, for a while I figured John was acting odd because he'd pushed himself so hard to meet deadline after deadline, that he'd settle down once the collection appeared in print, or when he handed in the next novel to his publisher. Besides, I'd only heard this stuff secondhand prior to my arrival in New York. Mutual friends and colleagues mentioned it obliquely; cocktail gossip that I largely ignored. Writers can be jealous bastards. Master exaggerators. You really can't believe anything they tell you.

The mystery came into focus when my agent Janet took me to dinner at a fancy New Paltz joint and casually mentioned John was *persona non grata* in Providence due to some criminal hijinks.

"That doesn't sound right," I said. "John's straight as an arrow. Besides, he hasn't gone to Rhode Island in ages."

Janet gave me a look. "Trust me, he was there last winter."

"If you say so."

"Well, I know he's your pal and all . . ." She glanced around the restaurant, then leaned in close and said, "Seems the authorities caught him lurking around Lovecraft's grave with a spade and a burlap sack."

"No way!"

"Hey, I'm not the one who makes shit up for a living. I'm tellin' you what Kasey over at Excalibur Books told me."

We had another martini and she went on to say that only the timely intervention by the chief of police (who was a huge horror fan) kept John's name out of the paper. I changed the subject to a discussion of my long overdue advance for my last horror novel. Meanwhile, I entertained visions of John tricked out in resurrection man gear as he haunted the back alleys of Providence in the wee hours. I also thought about his peculiar behavior around the house and the unfortunate fates of his closest associates.

God help me, I didn't leave well enough alone.

How I discovered the Bob Shaw tapes is a minor miracle, but I don't have time to explain. Doesn't matter, anyway. Doubtless John has since destroyed them, as he should've done in the first place.

Those recordings will haunt me as long as I live, which is to say, for a few more hours. If I'm lucky. My legs are broken from that mysterious fall I took down the stairs two weeks ago as I hurried to get the tapes somewhere safe. I can't prove there was a trip wire, of course. I realize now that the cop who came to interview me at the hospital might not have been a cop at all. John has a hell of a network of friends and associates. That network taps into student theater, you can bet. Explains why the cop looked so young, why there's been no follow-up. I should've checked the badge a little more closely. Should've made some calls of my own.

Naturally, John has proved quite solicitous as I lie in this small room, staring at ceiling cracks, dread in my heart at every footfall, every muttered conversation. He keeps me well stocked in pills and booze.

I may be delirious on painkillers and my half a bottle a day Jim Beam habit, but I keep one eye open when I sleep and a letter opener under my pillow. Only thing I know for sure: I won't go down crying and begging for mercy like poor old Bob did. The second John left this morning to run an errand, I dragged myself, James Caan style, down the hall to his office and got busy drafting this note on his Smith-Corona. No computer, no phone service at this big, ancient house at the end of a long, gloomy lane. The mailbox is way too far a crawl, even if the doors were unlocked. So I'll stuff this paper into a bottle and chuck it out the window into the stream that runs near the back porch. Been a lot of rain, lately, and the stream feeds into a popular duck pond near a major housing development.

Somebody will find it. The world's got to know. The world's got to believe.

I'm deathly afraid the fellows at Hippocampus will think this is a joke, a tongue-in-cheek send-up of my old friend, John. The ironic part is that no one might ever catch on to the fact I've gone missing. John's a pro at the game these days. I used to thank he watched *CSI* and *Cas-*

tle for a glimpse of those dreamy hunks, Lawrence Fishburne and Nathan Fillion. Well, now I know the truth. He was perfecting his craft in a perfectly innocuous manner.

Maybe people will wonder about certain inconsistencies in my prose style. Maybe the fact I won't attend any more conventions or do public signings will eventually raise someone's brow. And maybe not. This is the age of electronic correspondence, faceless commerce. It might be years before anyone suspects. Meanwhile, I'll continue to write stories, opine on various blogs, and render countless excuses for why I've returned to the Arctic and the life of a hermit.

I know my work will be much more self referential from now on.

John stood at the foot of my bed early this morning, silent while I drunkenly railed at him for his misdeeds. His expression was hidden in the darkness. I'm certain he smiled. I'm also certain the wheels were turning inside his recorder.

The last thing he said to me was, "Laird, tell me what it was like to grow up in Alaska. What's the weirdest thing that ever happened to you?"

—LAIRD BARRON

Acknowledgments

These last few years, I've been busier writing fiction than ever before. I've also been busier with writing-related activities—readings, interviews, conventions—than ever before. I've asked a lot from my wife, Fiona, and she's been unstintingly generous to me. Thanks, Love.

I've also benefitted from the love and support of my sons, Nick and David, as well as my daughter-in-law, Mary, and my granddaughter (!), Inara Mae.

Writing is, by definition, a lonely business. The friendship of fellow writers makes it feel less so. I'm fortunate to count Laird Barron and Paul Tremblay brothers-under-the-skin. Seriously—I love these guys. Nathan Ballingrud, Michael Cisco, Brett Cox, Richard Gavin, Glen Hirshberg, Sarah Langan, Nick Mamatas, Ian Rogers, and Simon Strantzas are pretty good, too. Oh, and if you'd told me that a book with my name on it would have an introduction by Jeff Ford, I would have accused you of taunting me, cruelly. Apparently, though, I have a balance on my karma from some incredibly good deed of which I'm completely unaware. Thanks to Jeff for taking the time to say such gracious things about my writing.

This collection's title, and that of the title story, is borrowed from the online journal of Caitlín R. Kiernan.

I count myself lucky in my agent, Ginger Clark, and her agency, Curtis Brown. Ditto the editors I've worked with: John Joseph Adams, Ellen Datlow, S. T. Joshi, Darrell Schweitzer, and Gordon Van Gelder. Ditto you: whoever you are, I'm grateful to you for the gift of your time and attention. Without you, books like this wouldn't exist, so thank you.

Publication History

"Kids" originally appeared in *Jack Haringa Must Die!*, edited by Nicholas Kaufmann (Merricat Publications, 2008).

"How the Day Runs Down" originally appeared in *The Living Dead*, edited by John Joseph Adams (Night Shade Books, 2008).

"Technicolor" originally appeared in *Poe: 19 New Tales Inspired by Edgar Allan Poe*, edited by Ellen Datlow (Solaris, 2009).

"The Wide, Carnivorous Sky" originally appeared in *By Blood We Live*, edited by John Joseph Adams (Night Shade Books, 2009).

"City of the Dog" originally appeared in the *Magazine of Fantasy & Science Fiction* (January/February 2010).

"The Shallows" originally appeared in *Cthulhu's Reign*, edited by Darrell Schweitzer (DAW Books, 2010).

"The Revel" originally appeared in the *Magazine of Fantasy & Science Fiction* (July/August 2010).

"June, 1987. Hitchhiking. Mr. Norris." is original to this collection.

"Mother of Stone" is original to this collection.

Called "an emerging master of the elegant macabre," John Langan has published a novel, *House of Windows* (Night Shade 2009), and a collection of stories, *Mr. Gaunt and Other Uneasy Encounters* (Prime 2008). With Paul Tremblay, he has co-edited *Creatures: Thirty Years of Monsters*. He lives in upstate New York with his wife, son, and an assortment of animals.

www.ingramcontent.com/pod-product-compliance
Lightning Source LLC
Chambersburg PA
CBHW080903250125
20852CB00036B/468